To

Hannah Gould

History comes alive through the stories of those who lived it.

Enjoy!

Thomas F. Linehan, Jr.

Thomas F. Linehan

The final approval for this literary material is granted by the author.

First printing

This is a work of fiction. Names, characters, businesses, places, events and incidents are either the products of the author's imagination or used in a fictitious manner. Any resemblance to actual persons, living or dead, or actual events is purely coincidental.

Hannah Gould is printed in Book Antiqua

In remembrance of Gloria Schwartz, a tireless proponent of Holocaust Education and one of the most courageous Jewish women I've ever met.

In remembrance of Samuel Makover, PhD, for his personal recollections of his life as a 19-year-old Jewish partisan.

With gratitude to the staff of The Tuttleman Library and The Holocaust Oral History Archive of Gratz College (Philadelphia, PA)

With gratitude to Mr. Alex Redner, Holocaust survivor, whose translations of Polish to English, and insights into the politics of the East European region during WWII were invaluable.

Praise for **Hannah Gould**

"*Hannah Gould* takes us inside the mind and heart of an extraordinary heroine. Hannah's harrowing story, grippingly told, is moving and powerful. Her transformation from sheltered young teen to fearless partisan fighter and leader is astonishing and inspiring. Hannah's a powerhouse and so is this book." **–Rabbi David M. Ackerman, Congregation Beth Am Israel, formerly Rabbi for National Outreach, Jewish Theological Seminary of America**

"This is a tale of a teenage Jewish girl in Poland at the outset of World War II who is traumatized by the cruelty of the Nazi invaders. *Hannah Gould* loses her family, and struggles to find her way to freedom and safety. The story, rivaling Anne Frank's experiences, follows Hannah and other Jewish refugees as they work their way through a maze of hazardous events, and engage in guerrilla warfare against the German enemy and their collaborators. Hannah encounters unforeseen incidents along the way that keep the pages turning to learn what more could possibly happen to this young, impressionable, yet spirited heroine." **–Thomas J Ryan, multiple award-winning author of *Spies, Scouts, and Secrets in the Gettysburg Campaign* and author of the *Civil War Profiles* weekly column for the *Coastal Point Newspaper* in Delaware**

"*Hannah Gould* – a powerful story of the coming of age and survival of a teenage Jewish girl, as she is orphaned and caught up in the upheaval of WWII Nazi-occupied Poland. Instinct, lessons learned and recalled from a loved father and a loving family, and an incorrigible will to press on against a hostile environment, see her through this turbulent epoch. Her journey, in the face of unendurable losses, obstacles, and bodily injury, can only serve as inspiration especially to modern youth, whether in challenged or privileged circumstances." **–Dr. Paula Bursztyn Goldberg, author of *CRC Handbook of Pharmacology of Aging*, and Polish Holocaust survivor**

Hannah Gould

PROLOGUE

In September of 1939, overnight, my world shattered like pieces of glass hitting the city sidewalk in front of our house. That's where my best friend Beila and I played our jumping games. We still hopped around on the cracked concrete sidewalk at twelve years old. I was not very worldly. But in the end, that may be what saved me, or at least my faith may have. I had to learn about the evil and the good in people firsthand. Sometimes I think everyone carries a little of both. Some just tilt the scale a little further one way or the other.

I always thought of myself as a survivor, but not a leader. Happy to let someone else protect me. Truth be told, I guess I never liked others doing for me either. If I appear conflicted with myself, well, one may begin to understand why the men in the forests of Belorussia initially thought me worthless as a fighter. I had to prove them wrong.

My name is Hannah Gould. I was born in Warsaw to a good Jewish family. My childhood was comfortable and loving. Papa saw to that. Our family kept the Sabbath and went to shul every week. And then the Germans came. People talked about Hitler invading our country. Mostly the older men talked. I think the younger ones didn't want to think about war. No one likes to think about death, especially their own.

Men were always a mystery to me back then. I learned quickly that some were not to be trusted and some I could trust with my life. War and all its craziness made it next to impossible for me to sort out my feelings.

As a young woman trying to make a new life after the war, I have little left of my childhood to lean on. I lost it somewhere in the forests east of my country or in the Pripet Marshes of Ukraine. Or maybe in the woods outside of Sokolka.

Or maybe I lost pieces of me all along the way.

Chapter One

The kitchen seemed more drab than usual as Hannah sat down at the table for breakfast. She looked at her parents. Seymour and Sara Gould stood facing each other from opposite sides of the room. They just stared. Hannah knew things had gotten much worse, but she had not wanted to think about it too much.

Only three months ago, everything changed. The fighting, the noise, trucks, airplanes, German soldiers on the roads. Papa said the Germans pushed the Russians back to Russia. Everyone tried to hide, but how do you hide from a war that's all around you? Now life was different in Sokolka, in the market, and on the streets.

"Papa, I heard you and Mama talking after I went to bed last night. We are in danger again, aren't we?" Hannah asked, glancing toward her father.

"Try not to worry, Hannah, we'll be alright," Seymour replied, rubbing his temples.

"Well, I am worried," Hannah said, twirling a lock of her hair around her finger, over and over.

"We don't want to scare you."

"You are scaring me," Hannah said. "But I'm fifteen. Not a child. I have to know what's going to happen to us."

Papa glanced at Mama.

"I thought we would be safe here, away from the city," Hannah said, arms folded across her chest.

Hannah noticed Mama nod to Papa.

"Alright, I have a plan for all of us. Let's sit and talk about it."

Papa and Mama took their usual seats. On the table sat a basket of rolls, butter, dry farina in Hannah's bowl, a glass pitcher of water, and silverware. No one felt hungry, least of all Hannah.

"We need to go through it together," Papa said, grimacing and lowering his head.

Hannah felt tension in Papa's voice and fought back the urge to cry.

"Why do we need a plan? Do we need to leave Sokolka?" she asked, looking back and forth at them. "The Germans? They're coming for us again. I knew it. I just knew it."

"Well, they might come, Hannah," Mama said, lightly resting her palm over Hannah's hand.

"It's always good to be prepared," Papa said, his face tight.

"Is it like before, when we had to leave home?" Hannah asked. She looked around the house at the pictures and wall hangings that were someone else's things.

"Yes, like Warsaw. Hannah, I had no choice and my boss offered us this cottage. He saved us. But now…"

"I don't want to move, but shouldn't we go before they come, Papa? There must be somewhere we can go," she said, searching his face for an answer.

"The Germans are all around us now, so there is no way out of here. No place is safe."

Hannah slumped in her chair. "Do we have to leave right away?"

"No, but maybe soon," Mama said, as she patted the back of her daughter's hand.

"Hannah, remember that patch of woods north of the park?" Papa asked.

Hannah shrugged. "I don't know." She thought a moment. "The blue jays…squawking at the squirrel's nest in the birch tree. Yes, now I remember it."

"That's the place," Papa said. "I'm going to hide some things for us there. If the Germans come and we are not together, we'll meet there."

"Papa, shouldn't we have left a long time ago?"

"I didn't think the Russians would bother us, and they didn't. But the Germans, well…if we try to leave now, we'll appear suspicious. We have been very lucky so far."

"They'll take us away somewhere because we're Jewish, and not because we're Polish. Isn't that right?"

"Yes. That is the truth of it. And what may have saved us so far is that I have never registered us as Jews and none of our neighbors have told them. Not yet, anyway."

"Is that why you wouldn't let me have any friends here? Beila was my only friend. Now I have no one. I thought you just didn't want me to meet gentile girls."

"I'm sorry we had to leave the Borowski family, back in Warsaw. And I know it was hard for you to leave Beila. But it was getting very dangerous for us there. We need to keep who we are a secret. I think you know that. But now I feel we are out of time," he said, lowering his eyes.

Everyone sat silent for a long time. Hannah stared at the bread on the table. *This is so unfair*, Hannah thought.

"So, what should we put in the hiding place?" Hannah looked around the room. "Most of these things are not ours."

Papa raised his head. A hint of relief showed in his face.

"Money, jewelry, and other things," he replied, leaning his elbows on the table.

"Maybe an extra coat or blanket," Mama said.

"We'll take the bicycles and go together," Papa said. "That way we all know exactly where to meet in case we are separated."

"Papa wants to go very early tomorrow morning, when it is still dark," Mama said.

"Yes, most people should be asleep," he said, nodding.

"Do we really have to get up so early?"

"It's important that others don't see us," Mama replied. "And I can't wait any longer to do this. I just can't."

"What should I take?"

"Whatever will fit in one small suitcase."

"I thought we weren't leaving?" Hannah said with wrinkled brow.

"We're not. We'll bury one case for all of us. I'm bringing a small shovel," Papa said.

"Let's pick out a few of your things for the suitcase," Mama said. Smiling, she put her arm around Hannah's shoulders and led her into the bedroom. "Your father and I already packed."

Papa placed the suitcase on Hannah's bed. Mama and Hannah looked through Hannah's things, thinking about what to pack. Papa put some money in and Mama parted with her grandmother's necklace. Mama put the necklace in Hannah's hand.

"It's very old," Mama said. "It was my Bubbe's pearl necklace."

The pearls were milky-white and the gold chain, 24-karat gold. "See the detail work," Mama said. "Each pearl has its own link and the links are all attached to make a chain. This piece should catch the eye of many."

Hannah remembered an old photograph that hung in the apartment in Warsaw of a bride in a wedding gown wearing the necklace. Mama said it wasn't her style, but it was all she had that was her grandmother's. It would bring the highest price.

"What are we going to buy with the money, if we can't be seen by anyone?" Hannah asked. "We can't just go to a store."

"Hannah, the money and jewelry is for trading with people for food or other things," Mama said.

"You mean so they will help us?" Hannah asked, looking through the doorway at Papa in the next room. "Even if they are afraid to?"

Mama glanced up at Hannah and nodded. She kept packing.

"Who would I trade with in town, Mama? What would I tell them?"

"If the time comes, you'll know."

"Some people seem alright," Hannah said. "But not people like that neighborhood policeman and his son.

"Stay away from them," Mama said. "Jewish people can't trust them. Everyone knows that man isn't a real policeman. He decided he was one on his own, but now nobody will stand up to him."

"He is mean and hates Jews," Hannah said. "I saw him in the village that time you sent me for bread and milk. I had to wear the blue ribbon and a braid like the gentile girls."

"Do you understand why?"

"Yes. So, I'd blend with the other girls."

"That's right. And blue is my favorite color. You know, 'Like a clear blue sky, Your Papa and I.'"

Yes, but I don't think a ribbon is going to make me look like the rest.

"What about this?" Hannah asked, reaching under her clothes in her dresser drawer and pulling out her necklace. The delicate gold pendant and chain from Bubbe Rachel was always her favorite. A little butterfly. On her tenth birthday, Hannah could still feel gentle hands resting on the back of her neck as Bubbe fastened the chain, then pressed lightly on her shoulders. *She said it's special, like me.*

"You could wear it instead of packing it, you know?"

"No, you're putting in jewelry, so should I," Hannah said, noticing the diamond and gold ring on Mama's finger. "You never take your ring off, not even to wash."

"Your father and I promised we wouldn't. Only by our passing would we do that."

"Papa always has his ring, even in the woods."

"The rings aren't the important thing. What's most important to us is you, Hannah."

Hannah placed her necklace in the little pouch with Mama's big necklace and they finished packing. Mama took the suitcase and left Hannah sitting on her bed. She felt better that they were doing something about the German problem, but the sickening feeling in the pit of her stomach would not go away. *What if I end up here alone? How am I going live? What will these people around here do to me?*

Feeling her stomach growling, Hannah decided she would try to eat some breakfast. She nibbled at a roll but pushed the farina aside. She never had a good appetite when facing troubles. Bubbe Rachel always said, *"Trouble can wait, your stomach cannot."* Hannah smiled to herself.

Glancing out the window, she could see the village houses in the distance. *How am I supposed to "blend in" anyway? The boys in Sokolka are always looking me over, like they do to the older girls. I don't like it. And then there's that policeman and his son.*

Hannah couldn't shake the thought of that awful day in the

village. She had tried to hurry so nobody would notice her. Hearing a commotion up ahead, she stopped. Peeking around the corner of a building, she saw the policeman cursing and striking the rabbi. Papa said the fake policeman suspected everyone of hiding Jews and was quick to bully anyone he suspected.

Well, sometimes I want to punch and kick the boy. It's so unfair. They can be nasty to us and we can't do anything to them. I hate it.

Hannah tried to forget the policeman and his son. She picked up one of her lesson books and stared at the cover.

All the rabbi did was to try to help a poor, old man lying in the street. The man wasn't even Jewish. And his son is a bully, too. He likes to push around the smaller boys in town like he is in charge. Someday I'll show him.

Hannah looked at her book again and started to read, but her focus drifted.

Most people in town leave me alone. But if things get worse? Some people know who we are. They just don't say anything.

Scanning the room, she saw no personal things to pack. Only her necklace from Bubbe, which must be hidden away.

Everything was ready for the morning. The suitcase was packed with a blanket, socks, and knit hats. An old family photograph tucked in a stained, manila envelope lay on the bottom. The necklaces and money were sealed in the glass jar. Papa said that eventually the moisture and bugs would get into the suitcase and ruin most of the contents. Hannah wondered how she would use these things if she were left on her own. *Maybe none of us will be back before it's all ruined. But then it won't matter. Papa is trying to make it right. I know.*

That night they all went to bed early, wishing the German problem would just go away.

Chapter Two

Hannah felt a slight jostling and opened her eyes.

"It's time, Hannah," Mama said. "Get dressed quickly. We are leaving in twenty minutes."

"Oh, yes, Mama."

Hannah sat up and slouched over the side of the bed. Her bare feet searched for her slippers and touched the cold wood floor. She pulled them back quickly. *Where are they? I left them right here,* she thought, as her left foot made contact. She wiggled her feet into the slippers, stood up, made her way to the bathroom, and began to wash-up with icy water hitting her forehead and cheeks.

I hate this cottage. I never wanted to leave home. The woods are alright, but not the rest. And why do we have to keep running away from Germans? Why don't they just leave us alone? Could this water – this whole place – be any colder? We should have stayed in Warsaw and hid with my friends, Beila and Sol. Too late now.

Hannah reached for the towel that hung on a hook too close to the tiny sink. It felt rough and cold on her skin. She thought how annoying it was that clothes got stiff from drying on the clothesline in the wind.

She never had to do much clothes-washing and hanging before. But Mama thought it a good chore for Hannah to learn. Over and over, Mama would say, "Someday you will have to wash your husband's clothes. So, be mindful of your chores and you will already know what to do later." *Well, I'm not even going to wash my own clothes. Certainly, not my husband's.* Sol Wertz from the old neighborhood flashed through her mind. No, she'd never marry *him.*

"Hannah, are you dressed yet?" Mama called from the narrow hallway.

"Almost," Hannah said. She didn't know what to put on. She brushed her thick, dark hair a few times and moved quickly to the little dresser for underwear and socks. The miniature closet in her tiny bedroom held a few blouses, sweaters, a few skirts and trousers. She remembered packing at home in Warsaw. There was so much left behind. No time. All her favorite things left behind. She put on her old worn trousers and dark green knit sweater.

Hannah emerged from her room ready to leave, needing only a coat and hat.

"Ready," she said, scanning the empty kitchen table. "Where is Papa?"

"I am sure you are hungry, but we will eat when we get back. He is outside. Let's go," Mama said, with a little frown. "I know, I don't like this either. Go."

. . . . .

Frigid March air stung her cheeks and forehead as she stepped into the early morning darkness. The stars were still sparkling around a dying, faded moon. Hannah felt the sharp stab in her lungs as she drew in a deep breath and exhaled white steam. It always seemed colder before the sun came up. Her bare fingers stuck to the frozen steel handlebar, stinging and burning her skin. A shiver rolled through her as tears formed in her eyes and then felt as if they had frozen on her cheeks.

Oh, I can't go for long in cold like this. Don't think. Just keep pedaling. Follow Papa.

The road beyond the lake that led into the forest park was of frosted mud and rigid ruts. They pedaled along, moving away from the town proper. Sokolka was still asleep. Hannah noticed a few birds hopping around, but otherwise all was still as Papa had hoped. The front fender of her bicycle rattled a little as the tire jolted through the deeper ruts. Hannah strained her eyes to find smooth spots for her tires. The three bicycles soon disappeared into the woods as Papa navigated the gravel road that quickly narrowed to a walking path.

Underbrush occasionally nipped at Hannah's hands.

Papa stopped finally to check behind for any followers and look for a good hiding spot. More trees were visible now as the night sky turned a deep gray. They were well into the woods.

My secret place is only a football field or so farther. I don't want them to see it. Maybe we can bury the suitcase here.

Scanning the area, she spotted a depression off to the right. The path took a sharp turn just ahead.

"Papa, what about that spot over there?" she said, looking up to see Papa with his arm and finger already pointing to the same place.

"We can find it because of the sharp—"

"Bend in the path," Papa finished, smiling. "She has learned well about the forest and nature, Sara."

"Yes. You may be right, Seymour. Your idea," Mama said.

Hannah had to smile, in spite of the reasons for being there. Their nature walks and stargazing had indeed taught her much about nature and the forests. Hannah wondered what Mama meant about Papa's idea.

Papa chose a spot between the roots of a big evergreen and chopped at the frozen surface. The shovel quickly found softer, black earth. He dug a shallow hole and wrapped the suitcase in burlap. Hannah watched as he positioned it in the hole and shoveled in the covering dirt. The air smelled earthy, blending with the crisp, clean forest aroma. It felt like old times for a moment.

Hannah helped spread dry leaves and sticks over the burial spot. They cleaned up quickly and pedaled back to the cottage. Only one early delivery man noticed the three riding, and he waved. Hannah saw Papa give a big wave back and a "good morning."

He probably thinks we are just a family going out for an early bicycle ride. Maybe Papa's idea is a good one after all.

. . . . .

Wednesday afternoon seemed normal enough. Hannah was studying in her room. But she could not help going over in her mind exactly where they buried the suitcase a week earlier. She imagined the path from there to her secret place. It would be easy for her to find both, even in the dark. She also traced the steps in her mind as they planned. She would go out her bedroom window, quietly shut it, and run to the big bushes behind the cottage. From there she would move through the woods, tree to tree until she reached the suitcase. Not telling Papa, she had a second plan if the suitcase spot was not safe. That was her secret hideaway, a little deeper into the woods.

Papa had given her homework assignments since they arrived in Sokolka. He said there was too much risk in Hannah attending the public school. She was reading through a chemistry problem when she noticed a sound, faint at first, but getting louder. She closed the book on her finger and stepped over to the window. Although the door was dusty, Hannah could make out the markings on the side of the truck.

"Papa, a truck is coming. Papa, I think it's the Germans! Where are you?" Hannah called out. Papa emerged from the bedroom and Mama from the kitchen.

"Hannah, go to your bedroom, quickly. You know what to do. The window in the back. Like we planned," Papa said, as he pushed the sheer curtain aside. "Yes, it's them."

A big gray truck stopped in front of the cottage. A staff car pulled around and parked in front of the truck. Two German officers strutted up to the cottage door. Hannah peeked out of the small window from her bedroom. The men wore hats with swastika emblems on the front. Soldiers were coming out of the truck with guns. Hannah felt her heart pounding as the banging on the door broke the silence. She tiptoed across the bedroom floor to the back window. Unlatching the lock, she started to push open the window and stopped. A soldier walked around the corner of the cottage to cover the backyard.

What do I do now? I can't get away like we planned. Hide?

All the worry, all the fear, the waiting and hoping was melting away. It was happening and nothing she could do would stop it. Hannah could feel tears coming. Papa opened the door and she felt bile burning in her throat.

"Seymour Gould?" the German asked.

"*Nein. Was ist los*?" Papa said. "What is the meaning of this?"

"I need to see your papers," the officer said. The man towered over Seymour, face rigid.

Hannah crept over to the bedroom door. She peeked through the crack in the door and watched. The German was looking into the living room from the doorway and focusing on Mama. She would be next.

Hide, but where? The closet is too small for me. Under the bed? Too many things stuffed under there. No. Behind the door. Maybe they won't see me.

"I am Polish, but the Soviets, they made me get a Russian passport," Papa said.

"Well, that would be alright, except the Gestapo knows who you really are. You are a Jew," the SS man said.

"We are not! You have no right."

Turning to his men the officer said, "Search the house and put them all on the truck."

A soldier came into Hannah's room and looked under her bed, then in the closet. He saw her cowered behind the door and grabbed her arm hard. She let out a yelp.

"*Raus*! Out," he said, pulling her into the living room and then out the door to the road.

He left Hannah standing at the rear of the truck. She looked into the open canopy and saw a dozen people crunched into the back of the truck. Papa and Mama were already inside. Hannah could not reach the first step to climb up. She felt hands on her waist. Launched into the air, she crashed down onto the truck bed, colliding with Papa. The soldier and the other guard then stepped up onto the back and held on. The engine roared and the truck started with a jolt.

They jostled in the back for twenty, maybe thirty minutes. People were moaning, some sobbing. There was a boy about fourteen Hannah remembered from town. He looked sick. Through the canvas canopy at the rear of the truck, she could see the countryside pass by. The fields were left behind and soon trees replaced farms. The truck was deep into woods when it came to a stop.

The soldiers got off the truck and started shouting orders.

"Get out! *Raus*! Move, move, move!" they yelled.

"Papa, what should we do?" Hannah asked. "Should we try to run to the hiding place? I don't know where we are."

"No, we must get out of the truck," he said. "Be careful to find the step and don't fall. I'll help your mother."

Hannah felt dazed at first but as she stood waiting the place came into focus. It was a park, a large clearing in the woods. There were two other trucks already parked, with people getting out and standing around. Many soldiers, holding guns, stood in groups. There was something in the ground too, very large. She could not see it, but piles of dirt formed a wall around the back side of it.

"Move, that way!" the soldiers shouted, pushing and shoving with their rifles, guiding everyone toward the thing in the ground.

"Papa, what is it? What is over there?"

"Stay close to me, Hannah," he said, as he put his arm around her with Mama on his other side.

Their group moved together toward the others. The German guards forced them into a single line. Hannah looked behind at the thing in the ground. It was a horrible monster like nothing she could ever have imagined. It did not even seem real. The pit, a huge hole in the ground, was half-filled with bodies, bloody and writhing.

Chapter Three

"*Achtung*! Remove all clothing! *Macht Schnell*!" shouted a German SS officer in a crisp black uniform as he paced up and down the line of villagers. He was tall and thin with a sharp jaw and bright, blue eyes. The German soldiers standing by wore black uniforms as well. Everyone carried a gun of one type or another, rifles, submachine guns, and pistols.

The SS officer screamed out again, "I said remove all garments. Now!"

"Papa," Hannah whispered. Her father was standing on her left and Hannah's mother stood on the opposite side of him, clutching her husband's arm.

"Be still, Hannah," Papa said quietly.

I can't undress in front of my father, she thought. *How can anyone expect a girl to do that?*

A stocky soldier stepped quickly toward them. He raised an arm high and slapped Papa across the face with the back of his hand. Papa's head turned slightly, but otherwise his body remained motionless. Blood trickled out of his right nostril and touched his upper lip.

"You have heard the order," he yelled. "*Macht Schnell*! Hurry up!"

Hannah shrank behind her father's thick, right arm as the gruff soldier moved down the line of villagers to inflict more punishment.

"Papa, Papa, help me! Help me!" she cried, tugging at his arm. "We should run! Run away. Don't let them do this to us."

"We have no choice," Papa said in a strange, faraway voice. "I'm sorry. I should have taken you away from here. It's my fault. All of it is my fault."

"No Seymour, it is not our fault," Mama said. "Remember the

plan. Do it. I am ready. Do it."

"Hannah, move behind me," Papa said softly. "Be quick, child."

Hannah's eyes darted around at the men and the woods. Everything was blurred. None of the faces seemed real. Like masks. They all had masks. Afraid to look back into the pit again where other Jews lay squirming in pain and crying out, Hannah was terrified that she might recognize someone, a friend or a shopkeeper.

But something drew her to look behind. No face was familiar. The bodies—they were naked, and their eyes just stared into nothing. She turned away and clutched Papa's arm tighter. *I will be there, too. Lying with all of them.*

The villagers disrobed. Hannah was afraid to look in her father's direction. It would be disrespectful and humiliating to Papa and her. She thought about the hiding place and how far away that must be. Hannah unbuttoned her blouse and waistline and felt her plaid wool skirt slide down her bare legs to the cold ground. *Papa, don't look at me.*

She could see the soldiers stepping into a line parallel to the villagers. A young German soldier stared at her. She covered her private parts the best she could. *Adonai, help us. The rabbi told us God would protect us. Help us. Help me now!*

The late afternoon sun hid behind thick clouds as the March air chilled Hannah's bare skin. The soldier's gaze paralyzed her.

"Papa, can't you do something?" Hannah said, looking straight ahead. "We can tell them where we buried our money and the necklaces."

"Hannah, they hate us. They only want us dead," he said, with such finality that Hannah felt fighting back was hopeless.

Young children cried and many women screamed and moaned. *I need to do something. But what? They have guns. Run away? Where? They will shoot us down.*

"Hannah, if you survive this, wait until all is quiet and then crawl away from here," Papa said, glancing in her direction then turning away. "Play dead if you have to."

"But I was going to speak to them and…" Hannah said, her eyes searching for anything that might stop it all.

"Listen to your father, there is no time. We have already agreed," Mama said, her voice quivering.

"Remember the plan. The forests we explored in the summers. You know those places, Hannah. Go as deep into the woodlands as possible," Papa said in a low, solemn tone. "Try to cross over the Soviet border into Russia."

"I don't know, Papa, I'm scared. I can't think."

"Hannah, remember the maps, geography. Keep heading east."

Hannah took comfort in the certainty in her father's voice.

There is no way to escape. I am going to die here. She drew a deep breath and let out a long exhale. Her breathing slowed and calmness came over her. She could see herself from a different place. She began to notice things. Some of the men had different uniforms. Their hats were black, and boat-shaped. They did not appear to be Germans, but seemed very eager to obey the German officers. A scruffy boy she recognized from Sokolka roamed around behind the group of soldiers.

*This is so unfair.*Then Hannah heard Papa say something.

"*Shema Yisrael Adonai Elo-hei-nu Adonai eh chad,*" he said, low and strong.

Yes, Papa! Yes. Adonai. Adonai, help us.

The Nazi officer began shouting orders again, and all the soldiers raised their weapons and pointed them at the line of villagers. Hannah could see the eyes of the men aiming at her, at Mama and Papa. They just looked like people's eyes, no different than anyone else's. The SS officer raised his hand. "*Feuer*!" he shouted.

Submachine guns, rifles, and Lugers blazed away cutting down mothers, fathers, and children. Everyone was screaming around them. Bodies were riddled with bullets as blood spurted from heads and backs and arms and legs.

Without warning Hannah was snapped behind Papa as a spray of bullets hit his body. Somehow, in spite of the racket, Hannah could hear Mama's cry as the bullets ripped through her body. Hannah pressed her face against Papa's soft bare back. More bullets tore through his body. A massive blood spurt exploded from Papa's neck, slapping Hannah in the forehead, stinging her skin and spraying into her eyes. She blinked trying to regain her sight. The blood on her face began to spread over her nose and dripped onto her lips. It felt warm. It didn't taste like anything. It was Papa's blood. She felt faint and nearly lost consciousness. The ground around her feet felt wet and sticky between her toes. She glanced down to see streams of blood, running down Papa's legs soaking into the dirt. Hannah realized that Mama was no longer next to Papa; she had stepped in front of him to help shield Hannah from the gunfire.

Pressed into Papa's back, Hannah felt the dead weight of his body shifting backward into her. They were standing at the edge of the monster in the ground. The gigantic grave. Hiding behind Papa's body, she glanced back to see wounded and dead neighbors in layers, lying in the pit. Papa's body keeled backward and together they drifted through the air. The drop seemed endless as if she were cascading down a dark, damp well in a nightmare. Hannah vaguely remembered a burning sensation running along her hairline, just above her left temple. Then nothing.

. . . . .

Bang! The loud crack of a German Luger only a couple of meters away jolted Hannah into consciousness. She felt cold and wet and suffocated by the weight of bodies piled on top of her chest, torso, and legs. Only her eyes and forehead were exposed to the air. She cracked open her eyelids. A uniformed man stood erect with feet apart on the dead and dying bodies in the pit. The form was blurred through the slits of her eyelids. The man was carefully scanning the bodies for any signs of life. Looking past Hannah, he smirked, then slowly raised his arm and pointed his Luger above and left of Hannah's head.

Bang! The sound was so close and loud that Hannah flinched and popped open her eyes. She heard a sigh as another villager expired from the gunshot. The standing man was the Nazi officer. She could see him clearly now. He was still scanning for more live victims when his gaze stopped and focused directly on Hannah's eyes.

She was out of breath and felt an overwhelming urge to gasp for air. If she moved or took a breath, he might see it. She lay motionless for what seemed a lifetime. Hannah thought she would never be able to forget that cold stare. Finally, the death glare withdrew from her. Papa moved. *He's alive!*

Wanting to shout for joy, Hannah could only allow herself a private relief. *Adonai* had answered her silent prayer and spared Papa. The Nazi raised his arm once more and pointed the Luger at Papa's head.

No! Hannah wanted to scream. *Please, no!*

Bang! The pistol did its work. Hannah felt Papa's body relax and the dead weight of it increased the pressure on her chest slightly. She felt hollow, like an empty bottle, a see-through girl. Nothing inside. Her lungs squashed like a deflated tire tube, and she tried to breathe.

In the corner of her left eye Hannah could feel a teardrop beginning to form. She must not move. A dead person's eyes would be dry. She was sure of it. Staring into the overcast sky, eyes still open, feigning death, Hannah could see the German's face in her peripheral vision. Maybe the man would not notice the suspended tear. But if it dropped from her eye and crossed her cheek, she could be next.

The German was precise in his killing duty and seemed to take pride and pleasure in it. He would not overlook the tear, a sign that she was still alive. Hannah thought this torture was worse than dying. Papa spoke to her just minutes earlier and now he was gone. The thought of Mama's face, her body torn open and lying above Papa, was beyond all coping.

Don't think of them. Don't think at all, she told herself, relaxing her face.

The gunfire was very sporadic now. Hannah kept focus on her face and shallow breathing. She heard men's voices.

"Ja, Ja," the Nazi officer said to another, content. "I am finished for now. More on the way. There is always more work to do. To the trucks."

Hannah saw a blur at the edge of her eyesight as the German stood up straight and stepped away. She felt the poised teardrop streak down her left cheek. She blinked and another tear dropped from her right eye.

"*Juden schwein*," Hannah heard a soldier say in disgust as the murderers walked across the pile of bodies and scrambled out of the pit. She heard truck motors start and more men shouting in German and another language, Ukrainian probably. The noisy machinery pulled away and trailed off. The woods were once again quiet, peaceful. But Hannah knew different.

The weight on her chest was suffocating and she nearly panicked. *Short breaths, quick and short. Papa and Mama and maybe others above. I can't breathe. Adonai, help me! I've got to get out of here.*

She remembered what Papa had said—wait until all was quiet and then get away to the forests. Tears were running down her cheeks. She wanted to lie there in the pit and cry.

Hannah felt a powerful voice from deep within. *No time for crying…do something. Now!* She pulled her trapped hands along her body. They slid easily between her father's body above and the corpses of the other villagers below on which she lay. Sliding her sticky, blood-covered fingers over her torso, she clawed and yanked at Papa's lifeless shoulder and pulled herself free.

Lying on her back atop the pile of bodies, Hannah breathed cold, clean air. Her mind sharpened and she could see herself as if she were far away, looking upon the scene. A terrifying dream. None of it even seemed real. She didn't want to see Mama's body. *I can't think about them. Not now.* Hannah could feel herself breaking down. The slightest tip and she would fall. *I'll fight them somehow. I'll find a way.*

Hannah struggled to stay focused. *Think, just keep thinking.* Hannah plotted her escape as if she were designing a solution to a problem at school. She slowly rolled over and rose to all fours scanning the horrific scene. She blinked hard to clear her eyes, but the tears would not stop coming.

She hunted for any clothes that might fit. Before they left, the Germans kicked some of the villager's things into the pit. Hannah found a young boy's shirt that fit tightly across her chest. The sleeves barely covered her wrists. The pant leg of a man's dark gray trousers protruded out from under a naked woman. Hannah pulled and pushed at the body while yanking the trousers free.

Sitting on the pile of bodies, she pulled the waistband over her knees. The woman's blood had stained a portion of the thigh on one leg. The belt was still attached to take up the slack in the waist. He must have been a small man. She thought they might fit. No, too long. She would roll up the cuffs. The shirt had small blotches of blood, some of which were still wet.

Her bare feet sunk into warm bodies as she scanned the pit. She needed a coat and her feet were freezing.

She stepped toward the edge of the pit. *Shoes. Have to find shoes.*

"How can I run away without good shoes?" she mumbled, confused, fighting to hold back the fear and panic. Hannah forced herself not to look at Papa and Mama. She would only look one last time when she left. She wanted to say good-bye to them properly, but there was no time, no way to dig graves. She had to be content that Papa and Mama would rest with their people. Tugging at legs and arms, she uncovered a woman who was looking right at her.

Is she alive? Can you see me, lady? She had shoes, house slippers. *Take them! What if she can see me? Oh, I don't know. Take them!*

Hannah yanked the slippers from cold feet. The woman did not move. The soles were soft, not good for running, but would have to do.

Off in the distance the noise of trucks echoed through the trees. The Germans were coming back. Hannah rode the panic rising in her body. Frantic, she looked toward the woods for a way to escape.

Which way to the forests? East and maybe some to the north? What route would be safe? The Germans, they must be everywhere. I don't know. Get out! Go!

Crawling on hands and knees, Hannah pulled herself up from the pit. Out of the corner of her eye she noticed movement and looked toward the park entrance. The village boy was still there, walking up the park road about fifty meters away. She focused on him. It was the village policeman's son. A man walked away in the distance. The father. The boy lagged behind, shuffling along. He looked back, their eyes met, but the boy seemed to be in a daze.

Hannah moved swiftly toward an opening in the woods. She stole a glance back to Mama and Papa, but could hardly make out their bodies among the pile of corpses. At least they were together. They would always be together now. Her stomach felt empty, body cold and numb. She didn't want to remember her family like this.

They died for me, Hannah thought. *I won't forget you. I won't. Go. Go!*

She turned and ran toward the woods. The lady's slippers were soft and she felt every rock and sharp stick. Her feet hurt already after only a few meters, but she swallowed the pain and kept moving. The boy cried out something and she looked back. He waved a fist and called after her to stop.

"They will find you and kill you too," he yelled.

Get away. Like Papa said. Run!

As she neared the woods she felt strange as if it all had happened before. Just for an instant, the fear stopped. Anger rose from somewhere inside. She could do this. Survive. And more. She felt a chill like when the blue-eyed Nazi's eyes shot through her. She could feel it in her own eyes. Losing focus, Hannah stepped on a stick and nearly lost her balance. She stopped and stood up, straightened her back, then stepped into the woods and disappeared into the trees and brush.

• • • • •

Shadows crossed the path that led deeper into the woods. The temperature began to drop. Long breaths pulled in lung-stabbing air. Hannah found something of a trail that deer or maybe people trampled down over the years. Rambling on in the dimming light, the sting of small tree branches and underbrush whipping her face and arms slowed progress. She stopped to think. *What should I do? They're gone. The plan. The suitcase. I can't get to it. It's the other way from here, I think.*

Hannah had no idea how far she had come. With nowhere to hide and out of breath, sides aching, she stopped and listened. Bent over with hands on knees, her heart pounded in her ears. The woods were still. Only her breathing broke the silence.

The boy in the park stuck in her mind. Like he said, they would chase after her. But maybe she had some time. They were too busy bringing more villagers to the park. She sat on the ground trying to catch her breath. Wrapping her arms around bent legs, Hannah huddled into a ball against the growing cold.

Papa, I'm afraid. I can't do this. Her eyes welled with tears. She rested her forehead on her knees and closed her eyes. *I want all this to go away. Make it go away, Papa.* Hannah stayed still for a few minutes. Everything around her looked the same. Dusk had turned to night. She glanced up through the boughs. No moon. The stars were clear, like Papa showed her with his telescope. She took a deep breath and let it out slowly. The sharp pain in her side was gone.

I need to move on, she thought. She remembered the nights in the forest camping. *Where is the North Star?* Searching the sky through the gaps between the tree limbs, she found it.

Hannah got up and slowly began to move forward. Trying to keep her wits, she focused on the star. *Papa, Adonai, are you up there somewhere? Stay with me. Help me find Russia.*

With no way to be sure anyone was following, she trudged on. The initial shock that had pushed her to escape the park was spent. She touched the left side of her head and then snapped her hand away. The pain was sharp and burning. Her head throbbed. Every few steps Hannah felt the sharpness of a rock or stick poking her feet. She couldn't move fast enough with the slippers and wondered where she could get shoes and warmer clothes.

The path through the woods seemed to narrow as underbrush blocked Hannah's way. Small branches whipped her face as she moved nearly blind through the woods. The stinging and burning was dizzying. *Where am I? The star. Where is the star? Now I've got myself lost!* Up ahead, through tears she spotted a twinkle of light in the distance—a spotlight. *Germans. They've found me!*

A rustling from behind disturbed the silent woods. Hannah wiped the tears from her eyes and tried to see through the darkness. Maybe it was a trap and they'd followed her from the pit. Her eyes had now adjusted to the darkness. She could see what seemed to be an area of dried mud with few if any leaves or sticks bounded by dense thicket. Her steps made no sound as she moved toward the brush a few meters off the path. The thicket was somewhat hollow inside. It was an ideal shelter for a rabbit or a fox. Hannah groped in the darkness for a small opening large enough for her to slip through. The only way in was from the back side, easily entered by a small animal, but barely large enough for even a small person.

It's a good hiding place. I hope no animals live in there. Please, Adonai. Please.

Lying flat on her stomach Hannah crawled on her belly through the little opening. The brush scratched her cheek, poked her head, and snagged her hair. Trying not to make a sound, she pulled her torso and legs through the briar-guarded opening.

Hannah curled up into a ball to keep her feet and arms from freezing. Then she heard the footsteps approaching at a quick pace. Two or three people moved along the path with wide strides, crunching leaves and sticks as they hurried through the shadows.

What if they heard me squirming into the thicket? She peered through the tight mesh of branches.

Three shadowy forms passed by. She had not heard enough to understand them before. Now at only five or six meters away, she knew. Three men, soldiers with rifles speaking Ukrainian. They said something about a boy and a girl and the woods.

They turned left to continue down the path and disappeared into the darkness. After twenty or thirty minutes, all was quiet. Somewhat rested, Hannah crawled on her belly out of the brush. She returned to the trail, but tried to move in the dark without a sound which was now almost impossible.

She realized that following them might not be best, but she didn't know where else to go. What if they turned around and caught her? She stopped to listen every now and again. The temperature continued to drop. It couldn't be more than ten degrees Celsius, she guessed. Her whole body seemed to ache now. Then, less than a hundred meters ahead, she saw another flash of light. The rustle of leaves came from up the path. From the light. Hannah froze. The Ukrainians were coming back!

Frantically searching for an escape path, she found none. She would have to stand her ground. Hannah picked up a pointed stick that lay nearby. She braced herself for the onslaught. Footsteps were close. She raised the sharp end of the stick at the sound.

A fawn hopped onto the path and stopped about three or four meters directly in front of Hannah. The animal had long soft ears and a twitching nose. The eyes were pure black dots. The deer looked startled. Hannah stooped over and supported herself with the stick. She let out a long breath and drew in the earthy scent of the woods. She stood up and dropped the stick to the ground without a sound. The frail baby deer hopped away. Shivering, Hannah watched it disappear into the darkness.

Chapter Four

A slight breeze rustled the trees and the speck of light up the path twinkled in the distance. The light did not move. No one would be out in the woods with a light just standing still. It was probably a farmhouse. With the thought of a warm hiding place, she slowly moved toward the light.

In fifty meters or so, she came upon a clearing. A house, lit inside, stood out against a wall of shadows. A well-worn little barn nearby looked dark and uninhabited.

If I could only get warm and maybe find some shoes. I'll never reach Russia without good clothes and shoes.

The barn sat in the shadows only twenty or thirty meters across the clearing. The dim light from the house did not carry the full distance to the barn, so Hannah hoped to dart in and out of the shadow lines to the barn door and slip inside without being noticed.

She lunged forward from the safety of the trees into the open expanse. Crouched in the long silhouette of the woodpile for a second or two, she ran for the barn door. The door latch was crude and squeaked as she lifted the handle. The rusty metal felt cold and rough against her skin. The door gave way, hinges creaked. As she slipped through the tiny opening, Hannah quickly peered toward the house for any sign that someone inside may have heard her. As she nudged the door closed, a spark of fear jolted her.

She saw a tiny dot of red light that glowed from the dark end of the porch. Could it have been a lit cigarette? Was someone standing outside in the dark, watching her? Maybe she just imagined it. She stood in the corner of the room and waited for someone to burst in to get her. She stayed behind the door and waited for her eyes to adjust to the dark.

I'm so cold and tired I don't care anymore. Maybe I should have died in the pit. At least we'd be together. No matter what I do, I won't beat them. Tears streaked across her cheeks. Standing silent, Hannah felt her heart beating, her lungs filling and expiring the sweet-scented air of the hay in the barn. It was warmer than outside. She wiped her face with dirty hands and looked around for anything that might be helpful. *Alright, stop the crying. Stop it. Be strong. You're stronger than them. Just keep going,* Hannah told herself over and over.

One dirty little window covered with cobwebs and a heavy coating of dust allowed only a weak stream of light from the house to penetrate the otherwise total darkness. Slowly her eyes adjusted to the pitch. She could make out a ladder that ascended into a dark loft.

The air smelled clean, not musty like the garden toolshed in Warsaw. Sol Wertz from the old neighborhood slipped into her mind. Eight of them used to hide in the toolshed, which smelled damp like rotten grass. Hannah climbed the ladder toward the dark loft. The ladder rungs pressed hard into her arches. The lady's slippers offered little protection. Her tattered feet felt like clumps of flesh and bone, cold and numb. The top of the ladder extended three rungs above the loft floor. Hannah could feel the ladder move sideways as she stepped onto the loft.

A large pile of hay took up half of the floor space. It smelled clean and fresh. Hannah burrowed a hole in the pile and nestled into it. The sweet scent of straw crept up her nose, and though the straw poked and scratched her skin, the warmth was heavenly. Shivering, she swept more hay over herself and lay still for a moment. Shallow breaths soon gave way to deeper, relaxed breathing. Slowly she could feel the tension release in her leg muscles as the insulating hay trapped her body heat.

This is better, Hannah thought as she began to feel the warmth from the blanket of straw melt away the numbness in her feet and calves. The cuts and bruises from her escape through the woods began to sting and ache as her body warmed. *I need shoes and better clothes. Russia is too far away. I won't make it like this. Papa, help me think of something.* Her head ached much stronger now. The crusted blood on the side of her face was jagged to the touch and the slightest pressure near the wound above her temple brought blinding pain. Maybe a bullet grazed her face.

Exhausted and hungry, she laid her head on the pillow of straw. A lone tear streaked down her cheek. Silently, softly, Hannah fell off to sleep.

. . . . .

In her dream, the old door to the basement which Papa never had time to oil, creaked abruptly. It took only a moment as Hannah sorted out dream from reality. Her eyes popped open. The barn. The creaky door. Someone was inside! Her spine and hair felt electric. *Don't move, don't even breathe.*

Footsteps cut the quiet of the night moving slowly toward the ladder. Toward her hideaway. Then stopped.

"I mean you no harm," the farmer said in a kind, even tone in thick country Polish.

The man could not see her and appeared to be talking to himself in an empty barn. But he must have seen her slip into the building. The cigarette…

"My wife, I don't know. She's scared of these Germans and Ukrainians," he said with no anger in his voice. "She might tell somebody, so can't let her know."

Hannah did not move, barely drawing a breath.

"I'm leaving you some bread and cheese and a cup of water," he said. "Take that old jacket that's hanging on the wall down here. I don't need it. Stay the night. Just don't let the wife see you."

Hannah heard footsteps, then silence.

"Is there anything else I can get you?" he said with such compassion, Hannah thought maybe she could trust the man.

His boots scuffed the floor. The door hinges creaked.

"Shoes," Hannah called out, her voice cracking. "I need shoes…please."

"Ahhh," the farmer said.

Hannah heard the barn door swing shut again.

What have I done?

Wild, raw fear shot through her chest, limbs, and head. She could hear her heart beating fast. She tried to draw a breath, but her lungs were already full.

Should I run? Should I wait to see what the man does? Can I trust him? He seems so kind. It was only a few minutes now since the man left her. Not knowing what to do, she sat up in the straw. Frozen, she stared into the shadows.

Stupid, stupid, stupid. I should never trust any of them. What am I doing? Stupid girl. Maybe he will come back with a gun and kill me. Be ready to fight. I need a club or a knife or something. She thought about leaving, but he didn't come back.

After a time, her heartbeat and breathing calmed. She remembered what Papa used to say: *"Do not act before you understand the consequences of your actions. Once clear, you can proceed with confidence, even with haste."* She thought he read that in a book.

She decided to wait and listen.

After half an hour with no sign of danger, Hannah decided to explore the barn again and she climbed down the ladder to the main floor. Besides, from the ground floor she had some chance of running out the door to escape. Also, to look for a weapon. Her eyes were now completely adjusted to the darkness. She could distinguish farm implements, a hoe, a plow, and some clothing on nails hammered into the wall studs. She thought the jacket that the farmer offered was hanging by the dirty window. As she reached for it her fingers touched the wall. The unfinished wood was very coarse and dusty from years of neglect. She expected the coat to smell musty or dank, but it didn't smell at all. She took it down off the rusty nail and shook it.

The muffled sound of the jacket being shaken might have been heard outside. She glanced out the dusty window. All was still. She pulled on the old coat and buttoned up the front. It was old and faded, but warm.

Hearing her stomach growl, Hannah realized she had forgotten about food. Groping in the dark, she nearly knocked over the bread and water sitting on an inverted pail in the middle of the dirt floor. Peering out the window again, the barnyard was quiet. The farmer was not coming back. Her stomach growled again. Hannah moved to the bucket with the food.

I'm sorry, Papa, but I have to eat. I don't want to, but I have to keep going. She smelled the cheese. The cheese was cold against her teeth, and the rich taste of it filled her mouth. A memory of home filled her thoughts. Bubbe Rachel liked to eat cheese with her Hamantashen. No one did that. Only Hannah knew her secret. One year, Hannah made Hamantashen for Purim for the neighborhood street fair. Bubbe Rachel, Mama, and Hannah were hard at work baking. The rolling pin slipped out of Hannah's hand, landing in Bubbe's favorite rose-petal mixing bowl and splattered dough in every direction. Clumps landed on the tip of Hannah's nose, eyebrows, and bangs. She expected Mama to be mad, but Bubbe and Mama looked at Hannah's face and burst out laughing. Hannah laughed along with the ladies. She got second place in the Hamantashen category. Absently, she tried to wipe dough from her brow. Scorching pain flashed across her mind. *Don't touch it! Leave the wound alone.*

Hannah sat still for a moment, then bit into the bread and chewed. It felt coarse on her tongue and somewhat dry, though not yet stale. Bubbe's bread was always chewy on the outside and soft inside. Regardless, the farmer's bread filled her stomach and for that she was grateful. The large tin cup was cold to the touch, and the water made her shiver as it flowed down her throat and settled uncomfortably in her stomach.

She finished the bread and cheese, but saved about half of the water. The food felt good, though she didn't want to admit it. But the persistent nagging in the pit of her stomach had nothing to do with food. Each time she closed her eyes, she could still see the gunfire and hear the thudding of bullets hitting Mama's body. That would not stop. *I'm going to have to do more than escape. Somebody has to pay for what they did to us. Someday.*

Without warning, the barn door creaked open and a husky shape stood silhouetted in the dim light. Hannah froze, then glanced around for anything that could be used as a weapon. Nothing. She slowly stepped away from the intruder.

"Don't be afraid. I've helped others, you know. I want to help you," the farmer said. "My wife is sick and went to bed early. I found my daughter's old shoes and thick socks. She is married and lives on her own now. Don't know if they will fit."

"Please don't hurt me," Hannah said, taking a step closer to the door. She wanted the shoes. Had to have them. She stopped. "I'll try them. Please, put them down and I'll get them."

"I'm not going to hurt you. You need help, yes?"

The farmer stood feet apart, a lantern in one hand. In the lamplight Hannah could see he was a short and stocky man with a fat, round face and blush-red complexion. With his barrel chest and tree limb-like arms extending into big, thick hands, Hannah thought he looked right for farming. She thought he seemed kind, but didn't know if she should trust anyone. She would have to wait and see.

The man raised the lantern and the bright light glanced off the wound and blood streaks caked across her cheek and forehead. He grimaced at the sight.

"You must be in a lot of pain," he said when he saw the blood. "I have clean rags in a bag over here." He motioned to the shadowy corner of room. "I'll clean it up."

The farmer's movements were slow and heavy. Hannah didn't know what to do. She was ready to run for the barn door. But the man proceeded without her consent and came to her with a white cloth. Hannah raised her arms to block him and took a step back. First dipping the rag in her water cup, he held the cloth up in front of her face and gestured. *If he wanted to hurt me, well...he could kill me with his bare hands.*

Hannah dropped her arms to her side. The farmer hung the lantern on a nail and moved close. He gently dabbed and wiped clean the skin around the wound.

"That graze looks nasty and needs a sterile touch," he said, looking over the oozing burn. "Infection will come on sure enough if left alone."

Hannah's head throbbed, the pain radiating down her cheek and into her jaw.

"I'll have to go back to the house for alcohol," he said, wagging his head. "Can't wake the wife though."

He turned and walked out of the barn toward the farmhouse, bent slightly forward with determination. Hannah moved to the door and peeked through the narrow opening. She watched him step onto the porch and go in. After a few minutes the window on the far side of the house lit up. Hannah jumped.

He woke his wife.

The farmer's words came flooding back and a new round of fear seized her.

What if she suspects? What if he tells her that a fleeing Jewish girl is hiding in their barn? *I am so stupid to think these gentiles will help me.*

As suddenly as the far window lit up, it went dark. Hannah imagined a shadowy figure peering out. She strained to make out a shape, but the distance and darkness were too much.

The farmer came out of the house carrying something. He had a heavy woolen jacket on and moved quietly and quickly to the barn. Hannah backed away from the door. The door creaked once as he squeezed through the opening.

"She woke up with me fumbling around in the kitchen for alcohol," he said under his breath. "I told her I had to ready my tools for tomorrow's work and she should go back to sleep."

"You're very kind, but I can't stay here long," Hannah said, almost in a whisper as she sat down on the pail. "Ukrainian soldiers were following me from the park. I'm afraid they will find me and bring me back to the Germans."

"You are a Jewish girl?" the farmer asked, looking Hannah in the eye.

Hannah thought her heart had stopped for a second. She just stared at him.

"The Germans and their friends warned us. I could be arrested or even killed for helping a Jew. But my friend was Jewish. He was a good a farmer, too. A good man.

"Was?" Hannah asked, barely getting the word out.

"Yes. They took him and his wife. His children, too. They never came back."

"Did you tell the Germans about them?" Hannah couldn't believe the words came from her own mouth.

"I did not," he said, wagging his head. "But that is when I started helping Jews when I could. "It is not right, what is going on here."

"Are you sure the family is gone?" Hannah thought maybe they fled to the forest. Maybe this farmer knows the best way to go.

"I closed up the farm and saved the animals. I know those bastards killed the whole family. I can feel it in my bones."

"Your wife is afraid they will hurt her, too. Right?"

"Forget them for now," he said while wetting the rag with alcohol. "They've probably given up for tonight. Too dark now. If anyone comes, I will tell them I saw no one."

He could be lying, but why would he do all this for me? He seems like a good man. I'm going to have to trust somebody or I'll never reach the forests.

She looked at the damp rag he held up in front of her face and then back at the farmer. She caught a whiff of the pungent chemical and pulled her head away.

"This is going to sting very strongly when it touches the wound," he said, holding the rag close to her head, "but it has to be done. Bite down on this."

Hannah bit down on a wad of cloth. The man gingerly rubbed the area around her temple and cleaned off the layers of dried blood. He dabbed the wound and Hannah pulled away and whimpered in pain from the blistering burn of the disinfectant. She felt nauseous and dizzy and like she was losing control. Another bolt of fear raced through her body.

If I pass out he can do whatever he wants with me. Be strong. Adonai, please help me.

Hannah instinctively reached out with her arms, hands groping for something solid to steady her body and keep from falling off the bucket. She found the farmer's forearm and clutched it.

"I am sorry…so sorry," the man said, with a grimace that seemed to match the strength of pain spiking through her head. "It will get worse without this. I am very sorry."

Hannah relaxed a moment as he stopped dabbing. She steadied herself, then nodded for him to continue. He waited. Hannah was suddenly aware of the man's muscles. Hard and powerful arms developed from a lifetime of farmwork.

He could easily overpower me. But his touch is light and his eyes are soft, like Papa's eyes.

Hannah looked up at the farmer. She felt tears trickling down her cheeks. Blushing, Hannah released her grip on the farmer's forearm. The wad of cloth fell out of her open mouth as she took in a deep breath and let it out slowly. He stopped and looked up.

"Please. Go on," she said, resetting the wad of cloth in her mouth. Hannah rested her hands in her lap and nodded to him.

The farmer finished the cleanup. From his pocket he took a small, blue-glass jar and opened it. With his thick index finger he scooped out some greasy gel and delicately smeared the remedy over the open wound.

"When my daughter was a young girl and scraped her knee, I would put this ointment on it. I called it 'tickle medicine' and she would stop crying and giggle. You remind me of her a little," he said, a smile breaking through his whiskered face, eyes sparkling.

He made a makeshift bandage from a piece of dull-gray cloth and fastened it around Hannah's forehead, covering the wound.

"You need to sleep now," the farmer said, motioning to the loft. "You will be safe overnight, I think. The straw is warm and clean."

Hannah began to climb up the ladder and heard the farmer pick up the dressings. He slowly shuffled to the barn door.

"I am Pawlowski," he said, glancing up to the loft.

"Hannah Gould," she said. "Thank you."

"Good night, Hannah," Mr. Pawlowski said and closed the barn door.

Chapter Five

A scratching sound overhead seemed distant. Then it stopped for a moment. Now it was close and obviously on the roof. Lying still under the hay, Hannah carefully opened her eyes. With only that slight movement of her eyelids, the wound came alive again. Her head ached.

She thought it must be a bird walking around on the barn roof. It was probably just before sunrise and nothing else seemed to be about. The loft was dim in the pale morning light. She breathed in a mixture of sweet and damp air. Sitting upright, a dizzying wave of pain rushed across the side of her head.

I made it through the night. Now what do I do? Should I leave here now or wait until dark?

Hannah looked at her dusty, torn slippers. She held her toes to warm them. Her feet needed more time to recover. Given the silence, all seemed at peace in the barnyard. But she needed to check outside to be sure. She carefully climbed down from the loft and winced each time her sore feet pressed into the dry, cracked rungs of the old ladder. She touched down on the barn floor and looked around, spotting a pair of scuffed women's work shoes. Men's tattered work socks with a jagged tear were draped over the shoelaces.

His daughter's shoes. They must have been handed down. They were poor people. Hannah remembered a farmer waving to her when she and Papa passed through the farming areas on the way to the forests for their weekend summer trips. Men, sometimes women, sweaty and dirty, worked the fields.

Some just stared at them in their car. They seemed angry. She doubted their children had nice shoes like her family did. Even before her shoes were as worn as these, Mama would give them to poor people in the city. Mama always said they weren't rich, but Papa made a good living. Hannah thought the farmers might hate her because she had nice clothes. Now she thought maybe she was wrong.

Looking around, Hannah spotted a bag and container sitting on the worktable by the window that wasn't there last night. *How did Mr. Pawlowski get these things in here without me hearing him? I have to be more careful. At least I can trust him.*

Even after sleeping fairly well, Hannah still felt drained. Another day of running seemed impossible. Her head ached even more than last night. It would be so easy to give up. But that wouldn't help anyone. Part of her felt like crawling back to the hay in the loft. Part of her pushed to go on. She ran her fingers through her hair in an attempt to straighten out some of the knots.

Looking around she spotted a clean rag folded on the workbench by the window. Also on the table was the bag which contained another piece of bread and more cheese. An old-fashioned canteen, full and cold, sat next to the bag. It looked like a relic from a past war. *He must have been an army man. Water for me in the woods. I wouldn't have thought of it.*

She peered out of the dirty, cracked window glass. There were a few chickens pecking the ground quietly and a cat lying in the yard. No one was in view of the window. She sensed no immediate danger. Moving away from the bench she found a relatively clean spot in the corner and sat on the floor. Her cup was refilled with water and after taking a few swallows, Hannah poured a little on the rag. She wiped her face and neck, careful not to disturb the makeshift bandage. Then, gingerly she cleaned her feet with the rag and put on the old socks and shoes. The fit was tight, but the thick socks cushioned her sore feet. She laced up the shoes and got to her feet. Her toes felt warmer. *I can even run in these shoes,* she thought, walking around the barn floor.

Look at me, with a boy's shirt and man's pants rolled up over the cuffs. Will I blend in with the villagers now? Stay away from people. Hide in the woods.

. . . . .

Outside the barn, Hannah heard voices. Deep voices. Men. She wasn't certain of the dialect, but not German. Maybe Ukrainian. Mr. Pawlowski said in Polish that he had bread and cheese in the house. They were very near the barn door. She dared not move around for fear of causing a sound. Hannah squatted and slowly lifted herself above the workbench enough to peer through the window. Three soldiers with guns followed Mr. Pawlowski toward the house.

Should I get away while I can or stay hidden? What if they come back and search the barn? What if they see me leaving?

She looked quickly for some sort of weapon. Hannah grabbed a pocketknife from the workbench and buttoned up her coat. Delicately prying open the barn door, the hinges creaked as she created a large enough opening to squeeze her body through. The early morning sun now lit up the barnyard. Cold, dry morning air touched her face and she blinked to improve vision. Once outside, she jerked her head to the left and right with eyes darting, searching for a way to go. Glancing toward the house, she saw the back of the last soldier stepping through the farmhouse doorway. Looking around she spied the woodpile from the previous night's escape and headed directly to it for cover. She was sure no one saw her.

Hannah could feel her heart beating like it might explode in her chest. She hesitated, checked the back door. No one.

Do something. Right now.

She spotted an opening at the edge of the woods. Maybe it led to a path. With the woodpile somewhat blocking the view from the house, Hannah scurried and bent over from the waist to reduce her visible height. About thirty meters across open scrub grass to the bushes and woods, she moved faster and faster. Feeling naked again, like the whole world was watching, she felt cheated. She did nothing wrong and shouldn't have to run and hide from anyone. It wasn't fair. But she kept moving.

With only three meters to safety, a woman screamed, "There, over there, someone is running into the woods!" The voice came from behind her, from the direction of the farmhouse.

No! Mrs. Pawlowski. Afraid for her life. What about me?

Hannah passed through the opening into the woods and quickly found the path that continued on from last night. She broke into a full run. The shoes were comfortable and she set a fast pace. The sun was on her right. She would need to find a way toward the sun, toward the east.

Afraid to slow down, Hannah could not tell if she was being pursued or not. She turned her head back and glanced over her shoulder, but she could not get a glimpse of the trail behind. She knew she had to get off this path; they would follow it, too. She had to look for a path east.

Continuing on, she eventually could not keep up the pace. Nearly exhausted, Hannah felt her body slowing down. Heart pounding and breathing heavily, she stopped and turned around. The path was twisted and ran up and down, so she could only see about a hundred meters in any direction. The rustling of feet over the last rise startled her.

They're on me! Hannah held her aching sides, gasping for air.

She turned and lunged forward, running along the path. Her feet felt like stones. Almost in a panic, she saw it. On the right, one branch of the path went up a short grade and quickly over a crest. She would be out of sight. She veered right and pushed herself to the limit to get over the crest. Once over, Hannah had nothing left to give. She stopped and bent over with hands on knees, panting hard.

A large tree off the path had fallen and lay rotting in a sea of brown leaves. She tramped through brush, leaves crunching and crackling toward the massive hulk.

Around the back side of it was a space created by the large tree trunk and a dip of the ground. It would shield her from the path. She heard muffled speech, then the thumping of shoes on the path. They were moving away. They must have missed the turnoff. *What if they come back?*

The depression would have to do as a hiding place. But the ground looked soggy and cold. Grotesque holes dotted the dirt, drilled by some wild thing. *Snakes. I hate snakes.* Papa always said that snakes and most small animals were more afraid of people than we of them. Besides, it was too cold for snakes. *Well, just in case.* Hannah picked up a twig and scraped and swatted the depression with it.

Hearing footsteps from over the rise, Hannah crawled on all fours toward the depression. Turning over onto her back, she squeezed her body between the damp ground and the underbelly of the hulking tree trunk. Still panting from the long run, she tried hard to calm down.

The sound of breaking sticks and crackling leaves stopped in the same spot on the path where she had been. A man spit and said something under his breath.

Hannah fought back tears. If they found her, she had no energy left for another run. Her head wound throbbed in rhythm with her pounding heart. Her feet hurt in spite of the shoes and socks. Tears welled up in her eyes. More crackling of leaves and her pursuer was on the move again. Hannah held her mouth to keep from making any audible cry, but otherwise dared not move again. Like in the pit, she lay like a dead person. The footsteps became more distant. The man was gone. Where were the others? She figured they must have stayed on the main path.

She waited. Hannah could only hear the breeze rustling through the trees. No voices and no footsteps. She wondered if she should move on. If all three followed her and then split up to cover this path, they would surely meet back here. *I've got to keep going on this trail. Dealing with one man has to be easier than three. Maybe he quit. Be careful.*

Hannah pulled and pushed herself out from under the tree and squatted low for fear the men might spot her from a distance. Dizzy from the wound and from standing up, she clutched the tree trunk for balance.

I can't just hide. Remember what Papa said. Go east, even if the Ukrainian might turn back and meet me. I'll run faster.

Hannah took a deep breath and stood erect. She continued on, stopping occasionally to listen. An hour later, the woods were brighter and the path ended at the edge. Beyond the trees sat a grassy meadow with cottages and small barns in the distance. A country road wove through the village. She wondered where the soldier went from here. Perhaps he knew the area and told the others to meet him in the village below.

Fighting her headache, Hannah neared the wood's edge. The morning sun poked through gray clouds, but struggled to burn off the overnight chill. The farmer's coat was warm. She grabbed the front of it to gather the material and tighten the fit against the cold.

Looking out from the trees, she could see that there would be no protection once outside of the woods. She had little choice. Russia was to the east. That is where she would go. Papa and Mama died for her. *Go east. Say it over and over. Go east. East.*

"East to the forests," Hannah whispered, as she stepped out into the open field.

Up ahead sat a weathered wooden shed at the edge of the field and woods about ten meters to her right. She hadn't noticed it before.

An image of herself and Sol Wertz peeking through the spaces between the boards of the garden toolshed in Warsaw stuck in her head. The soldier could be watching her. Like she and Sol had spied on people. She hesitated then took a step away from the shed.

A rustling from behind startled Hannah. A powerful hand clamped onto her forearm. Looking up, a soldier in black, the Ukrainian, grabbed for her throat. His eyes were wild, teeth clenched. His hand missed as she spun away. She kicked at his shins. He laughed and pulled her into his chest by her forearm. Pounding on his chest with her free hand had no effect. With both hands he turned her and wrapped his arm around her throat applying overpowering pressure. Hannah felt herself being dragged to the shed.

"You are the Jew that ran away," he said in broken Polish. "You see, you cannot get away. We will always find you Jews and kill you. But first I will take what I want."

Hannah tried to scream, but the man's forearm was choking her.

I can't breathe! Fight, fight, fight.

She kicked him with her heels and jabbed him with elbows, but nothing loosened his grip. In one powerful motion, he turned her around and pushed her to the ground. Hannah felt his crushing weight on her. Sharp stones and sticks poked into her back. Dry brown leaves surrounded her head.

He's going to kill me, she thought.

"Papa, Papa, Help me, help me!" she screamed.

The soldier raised his hand high. Hannah felt a stinging blow on her right cheek as the back of the man's hand slapped across her face. Stunned from the impact, she vaguely felt a tugging at her clothes. She felt his body pressing hard against her.

The man breathed heavy, short breaths. He pinned her collarbone with his forearm and groped underneath her shirt with his other hand.

Stop him. Hit him. A stick or a rock. She looked to her side. Her arms were free. *Can't reach anything. What else? Think...the knife. Get the knife.* She felt for the coat pocket. *Where is it? Please. Papa. Adonai. Help me.* Her thumb caught the pocket edge and she slipped her hand to the bottom. She grasped the cold metal object and pulled it out. Trying to hold the knife and pull open the blade with one hand would not work. *Two hands. Use two hands. How? How?*

The soldier pressed into her even harder. *It hurts. Stop!*

Use both hands. Don't let him see it. Be quick.

She raised both arms over her head. Fingers pinching the blade edge with her other hand, she pulled on it and the blade snapped into position. She dropped her arms to her sides.

Stab him. Stab him now!

The knife felt cold and hard. She drove the blade deep into the man's side. Startled from the stab, he stopped and propped himself up. Pulling the blade out, Hannah slashed across his cheek, catching his nose. She froze and stared at his face.

"Ahhh, ahhh," he howled and pulled away from her.

Blood started to seep from the cut. The soldier touched his hand to his face wound and blood gushed from between his fingers.

Hannah rolled sideways and sprang to her feet.

Run! Run! Run toward the farmhouse.

She leaped into the pasture and ran for her life. Jerking her head back, she caught a glimpse of the soldier starting to follow. He had one hand on his face and the other holding his side.

Hannah raced as fast as she could. The farmhouse was only about two hundred meters away now and she stole another look back. The soldier had stopped in the middle of the field and was bent over. She hoped the stab really hurt him, that he'd stop chasing her.

She kept running. *Hide. Can't let anyone see me. Not even these villagers. Any of them could tell on me.*

"Go east, east to the forests," she heard herself chanting under her breath as she ran.

Hannah continued to sprint toward the sun, her heart pounding in her ears and chest. In this daylight it might be better to look for more woods. She spotted a narrow country road that looped past the farm and split the group of cottages as it twisted its way to the hills farther east and then out of sight. A girl running through farms and down the country road would not go unnoticed.

Reaching the farmhouse, Hannah slipped behind it and leaned against the back wall of the house, out of the pursuing soldier's sight. Panting and dry-mouthed, she rested her head against the wall and gazed into the blue and gray sky above. *Quiet down or they'll hear.* The cold air burned her lungs with each gasp. Like spikes driven into her chest and more into her sides, Hannah fought the pain. She had to be ready to run again. Her temple and bruised cheek now throbbed constantly. Taking gulps of air and slowing her exhales, she tried to relax her stomach muscles. Afraid the soldier had caught up, she dared not peek around the corner of the cottage. Voices, some high-pitched and some low, broke the stillness. Men and women were going about their daily chores. The tiny village was awaking for the day. She had to look before someone found her and screamed. She slid her back along the wall, and turning, she peeked around the corner.

A man dressed in work clothes was carrying some kind of tool and chatting with a woman as she hung wet clothes to dry in the sun. Hannah pulled back behind the wall. No soldier. Just then she realized she was still clutching the pocketknife. Looking down at her right hand, the blade looked ugly with its sticky streaks of bright red. Her hand was smeared with the soldier's blood. Staring at the blade, she slowly wiped it clean on her pants.

Papa. I'm trying to do what you wanted, but I don't want to remember the blood. Are you looking away, Papa? I have to do things. I had to hurt that man. I have to steal things.

Closing the blade into the handle, Hannah gently slipped the little weapon into her coat pocket. She had never hurt anyone like that before.

Afraid to go on and afraid not to, she moved to the corner again and peeked. The man had left and the woman, having hung the last of her laundry, lifted her empty basket and sauntered toward the house. She seemed somehow untouched by the war going on around her. *She looks like Beila's mama,* Hannah thought. *How could that be? Maybe I could trust her? No, don't be stupid!*

Beyond the yard, a pasture. Empty. Hoping the wounded soldier and his friends had given up the search, Hannah was about to run again. As she started to pull away from the wall, something caught her attention and she stopped.

Strung along a clothesline like flags, women's overalls dried in the morning sunshine with shirts, socks, and undergarments. The overalls were more suited for a farmer's wife than a schoolgirl. But they probably would be a better fit and warmer than the small man's dress pants that now covered her legs. Even better, they were clean, no bloodstains.

Ready to run again, Hannah placed her shoe up against the house wall. She recalled the races against Sol Wertz across the garden in Warsaw—it was how she finally beat him to the other side. *Don't look, Papa. I need these clothes. I have no money to pay for them. The suitcase. Maybe I could make it right someday.*

She lunged around the corner, eyes fixed on the target.

Reaching the clothesline, Hannah grabbed the garment as she flew by and turned back toward the east. Clothes bounced up and down as the overalls caused a ripple effect along the rope. A few things fell. She grabbed a blouse that lay in a heap on the ground.

I am sorry for this. She imagined the farmer's wife picking up her wash from the brown grass and dirt.

Hannah reached the road and continued running up the lane as fast as her work shoes would carry her. She noticed a few peasants here and there among the cottages. A few stopped to watch the girl with a rag tied around her head clutching a bundle of clothes. Someone yelled out. She didn't understand what was said, or even if it was in anger or sympathy. No one could be trusted. No one.

Chapter Six

After running a half hour or so, Hannah could see trucks and other vehicles farther up ahead.

Soldiers, she thought. Most of the farmers here didn't have trucks. They might be army trucks.

Veering off the road, she ran to a small group of trees lying at the edge of a field of tall grass. Crouching low behind the larger of the trees, Hannah waited for the trucks to pass by. While catching her breath, she looked behind for anyone following. The field lay still.

She sat on the cool grass and quickly removed the man's dress pants. She stood for a moment, stooped over, and pulled the work pants over her bare legs. The material was still damp and felt cold and clammy. She had no belt, but her hips held them from falling down. A good fit. Maybe the sun would dry them before dark. Papa said to stay dry in cold weather or she would get sick.

Squatting low, watching and listening for trouble, her head and face ached. The soldier's slap puffed up her cheek which blocked her vision in one eye. The makeshift bandage that the farmer placed was falling down so Hannah removed it.

Trying to think through the pain and decide what to do next, she thought about the soldier back in the woods trying to kill her. But the whole thing seemed strange. He could have killed her right away, but he was doing other things. She felt the same way she did years ago when Sol Wertz pulled his pants down. They were alone in the garden toolshed in Warsaw. She ran home, not knowing what he wanted her to do. Beila tried to tell her. That's what girlfriends do. And now, with the soldier. Hannah shuddered, suspecting what it all meant. She tried to put it out of mind, afraid she might be right.

. . . . .

The truck was only a couple of hundred meters up the road and moving slowly. Startled by a swishing sound from behind, Hannah turned her head back toward the rustling.

Two soldiers were upon her. She tried to leap forward, but the closer one grabbed her around the waist and with powerful arms yanked her body up from the ground. Her back was against the strong man's stomach and she had no leverage to break his grasp. The other soldier ran toward the road and flagged the truck which stopped across from the field and waited.

How did they see me in here? They're going to hurt me, too. Get away. Kick him. Punch.

She squirmed and twisted to try and break free.

"Let me go! You're hurting me. Papa, help," Hannah yelled.

The man laughed and shouted something she didn't understand. Three more soldiers surrounded her now. It was no use, her stomach hurt, she couldn't breathe.

"You are coming with us, girl," one soldier said in Polish.

Hannah stopped fighting. Two men grabbed her wrists and with one behind and another leading the way, they motioned her to move to the truck.

I could stab them with the knife. But then they might take it away. Any of them could use it on me. No, wait for a better time. I hope they don't know that I stabbed their soldier friend by the woods.

She looked at her coat and hand for signs of the man's blood. A trace of caked blood lined the cuticle of her thumb and stuck in the folds of skin on her knuckles. The coat had a blotch over the right pocket. It looked brownish, rather than red.

At the truck, an officer said something and motioned Hannah to get into the back. She was sure they were Ukrainians, and wished she understood them better.

Six soldiers sat on the wood floor in the back of the truck. Mama would say each one looked like a schlump. But they didn't smell too badly. The lead man said something to the others as Hannah put her foot on the stirrup by the rear bumper and began to climb up. A few chuckled and she could feel their probing eyes. A hand on her buttocks and then a strong push sent her sprawling headfirst to the floor of the truck between the lines of seated men. They seemed to enjoy her plight. A few of the soldiers got into the truck behind her and the vehicle started to move forward.

As the truck bounced and jostled along, Hannah sat on the floor curled up in a ball with her head bent low between her knees. She shivered with fear that these men might be the same as the monster in the woods. Her head and cheek began pounding again from the rude shove and impact with the truck floor.

It seemed about an hour or so, kilometers from her home, when the truck finally stopped just outside of a small town. There were railroad tracks and a depot where signs in Polish pointed to loading areas. Though she had not seen a freight yard before, the place appeared to be as she would have imagined it. There were voices toward the cab of the truck, out of view. She thought she heard someone speaking German.

Where are they taking me? What are they going to do to me?

The truck started up again and she could feel it turn into a driveway. Facing to the rear, Hannah and the soldiers could only see what they just passed. More soldiers and military vehicles came into view. Some of the vehicles displayed swastikas. German officers and soldiers were pushing and shouting at townspeople.

The truck jolted to a stop with a squeal of brakes. The last man onto the truck jumped to the ground and saluted an officer. Then the leader reached into the back of the truck, grabbed Hannah's ankle, and pulled her across the dirty truck bed. She collapsed onto the hard gravel yard and started to cry.

A German officer signaled a stocky SS guard who hoisted Hannah up to her feet. Hannah was afraid to look the officer in the eye. She never wanted to see those cold eyes again. Half in a daze, she wondered if they all had that same stare. The German looked at Hannah sharply.

"Are you a Jew?" he asked, in broken Polish in a peculiar way.

What should I say? I did nothing wrong. This one looks like the SS officer at the pit. If I say I am, he'll kill me. It's not fair. I hate them. All of them.

Bent over, Hannah stood shivering, with teeth chattering and streams of tears cutting through the coating of dirt on her face.

"Ja, you are a Jew. I can see by your filthy appearance," he said in precise German.

He gestured to the guard and simply said, "Train."

Hannah felt her heart racing in her chest and a lump growing in her stomach. She fought back an image of a huge pit, even larger than the one where Papa and Mama lay dead.

They are going to take all these people to the woods and shoot them.

The soldier bullied Hannah toward an open cattle car, pushing and shoving her with his rifle. The railroad yard was an awful sight. Trying to stay with family, townspeople were being herded into the open freight cars of the long train. Above their pleading in Polish and Yiddish, the Germans shouted orders. A mother clutched her child, an old man seemed content to be huddled with the rest.

The place was so confusing. There was no time to think about hiding or getting away. Hannah didn't know where the train was bound, but what was happening seemed the same as before. Another pit.

. . . . .

A young man wrestled with two German guards in black uniforms. Hannah saw and heard from across the yard the crack of a rifle butt smashing the man's face. He dropped vertically in a single motion, legs collapsing under his body. His face was oozing blood.

About twenty meters from the train car, Hannah quickly glanced up and down the tracks. Her temple and cheek throbbed, but she tried to think through the pain.

Somehow she had to get away. Maybe under the train cars? There was no time left. She could see more German soldiers on the opposite side of the train. Pushed into the swarm, Hannah was swept up to the railroad car by the steady flow of bodies. The crude wooden step funneled the herd into the car. The woman in front of her tripped on the front edge of the floor and fell forward. The crowd pressed into Hannah's back and she tripped over the fallen woman and landed on flattened palms.

The splintered hardwood floorboards were coated with dried mud, urine, and smeared cow droppings. The smell was strong. Hannah tried to hold her breath, but soon gasped for air. She crawled to the back wall of the car. Her hands stung from slapping the floor. People flowed in through the doorway. Hannah got to her feet, back to the wall.

"Where are they taking us?" she asked an old man with a thick gray beard.

"Probably to die," he said, eyes shallow and tired.

"I mean, to what town?" she replied. He shrugged his shoulders.

"I mean east or west…" He stared at her saying nothing. "Never mind."

I can't stop this. Hannah's eyes filled with tears. The truck that brought everyone to the pit stuck in her mind. Tightly packed, the car left no room between bodies. In a stupor, she could only stare into the backs of the people wedged into her space. Soldiers were shouting outside. Then the big doors were slammed shut. Papa's voice echoed in her head, far away. He had given up. Hannah stood in the dim light, surrounded by sobbing, crying old men, women, and children. She looked into the faces. Worry and fear everywhere. A little child buried her face into her mother's skirt. *How could these Germans shoot little children? What is wrong with these people?*

She felt her shoes slipping into the spaces between floorboards of the car. The walls were rough and splintered from years of use. *People should not be in here. It's for animals. Now I'm trapped.*

The train started with a jolt, metal slamming into metal followed by an ear-piercing squeal. Tightly packed, everyone swayed together like one living thing. After a time, above the cries and yelling, someone called out, "Where are we going?"

A man said, "The train is moving north, toward Bialystok."

The air was stale and the odor from bodies already stifling. Hannah was stuffed in between three old men and a heavy, sweating woman. "No. Not that way," Hannah said. "Not north, go east to the forests, east." Irritated, she yelled, "I can't breathe. Give me some room." She squirmed and forced the men to open a tiny space around her. The woman would not budge. The bloodied face of the young man at the train depot reappeared over and over in her mind. *They'll do even worse to me if I don't get away. And I'm not going to die in some pit either.* She found herself looking up toward the ceiling near the back of the railcar. Her eyes had adjusted to the dim light. Sunlight streamed through a gap in the wall near the ceiling. A missing board. Of all the railcars, what luck to get this car, she thought.

The gap was large enough. She knew what to do to escape. She just had to decide to do it.

The train rattled along for an hour, loud and dizzying. The pounding in her head was sickening, the mix of smells nauseating, but the flow of air through the wall reaching her nose made it bearable. *These people can only guess what is waiting for them at the end of this ride. I already know. I've seen it. I can't stay with these people.*

Peering through the spaces between the planks that made up the cattle car walls, Hannah tried to focus her eyes. Trees rushed by. Woods lined the train tracks, now thick, dark and deep. The farmlands along the way had disappeared a long time ago. The only way to escape was to jump off the train, when it slowed down entering a village or city.

Now is the time. Go.

Hannah squirmed her way toward a tough-looking old man standing against the wall below the gap near the ceiling. Strands of barbed wire were wrapped around the opening, but the wire hung low leaving a space large enough for her to slip through. The car bounced and jostled her around as she squeezed between swaying bodies. Some looked annoyed with her, some continued to sob ignoring her.

"Where do you think you're going, girl?" a rosy-cheeked peasant woman said as Hannah pressed into her side. Looking away, Hannah squeezed her way to the back wall. Losing her balance, she fell into the farmer's chest. He showed no change of expression. He looked down at Hannah and their eyes met. She pointed at the opening in the wall with her face and eyes. Looking up at the hole, he said nothing, but shrugged his shoulders. Cupping her hands together, she motioned with her arms and hands mimicking a hoist that would lift her up toward the opening.

"There is no escape from this," he said in defeat. "The Germans, they are everywhere."

"Please help me," she said.

"You will be killed by the fall," he insisted.

Balancing on one foot, Hannah slid her other leg up along his stomach until her foot was about waist high. She looked away from his eyes toward her foot and then back to him.

His face was covered in doubt, but then Hannah felt a strong grip on her raised foot. The man motioned her to hook her arm around the back of his neck.

With one powerful thrust, Hannah felt herself rise up to and through the opening into the rushing wind streaming over the train cars running at full speed. She sat on her thighs for a moment balanced on top of the wall. As she pulled herself through the opening, she felt a tug on her blouse.

A sharp, stinging pain traveled from her side near the rib cage across her back. She reached a hand behind and felt the steely barbs on the wire that had ripped open her skin. She hadn't noticed the barbed wire nailed to the outside of the railcar walls. Bright red blood smeared the back of her hand and wetness spread over her side. The blouse stuck to her skin.

Hannah grabbed for the roof and tried to pull one leg through the opening. The cattle car was swaying and bouncing and the roar from the tracks and the wind was deafening. Her shoe was hung up on the same plank where she had been sitting. She couldn't twist her leg enough from that angle to free her foot. She was stuck. No amount of pulling would help. Hannah felt stupid and helpless.

How am I going to reach the forests if I can't even get off a train?

Her back and side stung and burned and the slamming sounds of the train worked against her. She could feel tears coming.

Oh no, you're not going to cry now. You try harder.

Placing the back of her shoe against the edge of the hole, she tried to pull off the shoe. Too tight. Then she felt pressure on her foot. The farmer inside slowly and gently turned and twisted her leg and foot through the opening. Her leg swung down along the outside wall of the car. At the same time her other leg slid along the wall board with her thigh catching the back side of her knee and checking her fall. Grabbing the top of the wall and lifting herself up, Hannah slipped her other leg over the wall and out. Fortunately, her feet landed on the only support available, the hitch that connects the cars together.

Hannah wanted to look around the side of the railcar just ahead but it was far too risky. Blinded by the forward car, she thought, *What now? When should I jump?* There was no way to know when.

For her to jump from the train and not be killed, she must know what is up ahead. There were wooden poles and steel railroad stanchions all along the tracks every so many meters. If she jumped at the wrong moment and hit a pole, she would be killed instantly.

After a few kilometers, Hannah decided she would have to do something. Her legs were aching. The train was moving too fast to jump now, even if she were to miss the poles and stanchions. She didn't know how much time she had until the train stopped. *If I jump off here, which way should I go? Can I figure out which way to travel without being seen? Papa, what should I do?* She hung on for a half hour more.

Finally, Hannah felt a slight decrease in speed. Then a sharp lunge forced her body into the car wall. She nearly lost her balance. They must have reached a town or a station.

There will be Germans or Ukrainians there. Jump off. Jump now!

There was no time to think about it anymore. As she leapt from the car hitch into the air past the blind end of the cattle car, in a flash a railroad stanchion whizzed by in front of her. She caught a glimpse of a few men at the edge of the woods near the railroad clearing, then the ground. Hannah hit the gravel hard, landing on her hip and shoulder. Her head bounced off the ground as she rolled and tumbled through the scrub grass, small bushes, stones, leaves, and sticks. Something bone-hard slammed into her brow. Then nothing.

. . . . .

Hannah woke looking at the leaves and brown dirt of the path that traversed through woods. The ground was spinning around in her head. She could feel the thick shoulder of a big man supporting her as the dead weight of her body bore down on her stomach. Only vaguely aware, she felt nauseous and did not even care to know who this powerful man could be as he carried her aloft on the run. Pain started coming from all directions—forehead, shoulder, hip, and stomach. She heard muted voices. A few men around them moved quickly, almost silently. Just before passing out, she thought she heard some Yiddish mixed in with Polish. Then once more, nothing.

Chapter Seven

The ceiling looked cracked and dingy. Cobwebs spanned the corners, and the old wallpaper reminded Hannah of her Bubbe Leah's house when the family would visit on Sunday afternoons. The walls, the furniture and chotskies were similar, except that Bubbe's house looked perfectly clean, nothing out of place. Too clean, like a museum. Like nobody ever used the bedroom.

Where am I? How did I get here?

Movement of any part of her body caused waves of pain. She raised her head enough to notice a patchwork of scratches and scrapes covering her arms. Her legs were covered, toes pushing the tan blanket up into two points. A white bandage covered her left elbow. Trying to straighten her elbow resulted in a jolt of numbing pain. Lowering her head back to the pillow, Hannah felt woozy as the wallpaper patterns moved slowly in circles. Lying still on the bed seemed to be the best thing to do.

Soon a tall, shapely woman about Mama's age entered the room. Her hair shimmered, deep brown and spun up in a perfect bun. Her figure was like in the picture of the American actress, Greta Garbo, which Hannah once saw. Beila showed Hannah her secret copy. Girls were forbidden to look at magazines of movie stars. Hannah had no magazines, save one in her hiding place in the woods. The woman's gaze through bright, emerald-green eyes seemed razor-sharp. She was sure the woman would know if Hannah told the slightest lie, her face pale beneath rouge, eye shadow, and eyelashes. The woman acted proper like Bubbe Leah, but there was no doubt this woman was in charge. Hannah felt she would do anything the woman asked. She wouldn't be able to say no.

"I am Barbara," the woman said, "No one here will harm you."

I'm so dizzy, I can't think.

"What…who were those men?" she asked. "Did they bring me here?"

"Yes, and you will come to appreciate them in good time," Barbara said with a warm smile. "Are you a Jew?"

Fear spiked through Hannah's mind. Her tongue felt suddenly thick and dry.

What if she works with the Nazis? Or maybe she is one and this is her way to trick Jewish people. Hannah looked for a way out, one door and one window, probably locked. She could hardly raise her head, let alone make an escape.

"I know you don't trust me now, but I am a friend," Barbara said. Her straight white teeth sparkled through parted lips. "You will learn that in the end."

That could be a lie, Hannah thought. *But I took chances with the good farmer in the barn, and anyway, what else can I do like this?*

"Yes, I'm Jewish," she admitted. "The Nazis and Ukrainians murdered my family in a pit, but I escaped."

Barbara stood quietly and listened. Hannah tried to hold back, but her story came pouring out.

"They hunted me and finally caught me and put me on a train of railcars with hundreds of us," she explained. "I was sure they were going to kill us in another pit, so I jumped from the train. But I guess you know that?"

"You were the only one to escape the train," Barbara said. "The only one to escape dozens of trains that we have watched."

We? Her and those men? Who are these people?

"You are a very special person, a special young woman," Barbara said. "I need special people like you. Rest now, your body and head need to heal, and in a few days we will talk. Trust me. My friend Ingrid has bandaged your bruises. She is a nurse, a very good one. If you have pain or need something, call out for her. You are safe with me and my friends. Know that if I were your enemy, you would already be dead."

Barbara stepped away and softly closed the bedroom door. Her last words were still stinging and echoing in Hannah's mind. This woman seemed kind, but she had another side. She was not like Bubbe Leah, or Mama, or any other woman she knew. She had secrets. Maybe she had even killed someone.

Too exhausted to worry about it anymore, Hannah yawned uncontrollably. She took short, shallow breaths to minimize the pain in her shoulder and ribs and quickly fell off to sleep.

. . . . .

After several days, Hannah was moving around the house with little difficulty. The place was becoming familiar. Ingrid told her to stay away from the windows. Someone might see her. One afternoon a couple of German soldiers walked by on the sidewalk below her window. Hannah hid behind the lace curtains. She was in occupied Warsaw, right under the noses of the Germans.

Taking care to stay out of sight, Hannah continued to roam the apartment. One photograph on the wall in the dining room stuck in Hannah's mind. A young girl stood in a fancy dress next to a man and a woman. A small family. They looked happy. Hannah wondered if the girl was Barbara.

Ingrid, the old maid that helped bathe her and treat her wounds, reminded Hannah of Bubbe Rachel, her mother's mother. She said little, but was gentle and expert in nursing her patient back to health quickly. Hannah's physical wounds were healing nicely, but Ingrid had no medicine to make the emptiness inside go away. It was always there, waiting to stain and squash any memories of home.

"I cannot tell you that your life will be easy with me," Barbara said. "More than likely, it will make you hate me for what I put you through."

"You've been kind to me. You saved my life. I couldn't hate you."

"In a few days, I am going to have someone here. A man. He is very good at what he does. He will teach you."

"What do you mean? Good at what?" Hannah asked, not sure she would like the answer. Barbara's eyes missed nothing. They read

Hannah's every expression.

"Killing," she said.

. . . . .

A few more days passed, and Hannah felt much stronger. The dizziness from moving up or down stopped. She needed to do something more than sit. She needed to reach the forests, to fight back for Papa and Mama. *I think I could do it. Kill those people at the pit. If I could find them. At least I need to try.* But the Germans had guns. She didn't know anything about guns and shooting. Maybe this man Barbara talked about could teach her. But then, would she do it? *Will I kill someone? I don't know. I'm scared. Maybe.*

. . . . .

On a Wednesday evening, Barbara sat down with Hannah after dinner.

"How do you feel, Hannah?" Barbara asked. "You look much better and seem to be eating well."

"I feel stronger, thanks to you and Ingrid," she said. "I think I'd be dead without you. You saved me from the Germans."

"You alone are responsible for your life," Barbara said, pointing a finger at Hannah's chest. "To survive you must watch out for yourself always and then for your comrades. You will save each other. I know it seems cruel, but protect *you* first, Hannah." Hannah nodded yes, but inside she couldn't agree.

"You must be a schoolgirl from a well-to-do family," Barbara said with a piercing gaze. "I am curious about you because girls like that would not usually have the courage to escape from a death train. You don't fit in with them very well, do you?"

"I guess not. Not very well," Hannah admitted. "I like science and real things. They talk about other girls and silly things. I don't like most of them. Maybe that makes me different."

Barbara smiled. "Do you know how to survive in the forests,

Hannah?" she asked, her eyes glued to Hannah's.

"Papa would take me," Hannah started, but felt her lip quiver and eyes tear. She could see Papa's face. It was painful to relive. The murders, her face covered in his blood.

"I-I'm sorry," Hannah said, holding her stomach with crossed arms, fighting back the tears.

"I know my questions are hard, but I need to understand what you know and what you have no experience with," Barbara said, her face showing no emotion. "You will make friends. Many of them are going to die around you before this thing is finished. I have lost almost all of mine. You can survive, Hannah. You just need a little help."

. . . . .

Sitting in the living room reading Barbara's handwritten notes about villages outside of Warsaw and farther east, Hannah was startled by a knock on the apartment door. It could be soldiers, or even the Gestapo. *Not again.* The cottage in Sokolka burst into her head. No way to escape. She ran for the closet.

Ingrid reached the door and looked back. Hannah was supposed to hide in a back room when anyone came to the apartment. From the guest closet, she peered through the crack in the door. Ingrid opened the apartment door and a chubby man with ruddy complexion and black wavy hair stood holding a suitcase in each hand.

"Pawel Friedmann. Barbara sent for me," he said, looking past Ingrid into the apartment. He had strong arms as the suitcases swayed slightly, noticeably heavy.

"Come in, mister," Ingrid said, motioning him to move quickly. He stepped forward as Barbara entered the room and placed a small revolver on the mahogany side table next to an old wedding picture in a tarnished silver frame. He set the suitcases on the floor.

"Pawel, thank you for coming," Barbara said as she hugged him for a moment and then stepped back. He seemed to be a relative or somebody close. They must have known each other a long time. He didn't look like a killer at all. But what does a killer look like anyway?

"Hannah, come out here please and meet Pawel," Barbara said, looking back at the closet where Hannah hid.

Now I feel stupid, hiding in here. Hannah opened the door to greet him.

Her face felt flushed and she looked away.

"Ah, Barbara told me to hide when…"

"When someone knocks. Yes, I know. A very smart thing to do," he said and chuckled. Pawel held out his hand to Hannah. His smile was warm, eyes kind and gentle. *How could he kill anyone? He's nice. I thought he'd be like the German officer. I don't understand.* She put her hand in his. The hand was thick and callused, but his touch light and warm.

"Use the kitchen, Pawel," Barbara said, pointing to the table. He nodded and moved the cases to the kitchen floor. Hannah sat down at the table and watched. Pawel popped open the lids. Hannah swallowed hard. Four submachine guns, several pistols and handguns, a knife, and an oblong object she thought might be a bomb sat before her. She stared into the suitcases, not able to shake the image of the guns pointed at her, Mama, and Papa.

"Don't be afraid, Hannah. Think of them as tools. Like a hammer or a rolling pin in the kitchen," he said. Hannah looked at the wooden roller sitting on the kitchen counter by the sink.

"These tools will become your friends. They can help you survive or kill you. You must always be in control. Never let the killing lead you."

Hannah had worried what Barbara might ask her to do as payback for her protection and nursing care. Barbara's words rattled around in her head. *She said she needed a girl like me. What is she going to make me do?*

After a couple of hours, Pawel left. He left the weapons so Hannah could practice and said he would be back the following evening to continue the lessons.

"Do you have any questions, Hannah?" Barbara asked.

Hannah hesitated, wondering whether she should ask.

"Who are you? Who is Pawel? I thought you were Polish people trying to hide from the Germans," Hannah said, looking at Barbara, then Ingrid. Ingrid smiled and walked away.

"We fight the Germans, the Nazis mostly, to win our country back," she said. "I think you want to help us. Am I right, Hannah?"

"I don't know. I mean, I'm not sure," Hannah said, glancing at the submachine guns on the table in front of her. *Papa, what should I do? Fighting the Germans wasn't what you wanted.*

"Perhaps I was wrong about you," Barbara said, cradling Hannah's chin in her hand. "It's alright. I can get you to Russia perhaps. If that is what you want." Hannah watched as Barbara turned and walked away.

Papa, forgive me, but I can't let it go. I have to do something for you. For me.

"No. I want to fight," Hannah said, picking up a submachine gun from the table and giving Barbara as fierce a look as she could manage. "I will fight them."

Barbara turned and their eyes met. Lost in those mysterious green eyes, Hannah hoped she could do whatever Barbara asked of her. She just couldn't say no to her.

. . . . .

Over the next couple of weeks, Pawel came nearly every evening to instruct Hannah in weapons. He brought different firearms so she could handle any gun they might scavenge from a battle. She could disassemble and reassemble one gun in the dark. As Pawel had said, the black steel weapons became familiar tools to her. They no longer looked strange and dangerous. He brought a Russian submachine gun and later a German one. One night he brought a German rifle, disassembled. She could load them, but had no way to test-fire any. She only hoped she could fire a gun when she had to.

Pawel taught her basics about hit-and-run tactics and how to attack the enemy on their flank. He focused on how to use and care for the weapons. He made diagrams on how to make and use bombs.

He said they were for the railroad. Someone would show her more later.

During the daytime, Barbara gave her ideas about how to survive in the city, in the villages, and in the forests. But mostly in the forests. She said it would be good if Hannah knew more about the villagers and farmers and how to get along with them.

"There are many of our people who don't like Jews. Many don't like Communists, like me. Some might say they hate anyone who helps the Germans. Don't trust them either. After they kill the Germans, they may come after you," Barbara said. She showed Hannah a map of the Warsaw area, east to the border of Russia and south to the Ukraine. "It is very confusing. You really cannot trust anyone," Barbara said, eyes glistening with excitement. "Except the people I send you to. You can trust them with your life."

There wasn't enough time to learn the languages and accents. She gave Hannah some basic understanding of first aid and treating serious wounds. The more she learned, the more dangerous it all seemed. Finally, Hannah couldn't resist.

"All these places on the map…there are fighters in the forests, right?"

"Yes. Many. But I cannot tell you exactly where," Barbara said.

"Who are they?"

"There are men from our defeated Polish army. There are Russians."

"Are there any…Jews?"

"Yes, some. I know some," Barbara said, putting her pencil down on the kitchen table. "They are very brave. They are like you, Hannah. Scared and alone and wanting to fight back."

"But you're here in Warsaw. I don't know what you do here."

"What I do does not concern you," Barbara said. She got up from the table and placed her teacup in the kitchen sink. "Sometimes it is better not to know too much."

The lessons went on for a couple of months. Barbara and Pawel taught Hannah about the German and Ukrainian military, how they acted and what to expect. Hannah understood that this was important, but she was getting confused.

"Listen, some Ukrainians, the Nationalists, they fight with the Germans. Remember, the black uniforms are the enemy. Treat them like the Germans," Barbara said.

Like the one who attacked me in the woods. What should I do if I meet him? Kill him, maybe?

. . . . .

One day Barbara returned from a late afternoon "meeting," as she called it. Hannah saw the quickness in Barbara's eyes. She remembered Papa's eyes as he moved to the door of the cottage to greet the SS officer in Sokolka.

"Hannah, we must leave now," Barbara said, as she rushed around the house for hidden items. Hannah saw her pocket her revolver and stuff a note down her blouse.

They hurried out the back door of the house across the small patch of lawn shielded by high brick walls. Hannah remembered sneaking out there at night a few times for air and to see the stars. She struggled to keep up as Barbara moved swiftly through an archway in the wall that divided the properties. She followed the grassy path between the flower beds and small garden of the house directly behind them. The path then connected to a stone sidewalk along the side of the neighbor's house and emptied onto the main sidewalk of Radna Street. It was the best way to quickly move from one neighborhood to another on a different city block without being noticed.

From behind, Hannah watched how Barbara moved. *How could I ever be like her? She's so strong. Not afraid of anything. I want to be like that.*

Barbara stopped suddenly and turned to face Hannah.

"Come my dear," she said in a strange voice as she waved Hannah to hurry up. Barbara sounded like an actress delivering a line in a play. Hannah thought Barbara's voice seemed so different. Everything she did was in secret, and now she was pretending to be someone else. Someone, like a…spy. *That's it! A spy!*

As Hannah stepped up, Barbara cradled Hannah's shoulders in her outstretched right arm and the two moved forward in lock step. Just then Hannah looked up to see two German officers stroll by in the opposite direction. The sidewalk was wide enough at the point of their intersecting so no one had to move. One of the Germans tipped his brim and smiled at Barbara.

"*Guten tag fraulein,*" the German said.

Hannah stiffened and was afraid to look into their eyes, but could not resist. Barbara offered a slight smile and tip of her head as they passed. Hannah could feel Barbara's arm smoothly increase the pressure on her shoulders as if to say, "Keep moving."

Much to Hannah's surprise, the German's eyes were not cold, but actually seemed relaxed, even kindly. It was confusing to see such a contrast between the killing monster in the black uniform at the pit, and this German strolling down the streets of Warsaw as if there were no war on.

How could this be? She looked back toward the German officers. *What kind of people are these? Warsaw is different now, but I still remember.* The sun would warm her face, as she walked up Browarna Street along the park with Papa, to Bubbe Leah's building. The Vistula River still flowed along in the distance. The park, the sidewalk, all looked the same. Why did her city feel like such a strange place, as if it were in a different country now?

As they walked Barbara explained that her people felt the Germans had grown suspicious. It was time for Hannah to move on anyway.

"Turn here," Barbara said without warning.

Hannah again felt a steering arm direct her shoulders to the right. They stepped into a narrow alley. A few meters ahead, a weathered door with blistering, faded red paint led into the back of a building. Barbara grabbed the rusty, dented doorknob that squeaked as she turned the handle. The pair quickly slipped out of sight through the doorway into a musty old abandoned storeroom. Dust coated the stored office furniture. Unused desks, chairs, and cabinets were neatly piled up along the wall leaving a narrow passageway toward the front of the vacant office building.

"I have to go now, Hannah," Barbara said. "Do not leave this room. Your life depends upon it. Just after dark a young man will come to take you away. His name is Itzhak. Do whatever he tells you. He will lead you to the etrad in the forests."

"Etrad? What is an etrad? Where is it? Who will be there?" Hannah pleaded.

"A detachment. Russians. Listen to Itzhak. He is a good man. A Jew."

Barbara opened a slit in the door and cautiously peered out. She looked back at Hannah with penetrating eyes that suddenly softened.

"You have some training now. With more field experience you will provide the enemy their just rewards," Barbara said. "You will get very good at punishing them. Be careful not to let your hate of these murderers take you down with them. Remember who you are, Hannah. Never forget how to feel life, how to love. Good-bye, Hannah."

Hannah didn't understand what Barbara meant. What did she say about love and hate? Don't hate more than you love people? Maybe. She knew she loved Papa and Mama. She had said she would help stop the killers. That's what she did know.

Barbara quickly peered through the crack in the doorway once again and then was gone.

Chapter Eight

Hannah stared at the beaten and battered old door through which her only friend in the world vanished. On the inside the door was a sickly greenish beige color streaked with blackened dents from furniture, and who knows what else slamming into it when stock was moved in and out of the building.

I'm like this door. Battered and then forgotten. I'm farther from the forests than where I started. She stood for a long time staring at the door. She felt the trickle of tears on her cheeks, making their way to the corners of her mouth.

Down the hallway toward the empty front offices, shadows began to creep along the walls and floor. The storage room was already dim. Hannah remembered the farmer's barn, the dusty workbench by the window, and the knife. There was no heat in the office building and the early spring night added a bone-chilling dampness to the stale air in the hideaway.

Resting her head on the oak chairback, she closed her eyes when the door handle began to turn and squeak. Hannah froze. The storage room was very dark now. She could see the silhouette of a thin man when the door opened. The dim alley lighting outlined his figure and then he seeped into the shadows as the door closed.

"Are you in here?" he asked in Polish.

Hannah made no sound.

"I am Itzhak," the man said, standing still.

He sounded young. Not much older than herself, Hannah thought.

"I'm Hannah," she said, gripping the armrests of the oak chair. "Barbara said you would come."

"We have to leave here quickly," Itzhak said, standing in the dark.

"I want to know where you're taking me," Hannah said as she got out of the chair, still in the shadows.

"Look, you will have to trust me," he said. "I know a little of your story. Our men found you by the railroad tracks. You told Barbara you wanted to help us. Is that right?"

He sounds alright. But how can I be sure? Well, who else would know I'm in here, unless someone saw me come in. What if he turns me over to the Germans. She stepped away.

"Hannah, I am a Jew," Itzhak said quietly, as if he could read her mind.

"Barbara told me, but there are Germans out there. They want to kill me."

"Yes, I am well aware of that," Itzhak said, chuckling. "And me, too."

"What should we do if we're seen or stopped?" she asked. "Who should I say I am?"

"Well, if I am any good at this, no one will see us. We will meet with others from our etrad, then make our way out of the city," he said, voice solid and steady.

Barbara said this etrad was a group of Russians and at least one Jewish boy. But it must be a lot of men. I'll be the only girl. I don't know what to do, Papa.

Itzhak took a step toward the door, opened it a crack, and peered out.

"Let's go now," he said and reached for her hand.

Barbara could be wrong about him. What choice do I have? Just go.

She moved forward and stuck out her hand. He grasped it and with a gentle tug started Hannah on a new journey.

. . . . .

Outside, the last bit of light faded into a clouded night sky. They slipped like ghosts through the shadows of deserted streets. The air was cool and damp. Shivering, Hannah drew in deep breaths. Steam exited her nose and mouth. Papa's trick to warm up usually worked, when the chill crept into the bones while gazing at the constellations on winter nights. Moving through the streets meant doing something. She didn't know where they were in the city. But it seemed that Itzhak planned to go east toward Russia. *Maybe later I'll sneak away from him in the forests, if I don't like him. I guess I'd rather be running somewhere than waiting in a hiding place until the Germans found me.*

Hannah noticed that it was much easier to follow someone else's lead than to make all the decisions. It was a relief, at least for a little while.

I do need his help. I'll stay with him until I can't trust him. Can't let my guard down though.

"If we are somehow separated, stay in the shadows," Itzhak said, almost whispering. "Follow this street out of the city to the north."

Hannah already felt disoriented because of the darkness and confusing city lights. She could see her breath forming as the night air quickly moved from cool to cold. Trying not to appear afraid, she kept silent and followed his lead.

"We may need to slip onto side streets that parallel the main street," he said, almost casually. "But that all depends."

"Depends on what?" Hannah asked.

"Patrols, dogs," he said as he scanned the next several blocks ahead.

The pair moved quickly through the streets. Hannah soon realized that this young man was very skilled at this game. He avoided the haze of streetlights while not stepping on noisy metal grates embedded in the sidewalk. Every move was planned and executed with precision. Her confidence in him was growing stronger with every intersection they passed through.

As they moved away from the last intersection, Hannah felt Itzhak's grip tighten and she was jerked sideways into a narrow alleyway between two buildings. The space was barely enough for one body to pass. Itzhak trailed his arm behind his back and pulled Hannah along as he led the way.

"They saw us, I think," he said as he continued ahead at a rapid pace.

Hannah felt herself stumbling over debris littered along the pavement of the tiny passageway. She could hear voices from behind echoing off the walls and then saw flashes of light panning the red brick walls of the buildings.

"A patrol, but no dogs yet. Lucky…so far," he said with excitement in his voice.

They kept moving faster and faster. Hannah could feel and hear her coat rubbing against the rough brick on either side.

"Almost there," he said. "A few dozen meters to go."

Hannah didn't think she could run much farther. Her knuckles on both hands had scraped the brick as they ran frantically through the alley. She was sure her hands were bleeding.

Finally, they burst into a large opening formed by several buildings. German voices were ringing from around every corner.

Now where? Hannah thought as she was jerked to the left.

"Down here!" Itzhak snapped, as he quick-stepped down a concrete stair heading for an open basement door.

Hannah slipped on the first step and fell headlong into Itzhak's back. She instinctively wrapped her arms around his waist to stop her fall. She found her footing again and moved forward on her own.

"Keep moving," he said. "Are you alright?"

She could feel fresh bruises on her knees and shins from the fall onto the sharp edges of the concrete steps. For a second, she envisioned the steep stairway up to Bubbe Leah's apartment, her fall, her shins stinging. They were late. Papa was mad. Bubbe scolded her.

"Yes, go on," Hannah heard herself saying between gasps for air.

The basement was dry and dusty. She held back an urge to sneeze. Muffled German voices were outside around the building now. Hannah and Itzhak huddled behind a fat column near the far corner of the shelter. The only light was a pale glow from a rusty lamp over the back door of the adjacent building. The dim light crept only a short distance into the cellar, so the back was dark. The place smelled dank and stuffy but was warmer than the night air outside. It warmed her hands and feet. She could hear her heart pounding loudly.

When her eyes adjusted to the darkness, she noticed that Itzhak was holding a pistol.

"You have a gun," she said, searching for Itzhak's eyes.

"Yes. You thought that I punch the Germans in the nose and they give up?" he replied, grinning.

Hannah reached into her coat pocket and touched the farmer's jackknife. It had protected her before. It was better than nothing, but no match for German rifles and submachine guns.

"I have a knife," she said, looking toward the light. *I guess he must think I'm a helpless girl. Well, I can fight, too. He'll see. I just wish I wasn't so scared right now.*

Squatting in the dark, so close to Itzhak, she had not thought of him as a soldier before. He seemed like one of the older boys at school in Warsaw. Or maybe he was older than she thought. *He's strong and really smart. But will he kill someone to get me out of here? I don't know.*

Suddenly, a man jumped from the stairway landing with both feet onto the basement floor. His heavy boots made an unmistakable thud that echoed off the walls and was quickly deadened. It was a soldier. Itzhak put his finger on Hannah's lips to ensure she would make no sound. She froze. The soldier moved cautiously with knees bent in a lowered stance. He panned the walls and dark corners of the shelter on either side.

It occurred to Hannah that she could see the German, but he could not see them crouched behind the pillar. Soon his eyes would adjust to the pitch black of the basement. If Itzhak were to fire his pistol, others would arrive and the shelter would become a death trap. They did not move.

Hannah took some deep inhales and exhales to quiet her breathing. Itzhak wasn't even breathing hard. She thought he must be very fit. If there was some trick to calm his body, she needed to know it.

She could hear the German soldier breathing heavily after the long chase. The man's boots clumped as he ventured a few more carefully placed steps. He was now across from the pillar where Hannah and Itzhak were hiding. She peered around the corner of the column toward the footsteps. She could see the shape of a man, a big man with feet apart, knees bent and facing the column. His silhouette moved slowly and his boot scuffed the concrete floor.

He sees us! Hannah thought. In a near panic, she tugged at Itzhak's sleeve.

Stop him! Shoot him! Shoot him!

Then from the stairway, another soldier called out in German.

"Hans, you in there?" a younger voice asked.

The second soldier must be by the steps, Hannah thought, afraid to peek around the pillar.

Hans, the silhouette, stopped and pivoted toward the stairway.

"*Was*?" he replied, somewhat agitated. "What is it?"

He stared at the pillar and the dark corner where he sensed his prey was hiding.

"The sergeant, he says to come now," the soldier said, "or we will have to eat rations. No good food left when we get back."

"Oh, tell him I don't give a…" Hans shouted. "Ahhh, never mind, probably chasing ghosts anyway."

"Those people are gone by now," the younger man said. "I want some hot food, let's go."

"*Ja, ja. Scheisse,*" the big soldier replied, spitting toward the pillar. "Shit. I'm coming." The man turned back one last time staring into the dark corner and the pillar for a few seconds.

Hannah thought her heart would stop. Neither she nor Itzhak had made even the slightest movement since the big soldier had set foot in the basement. But her left leg was going to sleep. She had an overwhelming urge to move her foot and get more blood flow in her leg. Itzhak seemed to sense it and silently placed his hand on her knee.

The soldier slowly backed away, turned, and moved with a quickening pace toward the stairway and his impatient comrade. With the sound of footsteps scraping the concrete as the two soldiers exited the basement, Hannah felt like collapsing onto the floor. Her hands were shaking as she pushed moist hair away from her forehead.

Itzhak removed his palm from her knee, and Hannah realized how tender his touch had been. His finger on her lips, his touch meant something. Sol Wertz kissed her once in the toolshed back home. Sol touched her lips and rested his hand on her shoulder. She felt something deep inside. Even here in this cellar, Itzhak's touch stirred the same feelings. The danger made it all the more exciting and confusing. *What does he want from me? Not sure, but I need him to get me away from here. Out of the city. Wait and see.*

The sounds outside were muffled. After five minutes it was silent again. They were probably waiting for them to come out.

"Time to move," Itzhak said as he took Hannah's hand and gave a gentle tug.

"We can't go out there yet, can we?" she whispered, glancing toward the stairway.

"This place is a trap. Besides, they're regular army. They don't care about us. Only about keeping the officers off their backs and getting food in their bellies," Itzhak said, his voice edgy.

He tugged again at her hand, a little stronger this time. He stood up and urged Hannah to leave.

Trying to lift herself up, her numb leg gave way and she began to keel over. Hannah felt Itzhak's arm wrap around her waist as he counterbalanced her body against his. She had never been so close with a young man before. His strong arm and stable stance braced her from falling.

"Is your leg alright?" he asked. "It may take a few minutes to stop the numbness. You won't be able to run like this." They stood together for a minute. Hannah exercised her leg, bending it forward and backward. Her bruised knee burned as she flexed the leg.

"I can feel the strength coming back now," she replied. "Let's go."

Hannah felt very awkward as Itzhak slid his arm from her waist. She was thankful for the darkness. She was sure her face and ears were flushed. They crouched and moved toward the stairway. When they reached the steps, Itzhak signaled Hannah to wait. He placed one foot on the middle step, lifting up enough to pan the area outside.

He looked strong and handsome in the dim light. With his pistol in one hand and signaling Hannah to come out with the other, he stepped into the alley ready for a fight. It was deserted.

"Stay close to me," he said, as he extended his free hand to her. Hannah stepped out into the night air. Much colder now, the dampness made her shiver.

Itzhak moved forward rapidly into another narrow alley. Hannah kept close enough to touch his back. Occasionally, she looked behind for anyone following them.

She had learned a few more things and that Itzhak was a different kind of soldier. He did not fit her image of a soldier. The Germans and Ukrainians did.

For the next couple of hours Itzhak and Hannah wound through the side streets and alleyways of the abandoned business district. As Itzhak explained to Hannah, neighborhoods might be more dangerous as the Jews of the city had been rounded up and held captive in the ghetto district. This left only gentiles in the residential districts. Some were hostile to Jews. Some, like the farmer's wife, were just scared of Nazi reprisals if they helped the Jews. Some were probably good people caught up in the madness. Itzhak said, "You can't tell one from the other, so avoid them all."

The landscape of large commercial buildings on the north side of the city began to thin out. As they slipped away from the city lights, the neighborhoods changed to homes and apartment buildings and then to farms and small villages. Itzhak was always moving, staying aware of potential traps and avoiding any locals. The moonless sky helped conceal them. By now, Hannah's scraped hands and shins were burning. She had left Barbara and the storage room many hours ago. Her stomach growled.

"Are we out of danger yet?" Hannah asked, slowing her pace.

"First rule of survival," Itzhak replied, "you are never out of danger."

"I don't mean to complain," she said, "but we haven't eaten anything for hours, and my legs hurt."

"We're close now," he said. "They will have food and drink. Maybe something for your bruises."

"How much farther?" she asked, walking faster to catch up to him.

"Maybe thirty minutes, less if we don't find trouble."

"Who are 'they' anyway?" she asked, looking into his eyes.

"Oh, friends, very good friends, you will see," he replied, scanning the ground ahead for trouble.

"You mean men, soldiers like you?" Hannah asked, hoping a woman might be with them.

"They are Jews fighting for their lives," he said, glancing over to her. "Like us."

So far Itzhak and Barbara had been true to their word. But Hannah had bad experiences with soldiers. She wondered what Russian soldiers were like. Hopefully, better than the Germans and Ukrainians.

What choice do I have? She tried to keep pace with Itzhak's strides.

They turned off the main route onto a country road. After a kilometer or so, two lights appeared on the road ahead. The lights grew nearer. Suddenly Itzhak veered off the road onto a path that ran between fields. It was bounded by a thin line of trees. About fifty meters in from the road, Itzhak stopped.

"Crouch down," he said.

Hannah could only think of the path she followed from the pit, narrowly escaping. She felt for the pocketknife. It was still there. The vehicle, a truck passed by and then squealed to a stop on the road about a hundred meters from the path. She could feel her heart thumping in her throat as the truck backed up with a high-pitched, mechanical whine.

"Be still," Itzhak said in a low voice.

The truck squealed to a stop once again, exactly in line with the path.

"They've seen us. We need to run, now!" Hannah whispered, frantic.

She could make out the silhouette of a small truck. It must be more Ukrainian soldiers on patrol. As she began to stand up to run, Itzhak grabbed her shoulder and pulled her down.

"Itzhak? Itzhak?" called a man from the road. "Give me a sign, if you are there," he said in Yiddish.

"Idiot! Of course I'm here," Itzhak said with a smile spreading across his face.

"My cousin, Joseph. This fool driving around in a truck on these roads," Itzhak said with a chuckle.

"These are the ones we are to meet, then?" Hannah asked, confused but relieved.

"They were supposed to meet me here on foot," Itzhak said to Hannah. "Not driving on the roads. Come on." They walked toward the road.

She noticed three others around the truck, laughing and joking as she and Itzhak approached. *I guess they're like Itzhak, sort of soldiers. But they act more like friends or relatives. He said his cousin. Why don't they seem afraid?*

"We will be seen if we stay out here much longer," Hannah said to Itzhak. "Aren't we in danger?"

"Oh well, we got tired of walking and this stingy farmer happened along with the truck," Joseph explained, always one to embellish a story. "So, we—I mean *I*—decided to borrow it for a while." He threw his head back and laughed.

"And where was this?" Itzhak asked, arms crossed, eyebrows raised.

"Oh, you worry too much, cousin," Joseph said. "He has many, many kilometers of walking to report the theft, I mean, the loan."

"I must apologize for my poor manners," Itzhak said, resting his hand on Hannah's shoulder. "This is Hannah Gould, one of the bravest girls I have ever met."

Hannah placed her hand over the graze wound above her temple. It was healing well, thanks to Barbara and Ingrid, but it still looked quite angry and red.

The boys said their hellos to Hannah. Boris, Schlomo, David, and of course Joseph. They were all so friendly, Hannah could not help but let her guard down a little. No one mentioned her wound.

Maybe they didn't notice my face in the dark. Or maybe they don't think

I'm much to look at.

"Get in, everyone," Itzhak announced. "I'm driving, that way we might actually get there."

"Oh, you always get to drive," replied Joseph with a big grin as he teased, poking a finger at his older cousin.

"Hannah, you can ride in front," Itzhak said, waving to her.

Hannah noticed that no one, not even Joseph, really challenged Itzhak. He must be the leader. Itzhak turned the truck around and they sped off into the night up the deserted country road.

A numbing draft streamed through the open window of the old, dented farm truck. Hannah turned the crank on the door, but it spun freely, long since detached from the window mechanism inside. Kilometer after kilometer, Hannah searched the black wall that lie past the range of the headlights. What would they do if they were stopped by a patrol? She squirmed in her seat, trying to get comfortable. The night air rushed by her ear. After a while the drone calmed her. She palmed her cheek to soothe the sting of the frigid air on her skin.

For a moment, she drifted back to a time with Papa. The winter night sky, way out in the country, was always the best way to view the heavens. Astronomy was not her favorite subject, but Papa liked to teach. That was enough reason to go. One night on the way back, the night air slipped through the open window of the car. With blushed cheeks, Hannah kept her face near the door and breathed in the evergreen scent. It seemed so long ago already. She didn't want to think about the pit. She tried to remember the good times.

"Where are we going?" Hannah asked, looking over at Itzhak.

"About forty kilometers north to Ciechanow," Itzhak replied. He did not look away from the road.

Itzhak seemed happy to be out of the city. Hannah wondered if he was thinking about her. Maybe he only wanted to keep her safe and that was why he asked her to sit with him.

The others were in the back of the little truck. They finally quieted down.

The jostling must be awful, she thought, looking over her shoulder. *I would be sick to my stomach by now. Maybe they're too tired to joke around anymore.*

Hannah sighed and glanced to Itzhak for his reaction. None. *Papa and Mama want me safe in Russia. I have to get there. But I'm so tired.* Hannah stared ahead absently at the monotonous country road lit by the headlights.

The shadows stream along the sides of the fenders, just as a wake forms around a boat moving through water. The motion and the passing river of roadway left her eyelids heavy. Then Hannah caught a sudden flicker of light and snapped to attention. It was way off in the distance. The road melted away into a curtain of black, and she felt her body lunge forward toward the dashboard. Itzhak must have seen it too and instantly responded by killing the headlights and slowing the truck to a crawl. Hannah glanced over her shoulder. Everyone in the back was up and ready.

"You saw it too?" Hannah asked, looking over at Itzhak.

"Yes. We are two, maybe three kilometers from the village. If we saw them, then they must have seen us."

"Who do you think it is?" she asked, feeling the fear rise in her throat.

"Doesn't matter. Could be a farmer or a patrol or Gestapo," he said, with no fear in his voice. "I have taken a big gamble, but now we must go on foot."

Itzhak turned the truck off the road into a wooded area. They bounced and swayed on exposed tree roots, sticks, bumps, and depressions in the ground. Hannah grabbed onto the doorframe to keep from sliding across the seat into Itzhak. As it was, their shoulders bumped several times. Unsure what her reaction should be, she decided the best approach was to ignore it.

"This will do," he said as he stopped the truck about fifty meters from the road behind a thick clump of trees.

"Everyone out," Itzhak said with authority. "Ciechanow is north from here."

Hannah watched the others grab their weapons and start toward Itzhak.

"I don't have a gun," she said to Itzhak.

"You will soon enough," he replied, waving to the others and pacing off into the shadows.

"Wait. Can you tell me why Ciechanow? It seems there are things you're not telling me. I'm scared." Itzhak kept walking away.

Maybe they don't trust me enough to tell me the whole plan. I guess I don't trust them completely either.

The little troop moved quietly and quickly in single file behind Itzhak through the trees and underbrush. Hannah followed in line behind Itzhak. She wondered why they were heading north and not east toward the big forests and Russia. *What is in Ciechanow? What is so important about a small village?* She brushed aside saplings and briars as she kept stride with the men. *They're Jews like me. I have to trust them.*

The group emerged from the woods and entered a field. They stayed close to the edge near the trees.

"We can make better time out here than in the thick brush," Itzhak said over his shoulder.

Hannah felt more exposed away from the woods. The long grass in the field swept around her legs. She visualized strolling through a shallow pond, but her feet were dry.

I'm on the run. But none of them seem to be running. They're fighters, not runners. That's why they're treating me differently? Or is it because I'm a girl?

They kept on for about an hour until Itzhak stopped, turned around, and faced everyone.

"The edge of the village is about three hundred meters ahead," Itzhak said lowering his voice. "I have to meet with Katzner. He has two or three new recruits. Maybe some news of the Russians, too."

Recruits? Russians? Hannah glanced around at the faces. *What is he talking about?*

"If all goes well, we will be gone within the hour," Itzhak said. "Joseph, take Schlomo and move off to the right."

"You are thinking trap?" Joseph asked, looking toward the village.

Hannah blurted out. "I want to go with them." She watched

Itzhak's expression change.

He hesitated. "No, you stay with me," he replied. "You have no weapon and would be no help to us."

Hannah shrunk back from his sharp words. Itzhak was already moving forward.

"He means in case of an ambush or to divert attackers," Schlomo said gently.

I thought Itzhak liked me… Hannah looked Schlomo in the eye and nodded. *I must have been wrong.*

She didn't want to look at Itzhak. Instead she glanced up at the younger David and their eyes met for a moment. His eyes held an awful sadness. Dark, bottomless pools set deep in his bright sand-colored face. Back at Barbara's apartment when she first arrived, Hannah glanced in the mirror as Ingrid helped her in the bathroom. Her eyes had looked the same.

Hannah decided that there was a lot more to learn about Itzhak. But now was not the time. This meeting felt dangerous. The whole mission was probably more dangerous than she realized. She tried to focus on staying safe.

What should I do if everything goes wrong? I don't want to be alone again. I need to plan better than Papa did.

Shadows of cottages appeared up ahead through the trees and brush. Hannah felt her mouth dry and her shoulders tense. The woods and cottages flooded her mind with images of the Ukrainian soldier and running to the village where no one would help her.

"It's a trap," Hannah said.

"No sign of that, be calm," Itzhak whispered.

"We will protect you," said David from behind her.

Joseph and Schlomo were about fifty meters to the right. Itzhak stopped at the edge of the woods near the rendezvous point and scanned the few cottages that were but outlines in the dark. He turned and motioned everyone to crouch down. Joseph signaled and then disappeared from sight.

"Katzner is supposed to show at three-thirty with some new people," Itzhak said in a whisper. "We are early. We'll wait. Keep watch."

The waiting seemed endless to Hannah. Her shins and knuckles burned from the scrapes she got on the chase through the alleys and basement in Warsaw. The waiting gave her more time to focus on her discomfort.

Papa always said that bruises hurt more before you actually see the wound. She had to stop imagining the worst. She could not resist a peek at her shins and rolled up her trousers to inspect the damage. Only red marks, not gaping bloody abrasions.

"Not bad at all," she said, whispering. A little smile formed on her lips. *Maybe I can be a fighter. I have to be tough. Like them.*

Finally, Itzhak motioned that someone had arrived at the backyard of the cottage. Hannah felt her chest tighten and swallowed hard. A tiny light—a flashlight—pierced the blackness. It disappeared and then reappeared for a moment. On and off, four times.

"It's Katzner," he said. "Everyone stay here. David, Boris, cover me."

"Itzhak, be careful," Hannah said. Putting her hand over her mouth, she could feel her face turn red. *Stupid. I hope no one heard me.*

Moving out of the woods toward the cottage, Itzhak entered the yard and approached the man in the shadows with the flashlight. They spoke quietly for a minute or two.

Then three figures emerged from the corner of the cottage to meet the two men. Hannah was startled. None of them appeared to have a gun. They moved slowly, stooped over, not like fighters. She felt her jaw relax as the men shook hands. Then the group, without Katzner, started back toward Hannah and David.

"Stop now or I'll shoot!" a man shouted in Polish, as he stepped from the shadows on the opposite side of the cottage. "Who are you? Jews maybe, sneaking around in the middle of the night? Looking for things to steal from us Polish heroes, I suppose."

"Uh, must be ZJ types or local police or both. Anti-Semites for sure," Boris said under his breath.

"Who?" Hannah whispered.

"Zwiazek Jaszczurczy, Lizard Union men," Boris said. "I've seen a few. Extreme righties. Hate us Jews and regular army, too."

Two other men stepped up next to the man. They all had weapons.

Hannah wanted to cry. The scene had turned to disaster. The awful ride with the Ukrainian soldiers in the truck and the German at the train station swept her away.

It's happening all over again! she thought, frantic and losing control.

Hannah jumped up from her crouched position. Pushed from behind, she fell forward into bushes, leaves, and sticks, as David and Boris rushed ahead with rifles shouldered.

"Don't move!" said someone from the direction of the ZJ men.

Getting control of herself, Hannah looked up in the direction of the voice. Joseph and Schlomo had their weapons pointed at the heads of the ZJ men.

"Drop your weapons," Itzhak demanded in Polish. "Drop them."

Hannah moved up to the edge of the woods to watch. David and Boris joined the group and overwhelmed the ZJ men. Scowling, the leader dropped his rifle to the ground. The others did as well and put their hands on their heads.

"Going to kill us true patriots, are you?" the leader said, gritting his teeth. "Only a Jew coward would do that to a defender of his homeland."

"I will give this anti-Semite his due," David said, resting the barrel of his rifle on the back of the man's head.

Hannah thought for sure the boys were going to shoot these men where they stood. She did not understand who the ZJ were, but they seemed to have no qualms about harming Jews. She didn't want to see any more killing. Itzhak leaned over and whispered into Joseph's ear. Joseph signaled David, Schlomo, and Boris, and they all marched the ZJ men into the woods and out of sight.

They don't want me to see the killing. She watched them disappear into the shadows.

Hannah expected to hear gunshots at any moment. Then it would be over. She moved closer to the others. Itzhak was speaking to Katzner.

"It's too dangerous for you to stay here now," he said. "You can join our etrad. I will see to it."

"No, I have come a long way for this rendezvous," Katzner said. "These are locals. They don't know me and I doubt they will follow me back."

"Well, suit yourself, but we can't use this place to meet again," Itzhak said.

"Be careful, my friend," Katzner replied, smiling.

"And you."

Hannah watched the middle-aged man slip away into the darkness behind the cottage.

Itzhak picked up the rifles and handed one to Hannah. "Do you know how to use a rifle?" he asked.

She took the heavy weapon from him. "Yes, Barbara and Pawel showed me things," Hannah replied, grabbing the stock.

They introduced each other to the new recruits. To Hannah, the lot of them seemed to be terrified. She understood. None were willing to accept the other rifles that Itzhak held out to them.

"This could make the difference between survival and death," Itzhak said, stiffly pushing a rifle to one man's chest.

"I have never held one before," the man replied, closing his arms around it.

"If not for yourself, then think of protecting the others," Itzhak said, glaring at him.

Hannah gripped her new weapon tightly. It was a little different than the one Pawel trained her with, but was mostly the same. It could kill people.

I know how he must feel. Hannah pulled back the bolt and checked the magazine for bullets. It was loaded.

Just then Joseph and the rest came out of the woods into the clearing.

Hannah wondered why they didn't shoot the ZJ men.

"We must move on from here," Itzhak said, motioning them to follow.

No one argued.

Chapter Nine

Itzhak led the way with David and Joseph acting as their rear guard. Hannah let her mind stray as they marched on in the dark unnoticed. The early morning air sent a chill through her body. The rifle weighed heavy on her arms, and the frozen stock and barrel burned her bare fingers. She changed her grip on the weapon every so often. Nothing would stop the cold from numbing her fingers and toes. *Why does it have to be like this?*

They trudged along through woods, long-grass fields, nasty scrub brush, farm fields and pastures. Lack of sleep brought on a headache. Memory of her head wound only made it worse. Each step became an effort. Images of Papa and Mama lying in the pit were draining, the marching endless. *Why do these people hate us and want to kill us?*

On and on they went, all night it seemed to Hannah.

"East to Russia," she chanted under her breath as her steps became slower and slower.

The man behind her accidentally bumped into her. He said nothing.

Hannah looked up ahead at Itzhak's back. The faint light on the horizon was already exposing their position. At last, Itzhak raised his hand by his shoulder and stopped the march. Everyone stopped behind him in silence. He listened for a moment and then turned to face the others on the path.

The village of Przasnysz, Itzhak's hometown, lay less than a hundred meters ahead through the trees.

"I need to check for survivors…my family," he said, scanning their faces.

"How do you want to approach?" David asked, squinting into the dim light for a way to go.

"Circle the shtetl from inside the woods," Itzhak ordered, pointing to David and Joseph.

Hannah looked ahead at the narrow trail which disintegrated into a mass of dry leaves, briars, and sticks. Tramping through the woods would be noisy. Early risers might notice the scouting parties. She was not sure what to expect when they entered the village.

Hannah thought about Papa and the things he taught her. Everyday things not taught in school. They might mean the difference between being caught and surviving in this new world. At least what the boys talked about also was on her mind. But she had to admit, she was usually a step or two behind them. She decided to be quiet for now.

"Look for any signs of the enemy, do not engage, and meet back here by seven," Itzhak said.

She could not help but watch Itzhak. He didn't look like a soldier, but he acted like one. Itzhak was smart and careful, but he took a chance using the farm truck on the road. If you took too many chances, one would get you in the end.

"Hannah, I need you to help Boris and Schlomo protect Katzner's people," Itzhak said.

"But I don't…" Hannah started to say.

"You are ready, you can do this," he said softly. Their eyes met.

He looks at me differently than the others. I can feel it. How is he ready to kill people in one moment and kind to me in the next? How do you want me to be, Itzhak?

"Don't leave this place unless you are discovered," Itzhak said. "If so, go back the same way we came in and I will find you."

Itzhak moved quickly away in the opposite direction from David and Joseph to encircle the village.

• • • • •

"When are they coming back? It is well past seven o'clock," one of the villagers said. "My wife is frightened that we will be discovered. So am I."

Not knowing what to say, Hannah looked over at Schlomo and gestured. He was looking past her toward the village and tilted his head back motioning her to turn around. All four stomped through the trees toward them. Hannah felt a load lift from her shoulders. *Itzhak, Itzhak, you're back safe. I want to tell you I was worried, but everyone is watching.*

The scouting party trudged through the woods up to the huddled group making no effort to be quiet. Everyone stood. The murmurs from Katzner's people faded away.

"Are you alright here?" Itzhak said, looking at Hannah.

"Some complained. And some worried that you wouldn't be back for them," she replied, slowly wagging her head. "Is there a problem in the shtetl?"

"I spoke with a gentile that I trust," Itzhak said, shaking his head. "No Germans in the area right now. But the Volksdeutscher, of course, have no qualms about turning us over to the 'authorities.'"

"Authorities! Ha! The SS and those miserable Ukrainians are not the law," Boris said, spitting on the ground. "We even have to watch out for our own countrymen. The hate goes deep."

"We shouldn't stay here then?" Hannah asked, relieved that Itzhak took back control of the group.

"My family lives near the center of town," Itzhak said, shifting his weight. "I need to look for them, then we will turn east to Bialystok."

"Where to now?" Hannah asked. "We are a big group and people will notice us moving through the shtetl."

"Very good, Hannah," he said, grinning. "You are thinking like one of us now."

Hannah did not know what to say, so she just nodded to him.

"Joseph, Hannah and I will go in," he said. "Boris, Schlomo, and David, take the others around to the east road and out of town."

"Where will we meet?" David asked, his eyes focused on Itzhak, ignoring Hannah.

"There is an old barn on the right along the east road about a kilometer from the village," Itzhak said.

"I know the one," David said.

"Get behind it and rest for the journey. We will meet up in an hour or two. With some food and water, I hope."

Itzhak said a few words to David in private and then turned back to the others.

"Let's go to my father's house first," Itzhak said.

Hmm. He hopes they will be there, Hannah thought, her stomach queasy. *I hope so too, but I wonder.*

David led the group off to the east side of the village with Schlomo and Boris protecting the rear. Hannah watched their villagers stumble along, complaining about everything. They looked weak and lost. *I suppose they're like I was. But I'm not so scared and weak now. Not anymore. Itzhak, Joseph, and the others are strong. They have no fear. How do I learn that?*

Hannah pressed her lips tight, squinted in the bright morning sun, and ignored her empty belly.

"This way," Itzhak said, moving forward into the village. "Try to keep your weapons out of sight. I don't want to attract attention."

Hannah saw Joseph slip the stock of his rifle up under his coat and he seemed to cradle it in his armpit. The barrel protruded from the bottom hem of the coat. At first glance, it was much less obvious. She did the same, but the barrel scraped the ground. The rock-hard wood felt cold at first. She pressed it between her bicep and rib cage. Actually, it felt more comfortable than she figured it would.

"Not many people about," Joseph said to Hannah, pointing out local sights. "I used to play in that field over there when I was younger."

"Are we going to your house?" Hannah asked Joseph, adjusting her grip on the rifle stock.

"Yes, and to the houses of my uncle and my father," he replied, glancing up side streets for any activity.

For the most part, the village seemed normal. Few townspeople were outside though. Several houses looked abandoned, closed up with nothing in the yards. Hannah wondered if Jews lived there and how friendly Joseph's neighbors were now. She thought about the farmer and his wife.

The narrow road through the village was crude and looked well-traveled. Paying more attention to the houses than where she was walking, Hannah stumbled on a jagged rut. She caught herself from falling forward.

Stupid! Some soldier I am.

As she refocused her attention up ahead, she spied a short, stocky figure. A barrel of a man, round face, dark hair, walked slowly along the edge of the road. Hannah gripped her rifle stock with her free hand, trying to figure out how she could quickly get the gun out from under her coat. She looked at Itzhak and Joseph. Neither seemed the least bit concerned with the approaching stranger. He could be another Volksdeutscher with friends waiting to attack them.

As they drew nearer, Itzhak grinned. "Mr. Petroski, I'm so grateful you're here," he said, spreading his arms wide, embracing the man.

The old man didn't smile. Hannah caught his glance as he straightened his back from Itzhak's hug.

"And who is this pretty young woman?" Petroski asked, looking at Itzhak and Hannah. "Are you and she…?"

Hannah heard the question and noticed Itzhak's cheeks were red. The bitter morning air had the same effect on them all. She wasn't sure if it was a blush or not.

"This is Hannah Gould," Itzhak replied. "Hannah, Mr. Petroski, a dear friend of my family."

"Known these boys since they were youngsters," he said, placing his hand on Itzhak's shoulder. "Those were good times then."

The old man's face relaxed a little and a warm smile replaced the wrinkles of concern that had made him look much older.

"It is not so good now," Mr. Petroski said, panning the streets for other villagers.

"Have you seen my father and mother or any of my relatives?" Itzhak asked. "I'm heading to the old house now.

Hannah thought he was a good son to come back here. She would want to save Papa and Mama if she could.

"They came here, that Nazi bunch," he said, eyes deep. "Weeks ago. I have not seen your people since. No one here goes out much."

The thought of her parents and the pit sent her mind reeling. The German's eyes. Hannah felt dizzy and stood still, feet spread apart for a moment. Then, realizing she had stopped breathing, she drew in a deep breath.

"Hannah, are you alright?" Itzhak asked, putting his hands on her shoulders.

"Uh…yes," she said, still dizzy.

Turning to the old man, he said, "She's been through a lot."

"These last few weeks have turned sour," Mr. Petroski replied, nodding to Hannah. "As I said, I have not seen your family, Itzhak. I hope they got out of here in time."

"I'm going to look around and take anyone I find with me."

"It is dangerous for Jews, Itzhak," Mr. Petroski said. "Do not stay long."

"I'll be quick," Itzhak said, nodding his head.

"The police cannot be trusted. Only the bad ones remain here."

"I know. Do you need protection, Mr. Petroski?" Itzhak asked, resting his hand on the old man's shoulder.

Hannah listened while scanning the houses. He seemed like a good man, but how many more could they take with them?

"No, I will be alright. But you, Itzhak…" Mr. Petroski said. "If they catch you, you will surely face the devil in them."

"Good-bye, my friend, and God protect you. Shalom," Itzhak replied, as he waved to Hannah and Joseph to follow. Hannah looked back as they walked quickly away. Mr. Petroski continued down the road as before.

. . . . .

The morning air was still numbing and stung Hannah's nostrils, burning in her lungs. They moved quickly to keep warm. Przasnysz was beginning to awaken. A few early risers were puttering around their cottages. Hannah was worried. Mr. Petroski's warning echoed in her mind. A villager looked up at the three strangers moving past his property.

Do they know we are Jews? How do they feel about us? Hannah was careful not to make eye contact.

The rifle under her coat now felt heavy. Hannah's fingers stuck to the frozen steel barrel and began to ache.

Itzhak turned up one more road and as he rounded the next corner, he stopped short. A faded white clapboard house sat near the road. A vegetable garden bordered the side of the house, left unattended with dried stalks and vines still waiting to be plowed under for the next growing season.

"There is no one home," he said, sadness in his voice.

"How can you be sure?" Hannah asked.

"They never sleep late. One or the other would be out and about," Joseph replied.

"Your mother and father you mean?" she said.

"Yes. Or my uncle who owns the house next door."

"Well, maybe they are sick or something," Hannah said, hoping to ease his worries.

Itzhak looked back at Joseph and Hannah. She could feel the disappointment in his eyes. Joseph pulled his rifle from his coat and signaled Hannah to do the same.

Itzhak reached the door of the house first. He tapped lightly and then turned the door handle.

I guess no one locks their doors here. Never any need to. Like Sokolka. Not like at home. Papa locked the house door at night. 'Warsaw is a nice city, but it is still a city,' he would say.

Itzhak motioned Hannah and Joseph to follow. Hannah stepped into the living room. It was dotted with little chotskies, family photos, and other items of no particular value except of course to the family that lived there.

Standing on an old, tattered rug that did not quite extend to the walls of the modest room, Hannah felt the draw of memories from her own home. This rug was a cheap copy of the beautiful, rich floor covering Mama had selected from the fine carpets section of the best department store in Warsaw. Hannah felt suddenly sick and weak.

She remembered when she had spilled a glass of milk which immediately began to stain the expensive rug in the den. It was simply an accident, but children were not supposed to be in that room. Mama was so upset she could not let it pass. Hannah remembered her punishment clearly. She was to never bring food into that room again. She loved to eat in the den with Bubbe Rachel. They would sit together with cookies and read after school.

She and Mama did not speak of it again. Hannah always thought there was more to it than the stained rug. Even as a teenager, it was never discussed. Now it could never be resolved. The worn pattern in the old rug beneath her feet began to blur as tears welled in her eyes.

"They're gone. Left suddenly, I can tell," Itzhak said.

Itzhak looked around and found a loaf of bread, slightly stale, in the cupboard and strong cheese, though not yet spoiled. There were carrots and potatoes in a basket under the counter.

"Let's take it all, Joseph," he said. "I doubt they will be back. Ever."

"Hannah, take that sack and fill it," Joseph said.

"But isn't that stealing?"

"My aunt would have given us whatever she had."

Hannah wiped tears from her eyes with her sleeve. Joseph grabbed two jugs of water that sat on the floor of the pantry. Hannah filled the sack with the bread, cheese, and vegetables and slung it over her shoulder. She balanced her rifle in her other hand.

"I'll check Uncle's cottage to be sure, then we go," Itzhak said, his words drifting off.

Hannah heard Itzhak's voice cracking as he spoke. *I can't keep from crying. He won't say it, but he needs someone. Maybe we can help each other.*

Itzhak said nothing more and left the house.

"Follow him, Hannah, I'll be right behind you," Joseph called out from another room in the house. "He's going to my father's house."

She stepped outside into the cold. Itzhak was already next door. The house was similar but painted a sickly pale yellow. Hannah noticed his hesitation, then he knocked on the door. As she approached, he turned the doorknob and eased open the door enough to poke his head into the room.

"Uncle, Auntie," he called. Then he disappeared into the house.

Hannah could hear Joseph behind her.

"Go on in," Joseph said when he reached her. "It seems quiet, but be careful."

Hannah stepped toward the door. A crack ran vertically from the top of the wood door to the door handle. The brass back plate behind the handle was tarnished and scratched. She pushed open the door.

Itzhak stood in the middle of the living room, looking worried and angry.

"Are they gone?" Hannah asked. "Or out to the market or something?"

She didn't know what to say, especially when everything seemed so bleak.

"They never go anywhere," he said. "They took our whole family away. I just know it."

Joseph moved through the house quickly as Itzhak was talking.

These two handle things differently. I haven't seen Itzhak like this before.

Joseph came out of a back room with a small bag. Hannah did not ask what he took. Itzhak sat down in the middle of the living room, grumbling something. Hannah stepped past him. The scratched hardwood floor, shellac coating worn through to dry wood in spots, extended down a short hallway to the kitchen. She could see Joseph through the kitchen doorway opening cabinets.

"Hannah, add this bread and these potatoes, beets, and carrots to your sack," Joseph said, a bit out of breath.

"We're taking this, too? What if we're wrong and they're coming back?"

"They are gone. Just take it," he replied, hurrying out of the house. "One more place to check, let's go."

Hannah headed for the front door. Itzhak now standing on the step, stared at her. He seemed lost in thought. Without a word, he turned and ran. Hannah started to follow him, but he glanced back and held up his hand to stop her.

"Hannah, wait here for a moment," Joseph said as he motioned her to stay near the side of the house out of sight from the road.

"Where is he going?" she asked, watching Itzhak stop at a light-gray house with black shutters.

"Oh, it's someone we know," he replied, looking toward the house.

"Another relative, then?" Hannah asked, moving close to the wall next to Joseph.

"Well, sort of, I guess," he said. "He needs to come back here."

"He's knocking on the door, but it doesn't look like anyone's home."

"Oh, come on, Itzhak, give it up."

"What do you mean, give it up?" Hannah asked, looking back to Itzhak.

"We'll talk later. A group of men are coming our way," Joseph said as he peered around the corner of the house. "Come on, Itzhak, now."

Hannah guessed he didn't want to talk about that house. He should just let it go, but something wasn't right about it. She squatted, leaned on the clapboards, and peeked around the corner.

"Look, here he comes," she said, watching Itzhak move swiftly through the yards, avoiding clotheslines, tools, broken bicycles, and other discarded junk.

"He must have seen them coming our way," Joseph said.

Itzhak approached from behind the house. He looked past Hannah to the road.

"Who are they?" Itzhak said, breathing heavily.

Itzhak looked shaken. Hannah wondered what was wrong. *It's something about that other house. I'm sure of it. Itzhak, wake up. We need to do something about these people.*

"Old man Straczynski and a couple of his miserable sons," Joseph said. "Hate that bunch."

Setting down her sack of food, Hannah raised her rifle.

"They are going to your father's house, Itzhak," Joseph said, as he carefully peeked around the corner.

"They didn't see us. Good. We'll go the other way. Stay behind the houses out of their sight. Follow me," Itzhak whispered. "No need to create a scene if we can avoid it. We are done here anyway."

Hannah picked up the food sack and slung the rifle strap over her shoulder. She followed Itzhak through backyards away from Straczynski. Joseph followed them, guarding their backs. The three moved swiftly staying out of sight by using the adjacent houses as cover. Hannah thought they were going north and would have to turn east somewhere to meet with the others.

As they moved on, Hannah realized she was smiling. She wasn't running for her life. Not like before. They were avoiding people on purpose. That's what fighters did.

Maybe I can fit in with these people and maybe even help. Those girls in school would be lost out here. They couldn't even tell which way was north. And I can't believe these older boys treat me like one of them. Not like a girl. And I know about the forest and camping. I can do this, Papa. Thank you, Papa.

Itzhak silently signaled to turn to the right and the three moved in unison from behind the shelter of the houses and into the road that ran through the village. As they crossed the main road heading east out of the village, shouts from far away startled everyone. All looked south from where the sound had come. The voices were muffled due to the distance. Angry-looking men were running toward them swinging weapons or tools of some kind.

"Hannah, you have the range. Can you fire your rifle over their heads?" Itzhak said coolly. "One shot just to scare them and we will see what they are made of."

"I've never actually fired a gun before, only make-believe with no bullets," Hannah said. "What if I miss and hit one of them?"

"Hannah!" Itzhak said loudly, unquestionably a command.

Hannah dropped the sack onto the dirt road and lifted the Mauser. She raised the bolt, pulled it back, and then pushed it forward. The mechanism clicked as it had done when Barbara and Pawel had trained her in weapons. She pulled the lever down to complete the action. She knew a 7.62 millimeter bullet was now ready in the chamber. She only needed to pull the trigger and the deadly projectile would smash whatever target the muzzle was aimed at.

She gripped the gunstock and lined up the sights along the barrel. She could feel her heart racing in her chest and pounding in her ears. She only vaguely heard Joseph's urgings. Hannah spotted a tree trunk behind the men. She aimed the sights to a spot just over their heads and center on the trunk. All seemed perfectly quiet in that instant. The world around her seemed to stop. Her focus was complete.

Pull it! Fire!

The blast was deafening, and the recoil smacked her right shoulder. The high-pitched zing of a ricocheting bullet broke the morning silence. The men in the distance stopped abruptly, hesitated, and scattered in the opposite direction.

After a moment, Hannah thought, *I did it. Somehow, I did it.*

She remembered the German Luger and the finality of the sound. It had taken her Papa's last breath. But the Mauser had a different sound. Her heart was still beating fast, but deep inside it felt good. It felt as if she had fired at the SS man. She finally did something to fight back and as scared as she was, it felt good.

"Bullies through and through," Joseph said in disgust. "Fine work, Hannah."

The three moved quickly along the east road, careful not to be seen. Up ahead was an old barn, as Itzhak had said. Behind it were the starving, complaining civilians from Katzner. Hannah no longer considered herself a civilian. Now she was a soldier in this new kind of army. An army made up of everyday Jews who were just trying to survive.

When about one hundred meters from the barn, Itzhak made a diversion into the edge of the woods. There was a narrow path through the trees and undergrowth that meandered in the direction of the barn. It reminded Hannah of her escape from the park and the Ukrainian.

"Joseph, Hannah, follow me," Itzhak said. "But stay back fifty meters or so in case I find trouble."

Joseph nodded and looked over at Hannah.

She suddenly felt uneasy. The food sack seemed to grow heavier as more images of the soldier stuck in her mind. She felt her pocket for the knife. It was still there.

Itzhak moved forward up the path.

"He's very careful," Hannah said to Joseph.

"Yes, and we are still alive because of it," he replied.

"What if our group has been discovered and someone is waiting to spring a trap on us?" she asked.

"Not likely, but better to be ready for anything," he said. "That way you won't be distracted by what you might find, when you didn't expect it."

"How do you learn that?" she asked, thinking about a trap.

"You can't. Just go by instincts," Joseph said. "You will see."

They followed slowly, low brush snagging at their pants. Then Hannah heard voices up ahead. She stopped on the path. Joseph noticed and moved close to her, resting his hand on her upper back.

"What is it?" he asked in a whisper. His whiskered cheek close to hers, she looked up, and their eyes met.

"I hear voices just ahead," she whispered, pointing toward the sky. The peak of the barn roof protruded above the evergreens. The white trim contrasted with the deep brown rustic clapboards. They were very close.

"Well, probably the group talking," he said softly. "Move up slowly, follow me."

Dry leaves and small sticks crackled and snapped under their shoes. When Joseph stopped abruptly, Hannah almost ran into him and caught herself from falling.

She peered again through the trees and brush looking over Joseph's shoulder. They strained to hear.

"You agreed I would transport you to Bialystok and East," Itzhak said flatly. "There is just too much danger in these towns around here. You will never make it on your own."

"We have not seen anyone since we left Ciechanow, and my husband's heart is not strong enough to go on much longer," said an old woman. "It's my husband. As you can plainly see, his breathing is labored even after resting."

"We did have contact with the local police in the village here and they were not friendly," Itzhak replied. "The reason you had no trouble is because we were off the main roads."

Joseph waved Hannah to follow him and the two broke out of the woods into the clearing behind the barn. Everyone looked in their direction with surprise. Hannah sensed that the food in her sack might help calm the discontented group. Glancing up at Itzhak, Hannah moved into the center of the gathering. Their eyes met for a moment and she detected the slightest of nods.

"This is not enough food for everyone," she said, while opening the bag. "So, we will have to divide it as best we can."

"How do we know that you three did not eat your fill earlier in the village?" another man said, grumbling to Itzhak.

"As with everything in life, there are times when you have to trust somebody," Itzhak replied. "Would you rather take your chances with the Germans?"

"Why would we lie to you?" Hannah said in defense of her comrade.

"Survival," the grumbler said.

I can't believe Katzner's people are so ungrateful. These are fellow Jews. I'm going to tell them, like Bubbe Rachel told those mean people a thing or two at the street market when they pushed me away and fought over the last vegetables.

"We risked our lives for you, to save others and scavenge food for you," she said, almost shouting.

She broke off pieces of bread and handed it to each one as she spoke. Then she sliced the cheese into small chunks with her pocketknife. She still felt guilty about taking the good farmer's knife.

Maybe the complainers would settle down with some food in their bellies. "It will be a farshlepte krenk to Przasnysz," as Bubbe Rachel would say—a long, slow pain in the backside. But Hannah wasn't supposed to know what that meant. Hannah loved Bubbe Rachel's spunk.

"How much farther must we travel?" the grumbler asked.

Itzhak looked around at the hapless group and said, "About a hundred kilometers."

"Ohhh," was the general expression of the group.

How are we ever going to make it with these kvetchers? At least I don't have to put up with them alone. I will get there, Papa. East to the forests near Russia. Maybe not the way you thought. But I trust Itzhak now. He will get me there.

Chapter Ten

After finishing the makeshift meal of stale bread, overly ripe cheese, and nearly frozen water, they set out from the barn. Itzhak decided to keep off the well-traveled east road during the daytime. About ten kilometers out near the end of the day, they came upon a big farm. The troop was exhausted and hungry. The man with the heart condition looked pale and gaunt.

"The sick man can't go on much further, not walking anyway," Hannah whispered to Itzhak.

"I know, I have been watching him," he said.

He signaled Joseph over and whispered to Hannah and his cousin.

"I have an idea," Itzhak said. "Can you two take the group back behind that rise into the next field and set up a camp?"

"But they can't walk another meter," Hannah replied, doubting she could get them moving.

"Everyone is hungry and has little willpower to go on. Hot food will give them the mental strength to keep going. Make a cooking fire," Itzhak explained. "In the dark, a campfire at this position could be seen from the farmhouse and even from the main road. There is a depression in the terrain over there. It will shield the firelight from all directions. And the smoke will not be very visible in the darkness."

"Oh, yes, the vegetables," Hannah replied. "Hot soup might revive them."

"I will take David, Boris, and Schlomo to the farmhouse and scout for better transportation facilities," Itzhak said with a glint in his eye.

Oh, so you leave Joseph and me with the complainers and head off on an adventure, she thought. *How fair is that?* She looked over the group and shook her head.

The young men started off into the dusk toward the farmhouse. Hannah hesitated, then ran to Itzhak.

"I have no pot to make soup, no way to start a fire," she said with arms akimbo, fists resting on her hips.

"Use what you have, you can do it," he replied with a big grin.

He put his hand on her shoulder and she felt a gentle squeeze. His eyes looked deep and kind, even caring.

Maybe that's what I want to feel. I wish I knew more about boys. Beila would know. But I'll never see her again. She would say he's romantic, whatever that means. Like a prince in a fairy tale. But I don't feel like a princess. Ohh…I'm so sick of these complainers. And I'm hungry too, you know!

She scanned the suffering, ungrateful faces of the group in tow. She took a deep breath and let it out slowly.

"I have vegetables to make soup," she said, "but we must move out of sight to create a cooking fire."

More grumbling was the response, but they slowly followed her while Joseph protected their backs. Moving the group fifty meters or so to the depression seemed to be nearly impossible. Each one had to negotiate the sloping ground to the bottom. The long grass was slippery but provided a soft ground cover. Hannah finally got them to cooperate and sit still. Joseph gathered some dry branches and pieces of bark along the edge of the woods that bordered the field. He pulled matches from his coat pocket and together they started a little fire. From the sack they filled in Przasnysz, Hannah pulled out a small metal pot by its split wood handle. With pressed lips and a wag of her head, she looked the pot over. Joseph must have slipped it into the sack. She rested it on the ground.

Potatoes, beets, and carrots would make a soup. Mama and Bubbe Rachel would have added onion or scallions, salt and pepper, and more, but Hannah had no seasoning. Joseph produced a wide-blade knife and violently skinned the potatoes and carrots. He sliced all the ingredients into the old pot that sat on the ground.

"Get a water jug and fill up the pot," he told Hannah. "Set it down in the fire."

"But it will spill," she said, looking at the fire.

"It needs salt," one woman said. She wagged her head with a disappointed scowl covering her wrinkled face.

"Here, stir it with this," Joseph said, handing Hannah his knife.

After a while the water was boiling and the smoke gave off a fine aroma. Stirring the mixture, Hannah watched the potato and carrots spin around. Bubbe's kettle was much bigger, but stirring the vegetables was always Hannah's job. Lost in the bubbling surface, she let it boil over, the broth hissing in the fire. She looked up at Joseph. He shook his head slightly. All the while, they ignored mettlesome comments from the hungry onlookers.

"We have no…" Hannah started to say, holding up the knife.

Joseph propped up a scratched and stained old silver tablespoon.

Hannah looked at it dumbfounded, not sure if she was really prepared to put that spoon into her own mouth. But she took the spoon and pot and made her way around the group. After a few refusals to eat, even the most stoic eventually gave in to hunger pains and ate from the same pot and spoon. The pleasure of warm broth and pieces of vegetables in the mind and stomach was too much to resist. Mama's Passover soup was all Hannah could think of.

"Thank you, my dear," the man with the bad heart said to Hannah. "I am so sorry for all this complaining."

He reminded Hannah of Papa. Kind and nice to be with, but more than that. The man understood what she and Joseph were trying to do for them.

I didn't think I could do this, Papa. But now it feels right to me. I can be a fighter like these boys, Papa. I think I can even get to Russia with them. I can do this.

Panning the complainers in the dim firelight, Hannah could see worry on their drawn faces.

"We have to help each other," she replied, her words echoing through her own head as if someone else had said them. She noticed Joseph smiling at her.

"We have to survive," she said. "That is how we will beat them."

"Ah, so young and yet so wise," the old man said, his head

nodding slowly.

A woody thud and squeak came from over the hill breaking the stillness. Then a rumbling sound approached the hill surrounding the depression.

Joseph and Hannah grabbed their rifles and aimed toward the noise.

The noise stopped.

"Joseph…it's Itzhak," Itzhak said, very slowly and clearly.

"Come," replied Joseph.

Hannah watched and listened intently.

Itzhak came over the rise pulling a utility wagon.

"As you can see, I was successful in 'borrowing' this practical vehicle," Itzhak said, grinning.

"Well, that's fine, but what would have happened if we were taken by the enemy and you walked into a trap?" Hannah said, still annoyed and not able to contain herself. She wanted him to stop treating her like a child.

I'm learning and quickly, too. I need to see more. I don't know the best way to do things, that's all. Why can't he just tell me these things?

"That is why Boris and Schlomo are behind you right now," he said, smiling.

"Oh, well, what?" she asked.

Hannah looked behind her to see Boris and Schlomo in position. They were diagonally across from each other with weapons ready.

Hannah looked behind at the two boys and felt her jaw tighten. *These are lessons I must learn.* She fought the urge to stomp her foot into the ground.

"Have you finished your meal? Ready to travel?" Itzhak asked the group.

"But you and the others had no soup," Hannah said, looking at Itzhak.

He pulled back the horse blanket to expose containers of fruits and vegetables.

"We found jars of canned fruit, many jars in the root cellar near the barn," he replied.

"We made a meal of it," Schlomo said, rubbing his belly with feigned satisfaction.

"I guess we have no other choice but to take their food," Hannah replied.

"We have more food for the journey," Itzhak chimed in. "More jarred fruit, stale bread, ears of corn, and a basket of apples."

"Yeah, we raided the cellar pretty hard," Boris said with a grin.

"That's stealing, isn't it?" Hannah said, frowning at Boris.

"We know this farmer. He would not hesitate to turn us over to the town authorities or shoot us in the back," Itzhak replied, looking her in the eye. "Besides, we are running for our lives and starving. He is not."

I suppose God knows we have no choice. But I'm sure Papa would say no.

"We need to travel in darkness, so everyone be ready to go," Itzhak said as he looked over the faces of the group.

Pointing toward the older man and his wife he said, "You will ride in the cart and keep the food from falling out."

The moon was mostly hidden by thick clouds and the early evening darkness cloaked the group in the shadows along the rough, dirt pasture road that ran parallel to the main east road. They set off for Bialystok.

. . . . .

Late into the night they ran out of pasture roads and the only option was to chance using the east road. The road was empty in both directions. The big advantage at night of course was in the clear, relatively flat terrain, vehicle headlights could be seen for many kilometers. An escape into the fields and woods that bordered the road would be quick.

Hannah felt her energy drain as the night cold set in. The warmth and hope from the small portion of hot soup had long since faded. She stepped up her pace and closed the gap between her and Itzhak.

"How long can we go on like this?" she asked. Itzhak turned his head back and slowed a bit allowing her to catch up.

"The cart is working well, don't you agree?" he replied. "The boys are taking shifts pushing and pulling it along."

"I know it's risky, but we made much better time with that old truck," she said.

"I would have taken a truck from that farm back there," he said. "But the battery was dead."

Hannah noticed the sly smile on Itzhak's face. The night sky was dim with only a sliver of moon to light the way.

Oh, he's always a step or two ahead of me. She tried to hold back a smile, but it just came out.

"You are very pretty when you smile," he said softly.

She looked around, but the others seemed not to hear. She wanted to tell him how she felt, but not here, not now. The others would tease her, or maybe tease Itzhak.

"Thank you for being so kind to me," she said, brushing her hair aside.

Oh, how stupid that sounded.

"How old are you, Hannah?" Itzhak asked, catching her eye.

Humm, she thought. *He'll think I'm too young for him.*

"I'm seventeen," she replied, her eyes trailing away from his as she spoke.

"Oh, I thought you were probably a bit younger, maybe sixteen."

He already knows. She glanced up at him.

"Well, I'll be sixteen in a few months."

I like him. I guess now he'll think I'm too young. The boys in school in Warsaw were so immature. Itzhak is amazing.

Suddenly, Boris called out from the rear.

"Lights, behind us!" he yelled. "One, then two sets of two following."

"Motorcycle, staff car, and troop carrier," Itzhak said. "Germans."

"What do we do?" Hannah asked, fear rising in her chest.

Everyone was in a panic, scattering about and confused. Hannah looked up the road. About fifty meters ahead was a stream. It crossed under the road, and the berm on each side formed a small depression where they might be able to hide. Otherwise, open fields bordered the road on both sides. There was no other place to hide.

"Itzhak, look, up ahead," she said, pointing out the spot in the dark.

"It will have to do," he replied, motioning everyone off the road. "Split up. Boris, Schlomo, David, take these three and get in position on the other side of the road."

They helped the older couple off the cart and pushed it a short distance into the open field. Hannah's eyes met Itzhak's and she nodded toward the ditch and stream. He nodded back.

"Come with me," Hannah said to the other four.

Itzhak and Joseph got into position lying in the field with weapons ready. Hannah stepped down into the ditch and stream. The sides were a bed of nearly frozen mud. Her shoes sunk in and icy water from the stream filled them soaking her socks.

"Get down! Get down on the ground," she ordered the hapless couples.

"But it is dirty and wet down there," the old woman said.

The men climbed down the embankment and leaned their backs against the sloped ground. Their shoes were planted in the mud and their legs bent at the knees. Hannah figured they were low enough not to be seen from the approaching vehicles. But the old woman was still standing!

"Squat, sit, anything!" Hannah shouted at the woman.

The headlights from the vehicles dropped as the road dipped down. When the first vehicle came over the rise, Hannah knew this stupid woman would be exposed. She only had a second or two.

Hannah reached out and grabbed the woman by her ankles. She lunged backward toward the stream, and the lady's body dropped to her rump.

"Ohhh!" the woman exclaimed in shock.

Hannah continued to pull her, as the woman slid on her back down the slope next to the men as the light came over the cresting road. It glanced off the woman's hair and blinded Hannah for a moment.

A motorcycle roared past them and then slowed momentarily. A big, black Mercedes whooshed by. Hannah caught a glimpse of military hats.

Must be officers. She was too afraid to raise her head above the berm.

The third vehicle was a small transport truck or large automobile, open with several passengers in the back. It was slowing down in response to the brake lights of the Mercedes just ahead. Hannah spotted men with helmets as they flashed by in the dark.

Soldiers. They're stopping and coming back.

She moved to the other side of the stream embankment and cocked her rifle. Her chest felt like it would explode, heart pounding furiously.

Breathe, breathe before you pass out…breathe, stupid!

Hannah watched the brake lights in the distance. They dimmed and then after a few seconds disappeared. She took a gulp of air and coughed.

"Why are you treating me so cruelly?" the old woman moaned. "You are nothing but a ruffian, like those young men that lead you around."

"Are you hurt?" Hannah asked, hoping the old lady was at least physically able to go on.

"Oh, I may never walk again," she replied, trembling and rubbing her hip.

"Let me help you up," Hannah said, holding out her hand.

Itzhak sauntered over to the cutout where Hannah and the others were still hiding. He didn't seem worried a bit about the German patrol returning. The memory of the pit and the German's steely eyes came to mind. A numbing shiver rolled through her body.

"They seem too much in a hurry to worry about us," Itzhak said, gazing down the road into the darkness.

"But what if they do come back or another patrol comes along?" Hannah asked.

"Everyone, back into position. We are moving again," Itzhak called out.

To Hannah he said quietly, "We have to take advantage of the darkness. I have to keep them moving. And Hannah, those Germans? They're gone for now."

Hannah had to agree and helped the boys round up the others. In spite of wet shoes and socks, the troop was moving as before, along the east road in the darkness.

Chapter Eleven

It was an hour later when a rattling farm truck came lumbering along the route. Itzhak dispersed them to the sides of the road as before, although this time there were ample trees and scrub brush to hide behind. Hannah and Joseph led the older ones to hiding places behind the trees, while Itzhak, Boris, and David uprighted the cart in the middle of the narrow country road. Everyone then hid with weapons ready. Hannah and Joseph were on the opposite side of the road from Itzhak and the others. All hoped this would cause the farmer to stop the truck to move the cart out of the way. The plan was simple, but Hannah wondered what Itzhak would do if the man didn't stop.

The truck lumbered over the crest in the road and crawled to a stop with the motor idling. The driver, a middle-aged farmer, nervously peered out either side of the open windows. Then he turned the steering wheel sharply and stepped on the accelerator. The truck started around the cart with wheels digging into the loose dirt on the shoulder of the road. Itzhak and Joseph lunged from hiding and headed toward the road from both directions. Hannah could see Itzhak jumping onto the running board of the truck. Joseph lost his footing and fell flat on his stomach. His pistol jolted from his hand and skidded onto the road.

"I'll get it!" Hannah yelled, dropping her rifle next to Joseph, launching herself forward into the road. She scooped up the pistol and jumped onto the truck. Her right foot landed securely onto the running board in stride. Grabbing the doorframe, Hannah pulled herself up onto the truck. As Itzhak did on the other side, she thrust her pistol to the man's temple.

"Stop!" they shouted in unison.

The farmer looked terrified, his hands frozen on the wheel. But the truck was still moving. He would not stop, or could not. The truck bounced over ruts and Hannah was afraid she would fall off the running board. She thrust her head and shoulders through the open window, the top of the door pressing hard into her stomach.

"Stop the truck!" she yelled, teeth grinding together.

She turned the pistol from the farmer's temple and pointed the muzzle between his eyes.

"Stop now!" she said, "or I'll kill you."

The farmer stopped the truck. Itzhak reached across the farmer and moved the floor shift to neutral. Hannah glanced over and caught his expression. Itzhak looked shocked and then a little smile appeared.

"Get out," he said to the farmer.

Hannah's and Itzhak's eyes met for an instant. She removed the gun from the man's face. The farmer put his hands up and looked at Itzhak. Hannah aimed her pistol at the man's temple again, and Itzhak stepped off the truck on the driver's side. The farmer got out of the truck and Itzhak took him away.

"Load them in, Hannah," Itzhak said as he wrenched the man to the opposite side of the road.

Hannah went back to the others and got everyone into the farmer's truck as Boris and David pushed the cart out of the road. Itzhak left the man standing by the side of the road and sat down in the driver's seat. The gears ground and clinked in the old transmission, and with a jolt the truck started down the dark road again, heading east. Hannah sat between Itzhak and David, shoulder to shoulder.

About four in the morning they crested a hill. Hannah could see a town on the horizon. She could not resist, breaking the long silence in the cab. "Is that...?"

"Yes, Bialystok," he replied. "We have made very good time."

"I did not think the old wreck would make it this far," David said with a big smile.

They drove through the early mist, the truck droning on as it had done all night.

"We are to meet with Jacob and his brothers near the edge of the forest east of Bialystok," Itzhak explained. "They are getting a few fighters out of the ghetto there, hopefully."

"What then?" Hannah asked.

"Then we go deep into the woods," replied David. "And hope our brother Poles and the Russians still see us as comrades."

"You mean there are Russians in our forests, too?" she asked, eyes wide open.

Itzhak looked over at her and smiled. He tapped her knee with his finger and nodded.

Hannah wondered if the tap was one of friendship or something else. They had been through a lot in a couple of days, only a few hours actually. Since the farmer in the truck, she already felt part of the group. Jumping onto the truck and holding a pistol to a man's head was crazy. But everything was dangerous. Doing nothing was dangerous, too. Still, there was something exciting about fighting back.

Hannah gazed through the smudged, cracked windshield, hypnotized by the dull roadway streaming under the dented hood as they drove on through the damp air just before dawn.

They could meet another German patrol at any moment. But that didn't seem to matter as much. The group would protect her. It was so hard being all alone, making all the decisions. Hannah liked having others around her. She never liked many at school. Esther Kronsky hated her. And that Ruth Furmann. Ugh. And their stupid friends. They were so mean to her. Papa knew what she liked, too. Science and history, things that mattered. Who cared what color hair ribbon matched a dress anyway? They made her dance at those Bar Mitzvahs with those stupid boys.

Hannah glanced at David. His head was resting on the doorframe, eyes closed. Itzhak checked the mirror every so often.

They are older. Itzhak, David, and even Joseph. Nothing like the others. Besides, we're on a mission, saving other Jews. Papa would understand. Mama would not.

Far ahead, lights appeared for a moment and then disappeared. Hannah turned to Itzhak and was about to speak.

"I saw it," he said coolly. "David. Be ready to jump to the rear and get the rest out of the truck to shelter."

"Understood," he replied.

"Germans?" Hannah asked, straining to see the road up ahead.

"Not sure," he said. "I'm chancing it's a farmer, out early hauling crops to market."

"How can you be sure?"

"Can't, but the time is right," he said, two hands on the wheel.

The truck maintained speed down the road as the oncoming vehicle came over the crest of the hill. Two headlights, somewhat dim, continued to move toward them.

"Hannah, if something happens to me, you need to drive on past Bialystok as far east as this road will take you. Abandon the truck inside the edge of the forest and head in on foot," Itzhak said. "Any of the boys can lead you to the encampments."

"But I'm not a leader," she said. "David or Joseph are certainly better than me."

"I want to get the older people to one of the bigger etrads, to the Bielsky brothers if possible," he replied. "They will take care of them."

"But they won't listen to me," she said, her voice high.

"Look, you are far better at handling them than you think. Certainly better than the rest of us."

Because I'm a girl, I suppose, she thought, pressing her lips together tightly.

The approaching vehicle lumbered along and finally passed by in the opposite direction. Hannah got a good look at the driver and the cargo. It was indeed a farmer, who looked a little like Papa. The truck bed was full of hay. The man did not seem a threat. But Hannah remembered the farmer's wife who panicked and told the Ukrainian soldiers about her. She remembered one of Barbara's warnings that the most innocent situations can quickly turn on you. If that farmer just mentions to the wrong person that he passed a group of people in a farm truck on the east road, who knew what would happen. But Itzhak was smart.

"Nothing will happen to you," she said, looking up at Itzhak's face.

Their eyes met once more and Hannah still wondered about Itzhak's tap on her knee.

"We originally planned to slip into the Bialystok ghetto and recruit a few more fighters, but I cannot do that carting these people around," he explained.

"You just walk into a city full of Germans?" she asked.

"Not exactly. We sneak in at night," Itzhak said, smiling.

"We use these," David said, holding up a pair of wire cutters.

"What if you're caught?" Hannah asked.

"You only get caught once, Hannah," Itzhak said, looking over at her and then back to the road ahead.

She nodded. He did not have to explain.

"But since Jacob is going in and we have this lot with us," he said, "whoever he finds will have to do."

"Who?" she asked, wagging her head.

The predawn morning sky was dim and the cover of darkness melted away rapidly. Hannah began to feel uneasy as they skirted the city.

"I am taking a back road around to meet Jacob," Itzhak said. "Probably better if you don't know him."

Itzhak slowed and took a right turn onto an old farm road. The road began as worn pavement, then quickly degraded into gravel with potholes. The deep depressions from years of tire wear and the occasional mud puddle jostled the old truck up and down and side to side. The occasional groan from the rear of the truck was a clear reminder of their discomfort. The pace along the old dirt road was slow.

Eventually, Itzhak made a series of left and right turns. The roads were getting deeper into the farmland and woods. As daylight began to uncover the road ahead, Itzhak switched off the truck's lights.

He knows how to keep us hidden, even in plain sight. Everything he has been doing is common sense. I only need to watch and learn.

Finally, Itzhak pulled the old truck off the farm road about fifty meters and stopped in a clearing. He left the motor running and the three got out of the cab. They stood in a small field blanketed by coarse, dead weeds. It was a drastic change from the supple summer grasses she remembered. Hannah and Papa had taken walks in the summer woods searching for birds and insects of all types to match up with their nature books. The memory was now sweet and painful. She walked to the back of the truck to see how the group had made the trip. She felt guilty having had the luxury of riding in the cab with a cushioned seat, even though it was scored with jagged splits in the cloth with stuffing protruding. The springs poked her buttocks most of the way. Even so, it was still far better than bouncing around in the hay on the hardwood, mud-caked truck bed. They all looked worn out and too frazzled to even complain. Boris, Schlomo, and Joseph looked disgusted. Joseph rolled his eyes as he passed Hannah. It was easy to see the trip in the truck bed had hardly been pleasant.

"Joseph, Boris," Itzhak said, "take Hannah and the rest to our camp. I have work to do. David, we need to go into the ghetto."

"But you said that could wait," Hannah said.

"There is something wrong. Jacob should have been here or left a sign." Itzhak pulled Joseph and Hannah aside.

"Joseph, try to get them to Bielsky, he said softly. "And try to stay clear of the Home army and the Russians."

"I understand," Joseph replied.

"If we don't come back," he said, "report in to the commander." Joseph moved away.

"Be careful," Hannah said to Itzhak.

She felt her face flush and looked around, but no one seemed to notice. Itzhak and David were already getting into the idling truck.

Hannah suddenly felt as alone as she had when she crawled out of the pit. She turned back to see the old farm truck pulling away down the dirt road. *Itzhak, come back.*

Hannah looked at the group and let out a sigh.

"After a short rest, we must get them ready to travel," Joseph whispered to Hannah.

"Do we have any food left?" Hannah asked.

"Some jarred fruit is all," Schlomo replied with a shrug. "I hope enough. For strength, I mean."

"Not much of a breakfast, but it will have to do," Hannah said, looking at the glass jars. Bubbe Rachel and Hannah used to eat peaches right from the jar when Mama wasn't around. Mama would have had a fit, but she never saw them do it. "I'm not sure they can go much farther without some food."

Surveying the area, Hannah spied a little clearing. Just off the edge of the field was a fallen birch. The trunk formed a natural bench.

"Listen, everyone," she said, raising her voice, "we are going to take a short rest."

"I know the truck was a blessing, but most of us are half dead from the bumps and the cold," said one man, waving her off.

"I am cold and starving," said another, her eyes pleading for Hannah to help her.

Hannah took a step toward Joseph.

"Who is Bielsky?" she whispered.

"There are Jewish brothers, farmers, in the forest near our camp. We hear they are taking in Jews. They are not fighters like us," Joseph replied softly.

"Can we find them?" she asked. "And will they take these older people?"

"I can get us there, but..." Joseph shrugged his shoulders and grimaced.

It's probably not safe to stay here long, she thought. Hannah looked over at Boris, who was already motioning her to hurry.

"We will have some fruit for nourishment," she told the group.

"Do you have enough for everyone, dear?" an old woman asked. She peered around Hannah to see what Boris was holding.

Hannah felt bad for the older Jews. They were like Bubbe Rachel and Bubbe Leah. She tried but had no way to make them comfortable. It was so hard to be the leader. And Itzhak was counting on her.

"Please sit down over there," Hannah said, pointing to the

downed tree. "We will pass out the food."

"Oh. So hard," a man said as he lowered himself onto the rough bark.

"For me, too," the old woman added. "But I'll live, don't worry." She flicked a hand toward Hannah. "See to the others, dear."

"Alright, alright, I know everyone is in pain. We have come a long way," the sick old gentleman said. We could not have gotten here without these brave young people. They are doing us a mitzvah, a good deed. Have some *rakhmones,* some pity. Let's try to help them help us."

The man coughed and wheezed in obvious pain. The others stopped talking and nodded their heads to each other in agreement. Hannah looked at Boris and Joseph and knew she had found her place.

Smooth-skinned peaches and rough pears slid over her tongue. The nearly frozen juice filled her mouth making her teeth throb. A stomachache was in the making. The memory of the ice water from the farmer's old canteen in the barn stuck in her mind. *I won't give up like Papa did. I'm strong, strong enough.*

Hannah and Boris passed around the last of the fruit. They all sat quiet, looking exhausted. The old gentleman finally regained control over his coughing.

"Thank you, my dear," he said as Hannah handed him the fruit jar.

"You're welcome, mister," she said, taking a step back. She felt a strange calm inside, satisfied, as if she had won something. Like the games they played in the summer garden—her, Beila, and Sol Wertz. Especially the time when she finally beat Sol at soccer. She was not the same girl. Now it was different.

Boris stepped over to Hannah and leaned into her. "We cannot stay here any longer," he said, voice muffled. "Can you get them moving?"

"Give them another minute or two," she replied. "They're very tired."

"Only a few minutes more, then we must go," he said, looking around and then pacing the perimeter.

Hannah nodded and looked at her shoes, scuffed and smeared with mud. The slippers she pulled from the dead woman's feet broke into her mind. *Do these old people know who we are fighting? I do. I can't even sleep through the night anymore. Those eyes staring at me.* She reached for her rifle, hand shaking. Slinging the strap over her shoulder, she faced the group.

"Please finish quickly, everyone," Hannah said. "And get ready to move out."

Her order was met with a chorus of low groans. Nonetheless, people got up from their tree trunk seats looking a little refreshed and stood waiting for the teenage girl to give the next order. Hannah nodded to Boris.

"Follow me," Boris said to the group and started on a path that quickly led them into the woods.

Hannah and Joseph waited until all were walking in single formation and they took up the rear guard.

"Hannah, the Home army sometimes patrols here," Joseph said, "looking for Germans, Lithuanians, or Ukrainians. All the same as far as we're concerned."

Hannah remembered the Ukrainians at the pit and the one that attacked her at the edge of the woods and the others that picked her up on the road and brought her to the Germans at the train station.

"Who is the Home army?" she asked Joseph.

"After the Germans overran our army in '39," he explained, "they went underground to fight back, secretly."

"You mean the Polish army is out here in the forests, too?" she asked, squinting into the shadows. "I guess I thought they were all killed."

"I never really thought much about it. War seems so stupid," Hannah said. "Why do people want to kill other people? I'll never understand it."

"I heard a truck far away, a little while ago," Joseph said. "It could have been any of them."

"But isn't the Home army on our side?" Hannah asked, tilting her head.

"Well, some like us and some hate us. Some don't care what happens to us. Always be on your guard, because you can never be sure."

"But we are Poles, too," she replied.

"Yes, strange, isn't it?" Joseph said, lips pressed together, wagging his head slightly.

As they walked, the woods became cooler and darker. Hannah tried to remember the things she learned from Itzhak. The lessons that Papa taught her would no doubt help as well. Finding natural trails through the trees and underbrush was easy. The forest felt like an old friend as they plodded along.

Everyone seemed to accept their plight and walked in silence. They made progress for several hours of work fighting off briars and brush and branches. As for herself, Hannah was travelling east, doing what Papa wanted. She held back tears as she brushed aside bushes and small tree branches that constantly slapped and scratched at her face and arms. The group kept moving steadily, the old people groaning here and there.

Chapter Twelve

"Halt!" yelled out a burly peasant, stepping into view from behind a large spruce tree. He did not look military, but neither did Hannah and the others. He wore a Polish army cap cocked to one side and pointed a submachine gun at the group. Others from his ranks stepped out from behind trees pointing their weapons. Joseph, Boris, and Schlomo wheeled about and pointed their weapons at the aggressors. Hannah was caught unprepared with her rifle slung over her shoulder. She froze in place noticing another man with his rifle pointed at her head. The old people made a collective gasp, afraid to move or say anything. More Polish men appeared behind the boys. Hannah saw their faces and knew that they were overpowered. Everyone would be shot down.

"We are from the Obiesk etrad," Joseph said, his voice strong and bold. "Why are you interfering with our mission?"

"You look like Jews," the leader said with a half-hearted chuckle. "You have no mission."

"We are Poles, like you," Joseph replied. "And we are all fighting Germans, and Lithuanians and Ukrainians."

"I think you are a bunch of spies, trying to locate our positions and report back to your Nazi commander," the Home army officer replied. "Put down your weapons or I will cut down the lot of you."

"I have civilians here," Joseph said. "They are no threat to you."

"Neither are you," the officer said snidely.

Joseph lowered his gun and glanced over at Boris and Schlomo. They did the same.

"Drop your weapons on the ground," the officer said, glaring at Joseph and the others.

"No, you know we fight the Germans," Joseph said firmly. "If we run into Germans or their comrades, you will need all the firepower you can get."

"I don't trust you Jews," he said, holding his position.

"I don't trust you either," Joseph said, glaring back with fierce eyes.

"You are a brave one," the officer said, half-smiling with clenched teeth.

The man nodded his head signaling his soldiers to start moving into the woods. Hannah watched Joseph and the officer intently for any sign of easing the standoff. She could not hold her breath much longer.

"Keep your weapons down," the officer said after a long pause, "or my men will cut you to pieces."

Hannah could feel sweat running down her sides from her armpits.

Move forward, Joseph. We have no choice.

Joseph glanced at Hannah, Schlomo, and Boris. He nodded to them and took a step, following the Home army men as they led the way. Everyone let out a nervous breath and joined the line, in single file. All except the sick old man. He leaned on his wife for support. Hannah stayed behind the older people to at least give the impression of protecting them from the Home army men. She heard a comment or two from the men behind her—something about how their commander would enjoy this girl. She checked for her jackknife, her hand shaking in her coat pocket. Where was Itzhak? She might not see him again. Or even worse, he might not want to see her after these people did things to her.

Hannah tried to settle down and think like Itzhak. *If they start shooting us, what should I do? Try to run for cover and then shoot at them. They'll shoot me in the back trying to escape. What else? There are too many of them.* She waited and watched as they moved deeper into the forest. There seemed to be Polish Home army men everywhere. An hour into the deeper woods, the troop began to encounter outposts with sentries. Passwords were spoken and they moved on. The older people groaned a little, but none seemed brave enough to complain to their captors. Hardly anyone from either group spoke at all.

Hannah surmised they must be close to their camp. These men must keep watch for enemy soldiers in the area.

Sure enough, not five minutes more on the trail and the group broke into a clearing in the forest. From what was visible, Hannah guessed that the camp was about one hundred meters square. Men with weapons were plentiful. Many soldiers turned and looked curiously at the strangers who were bounded by their army comrades. Most turned back to their tasks, sensing no danger. Hannah felt the stares of a few. A pretty young girl in a sea of grimy soldiers and a few old civilians stood out.

"Wait here," the Home army officer said gruffly as his men stopped and corralled Hannah, the boys, and the elders. Joseph looked unflappable, as if he had been in this situation before many times. He assumed a wide stance, boots apart and submachine gun pointed into the ground. He looked confident, surprisingly relaxed, but ready at a moment's notice for any action. Hannah wondered if Itzhak would come back to rescue them. Would he even know how to find them?

The officer walked away toward a military tent and spoke softly to the soldier standing at the opening. He stepped inside. There was some grumbling and then the officer and his obvious superior emerged from the tent.

"Commander Bartowski will decide what we do with you," the officer said.

Bartowski was a round, middle-aged Polish army officer, who at first impression appeared tall. His face was round like his belly, of ruddy complexion with thick lips and topped with light brown, thinning hair. He sounded angry and looked and smelled like a drinker.

To Hannah he seemed a nasty sort of man. He was probably her father's age, but acted very differently. The man paraded around, his puffed-up chest almost protruding as far as his belly. Hannah could only think of the fat man on the street corner that she and Mama had to pass each time they went to the kosher butcher. The streets in

Warsaw looked the same, but the people seemed oddly different. It was just before they moved to Sokolka.

This awful man is deciding what to do with us?

The commander took bold strides up and down the line of captives.

"What do I need of these Jews?" Bartowski shouted, waving his right arm about. "Will they fight?" he asked the squad leader. "I think not."

"But, Commander, they walked into our territory," the officer stated.

Bartowski looked in disgust at the old man and his wife and then suddenly noticed Hannah. His eyes quickly scanned her body and a sly grin appeared, only for a moment.

"What of these old Jew peasants?" he asked, turning away from Hannah. "What am I supposed to do with the likes of these?"

Joseph stepped forward and looked the commander in the eye.

"Your people brought us here," Joseph said. "Why don't you let us return to our etrad and be done with us?"

Commander Bartowski grunted and his face grew hard and even redder as he paced toward Joseph.

"You dare to tell me what I should do?" Bartowski shouted.

Joseph did not move. The expression on his face did not change.

Bartowski stopped in front of Joseph and thrust his face to within a hair of Joseph's nose. "I'll decide what I please," Bartowski said, hands on his hips.

"What difference does it make whether I fight Germans here or twenty kilometers from here?" Joseph replied, eye to eye. "The object is to kill them before they kill us, is it not?"

Bartowski stood silent, glaring at Joseph. Then he burst out laughing.

"This young Jew has a point," he exclaimed, straightening up and backing away from Joseph.

"But it is one thing to say you can fight and quite another to do it," the commander declared. "You will have your chance tonight, my Jewish comrade."

"What are you talking about?" Joseph replied, glaring at the officer.

"You and your friends will accompany Chenek here on a mission and we will see if you are what you say," Bartowski said, eyeing the crowd.

Hannah feared the vile commander's real purpose and motioned to Joseph not to agree to this order.

"If we do this, I expect you will keep your word and we will be gone by morning," Joseph said.

Bartowski shrugged his shoulders and grinned as he walked away.

"Oh, and the old ones will stay with me in case you feel a sudden urge to slip away from my men in the darkness," the commander said.

"Leave them alone, they can't hurt you," Joseph replied.

Bartowski ignored him and walked away, shifting his weight from side to side.

"Ah, and this one will stay here to help comfort them," Bartowski said, pointing to Hannah. "Take her weapon, Chenek."

Hannah felt the weight of her rifle lift off her back. She grabbed for the shoulder strap, but Chenek snapped it out of her hand.

"I need my rifle to defend them," Hannah said.

"Oh, don't worry, we will protect you," Chenek said with a little smirk.

Neither you nor your filthy commander will do anything to me.

She watched Bartowski slip into his tent and the confrontation seemed over. Joseph, Schlomo, and Boris would go on a mission of some sort with Chenek and his men. She would have to deal with Bartowski and his men and of course keep her group of peasants alive. Somehow.

Where is Itzhak? she wondered. *Can he even find us?*

. . . . .

The last spikes of sunlight shot through tree trunks as the day ended. Darkness quickly filled the gaps. Campfires sprung up around the clearing. The little fires cast shadows on the tree trunks and evergreen branches overhead. The camp looked like a cave. Chenek ordered his men to pack up and move out. Hannah remembered what Joseph had whispered. They would probably try to shoot him in the back. If the three didn't return, she wasn't sure what to do. Hannah couldn't sit still. She got up and paced in their small section of camp. *I wish I could shut my eyes and this would all go away. I just want to be a girl. Why do I have to be here?*

Tired of pacing, she sat with the older people. With the whole camp watching, maybe the disgusting commander would leave her alone. But Joseph and the others were gone. She was on her own.

A couple of hours passed. The camp was as dark as pitch, except for a nearby fire in the center of the clearing. One of the camp men walked over with two soup bowls. Hannah tried a little. The broth warmed her stomach, but the soup was thin. She passed her bowl on to the sick old man sitting next to her. She closed her eyes and let out a long breath. *Joseph should be back anytime.* She tilted her head back. Hearing someone approach, she sat up straight. A Home army soldier approached from the direction of the tent. Firelight reflected off his submachine gun as he passed the campfire.

"Commander Bartowski wants to see you in his tent," the man said.

"See me for what?" Hannah replied, voice cracking. She looked at the old ones hoping someone would say something.

"I don't know," he said. "Now."

Hannah's heart sank. The memory of the Ukrainian on top of her was still raw.

"Maybe he has some news about the mission," the sickly man said.

He probably said that to make me feel better. Bartowski wants to hurt me. Keep away from him. I'll scream. But who'll help me?

Getting up from the ground, Hannah moved slowly and followed the soldier toward the tent. Her mouth felt dry and she swallowed hard. At the entrance, she stopped and stood still for a moment. She felt like a character in a book. But she had no lines to say.

The sentry gave her a sharp push and she stumbled forward into the tent. Hannah caught herself with a quick step to keep from falling.

Commander Bartowski was seated on a wooden folding chair, leaning back away from the small, wooden table in front of him. The tent was dimly lit and smelled of canvas, damp earth, tobacco smoke, and liquor. Hannah noticed a nearly empty bottle sticking out of an army satchel behind the desk. At Bubbe Leah's shiva, bottles of schnapps sat on the side table in the dining room. The old men drank vodka. They smelled of it. Papa didn't drink it.

"Ahhh, come in, my dear," the commander said with an air of cordiality.

Hannah eyed the red-faced oaf. She felt the blood rush to her head in a dizzying flush, a panic leaving her disoriented.

"Sit down over here," he said, offering her a stained pine field chair.

The tent stopped spinning and the commander's words began to make sense. She looked at the chair that was hardly more than an arm's length from him.

This is too close. And he smells like schnapps.

"Sit over here next to me and I will tell you about the mission your comrades have undertaken," Bartowski said with a toothy grin surrounded by a forest of black whiskers. He rotated his hand at the wrist waving her to come forward.

His eyes were bloodshot and movements awkward. His prominent nose glowed quite red. She had seen an uncle a bit tipsy once. This one looked the same way. She felt for the utility knife in her jacket pocket. Empty. *Where is it? It's got to be here. Try the other one.* She slipped her hand in the other pocket. *No. Gone.*

She scanned the tent for a weapon. Anything hard she could use to swing at him. The small kerosene desk lamp on the little field table was not enough to stop this man. But the lit kerosene could set him on fire. *It might be enough. Maybe distract him so I can get out.*

"Where have you taken them?" Hannah said, carefully moving around the table toward the field chair.

The large man chuckled, obviously enjoying his little game. Hannah reached for the top panel of the backrest of the chair and pulled it toward her. She positioned herself farther from the little field table between them.

If he tries to grab me, I'll take the lamp and hit him in the head with it.

"You know, I have a daughter about your age."

Hmm. I wonder if she's afraid of him, too. Hannah stared at the grotesque face, ready for him to make any kind of move.

"When will my friends be back?"

"My daughter. She doesn't like the cold. She would like to sleep in the tent where it is warm. Maybe you would like to do that?"

"No. I like the cold. What have you done with my friends?"

Bartowski smiled and nodded. He waved a finger at Hannah.

"There are German supply trains not far from here," Bartowski said. "We Poles blow them sky high."

"My group has strong fighters," Hannah replied.

"Your comrades are helping us tonight in our glorious work," Bartowski said. "If they don't get themselves killed on the way, that is."

He grinned taking much satisfaction in scaring Hannah.

"When will they return?" she asked, trying not to show any fear.

"Soon enough," he said gruffly. "Not your concern. I see you are very young to be so bold. I suppose you think you are a fighter, too? Well, we shall see."

Hannah bristled as Commander Bartowski stood up, straddling his chair. He swayed slightly and then regained his balance.

"What of these old ones with you?" he asked.

"We were bringing them to safety in the forests," Hannah replied.

"Ha! What safety?" he exclaimed as he staggered around his chair.

"The Polish Home army is the only one who can protect anyone out here."

Hannah didn't know what to say. She was not sure if Bartowski knew of the Bielsky brothers. She was afraid to tell him where they were bringing the old people.

"And as for you, my little Jew," he said, lunging forward. Hannah felt thick hands and forearms as she fell backward under his tremendous weight. She stabbed the air for the lamp, but couldn't reach it. He was on top of her. The Ukrainian soldier's face raced through her mind.

Not again! I've got to get out of here. My knife. Where's my knife?

In a panic, squirming to get free, she felt Bartowski's hand slip under her jacket. The weight of the man was suffocating, his breath overpowering. Her stomach wretched. Sour, burning bile rose in her throat reaching her mouth. She tightened her tongue to hold back the vomit.

Suddenly, Hannah heard the unmistakable metallic sound of a revolver being cocked.

The commander abruptly stopped pawing at her.

"Get off the girl or I will blow your brains out," a man said.

The voice was so familiar, but her mind was racing.

"Get off of her!" Itzhak commanded.

Hannah felt a great weight lift from her body and her mind came back into focus.

"Itzhak. Itzhak, you found us. I was afraid they would kill us all," Hannah said, her eyes filling with tears.

Itzhak's eyes were hot when he turned away from the commander. He continued to point his gun at the man. Hannah began to raise herself up from the ground and she grabbed Itzhak's outstretched forearm. Their eyes met as he pulled her up. She could not hold back any longer. Burying her face into his chest, she sobbed uncontrollably. Everything came pouring out. She vaguely heard Itzhak's words as he moved her out of the tent.

"I have plenty of firepower," Itzhak said loudly so all could hear.

"My men will—" Bartowski started, but was cut off.

"Your men are surrounded by my fighters," Itzhak said, hand sweeping the perimeter. "Not with old men and women. See for yourself."

Bartowski stumbled out of the tent and looked around. He immediately realized it was no bluff. David, Joseph, Boris, and many more that Hannah did not recognize stood at the ready, weapons pointed awaiting Itzhak's next command.

The anger seemed to melt from Bartowski's face as he realized it was at best a standoff and at worst, he would probably lose the fight.

"We are leaving now," Itzhak said. "And you will stand down."

Hannah regained her composure and moved away from Itzhak. *He doesn't need me hanging onto him while trying to put up a strong front.*

"So perhaps you are right, my Jewish friend. Why reduce our numbers and leave fewer of us to provide the Germans their just rewards!" Bartowski said so all could hear.

Hannah held her breath as the two adversaries held their positions.

"My thoughts as well, Commander," Itzhak replied with an exaggerated smile. "They deserve so much more pain and death from us!"

This awful man turns everything around to his favor. A valuable lesson to remember, even though it comes from a beast.

"Chenek, move your men away," Commander Bartowski ordered, then he spit in the dirt near Itzhak's boots.

Chenek's men lowered their weapons and moved to one side of the encampment.

"David, Joseph, Hannah, get the old ones, we are moving out," Itzhak said and gave a nod to Bartowski.

Hannah felt somehow ashamed that she had failed everyone. How would Itzhak and the boys and even the older people see her now?

Some tough fighter you are. Crying like a little lost girl. You are pitiful. A pitiful little baby.

Hannah dragged herself, empty, toward the old people to help David and Joseph get them moving. *I've let them all down. They must think I'm worthless.*

Someone handed Hannah her rifle and she slipped the sling over her head and across her shoulder. The sickly old man needed help getting to his feet. Hannah grabbed the man's arm and his wife took the other. They hoisted him to his feet. He was very weak. Hannah grabbed his wrist, tucked her shoulder into his armpit, and pulled his arm across her shoulders. He groaned as she raised him up. His wife took his other arm but could not match Hannah's strength. Together the three moved forward.

They soon passed the commander's outposts and turned northeast, deeper into the forest. Once out of Bartowski's territory, Itzhak stopped to rest. Hannah heard him dispatch men ahead and to their flanks, right side and then left. Two of the new men came up to Hannah with a tattered canvas sheet. A third man handed them two trimmed tree branches. The men slipped the straight poles through loops sewn into either side of the tarp. A stretcher lay on the ground at her feet. Hannah nodded. The old man moaned when they hoisted him up, but the sagging canvas worked well.

After a few minutes, Itzhak called everyone to move out again. Hannah rotated her shoulder and the bones cracked. She didn't know how much farther she could've carried him. At least she did that much to help. She overheard men call each other partisans. *Well, we are more than a bunch of Jews. I guess we even have a name. Partisans. I like the sound of it. But the important thing is not to be alone.*

Itzhak traveled at a steady pace, occasionally allowing brief rest stops and then moving on. Hannah began to notice things. The slope of the ground and types of trees all looked so familiar.

Papa's lessons. I can do this. Yes, I know what to do here. One thing is the same for all of us – escape the German murderers. But no, more than that. What did Bartowski say? 'Give them their just rewards.' Yes, somehow. Papa would not approve. But the German killers have to be stopped. I have no one left. Maybe this is the way it was meant to be. Bubbe Rachel would say that. Is that what you want me to do, Adonai? I should do what has to be done?

. . . . .

The march continued for a couple of hours. When Itzhak halted the column, they dropped to the ground exhausted. Itzhak approached Hannah and took her aside.

"Hannah, we need to separate the old people from the etrad and get Bielsky to take them in," Itzhak said. "More fleeing Jews like our friends here are not what he wants or needs, I suspect. I know his sentries are placed over the next hill through these woods. They will question our old ones and see they are no threat. If we are not with them, Bielsky will have no choice but to take them in. I hear he is a good man and is protecting the local Jewish villagers."

"But what should I tell them?" Hannah replied, not wanting to abandon these fellow Jews out in the woods, alone and defenseless.

"They trust you more than me," he explained. "They will believe you."

"You want *me* to explain it to them?" she protested.

"Yes, tell them to follow that path over there and they will find an encampment to shelter them," he said.

"How can we be sure they will make contact with Bielsky's men?" Hannah asked. "I don't feel right leaving them alone in the forest like that."

"I'll leave Boris behind to track them from a distance," Itzhak said. "He will confirm it."

"I guess so," she replied, looking over Itzhak's shoulder at the sick old man.

"Hannah, they can't stay with us. We are a fighting unit," he said. "They would not survive with us."

Facing her, Itzhak put his hands on her shoulders and looked softly into her eyes.

"We can't save everyone, Hannah," he said. "It will only get harder from here on. I need you to be strong."

Hannah searched Itzhak's eyes for some other way. There was none.

"I'll tell them," she said.

Hannah sat the old people down off to the side to talk with them.

"We are going into battle shortly and we cannot take you any farther," she explained.

"You mean you are abandoning us out here?" the old woman asked, shaking her fist at Hannah.

"We should have known better," said another.

The sick old man raised his hand. "Wait, let her talk."

"Thank you," Hannah replied. "There is a group through these woods that will take you in."

"What? There is no one else out here. It's a trick," someone said.

"A man named Bielsky has a large camp and is protecting many Jewish villagers," she said. "You can join him, but you will have to ask him yourselves to take you in."

"Yes, yes, I understand," the sick man said. "We will be alright. God will provide. Do as the girl said."

After their arguing and bickering died down, Hannah stepped away from the group. She motioned them to follow her. Two men dressed in suits and ties took up the makeshift stretcher. They looked like city people and wouldn't survive for long out there. Another man led the group behind Hannah. About a hundred meters down the trail, Hannah waved them by.

"Just keep walking on this path and you will find Bielsky," she said, hoping they would believe her, hoping Itzhak wasn't lying.

Some scowled as they passed Hannah. One gave her a nod. The man on the stretcher grabbed her hand for a moment and whispered a thank you. As Hannah turned to go back to the main group, she spied Boris. He was skillful in moving and hiding.

Itzhak must have told Boris to let me see him. Itzhak understands.

When she got back to the main group, most were already on the trail. She thought they were moving farther south. David and Joseph and a few others waited for Hannah. They joined the march together. Without the old ones, the men moved rapidly. She was grateful she had spent all those summers with Papa exploring nature in the forests. Most of the girls in her school classes would have given up long ago. There were no other girls or women and the men in this group were young and appeared athletic. She wondered why these men were looking at her. She hoped none were like that awful Bartowski. But Itzhak would protect her. Maybe they just thought she would never be as good as them. Hannah pushed herself to keep up. By sundown they had reached the etrad encampment.

Hannah passed a few sentries before the troop reached the clearing. Some glanced at her, others stared.

Do they look because I'm a stranger or because I'm a girl? I feel like sticking my tongue out at them. That's what Beila would do. Probably wouldn't scare them much. Sometimes I wish I could be like her.

Chapter Thirteen

The encampment was thinned of spruce trees, and the black earth rolled gently through the whole area. Underbrush was cleared back and piled along the periphery to give natural cover. Three men were working pots around the fire. In the back of her mind Hannah remembered her little cooking fire outside of Warsaw. A campfire can be seen for a distance, even in the forest. The walls of underbrush have a purpose. She had learned a lot.

Hannah found Itzhak talking with an older man. He had dark hair with gray streaks and looked to be about Papa's age. She wondered if he was the commander of the group, or etrad.

Hannah noticed that Itzhak's men had all dispersed when they entered the camp. Other men stared at her as she walked into the open from the trail.

"Don't worry about them," David said, looking around. "They are just being boys. Curious about women out here."

"They will get used to you soon enough," Joseph said, touching her shoulder. "We know what you can do."

"There are no other women or girls here?" Hannah asked, stomach unsettled.

She knew it would be mostly men, but never thought she would be the only woman. Thus far, she had not had very good experiences with soldiers. Hopefully, things would be better with Itzhak and his group. The Russian soldiers were uniformed, real army. The rest in the camp seemed out of place. They looked like villagers and city people thrown together. Except for the war, none would have ever met.

Is everyone here Jewish? Who can I trust?

"Hannah, this way," David said, waving her forward toward a

quiet-looking section of the encampment.

Hannah followed and they all sat down to rest. Tired and a little sweaty from the long march, she slipped her rifle strap off her shoulder and opened her coat. Boris handed her a tin cup of water. The water was chilled and felt smooth over her tongue and dry throat. But after settling down for an hour, Hannah could hear her stomach growling. *What do they eat out here, berries?*

The thought of berry-picking brought back an old memory. She and Papa looked for forest plants and animals. He pointed out edible berries and mushrooms, also poisonous ones. It was difficult, but not impossible to survive in the forests. She forced the thought away and scanned the campground.

A couple of men glanced her way smiling, but most had stopped staring. She guessed they were all fighters. But what did a fighting unit actually do? Itzhak's words were as troubling as encouraging.

. . . . .

As the sun dropped low, the last streaks of sunlight sparkled through the brush. A man lit a campfire. Hannah worried that the fire would be seen from a distance. But no one in the camp seemed the least bit concerned. Boris handed Hannah a tin can. The paper label glued around the side was faded and difficult to read in the fast-approaching dusk.

"Soup, vegetable soup," Hannah said with a little smile. "I guess we don't need to pick berries."

"Compliments of the local villagers," said Boris, chuckling. "Whether they like it or not."

"Well, I guess you can't very well go to the market for soup," she replied, shaking the can. "Do they just give you food?"

"Yes, wouldn't you if you had a pistol pointed at your head?" he said with a grin.

Hannah looked away. She didn't like the idea of stealing food at gunpoint. It wasn't right.

"We have learned who our enemies in the village are and the ones who feel bad for us," Boris explained as he pried open a soup can. "We take only from German sympathizers. Our people have a lot of different enemies. Not only Germans, you know."

Boris handed Hannah a can opener. She watched the others and worked on cutting off her can lid. She placed the open can on the edge of the campfire as the others did to heat their supper. Boris produced an ornate silver spoon and put it in his tin can. It looked like Bubbe Leah's special silverware, but it needed a good polishing. The spoon looked out of place sitting in the soup can.

"Where did you get the spoon?"

"I bagged my silver in a raid on a Volksdeutscher," he replied, his hand poking around in a gray felt bag. "Those Poles think they are better than us just because of some German blood in them. None in me. You learn to get what you need out here." He pulled another spoon from the bag and stirred Hannah's soup. When they finished eating, it was dark. Where would she sleep? The morning dew made everything damp and frigid. It would be a miserable night and she needed a sound rest.

Itzhak came walking over, jaw set, his mind obviously somewhere else. Boris stood. David, Joseph, and Schlomo all sat and looked up at the tall figure. He stopped and stood over them. The last remnants of daylight faded quickly behind his silhouette.

Hannah was not sure whether she should stand or sit. It felt as if they were soldiers in an army who stood at attention when an officer approached. But Itzhak had no uniform. No one called him an officer. Just as she decided to stand up, Itzhak squatted and began to speak.

"We have a concert to prepare for," he said, face tense. "The bags and triggers are prepared."

"When?" David asked.

"We will move out just before first light," Itzhak replied. "Get to sleep early. Daybreak will come quickly."

What is he talking about? Concert, bags, triggers! Hannah didn't want to sound stupid, but they had no musical instruments. How would a concert help defeat the Germans? That made no sense. Maybe they'd tell her tomorrow.

"Hannah, come with me," Itzhak said as he stood up.

The others moved toward lean-tos or tiny huts made from pine and ash logs. Crude shelters, but far better than lying in the open.

A few meters away sat another hut. Itzhak walked directly to it.

This was made for two, Hannah thought. Suddenly, it all made sense. *This was his hut. Am I to sleep with him?*

"You sleep in here. Keep your rifle loaded and ready for action," he said. "This was another soldier's shelter. He was a good friend. It's yours now. Good night."

"But won't the Germans find these huts? These things won't move easily like tents. The Germans will know we live right here, won't they?" Hannah asked, looking around the camp. "There must be thirty or more Russian huts plus a dozen more for us Jews. I'm sorry, but I guess I'm a little scared."

"The Germans are afraid to come this far into the forests. When they come, it's thousands," Itzhak said, fists on his waist. "We will abandon camp if that happens again. You are safe, Hannah. Go to sleep."

Itzhak turned and walked toward another hut, about the same size as her new home. Hannah watched. He never turned around. Then swinging open the gate, he disappeared inside. She felt strangely disappointed that her imaginings were only that. But what would she have done if she had been right?

I still don't understand him. A glance, a touch here or there, maybe I'm wrong.

Except for Aaron, Beila's cousin, and maybe Sol Wertz, she never had any feelings toward other boys. But Itzhak was not a boy. She could learn a lot from him. She peeked out of her hut at Itzhak's hut. No sign of him. She decided to get settled.

Hannah checked her rifle to be sure it was ready. She took off her shoes and coat. A crude bed of straw with a thick quilt over it formed a makeshift mattress. It was musty and faded. Not very inviting to someone used to fine clean linens. The smell reminded her of the farmer and the hay in his loft. It seemed a lifetime ago. Her schoolmates would never be able to lie in a bed of straw on a musty mattress in a hut. Those girls would be lost out here, but not Hannah. It felt a little like home to her.

Tired and aching and still hungry after the soup, she lay down on the bed. An old gray wool blanket hung from a rusty nail. Not certain how clean it was, she draped it over her legs and feet. Then she pulled her coat up over her like a blanket.

I'll never be able to fall asleep in here. She gazed about the hut. *This is not what Papa meant I'm sure, but I did make it to the forests. And not far from Russia either.*

She allowed herself a little victory smile and tried to ignore the faint wisp of steam from her nose and mouth as her breath hit the air. Shivering, Hannah pulled her coat over her chin and closed her eyes.

. . . . .

About an hour of thought-chasing was enough. Hannah sat up in bed, mind racing. She pulled on her shoes, then slipped cold hands through coat sleeves and buttoned up. The hut door, hung by leather-strap hinges, flopped open as she emerged from the shelter. The camp section was quiet. A lone shape sat huddled by the small campfire. A blanket for a hood covered his head. Hannah stood on the other side of the fire. Light and shadows reflected off the hunched man. He lifted his head from under the blanket, his face illuminated.

"Hello, Hannah," Joseph said. "I guess you couldn't sleep either."

"Oh, Joseph. I didn't know it was you." Hannah looked for a place to sit. "I was afraid. I mean, afraid of bothering you."

"It's alright to be afraid, Hannah. I found that out for myself a while ago."

Hannah started to sit, but Joseph patted the ground next to him and looked her in the eye. "Please."

"Alright, thank you," she said. Maybe sitting close together would be warmer and their voices might not disturb the others.

"Cousin Itzhak said fear is a good thing, if it keeps you on your guard. But deadly if it paralyzes you. He likes big words, my cousin."

A smile spread across his face. His eyes reflected the flames from the fire.

A giggle got past her guard. She stopped it short. But Joseph's smile was warm and playful. It had been a long time since anything felt fun. For a moment, he seemed like Sol, or Beila or Aaron—someone her own age. A faint smile crossed Hannah's lips.

Joseph picked up a stick and threw it into the fire.

"You know, I met a girl once who never smiled," he said, leaning over to see Hannah's face. "She was from my village. I thought she was angry and I wanted to make her happy, but nothing I tried would get her to smile. I tried being kind, but she said I did not really care about her. Then I tried being funny, and she said I was just stupid. Finally, I asked her why she did not like me. She said she was waiting for the right boy to come along. One day on an errand for my father in another village, I saw a pretty girl who smiled all the time. I found excuses to go to that village. I asked her to meet me by the pond nearby and eat lunch."

"What did she say?"

"She said yes, she would meet me. I still remember her smile."

"Did you have lunch then? By the pond?"

"No. I waited for hours. She never came."

"Did she change her mind?"

"I found out later that her father took her and her family away. The Germans were coming. I never saw her again. When I returned home that day, I passed by the girl who never smiled. I waved to her and I smiled, but she turned away. She always looked toward the house of the older boy across the village."

"Maybe she was confused. Maybe she didn't know what she really wanted," Hannah said, glancing over at Itzhak's hut.

"My brother and cousin took me to the forests. I knew I would never see her again. Sometimes I think about that day."

"Well, I smile sometimes, don't I?" Hannah asked, staring into the fire.

Joseph hesitated. "I think you are sad. I think your smile is trapped inside you. When your smile finds its way to your face, you will be even prettier than the girl in my village. The one who never had lunch with me."

"You remind me of someone."

"Oh? Someone nice, I hope?"

"A friend from Warsaw. My friend Beila's cousin, Aaron. He was nice to me, but I don't know what happened to him. We left the city."

"Yes. I know about leaving friends. Mine are mostly gone. I guess they left me. Then I followed my cousin out into the forests. Our families are…well, you know."

Hannah looked up toward the huts. "What about Itzhak? He seems to be a good leader. He took me from Warsaw. He never makes a mistake."

"Yes. He is smart and brave. People listen to him. But even he makes mistakes sometimes."

"What kind of mistakes?" Hannah asked, tilting her head, searching for Joseph's eyes in the firelight.

"You will see. I don't want to talk about Cousin. Tell me about your friends."

Hannah pushed her feet closer to the fire and sandwiched her hands between her thighs.

"I am so stupid. You are freezing out here. Come, share my blanket," he said, getting up and moving close to Hannah. He draped the blanket over her shoulders and across his own. Hannah looked at his face.

Is he like Sol or Aaron in the storage shed? What is he going to do now? I thought Itzhak liked me. But now I don't know.

"Your friends in Warsaw?"

"Oh, yes, you mean Beila, Sol, and Aaron," Hannah said, pulling the blanket up around her neck. "There was a storage shed in the courtyard. We could see out between the gaps in the planks. Spy on the neighbors. We were children. We played there a lot. It was fun."

"I would think you even laughed and smiled."

"I did until Sol…well, things changed."

"What things?"

"Oh, I don't know. Just things." Hannah said looking away. "I don't want to talk about it. Maybe I should try to sleep now," she said, lifting the blanket from her shoulders and standing up. "Thank you for talking with me, Joseph. I miss my friends. I think you would like Beila."

"If she is like you, then I would. Tell me about her sometime."

"I need to sleep. Good night." Hannah turned to go, then looked back. "I will."

"Good night, Hannah." Joseph smiled and then pulled the blanket up, covering his face.

Hannah headed for bed. She glanced to the right. Itzhak's hut sat a few meters away in the shadows. *I wonder if Itzhak would mind if I spent time with Joseph? I wonder?* She stepped into her hut, slipped off her shoes and coat. Exhausted, she drifted off to sleep.

. . . . .

The rustling of men's shoes and muffled voices disturbed the silence of the woods. *Is it time already?* She lay still in the dark with her eyes mostly shut.

Her mouth felt gummy and in need of a brush and toothpaste. For the most part, it had been a sound sleep. She hoped for at least six or seven hours. The morning chill and emptiness in her belly weighed on her. Hannah sat up and fumbled for her shoes. The hut was cold and drafty. She shivered and slipped on her coat. She squeezed swollen feet into frigid shoes. Trying not to think, she pushed open the crude door and stepped outside.

"Oh, there you are," said David as he paced by her hut. "Get your rifle and follow me. We have a mission."

She had to urinate very soon or risk a pant-wetting. There was nowhere for a girl to go. She had noticed a latrine not far from the Jewish section of the camp. There were many more in the Russian area, but no Jews seemed to go there. She didn't want to sit where the men went. Remembering the camping trips with Papa, she had learned to squat. She needed to find a bush now!

Hannah rushed into a thicket. Men were moving through the

camp, not really paying any attention to the bushes. She pulled her pants down and squatted surrounded by the brush. Looking around to see if anyone was coming, she smelled the faint odor of urine beneath her. A little steam rose as the warm liquid contacted the cold ground. No toilet paper, so she stood up and pulled up her panties and pants all in one motion. It was a familiar relief, an empty bladder. No one saw her, she was sure. Grabbing her rifle, she moved deliberately into the camp in David's direction.

Hannah rushed along toward the edge of the camp and spotted David, then Itzhak and the others. She felt uneasy joining with strangers in the group. Seeing scowls and hearing comments about having to protect a woman on their mission did not help her confidence.

"Where did you go? I thought you were right behind me," David asked.

Hannah could feel her face blush. The men were all looking at her. *I can't tell them what I was doing. They'll have a good laugh.*

"Oh, I went back for some extra bullets," she replied, patting her coat pocket.

"Here, take this," David said to Hannah, holding out a brown army satchel.

She slung her rifle over her right shoulder and took the bag from David. It was heavy and had a musty odor. The bag would be difficult to carry on a long march. She slipped the frayed strap over her left shoulder. It dug into her collarbone and pulled her left side down. She nearly lost her balance.

"Oh, look, our little kitten falls over with one bag. Where is Mama Cat? Maybe she can help."

Hannah could feel her face redden and the laughing only made it worse. *Ha, ha, ha. Stupid oafs. I'll show you what a cat's claws can do. Just you wait.* She tried to get the bag better positioned on her shoulder and it slipped off and pulled her to the ground. More laughs.

"What is this?" she asked, tugging on the straps.

"Gunpowder," one man said, grinning. "Don't get near a match or we'll all be part of the concert." Hannah looked at the bag and lowered it to the ground. Stepping away from it she heard the loudest laughs of all.

"Alright, enough!" David shouted. "You've had your fun. Time to go."

Joseph came up to Hannah and pulled the bag from the ground. "Never mind them, Hannah. It will be alright," he said quietly.

"Look, the hero comes to rescue Cinderella," one man said.

David gave him a look and pointed his finger at the man. The scruffy fighter mumbled something and took a position in the line. Itzhak approached the group. "Ready?" Itzhak asked as he walked past Hannah and took the lead.

"Yes, Cousin," David said, falling in behind him. The others followed David. Lastly, Joseph moved out, waving Hannah to follow. As always, Boris took up the rear-guard position. Nine men and one woman with an explosives bag or two over their shoulders left the encampment. No one smoked cigarettes.

They moved swiftly, almost silently through the woods. No one spoke. No one made much noise with their boots either. She could not stop mulling over the men's laughs and the kitten jokes. *I was so stupid back there. They're never going to accept me now. Oh! Mama's little kitten! Now I'll never fit in here.*

A rabbit jumped out of a thicket and zigzagged away from the line. Hannah jerked her rifle toward the fleeing animal. They moved on through the forest. In spite of the men's jeering, Hannah felt well-rested and easily kept up the pace. The strap of the cumbersome bag tensed her neck muscles. The first sign of a headache had already begun, throbbing behind her eyes. After an hour, Itzhak stopped the group. He gathered everyone together and signaled them to squat and be quiet.

"The tracks should be one or two hundred meters ahead," Itzhak said, voice muffled. "You three move about a hundred meters to the right. Boris, take two and move a hundred left, and everyone else converge on the tracks. David, Joseph, Hannah, follow me straight ahead."

"What if the German guards are in sight?" Boris asked. "Do we take them or hold fire?"

"The transport should be coming through here about 6:45, according to the Russians," Itzhak explained. "We cannot be seen by the sentries or the mission will fail."

"Understood. I will watch for your signal when we make the tracks," Boris said.

So, we're going to blow up an enemy train. But how do we do that with Germans watching the railroad?

"Go. Now," Itzhak shouted to the two flanking teams. He waited several minutes to give them time to reach their positions.

"Follow me," he said, glancing at Hannah and the others. He turned back toward the tracks, then started forward.

They tried to be careful, but the leaves and dry sticks crackled and snapped beneath their feet. The air was cold and crisp, too cold for early May.

Itzhak reached the clearing first and signaled his team to stop. Hannah could now see the narrow cutaway through the forest with the railroad tracks running down the center. She moved up closely to the edge of the woods and squinted up and down the tracks. There were no Germans in sight guarding this section of rails.

"How did you know the Germans would not be here?" Hannah asked Itzhak.

He smiled and said, "Good, very good, Hannah. You're thinking like a leader. See how the tracks slope up the hills in either direction?"

"Yes. But why wouldn't they put guards all along the railway?" she replied.

"They cannot spare even one man to cover these tracks way out here, and it is a long rail line to cover," he said.

"Oh, I see the dip in the ground. The enemy can't see us from far away."

"Exactly," he replied, nodding his head. He smiled.

Hannah watched as Itzhak signaled the other two teams who each sent one man carrying all their explosives. They met in the center near Itzhak, and then rushed up to the track and shoveled crushed stone and dirt from between the thick wood railroad ties.

"What should I be doing?" she asked, looking back and forth between Itzhak and the young men with the shovels.

"Keep watch for any sentries that come over the rises in either direction," he said.

"I will," she replied. She found the sabotage work going on just twenty meters in front of her more fascinating.

The young men worked quickly and soon had a large hollow dug beneath the near rail. They packed the hole with the bags of explosives. They knew just what to do. The man with the kitty jokes laid a line of twine from the bomb across the railroad cut. At the edge of the woods, he brought the pull rope to Itzhak.

"Everyone, move back to the tree trunk behind us," Itzhak said, pointing to the natural shelter.

Hannah saw the huge, fallen tree when they approached the area, but not as a shelter from bullets. She told herself not to miss things like that again. The tree would be good protection from the explosion. Nothing from a distance would penetrate a thick tree trunk.

"Is it time soon? For the train, I mean?" Hannah asked.

Itzhak looked worried and kept checking his wristwatch.

"A little past seven," he replied. "The intelligence is fairly reliable and so are the Germans. Maybe there was a schedule change."

"Look, one of our men is going to the tracks up ahead," Hannah said, pointing to the forward team.

The young man crouched down and rested his head on the steel rail.

"What is he doing? He'll be seen and expose us all," she cried.

"No, no. Jacob's putting his ear on the track," Itzhak explained. "The sound and vibration of the train can be felt and heard through the rails for a long way."

"Look! He's waving!" Hannah exclaimed.

"It's coming. Almost time for the concert to begin."

A faint whistle sound broke the early morning stillness. Hannah could feel her heart pounding.

"Here, take this and wrap it around your hand," Itzhak said to Hannah as he handed her the twine.

"What, what do you mean?" she replied, looking at Itzhak and the twine. "I don't know what to do with that. Not me!"

"When I tell you to pull on the cord, you pull and keep pulling until you feel it snag and then go free again," he said.

Hannah watched her hand shaking as she wrapped the twine several times around her palm. It was coarse and felt scratchy.

I wonder if the cord is going to pull me down when the bomb explodes. What if I do this wrong and we all blow up or something?

"What is on the other end of the cord?" she asked Itzhak.

"Detonator, a grenade to ignite the powder," he said as he scanned the horizon for the train to appear. "Just pull when I say and only when I say."

Oh, I don't know if I can do this. I am so scared.

Suddenly, the massive black engine poked its face over the rise. The pounding and squealing monster was a half-kilometer away and already seemed invincible. How would these little bags of gunpowder stop this huge iron machine?

"Steady, wait, wait," Itzhak said.

Hannah was afraid to do anything but focus on Itzhak's mouth. The engine and trailing cars rolled over the spot where the bomb lay. She peeked up at the train and then quickly back to Itzhak's face. In a moment, it would be too late! When? Now?

"Pull! Pull!" Itzhak screamed.

Hannah pulled the twine with everything she had. It went taut, something snagged and then popped free. The shock wave sucked the air right out of her lungs. And her diaphragm punched up into her stomach. Itzhak's body came flying into her. They went to the ground with her face buried in his chest. Debris blasted the thick tree trunk, shooting overhead at tremendous velocity. Dirt and dust and stones rained over them. The groans of bending steel and crashing train cars roared through the trees.

Itzhak rolled off Hannah and looked up, a huge grin on his face.

"Perfect!" he exclaimed.

Hannah gasped for air, her stomach and diaphragm finally releasing. Her head ached, jolted by the concussion from the blast and the huge sound. It was the loudest thing she had ever heard. Everything seemed to be in slow motion. She could see Itzhak's mouth moving but couldn't hear his voice. If only the ringing and ache in her ears would stop. Dazed, Hannah leaned on the tree trunk and got to her feet.

As the dust began to clear, she could see the railroad cars lying on their sides or upside down, some sideways straddling the tracks. Her hearing was slowly returning. A man screamed in pain from somewhere in the wreckage. She looked around for the team. Boris, David, and Joseph were all there. Itzhak had left to inspect the damage and rushed back.

"We are finished here. What a great concert!" Itzhak shouted.

Some of the boys raised their weapons over their heads in victory and defiance. One or two patted Hannah on the shoulder and congratulated her for the fine work she had done.

"I hear someone crying for help," Hannah said, scanning the train wreck for survivors. Papa would try to help. But a Nazi?

"Oh, just a German, he deserves what he gets," one of the men said gritting his teeth.

"Hannah, this train carries supplies to the German army to help them kill us," Schlomo explained.

"Our mission is over," Itzhak said. "Everyone is accounted for; let's move out."

"We need to help the wounded," Hannah said, looking at Itzhak.

"Cannot do that. Return to camp," Itzhak replied, voice hard.

"Go ahead and I will follow behind you," she said.

"There will be Germans coming here in minutes."

Itzhak shook his head, realizing he could not leave Hannah and he could not stay there much longer.

"Alright, spread out and find the German, quickly," he shouted. "Be careful."

Everyone turned and headed for the wreck. In a couple of minutes, David called out. "He's over here," he said, bending over the soldier and checking his pulse.

"He passed out, probably in shock," said another.

Hannah ran up to the spot. The German was crushed between two railroad cars and impaled with a twisted length of angle iron.

"Nothing we can do to save him," David said, looking at Hannah.

Hannah expected him to look like the monster at the pit, but he looked like a regular soldier. Now she didn't know what to do.

"Is he a Nazi?" she asked.

"No, regular army, but he wouldn't hesitate to kill us," David said. "One less to worry about, as I see it."

Papa, I killed this German. I killed a human being. He wasn't the one that killed you. Am I bad? It feels awful.

She scanned the scene again.

No. I had to do it. I'm sure of it. Could I do it again? I don't know if killing them matters anymore. She had kept her promise. She made it to the East. Not quite Russia, but as close as she needed to get.

Boris called out. "Germans, over the rise, coming this way."

"Move out. Now!" Itzhak shouted.

Hannah grabbed her rifle and followed Joseph and David as everyone hurried through the trees and underbrush. Itzhak moved fast and they quickly put distance between themselves and the train wreck. As she ran and ducked and swatted at low-lying tree branches and thorny bushes, the sting of killing became a numbing memory. She felt better when not focused on the soldier and kept her attention on the escape. Could she do it again? The question repeated as she ran. She didn't want to admit that she was now a killer.

A soldier, that's what I am. Just a soldier.

No one pursued the team and they returned in the afternoon to the etrad encampment. There were no casualties and the mission was very successful. Itzhak reported to the Russian commander. Everyone congratulated the team with smiles and well-meaning jokes. A bottle of schnapps and Russian vodka was passed around, too. Hannah did not drink. Only wine at Shabbat was allowed and she felt that that was her only connection back to Papa. At home, he always let her say the Kiddush and drink the cup of wine.

"*Baruch atah Adonai, elo haynu…*" she chanted quietly to herself and then had to stop. She slipped into her hut and could no longer hold back the tears.

Chapter Fourteen

Hannah was happy to be back safely. Most were in a good mood. The image of the German dying on the rails stayed with her. That none of Itzhak's people were injured didn't console her. The emptiness inside would not go away.

Watching Itzhak, Hannah could tell he seemed restless. The mission was a huge success. It was a fine time to celebrate. But something was wrong. The Russians passed around vodka again. They rarely missed an opportunity. Several bottles made it to Itzhak's group.

David took a big swig from the bottle. "Excuse me, Hannah, would you like a taste of this fine Russian stock?"

"No, thank you," she said as she kept an eye on Itzhak.

Itzhak looked upset. She was sure Joseph knew why, and he didn't want to tell her the other night. There was so much she didn't understand.

. . . . .

A few nights later, Joseph was sitting by the campfire, finishing his last spoon of broth. Hannah looked over at him. She wrapped a rag around her hand and pulled the hot soup can out of the fire. Three men finished eating, got up and walked away, leaving Hannah and Joseph alone.

I wonder what he thinks of me since we talked. I can't tell him what Sol did. I only told Beila. I can't tell a boy. It's a secret.

"Watch out or that rag will catch fire," he said, glancing over the flames. She nodded. The soup didn't smell quite right, but she slurped the broth from the spoon anyway. Her belly was warmed but not full. The bland mixture of potato chunks, carrots, and a few beans did not satisfy.

This soup is awful compared to Mama's, she thought. But she shouldn't complain. She hadn't brought them any food. Papa would say she was selfish and ungrateful. He would have told her to keep quiet and finish it. And he'd have been right.

Hannah squirmed in her clothes and felt very dirty. Then she began to wonder if the smell was not from the soup. She had no bath since Barbara's apartment in Warsaw. When Joseph was not watching, she pulled her coat and blouse away from her chest and sniffed. Ugh! A mixture of sweat and dirt. It was not as bad as some of the others, but very embarrassing all the same. She couldn't get too close to anyone, especially Itzhak. He didn't seem to smell. What if Joseph noticed? The smoke from the fire smelled like pine trees. She decided to stay near the fire.

She looked across the camp past the Russian huts. Someone said a small stream ran by the north end of the camp past the Russian section. She had not seen it yet. The Russians were very protective of it. The cooks used it for cooking and cleaning. *Maybe I could do a little cleaning up by the stream. But if they see me they'll stare at me and make jokes. Or maybe worse. Maybe I can try at night.*

"I don't mean to be a pest, Joseph, but could you explain something?"

"Oh, yes, I guess we are not so good with new people," Joseph said. "What?"

I can't ask him about a bath, how am I going to say that? Maybe I can just work up to it.

"Why don't the Germans just come into the forest and attack us?" she asked.

"Funny thing that is, we fight hard, anyway we can," Joseph said. "We know the woods, hiding places, the swamps, and we even put up with the mosquitos in the summer. We chew the Germans up when they come in here. And the mosquitos eat them alive."

"But we have to live with the bugs, too, right?"

"That's right, we 'have to' and they don't."

"Never?" Hannah asked.

"Oh, no, they come with full strength, thousands of men, artillery, tanks, armored carriers, anything that can get through the trees and the marshes to the south," he replied. "When they come again, we will run for our lives and hide."

"That's what Itzhak said. They were here before, I guess? When will they come again?"

"Don't know, could be anytime. Probably before the bugs get bad," Joseph said, laughing.

"Even after we blew up their train?" she asked.

"Oh, well, yes, that might push them to come sooner. But don't forget about the Ukrainians. They don't mind the woods, the swamps, or the mosquitos. They hate us more. Nasty bunch," he explained.

"What about our camp, the huts and all this?" Hannah asked.

"What about it?" Joseph said, looking around.

"You just leave it all and run?"

"There's nothing here worth anything. We'll build it here again, or somewhere else. Whoever is still alive will anyway," Joseph said, looking away.

"Joseph, I need to ask you something. It's kind of personal."

"Oh, what?" he replied, eyes narrowing.

He is younger than the rest, and very kind I think. I hope he won't laugh. Just ask.

"Well, I need to wash up."

"What do you mean?" Joseph asked.

"Ah, I mean really clean up," she said, avoiding eye contact.

"Oh, you mean like a bath?"

"Yes, well, like a bath," she replied, blushing.

"Oh, oh, I forget you're a girl," he said. "Well, in the summer we just go in the ponds south of here."

"But it's too cold now," she said, her eyes pleading for some help.

"Well, ask Itzhak," Joseph said. "He knows lots of people."

I can't ask him that. I will not.

"Ah, ah, he's too busy. Maybe someone else knows somebody in one of the villages?" she asked.

"Oh, yes, I think I understand. You are afraid they will make jokes?" he replied, smothering a smile.

"Umm, yes."

Now he knows. If he tells any of them, I'm in trouble. Oh, bad, bad.

"Let me think about it," Joseph said. "Maybe there's something I can do."

• • • • •

The following night was cold and still. Everyone had settled down for a good sleep. Hannah lay quietly on the straw and quilt mattress. Another night, dirty and uncomfortable, she started to drift off to sleep.

Bang! A gunshot echoed off the trees, ringing through the camp. Hannah sat up in bed, startled. She grabbed her rifle, and crouching, she pushed open the door to her hut and stepped into the shadows. The remains of the nearby campfire gave off a dim hue. Hannah strained her eyes to see where the attack was coming from. Men were running by. She looked behind to see Itzhak stumble out of his hut, pistol in hand. He stood for a moment swaying and then fell to his knees.

Is he shot? Maybe he's hurt?

She ran over to help him. David came running from the other direction. Hannah heard a commotion behind her—two men, Russians—arguing about something. David got to Itzhak first and kept him from completely falling to the ground. Hannah grabbed his shoulder to steady him. Itzhak looked up with groggy, bloodshot eyes and said nothing. His arm was limp and the barrel of his pistol rested in the dirt.

"There is no danger, one of the Russian sentries fired at his own man, I think," David said. "Help me get Itzhak on his feet."

Men half-dressed carrying rifles and submachine guns dragged themselves back to their shelters. Hannah looked up at one Russian she thought would help her, but the man kept walking. She pushed her shoulder into Itzhak's armpit and tried to stand up. He was heavier than she expected. She also caught a whiff of liquor as he exhaled. He leaned into her putting his full weight on Hannah's shoulder. As she started to collapse under the load, David hoisted Itzhak's body taking much of the weight off her. Together they carried him, feet dragging to his hut.

"Lay him down here," David said, motioning with his head. David knelt on one knee and Hannah did the same.

"We have to get him into the hut, yes?"

"Grab him by the boots, I'll lift from the top," David said, as he swung open the hut door. He snatched the pistol from the ground where it had dropped from Itzhak's hand and tossed the weapon into the hut.

"I see."

"Ready? Lift."

David tripped on the makeshift mattress and fell backward into the bed. Itzhak groaned from the jolt, but offered no other signs of life. Hannah held fast to his boots and was pulled forward to her knees.

"He'll probably puke all over me now…shit," David said. "Do I need this?"

"Can you pull him farther, so his feet don't stick out of the hut?" she asked, wiping grimy hair from her eyes with the back of her hand.

"Yes. One last pull. Lift the boots. Ready. Go."

Itzhak's slumped body slid back just far enough for Hannah to get his feet inside the hut.

"It'll have to do," she said.

"Now bend his legs a little, so we can shut the door."

Hannah lifted Itzhak's boots and kinked his legs at the knee.

"Alright, let's get out of here. Damned Russians," he muttered under his breath.

They stepped around Itzhak, bent legs and all. Hannah gratefully closed the door of the hut.

"He will be alright in the morning," David said, scanning the camp. Most men were back, and a couple of officers stood talking in front of the commander's tent.

"It only took a minute to get him settled down. I've seen worse. We try to keep it from the Russians, but most of us Jews know."

"Know what? What's the matter with Itzhak?" Hannah asked. "You're scaring me."

"Come on over here by the fire, away from the others. Enough excitement for one night, don't you think?" David said with a sad smile.

"Tell me what's wrong with him."

"Ah, well, I guess you're one of us now," he said, shrugging his shoulders. "There's some history with my cousin."

"You see, it is all about Zosia. Her family lives in our town. They were in love, Itzhak and Zosia. It all went bad."

"What went bad?"

"There was no doctor. And the midwife was old. They couldn't stop Zosia's bleeding. It wasn't Itzhak's fault. Well, not exactly," David said.

"Wait, wait! I am so confused. Start from the beginning. Tell me why Itzhak is like this tonight."

"The women said no men in the room, but Itzhak went in anyway," David said. "I was outside the house, but I heard lots of yelling and cursing. It was very bad."

"What women?"

"They say he kissed Zosia's mouth, but she was already dead," David said, raking his fingers through his wiry light brown hair. "Itzhak ran out of the house in a fit, screaming and tearing at the air. I never saw my cousin like that before. I saw him later that night, drunk on kosher wine. He never drank before, except maybe some wine from the Kiddush cup at Passover."

"Why was she bleeding? I thought babies were born without much bleeding?"

"Hemorrhage. Lots of blood. Zosia's parents…they blamed Itzhak," David said, staring into the campfire. "They didn't have anything against him until they found out Zosia was carrying his baby. Then they—well, mostly the father—had no use for him. Zosia loved Itzhak, but she was too young to go off on her own with the baby. She needed family help."

"He could have told them it wasn't his fault that she was bleeding, right?" Hannah crossed her arms over her torso and tucked her bare hands into her armpits. With knees bent, she bounced up and down on her legs, shivering.

"The parents said he killed their little girl. Itzhak tried to talk with them many times, but they pushed him away."

"The baby? Where is his baby now?"

"The baby lived, the old woman cut him out of Zosia after she was dead."

"No wonder," Hannah said, glancing into the shadows at Itzhak's hut.

"At least that's the story I heard. I was outside the house. None of us men saw any of it firsthand."

"Did Itzhak try to help with the baby later on?"

"Yes. They would not budge. Her parents named the baby Piotr," David said. "They are Christians."

"Where do they live now? Where is the baby?"

"Just five houses from us, same place as before."

"In the house that Itzhak visited before we left your village? No one answered the door."

"Yes, that is their house. Well, now you know. You can't tell him or anybody what you know about this. Especially the Russians. Wouldn't look good, him being the leader."

"I won't."

"Time for me to get some sleep. I'm sorry you had to see this. Good night, Hannah."

"David, thank you for telling me."

David nodded and started to walk away. He stopped and turned.

"Oh, Hannah."

"Yes?"

"Zosia."

"Yes?"

"She looked just like you," David said, holding his hands out to about Hannah's height.

"Really? You mean my size?"

"Yes. And Zosia had your long, brown hair, round face, and eyes looking to please. Eyes that some men can't resist."

"But I don't..." Hannah started, looking down at the dying embers lining the campfire.

"You are young. Someday you will understand." David left and faded into the shadows.

"Oh," Hannah said, to no one.

Chapter Fifteen

After the massive train wreck, Hannah's name floated around the etrad and beyond. Even the Russians and the nearest Polish Home Guard partisans heard about the fierce Jewish girl who blew up the big German supply train. Hannah could not believe her ears as the word spread.

It was nothing like that, she thought, when first hearing the tales. She pulled a rope and was knocked off her feet. Other than getting dirty and almost getting them caught, what did she do?

The stories spread and with less and less truth in them. At least rumors kept everyone's mind off their own death or worse, being captured alive.

I hope the Gestapo doesn't hear it. They might just come looking for me…again.

Everyone expected that an Aktion was imminent. But nothing happened.

The summer was hot. A welcome change from living outside during the freezing winter. But with the heat came humidity and with that, lots of sweat. There was no way for Hannah to escape the mosquitos. The Russians continued to bring in more and more soldiers. Itzhak said that Sakaloff was getting attention from Moscow and focused on building up his ranks. He had little time or interest in pestering anti-Semites. He was happy for Itzhak to do what he wanted, as long as the Jews were ready to join in anytime a big mission was planned. Hannah passed the summer doing forays to get food and harass the local German-leaning villagers. Big anti-Semites who needed a lesson.

• • • • •

The leaves were turning from green to orange when Itzhak heard that Sakaloff and Moscow decided they should hit again before the Germans could organize another large strike. It had been months since the big concert, but winter was coming on and the snows and numbing cold would stop all activity soon. He wanted to add as much pain as possible to the German soldier's life. If they were denied food and warm clothing, the weather might reduce their will to fight. Itzhak agreed, and gathered his Jewish comrades together.

"We have an end of year concert to do," Itzhak said, trying to sound encouraging.

"We hurt them badly last time, but that was months ago," David replied. "I expected them to come in here by now."

Hannah listened and wondered how much they could push before it all came crashing down on them. But she had decided weeks ago that being a partisan was to be her new life, as long as she could stay alive. She had nothing else to hope for. She kept the secret about Itzhak to herself.

"When do we go?" Hannah asked with no expression.

Hannah noticed that everyone looked at her differently now. It was uncomfortable. She led her own little group on small missions all summer. She took control. It felt right then, but maybe she took too much control. Hannah thought that some seemed embarrassed that she was telling them what to do. She could feel the resentment from one man. She overheard a couple of the boys saying that she had more steel in her than all the rest combined. It felt good and troubling at the same time. She decided to keep quiet and see what happened.

• • • • •

"New orders from Sakaloff. We expect another supply train in two days," Itzhak said, looking for support from his group. "We must prepare for another concert."

"Who is going?" David asked, checking his submachine gun.

"You, Joseph, and Hannah," he said. "Everyone get ready to move out."

"Powder?" Joseph asked. "We used a big load last time."

"There is too little left over. Time to see our friends," he replied. David nodded.

Hannah noticed that the usual twinkle in Itzhak's eye was not there. She was worried.

"Where are we getting the powder from?" she asked, scanning the faces around her.

"I will tell you on the way," Itzhak said. "We must have it by tomorrow for the mission. No time to waste."

Hannah and the boys got their things together and by midafternoon, the four set out into the forest. It was maybe an hour when they approached a small village. Hannah thought it looked suspiciously quiet. She remembered the farmer's wife and the people in Itzhak's town that tried to attack them. You could not be too careful, and Itzhak was a master at the game. He decided to wait and watch. No one argued.

"What is the secret about the explosives?" Hannah asked, catching Itzhak's eye. She wanted to know in case she was to run a concert someday.

"When the Germans overran our country in '39, they all left their ammunition behind, artillery shells mostly. The villagers and farmers searched the battle sites and hid the shells in stockpiles."

"They had to keep it away from the Germans and their miserable friends, the Ukrainians," Joseph explained. "Worse than the Germans, but I suspect you know that." Hannah glanced at Joseph. *I can't tell anyone. He can't know about the soldier in the woods. I'd rather die than have Itzhak and the others know.*

"Maybe our people could use the shells again when we push them back someday," David said.

"Or maybe we can use them right now," Itzhak said with a little smile. "What do you think?"

"Who has the shells, Itzhak?" Hannah asked.

"We know these villagers stored away a lot of shells and maybe grenades. According to Sakaloff, Russian intelligence marked the villager in the big white cottage at the far end of the street. He is Boleslaw Kazieba. Not a big friend of ours. He will need to be persuaded."

"What are we waiting for?" Hannah said, feeling strong.

"Nothing," he said, grinning at Hannah. "Let's go. Joseph, watch our backs."

It took less than an hour to reach the village. They stepped out of the woods and moved quickly and deliberately to the big cottage.

Hannah scanned the road through the village and the spaces between the houses for trouble. No one was outside, which seemed a bit strange. The sun was low in the mid-December sky. Shadows were cast over the village and the houses. Something didn't feel right. It looked like the village where she grabbed clothes from the clothesline and then those Ukrainian soldiers caught her. All the villages looked alike. Itzhak glanced around and then knocked on the door. Hannah noticed someone move the faded lace curtain and peer out the window near the front door. Without thinking, she smiled and dropped her rifle below the window out of view. She made eye contact with Itzhak and he understood.

"What do you want?" asked the woman inside, not opening the door.

"I am Itzhak Grozsman," Itzhak said, gently placing his hand on the black metal doorknob. "I need to speak with Boleslaw Kazieba."

"My husband will be home soon," the woman said. "Come back later."

"Itzhak, a man is coming toward us on the road from the other side of the village," David whispered.

"Alright then, Mrs. Kazieba, I'll return later with my sister to speak with him."

Itzhak signaled Joseph and Hannah to walk past the window and act like they were leaving, and then hide against the back wall of the house. None of the four were visible to the man walking on the road.

Hannah waited, glancing at Joseph occasionally. She kept watch for anyone who might see them hiding. A shadow cast over them and it felt much colder squatting in the shade than on the sunny side of the building. The sky above was clouding over and looked as if winter had already arrived. It was only a few days away. Then living in the forests would be hard.

Joseph put his forefinger to his lips and pointed toward the front door. Hannah could hear shoes crunching on the gravel walkway leading to the front of the cottage.

"Oh!" said the man as he caught sight of Itzhak and David.

"I am—" Itzhak began to say and was interrupted.

"I know who you are," the man said. "You people blow up trains and then the Germans come strutting into our villages looking for partisan collaborators."

"Well, I am sorry for your inconvenience," Itzhak said, "but we must do our part to take back our country."

"You are Jews? Yes?" Kazieba asked with a little smirk.

"That is no concern of yours," Itzhak replied. "Now you are going to take us to the munitions stockpile."

"The what? I do not know about those things," Kazieba said, glaring into Itzhak's eyes.

At that moment, Hannah and Joseph came around the corner and joined the others. Joseph opened the door, raised his submachine gun, and stepped into the house.

"Say good-bye to your wife," Hannah said in a tone that even frightened her.

Kazieba's expression changed as he glanced toward Joseph and Hannah.

"I have reliable information that you led the effort to seize and hide the artillery shells," Itzhak said, nodding in Hannah's direction. "You know she killed fifty Germans a month ago. I can't stop her, they murdered her family."

"Itzhak?" Hannah called from inside the house.

"Kill her," he said flatly, staring coldly into Kazieba's eyes.

There was a deathly silence that seemed endless to Hannah. Through the open door, she could hear Itzhak and Kazieba talking. *What am I going to do if the husband doesn't give in? I can't kill his wife in cold blood over artillery shells.*

"No, wait!" Kazieba exclaimed.

"If you lie, I will send her back here in the night and she will kill you both," Itzhak said.

"No, no, I will take you there," Kazieba said. "You can trust me."

We don't trust any of you villagers.

"Leave the woman alone. Boleslaw has reconsidered and is going to take us to the shells," Itzhak said, loud enough to be sure Hannah and Joseph would not harm Mrs. Kazieba.

"I know that you were with the Polish army and were saving the ammunition for their victorious return," Itzhak said while gesturing to Kazieba to lead the way. "We are actually fighting for the same side. We are comrades."

"You are Jews working with the Russians; you're not our kind," Kazieba replied.

David grunted.

"We are Polish Jews and you're Polish countrymen. We are being hunted by the Nazi Germans," Itzhak explained as they walked. "We are fighting to survive any way we can, and if that means with the Russians, then so be it. Besides, they have been good to us in this fight against the madman Hitler."

"The Russians have been horrible to our country, and you Jews have brought the Nazis here to terrorize us good citizens," Kazieba said.

"Ahhh, but we are good citizens, too," Itzhak countered with a grin. David nodded and patted Itzhak on the shoulder.

The five entered the woods behind a small cottage about two hundred meters from Kazieba's house. Hannah scanned the village for anyone who might be following. All was quiet. The sun was setting. It would be dark soon. The shadows already covered the forest floor as dry leaves crackled under their feet.

"How far is it?" Itzhak asked.

"Not much farther," Kazieba replied. He reached out to bushes and small trees to keep his balance, while walking over leaves, sticks, and uneven ground.

They went on for twenty or thirty minutes.

I wonder how Itzhak expects us to carry the shells any distance. What if they are big ones? How many could each of us carry? And what if we run into trouble? Then what?

Finally, Kazieba stopped.

"Here it is," he said.

They all looked around through the dim light for the stash. Hannah noticed a depression off to their left with large trees, ash, maybe fir or pine laid across the small crater. They were cut down rather than fallen naturally. She could tell the pile did not look right. Her nature walks with Papa did have a useful purpose after all. She understood the forest. Her purpose had been only to spend precious time with him. The biology lessons were secondary.

"Over there," Hannah said, pointing to the depression covered with trunks and branches.

Joseph jumped ahead and started down the slope into the depression to inspect the hideout. There was a large area, like a cave beneath the tree trunks. It was too dark to see into it.

"Wait! Joseph, stop!" Itzhak exclaimed, looking at Kazieba's expression.

Joseph stopped short and looked back at Itzhak.

"Let's have Comrade Kazieba go in first," Itzhak said.

"You think it is a trap?" Kazieba asked. "You do not trust your new comrade?"

"One can never be too sure in this business," Itzhak replied, pointing the barrel of his gun at the man.

I would have gone right into it myself, Hannah thought. *Never trust a stranger.*

"Alright, alright, I'll go in," Kazieba said as he proceeded slowly down the slope.

He entered the hidden store bumping his forehead on the log roof. Poking his head outside, he looked at Itzhak and shrugged.

"See, nothing to worry about."

Hannah followed him down and stood guard outside while Joseph went in.

"It is big, maybe five meters across and two deep. Many shells, maybe a hundred or two," Joseph called out.

"Grenades, mortars, any other explosives?" David asked.

Hannah and Joseph crawled over the stacked pile of artillery shells. He flicked on his cigarette lighter and held it up over the pile. Hannah gasped, thinking the flame would ignite something and the whole place would blow them apart. They saw a heap tucked behind the stack of shells. There were army satchels and a few rifles, tattered clothing, and straps. None of it looked to be in working order.

Joseph reached out and pulled on a satchel, dragging it over the shells. The familiar clink of metal hitting metal caught Hannah's attention. The bag had a swastika insignia on the outside. She pulled open the bag to see loose bullets, empty magazines, and a couple of precious grenades.

"Let's get out of here," Hannah said, squinting at Joseph. "This place is scary."

He put out the lighter and they backed out of the shelter. Kazieba had already climbed back to where Itzhak and David stood. Hannah held up the German satchel.

"A couple of grenades," she said, peering into the bag.

"Well, comrade, I see you are a man of your word," Itzhak said. A smile peeked through the corners of his mouth.

"How are we going to carry all this back?" Hannah asked, one foot at the bottom of the slope and the other resting on the rise toward Itzhak.

"We only need six shells and those grenades," he replied. He motioned to David. David pulled a familiar canvas sheet out of his knapsack and picked up the two sticks he had whittled into poles while Hannah and Joseph explored the stash. David and Itzhak put the poles through the loops of material on either side of the canvas rectangle which was spread out on the ground.

"A stretcher—smart, very smart," Hannah said, smiling and nodding.

"Huh," Kazieba uttered.

"You three load up the patients, six shells should work fine,"

Itzhak said. "And don't forget their play toys, the grenades."

They all worked quickly. Then Joseph and David took the poles in hand and raised the booty up on the stretcher ready for the return journey.

"We are going back toward the village to escort our comrade home. I want to be sure he arrives safely to Mrs. Kazieba," Itzhak said. "Go ahead, Boleslaw, and keep moving."

It was dark when they spotted the lights of the village ahead through the trees. Hannah could hardly see anything behind them. As the rear guard, she felt worthless. The boys carried the heavy stretcher.

"Well, we bid you a fond farewell, Comrade Kazieba," Itzhak said in jest.

"I will remember you," Kazieba said. "Someday the tables will be turned in my favor."

"Then I hope you will consider us as fellow comrades together defending our nation," Itzhak replied with a slight bow. "To Poland."

Kazieba frowned at them and left walking heavily toward the lights. When he was out of earshot, Itzhak told the boys to put down the stretcher and rest a moment."Hannah, do you think you could find the stash again?" Itzhak asked.

"Oh, I don't know, it's so dark," she replied. "Why?"

"Sakaloff needs to send another team to retrieve it before Kazieba and his friends relocate it," Itzhak said. "I don't have anyone else I can spare."

"I'm not sure I could find the village," Hannah replied.

"The Russians can get you to the village, but they don't know where the stash is located," Itzhak explained.

"I understand. That's not what worries me."

"What then?"

"Will I have a problem with the Russians like with Commander Bartowski?" Hannah asked.

"No, you should not, but I will speak with Commander Sakaloff, be sure of that," Itzhak said. "They need us to find the shells. It will keep us Jews in good stead."

"Yes, but once I point out the hideaway, they no longer need me," she replied, frowning.

"Don't worry, I will see him," Itzhak said. "Time is wasting, let's go."

Itzhak led the way back in the dark. There was no moonlight to guide them. They all seemed to know the forests very well. As she walked behind guarding the rear, Hannah kept thinking about the Russian men in the camp. She could fight Nazis, Germans, or Ukrainians with help, but trying to defend against getting shot in the back by your own comrades…that might be too much.

Where's my pocketknife? She patted her jacket down once again as she walked.

Her hand bumped into something hard with weight along the bottom seam of the coat. The knife must have somehow slipped through the pocket and was lodged inside the fabric of the coat. She felt the right pocket and found a tear in the back edge. She would get the knife out of there later and switch pockets.

After hours of groping through the forest, being swished and poked in the face and chest and legs with small tree branches and brush, they spotted a glow up ahead. Three men stepped out from behind thick trees.

"Your name?" one man asked in Russian, as he pointed his submachine gun at Itzhak's face.

"Itzhak Grozsman," Itzhak said coolly.

"Pass code?" the Russian said in Polish.

"Sakaloff," Itzhak replied.

"Ah! Welcome, comrade!" the Russian soldier said, grinning and lowering his gun. "What do you have here?"

"Fireworks for the next concert," Itzhak said in Russian.

They know we're not Germans. Why scare us half to death? I thought this was our home.

They walked into the camp exhausted. Hannah sat down to rest with Boris, Schlomo, and a few others. Itzhak had continued walking directly to Commander Sakaloff to report on the mission. David and Joseph took the stretcher of artillery shells to the back of the camp where some Russian men were sitting around a small fire. Hannah did not want to know how they would get the gunpowder safely out of the shells and into the bags and satchels. It sounded death-defying and not something she wanted to do.

It was hours past suppertime. Everyone in the camp had eaten, so asking anyone for supper would be pointless. Of course, it would be soup. Every meal was soup. Fortunately, Itzhak found some food and came back quickly.

"On the other side of camp, see the old Russian cook. He has some soup left over," Itzhak said. "I will be there soon."

"Who is this cook?" Hannah asked, looking to the right of Sakaloff's tent toward the Russian cooking area. So far, Hannah stayed clear of the Russian officers and men as much as possible.

"Don't worry, I know him," Boris said. "As Russians go, Vladimir is a good man. We can trust him."

Joseph and David strolled up. "Where can we get food?" Joseph asked.

"The old Russian," Boris replied. "These Russians have been good to us. Mostly because we help them kill Germans."

Hannah, Joseph, and David followed Boris to a little nook on the other side of the camp. There were about a hundred partisans now, mostly Russians, some Poles, and some Polish Jews. As they walked through the camp, Hannah could not help but notice the different uniforms. Full Russian uniforms, some men with just the jackets or pants from the Polish army, and civilians who fled into the forests to escape the Germans.

"I didn't have time to see all the different people here before now," Hannah said. "How did these people get here?"

"The Russians, you mean?" David asked. "Remember as I said before, after '39 and '40, the Germans had driven us Poles underground and pushed the Russians back to Stalingrad, maybe even Moscow by now. And you know why we Jews are here."

"Everyone hid and then made their way to the forests?" Hannah asked.

"Well, we did that. We had no choice," David said. "The Russian army was not beaten, only pushed back. In these woods they're fighting a guerilla war, as they see it."

"What is that?" Hannah asked.

"We hit and run, hide in the forests, strike, blend into the villages," Joseph said, striking palm and fist together. "It is very difficult for the Germans to catch us."

"But when they do, we get tortured and then hung in the village square," said Boris. "Don't get caught."

"You know they are afraid to come into the forests without a big force," Joseph said. "But always remember the Ukrainians will. That's why they are so dangerous."

Hannah remembered the men at the pit. Some were not Germans, but they were eager to join in the killing. Her attacker she was sure was Ukrainian. Also, the three soldiers that tracked her through the woods from the farmer's barn. And so were the others that grabbed her in the field and took her to the Germans at the train depot. They were all from the same group, combing the area for runaways.

I was so stupid to think that Papa could give them money and they would leave us alone. Papa understood what was happening. They just want us Jews dead. Well, they're not taking me. Not without a big fight.

Walking through the camp assembly area and right of the Russian officer's huts, three cooking fires burned low behind six more huts. The cook's section. Wrought iron bars and hooks straddled the fires. Bubbe Rachel's old cast iron cooking stove flashed into Hannah's mind. The stove was no longer used and sat in the corner of the kitchen waiting to be thrown out someday. Hannah wanted to make Hamantashen for Purim in the old oven, but Mama said the modern oven was safer.

Hannah walked behind the men and peered around them as they approached the first fire. An older-looking soldier with deep wrinkles outlining his face was bent over a hanging black kettle. Red embers glowed bright below and steam rolled up from the open pot. The fire glow reflected dimly off the cook's face, but his eyes shone bright and sharp.

That must be Vladimir the cook, Hannah thought. His apron, no longer white, looked like someone took paintbrushes and smeared the cloth with many colors.

"Good evening, gentlemen," the old cook said in Russian.

Hannah stepped up from behind David and the man got a first look at her.

"Oh, pardon me, miss," Vladimir said with the kindest smile. "I did not see you there in the dark. And how could I not see such a beautiful face."

Hannah could understand Russian fairly well, certainly better than she could speak it.

"Thank you, sir, you are very kind," she replied in broken Russian, feeling her face redden.

"You have come back late from a mission, no?" Vladimir asked.

He seemed to know all about their foray to the village and munitions dump. Hannah assumed he must have been a powerful fighter. He still looked muscular and tough, not at all like a cook. His black hair was peppered with gray. The deep lines in his brow and cheeks could not hide behind bushy eyebrows or the shadow of whiskers darkening his thick, weathered complexion. Soldiering was a hard life, and he must have seen plenty of pain and suffering and killing. Hannah was so lost in the sadness of his eyes, she had to look away.

"You must be very hungry, yes?" he said to Hannah.

"Yes," she replied and lowered her eyes.

"You fighters would like hot soup as well?" he said as he ladled out the broth and vegetables.

They nodded and held out tin cups.

The steam rose from Hannah's cup and she wrapped her cold palms and fingers around it. She spooned into her mouth chunks of potato, carrots, and more. The spices were unfamiliar, something Russian she figured. It tasted better than any canned soup.

The first sip is always the best. Papa would heat the kettle over the campfire. But they rarely went when it was this cold. Hannah would clean up after they ate. He would dip Bubbe Leah's fancy tea strainer in their cups. If she ever found out…they laughed and laughed. The orange tea was Hannah's favorite. It even warmed her toes. She remembered the stars poking through the tree branches and Mama's sweet ruggalagh for dessert. It was wonderful just to sit with Papa, smell the pines, listen to the still forest. They never talked much. They just felt the same things together.

Hannah glanced up through narrow gaps between the tree branches above. The reflected firelight formed a roof of dark green over them. Thick clouds smothered the stars and the roundness of the moon appeared distorted through the haze. She smiled to herself, thinking that good times should be remembered.

They all finished their soup, bid good evening to Vladimir the cook, and strolled back to their sleeping quarters. The camp was quiet. Hannah had the worries of her follow-up mission with the Russians in the morning nagging at her. Exhausted from the day and night, she needed sleep. She felt dirty and smelly as she lay down in her hut. Overtired, she lay restless, her mind dreaming up the worst outcomes. At some point in the night she must have dozed off.

"Get up! Get up!" said a man in Russian, with his torso leaning through the doorway of Hannah's hut.

"What, where?" Hannah replied, disoriented from sleep and a bit nauseous.

"We must leave now. You must show us the artillery shells," the Russian said impatiently. "You must come now. Quickly."

"Oh, yes, the mission, I will come," Hannah replied wearily. "Yes, yes."

She pulled on her shoes and coat. She could feel her full bladder. The soldier moved back from the hut and waited.

What am I going to tell this man? I can't go anywhere until I visit the bushes.

As Hannah emerged from the hut, the soldier firmly grasped her forearm and began to lead her along toward the other side of the camp.

"No! I can't go yet," Hannah exclaimed as she pulled away from his grip.

She tried to gesture to him that she needed to squat. She stopped her feet and braced herself. The man seemed utterly confused.

"Let go of her," said a tall, young Russian soldier, actually an officer.

"She needs a minute to relieve herself," he said in Russian with a calm smile.

"Oh…oh, yes sir," the soldier said, first dumbfounded and then embarrassed.

"Thank you, I will only be a moment," Hannah said.

She escaped into her private bushes and wasted no time.

How am I going to look this young officer in the eye? Oh, this is so embarrassing, and he is so handsome. I'm such a mess. Dirty hair, dirty, oh, dirty, smelly everything.

Afraid to look at the condition of her hair, she tried to comb out the greasy, twisted stuff. Her fingers combed through the strands filtering out the grit that lay deep near her scalp. The train explosion had added considerable dirt to an already ugly situation.

Hannah pulled up her trousers and got herself together as best she could. She stepped out of the bushes and looked around. The officer was gone. There was only the persistent soldier, pacing back and forth in the dim morning light. Seeing her, he moved away and waved her to follow. Hannah quickly stepped into her hut, picked up her satchel, slung her rifle over her shoulder, and started off. None of Itzhak's company was around.

This doesn't feel right without Itzhak and the boys. What do these Russian men think of me? Well, I guess I'll find out.

It was just before daybreak and difficult to see anything in the camp.

This Russian is a pesky one, yes, I see you. I'm coming. She wondered if he was as embarrassed as she was back there. He didn't say anything. Well, what would he say anyway? More important to her was what that handsome officer thought.

The impatient one had nearly reached a band of men standing around in the dim light. Hannah changed to a half-run and caught up as the mission leader was about to start off.

"What? A girl? How are we going to make any time?" one

Russian soldier said, spitting on the ground. "Dragging this one along will get us killed for sure."

"Hey! Shut your mouth," the leader said, glaring at the discontent. "She is the one who knows where the target is, unless you know better?"

The officer glared at the man and scanned the faces of the others. "No, I thought not." The officer moved to the head of the line.

The complainer's face froze in a scowl as he stared at Hannah, then he turned and walked away.

I guess I better not say anything.

She could hear the man grumbling and talking to himself in garbled Russian. She only understood a little, something about waiting for the something, something waif. Maybe she was better off not knowing some of those words.

They began at a quick pace in single file. The angry soldier was close to the mission leader near the front. She was happy to be away from him. Hannah didn't think she could keep up. Already tired from lack of sleep, she worried all night about being alone with the Russian team. And a second day at this pace was too much. She was sandwiched among the soldiers, closer to the rear. She stared at the back of the man directly ahead. He and all the Russians wore brown Soviet army uniforms.

I don't look like them. I hate to stand out. People always pick on you when you stand out. Beila liked to wear bright colors, dresses and blouses. She liked people to notice her. Not me. What if we're captured? I'll be the first one they hurt.

Hannah occasionally caught sight of the young officer who rescued her. He was positioned a few men behind the complainer and looked tall and rugged as he moved with ease through brush and around trees. She couldn't help herself from taking a few quick peeks at his form. He was striking, muscular with blue eyes, clear and bright.

She doubted this Russian officer was Jewish and she wondered if Itzhak knew him.

Suddenly the column stopped and Hannah nearly ran into the

man just ahead. She looked around. They must be very near Kazieba's village. Nothing looked even the slightest bit familiar. Fear rose in her chest, and she forced a breath. Her greatest fear had been that she wouldn't find her bearings and the Russians would take out their frustrations on her. It was happening!

Hannah heard some mumbling from the front of the line and word was passed along to her.

"Go up to the front. The Commander. He wants to talk to you. Go," a man said in thick, rural Russian as he nudged her forward.

The soldiers were all looking back at her. Some motioned with hand waves for her to come forward. Hannah could feel the fear rising again, now in her ears; she could hardly hear. Everything seemed to move so slowly. She wanted to cry, but got control of herself by biting down on her tongue.

Focus. Focus on the pain. Clear your head. Look around. Crying won't help. Nothing will help except finding the artillery shells.

She tried to clear her head as she squeezed past the men to reach the commander.

"Ahhh, there you are," the commander said in Russian. "We are close to the village now. Do you recognize this place?"

Hannah was not sure what he said. He was not angry, just very direct. She shrugged and gestured to him to go on farther. He pointed to the ground directly behind himself. Obviously, he meant her to stay with him. He moved on cautiously. The village became visible as they approached the edge of the forest.

"The big cottage, big house…" she said in Polish, "Where is it?"

"What?" the commander asked in Russian. He motioned the men behind Hannah and the young man approached.

"Yes, sir?" he said in Russian.

"Yuri, ask her what she means about a house," the commander replied. "There are many houses here."

"Why is a particular house important to you?" Yuri asked in pristine Polish.

Hannah felt embarrassed that she had to have him translate Russian for her.

So...his name is Yuri. He must think I'm an idiot. Say something. Think.

"We must have approached the village from a different direction," Hannah explained, her panic pushed aside. "It doesn't look familiar from here. Maybe if we could find Kazieba's house, I could find the storage place from there."

Yuri turned to the commander and explained quickly in Russian. They bantered back and forth as arms were swung and fingers pointed. The speech was rapid and Hannah only understood a few words. The commander seemed annoyed. Yuri looked at Hannah.

"Well, we are going into the village—you, me, and two comrades," Yuri said in Polish, "and find your house."

"I will know the way from there," Hannah said, trying to sound positive. None of the men looked happy about splitting off from the main group. It was easy to tell they thought she was to blame.

Yuri waved Hannah on and she followed with two men trailing her. Hannah peered down the dirt road that cut through the village. It was quiet as before when they called on Kazieba. But his house was not in sight. About a hundred meters at the end of the dirt road was another dirt road crossing. As they approached the intersection, Hannah could see more cottages along that road as well. Then, there it was. The big cottage was behind them on the side road.

Over there! Oh, thank you, Adonai. Go past it to the woods behind. Yes. That's it.

"This way," Hannah said with a smile and a glance that caught Yuri's eye.

"Ah, this way," Yuri said in jest, with a smile of his own and motioning the others to follow.

Hannah blushed.

Oh, how embarrassing to be lost and then so easily find your way. He must think I'm a stupid thing. Well, he should try to find a place in this forest where he was only once before and in the dark, too. Not so simple.

Yuri said something to one of the men as they moved down the road toward the opening in the woods that Kazieba had taken. Hannah noticed their comrade moving swiftly back toward the commander's position. The main group would follow no doubt. As Hannah approached the edge of the woods, she remembered an odd, twisted tree. From there a path started that would lead them from the village nearly to the stash of artillery shells. The *target*, as Itzhak and Yuri would say. She wondered what Itzhak and the others were doing. No one seemed to tell her anything. Too many secrets.

Maybe they still don't trust me. No, it can't be that. How long since Warsaw, and we've been through many things together…dangerous things.

Hannah was still thinking about Itzhak and Yuri when the path ended at a large birch. They were somewhere near the hideaway, but it looked different. Had she missed a turn? No, it was the right place, but somehow different. The stash should be off twenty meters to the left or so. Why did the path stop here now?

"Don't move or we will kill all of you," said a stocky, middle-aged man, gruff and arrogant-sounding.

Before Yuri could act, six or seven soldiers jumped out of the brush and trees. Hannah recognized the uniforms. She had seen them before. Ukrainians. The dark holes in the barrels of their rifles and submachine guns were all Hannah could focus on. The enemy surrounded them. They were outnumbered.

Hannah caught Yuri's glance and eye movements. The commander and the others were following and would walk into this trap.

We need to make noise, to warn them, Hannah thought. *But how? If shooting starts, we will be the first to die.*

Yuri spoke loudly in Ukrainian, "You are surrounded. Put down your weapons!"

A huge grin covered the face of the Ukrainian squad leader.

"It is you who are surrounded, comrade," he said, "and I will take full advantage."

A couple of the Ukrainian soldiers chuckled with delight. There was little love between them and the Russians, particularly after the Ukrainian Nationals decided to side with the Germans. Getting the upper hand on the Russians was always a treat. The squad leader looked curiously at Hannah.

Kazieba must have told them where the artillery shells were hidden. Why else would they be here at this very spot? *What a traitor.*

Then she spied Kazieba. He was sitting at the base of a nearby tree with a guard standing next to him. He looked beaten and bloody. His hands were tied behind his back and his head hung low. He looked to be in pain. Raising his head slightly, they made eye contact.

He isn't a traitor at all. They beat him. Maybe he was right that we bring trouble to the villagers. What other choice do we have but to fight back? They will just kill us anyway. The pit proved that.

"Drop your weapons, now!" said the squad leader, pointing his submachine gun at Hannah and the others.

Hannah glanced over at Yuri, wondering what they should do.

Yuri's face was stern. He did not move. There was an awful silence.

We are dead. All this way for Papa and Mama and then to end like this.

Suddenly, a clicking sound was heard, metal to metal…then another and another. The sounds came from all around the group, behind the Ukrainians. The smile left the squad leader's face. He slowly scanned the woods just beyond his men. Russians in uniform appeared, weapons cocked and ready. Silence.

"As I said," Yuri repeated. "It is *you* who are surrounded."

Hannah held her breath.

"Put down your weapons and move to the side," the Russian commander shouted in Russian. "Or you will be cut down."

First hesitating, then lowering his gun, the leader complied. He grunted a short order to his men and they did likewise.

Hannah could barely force herself to breathe again. She was sure it was the end.

The enemy was moved along the trail into the woods by some of the Russian soldiers and the commander. Yuri and a few men stayed with Hannah.

"Well, where is the stash?" Yuri asked Hannah.

Hannah felt light-headed as she slowly adjusted to the circumstances. The weight of sure death still lingered in the air. She closed her eyes. *I thought I was dead, Papa. I thought I would be with you when I opened my eyes. But I wasn't afraid like before. I wasn't afraid to die, Papa.*

She opened her eyes and stared at the dry leaves around her shoes.

Get control of yourself. Quickly. They're watching, testing.

Hannah turned to Yuri.

"Now, it is your turn to ask a stupid question, no?" she said.

Hannah pointed to the spot about twenty-five meters away. It was beautifully camouflaged. None of them had noticed it before.

"There," she said with a big smile.

Gunfire broke the calmness of the forest. At first Hannah thought they were under attack. Instinctively, she crouched low to the ground and raised her rifle. Then she realized what had happened. The Ukrainians were no more.

She could feel the small victory draining from her smile as the echoing gunshots filled the park and her family's bodies filled the pit. She was taken back in an instant. Dumbstruck, Hannah dropped to her knees, frozen in the moment. Yuri saw her face, the shock that hit her. He could only guess why. Something powerful shook Hannah as she cowered on the ground before him. The brave girl he thought he was beginning to understand looked defeated and crushed under some huge weight.

Hannah stared into nothingness. Her eyes fixed on Yuri's boots. After a moment she glanced up and her eyes found his. They were soft and kind. He seemed to understand. She didn't want to know how. She just felt it.

"Why?" Hannah asked, closing her eyes. "Why does it have to be like this?"

"I don't know," Yuri said shaking his head. "It just is."

Yuri extended his hand to Hannah and she stared at it. He leaned over and gently gripped her forearms and pulled her up from her knees. On her feet, Hannah looked around and forced herself back into the moment. *I can do this now, Papa. I will.*

"Now what do we do?" she asked.

Yuri watched her, amazed at how quickly she got control of

herself.

"I'm alright. I am," she said, straightening her back and slinging her rifle over her shoulder.

"I believe you. I do," Yuri said in clear Polish.

. . . . .

The commander and the rest of Russian soldiers came back through the woods. Hannah had not noticed before, but Boleslaw Kazieba was still sitting at the base of the tree where the Ukrainian guard left him.

"Should we kill this man? Who is he?" the commander asked Hannah.

Hannah was unsure of his question and frowned. Sensing the importance of the question, Yuri quickly interpreted.

Kazieba looked frightened. His previous captors had died a violent death. Now would his new captors do the same for him? He looked at Hannah with pleading eyes.

"No, he led us to this hiding place," she said. "Please, let him go."

The commander glared at Kazieba for a long time, then raised his submachine gun and pointed it at his face.

"If I see you again, comrade, you will become a dead man," the commander said. "Tell no one about us. We know your village, your house. Now go."

Hannah hoped the Russian would not shoot him in the back as he walked. Kazieba must have understood, as he struggled to his feet and limped away toward the village.

"So where is the ammunition?" the commander said in Russian, looking at Hannah and Yuri.

Hannah pointed to it and began walking toward the depression in the ground.

The commander grunted something to his men and they all descended upon the hidden stash. In short order they loaded up stretchers piled to the breaking point with artillery shells. One Russian had a collection of submachine guns, pistols, and rifles confiscated from the dead Ukrainians. Yuri grabbed a submachine gun and handed it to Hannah.

"It's a PPS-42, a good Russian make. You will be much more effective with this. Give me the Mauser." She took the weapon and handed over her German rifle. She had learned the code of the partisans. New recruits had to find or take their own weapons from the enemy. The gun had far more firepower than her rifle. In close quarters, the weapon made all the difference. Even better, the Russians had plenty of ammunition for it.

Back in Warsaw, Barbara and Pawel had taught her about guns and tactics with pictures and diagrams. She was scared half out of her wits back then, but she focused hard on the lessons. She knew her life would depend upon knowledge of guns and such. The lessons were cut short when Barbara had to move quickly to avoid capture. Hannah could not see herself shooting another human being or even an animal, but the enemy obviously had no second thoughts about killing her.

She looked over the weapon as Pawel had taught her. The lessons rushed back as she found the magazine release, checked the chamber for a round, pulled back the slide bolt cocking the gun, and flipped on the safety. She nodded to Yuri as she saw the men do with each other. He was smiling. He nodded back with approval. He had never seen a girl handle a weapon like that before.

The trek back seemed to go much faster than the march to the storage area. Danger was everywhere, but Hannah felt relieved, even light. She had found the target and so far the mission was a success. If it weren't for the emptiness in her belly over the execution of the Ukrainian soldiers, she could be happy. Even so, the fear of the Russian men not accepting her was gone. A little smile crossed her lips as she stepped over a crooked stick in her path. She was given the rear guard with another soldier. She used to think it was the lowest position in the rank. Now she understood it was one of trust. He watched her, then nodded. She nodded back and checked the path behind them. No one was trailing the group. They were safe for the moment.

. . . . .

As they approached the camp, they were challenged by sentries. There were words exchanged up at the front and the line started moving again. They entered the camp carrying the shells and some of the men in the camp raised their fists and shouted, "Victory!" in Russian.

Itzhak, David, Joseph, and the others were back. They waved Hannah over to their section of the camp. Hannah couldn't hold back a big grin. Boris pointed to the submachine gun, laughed, and nodded. It was so good to see them all safe and unharmed. Hannah sat down next to David. Joseph handed her a steaming cup of soup. She couldn't remember when plain vegetable soup had tasted so good.

Another concert before winter was rumored. They had plenty of explosives now. In the last few weeks, the nights were growing colder. Hannah worried that she might not manage the winter in the forest. If she got sick, the cold would become the enemy, not so much the Germans and Ukrainians.

Talk in the camp was open and sometimes brazen. Hannah felt that bragging would sooner or later turn against people with no respect for what could happen. Boasting means not being on your guard. *Papa, you used to say that Adonai protects people who are humble. I don't know anymore, if all that's true. Maybe some of us have to act like those Nazis to beat them.*

Many joked that the Germans hated the summer in the swampy forests. The heat and humidity were bad, but the mosquitoes were worse. Nor was there any shortage of water snakes in the swamps and pools of the low-lying areas. Anyone who didn't have to stay would gladly leave.

Some thought the Germans might plan another "Aktion" into the forests before spring. Hannah had only heard about those attacks from Joseph. But the Ukrainians? He said they were always a threat.

They were not afraid of the Russians or the Polish Home army survivors and especially not Jews. Even in the summer, they were in the forests and swamps, trying to impress their German friends. Hannah took it all in and waited. She knew firsthand that some of the orders came from the Warsaw spies, like Barbara.

Chapter Sixteen

Hannah sat alone on a tree stump outside of her hut, thinking of the last mission and how badly it could have gone. Itzhak strolled up.

"Hannah, Joseph tells me that you want a bath," Itzhak said.

No! He didn't, I told him not to tell. Hannah could feel her cheeks getting red. She looked around to see if anyone was listening. No one was. She put her hands over her cheeks and looked up.

"Well, yes, it's been a long time…since I have been, well, clean," Hannah said, hoping he wouldn't speak too loudly.

"Oh, oh, yes, I see, we probably don't smell very good out here, is that it?" he said, eyes searching for her to confirm his suspicion. "And, well, you are a girl and all."

"Yes," Hannah said, putting her hand over her eyes.

I can't believe how hard this is. Help me please.

Itzhak paced back and forth for a moment, thinking, seemingly talking to himself inside.

"I know. Yes, I know a peasant woman in a little hamlet west of here," he said, pointing with his finger.

"She is a gentile and hates the Germans even more than I do. Her daughter was killed by a stray bullet during the German invasion in '39 and the son-in-law was killed on the front lines. Husband gone a long time ago. She has only her grandson left. She will help us. Help you."

"Where do I find her?" Hannah asked, shrugging her shoulders.

"No, you can't go alone," he replied. "Take a team with you."

Take a team with me! What? On a mission to give me a bath. Ohhh!

Standing up and facing Itzhak, she looked him in the eye.

"I am not taking a team with me for this," she said, turning her back to him.

"Well, what then? You can't go alone. Too dangerous."

She spun around and said, "I'll take Joseph since he already knows. And one of our young fighters." *Someone who doesn't know me.*

"Just the two, alright?"

"Ahh, alright. I'll talk to Joseph," Itzhak said. "Today may be the best time. Nothing much happening right now anyway."

"I'll get my things ready. Can the woman wash clothes? Mine are filthy," she said, swatting dust off her trousers. She remembered when Barbara's nurse brought in clean clothes, underwear too, after she jumped from the train. It was the last time she felt clean clothes on her skin.

The bloody clothes. No. I don't want to think about them. Forget them.

"I don't know, I'll work on that, too," Itzhak said, a look of frustration covering his face. He shook his head and walked away mumbling something. Hannah didn't want to hear it regardless and walked the other way, wondering if she pushed him too far.

. . . . .

Later on, Hannah came out of her hut and stretched.

"Hannah, I have good news for you," Joseph said, sauntering up to her.

"About what?" she said, looking up at his smiling face.

I talked with Itzhak and there is a villager woman who can take you in for a bath."

"Yes. I know. We talked," Hannah said, almost whispering and looking around for anyone too close. "I hope you know how to get there."

"Oh yes, it's easy. Unless we find some Nats on the way."

"What do you mean, 'Nats'?"

"That's what I call them, Ukrainian Nationalists, that nasty bunch," Joseph said, pointing his gun into the trees, pretending to shoot them.

"Ah. And the woman, do you know her?" Hannah asked.

"I know the one he means. The old woman with the little

grandson."

"But you don't *know* her? Not enough to ask if I can…I mean, you know."

"Itzhak said to use his name. He did her a big favor. She will help you."

"When can we go?" Hannah asked, trying to keep Joseph focused.

"Well, he had a package for me to pick up from the Russians, then we can go. Give me a few minutes, alright?"

"Is it far?"

"Not far, but we need to be careful, of course. I'll meet you here by your hut."

"Thank you."

Hannah watched as he strode away across the camp. Her clothes were filthy. She didn't want to take a bath and get back into them. Maybe they'd pass a clothesline along the way…

Hannah entered the hut and checked her submachine gun. She wanted to be ready for Joseph. They had to try to sneak out of the camp so none of those men would know what they were doing. If any of the Russians saw them…well, that was too embarrassing to even think about.

When it was almost noon Joseph showed up at her hut with a young Jewish fighter and three young Russians, all armed and ready for the mission.

"Hannah, are you in there?" Joseph called.

Hannah opened the door and stepped out.

"Who are all these…" she stammered, scanning the smiling lot of them.

I'm going to get Itzhak back for this! What am I going to tell them this mission is about? Well, they probably already know!

Hannah pouted, shut the door of her hut, and stared at the bunch of them.

"Let's go. Joseph, do you know where the woman lives?"

"Yes, and Itzhak said to give you this," Joseph said as he slipped a satchel from his shoulder and handed it Hannah.

"What's in it?"

Joseph shrugged and waved the squad to follow. Off they went to the west.

The day was sunny with blue sky overhead. The forest air smelled fresh and clean. In less than an hour they were upon the edge of the village. The woman's cottage was on the outskirts, set apart and mostly hidden from view. Hannah surveyed the area.

This is a good spot, no one likely to notice us back here in the trees away from the other houses. But they still need to be on watch.

"Joseph, keep a good lookout."

"Yes, I will take care of it. This village is not a problem though," he said.

"You never know," she replied. She peered through the gap between the mold-covered dull-brown house siding and the bare lilac bushes at the edge of the yard.

Joseph stepped up to the front door of the cottage with Hannah at his side. "Let me speak to her. I think she will remember me from before."

"Alright, but I'm staying right next to you," Hannah said, looking back at the three Russians standing around joking with each other.

Joseph knocked on the door, but no answer. He knocked again. Waited. They were about to leave when the door creaked open. A little boy looked out and said, "Wait. Grammy is coming."

"Hello," Hannah said with a smile.

"Who are you?" said a middle-aged woman, moving the boy around behind her.

"I am Joseph. Itzhak sent us."

"Itzhak, yes, I remember you. You are his cousin I think?" she said. "He is a good young man. What can I do for him?"

"For her," Joseph said, looking to Hannah to say something.

"I am Hannah, Mrs…?

"No names. It's safer that way."

"I, well…Itzhak thought that maybe you could help me get cleaned up," Hannah said quietly, glancing back at the Russians. She hoped the woman would understand.

The woman looked at the young men and back to Hannah.

"You and the other boys, you wait out here," she said to Joseph, her face set like stone, eyes glaring.

Joseph backed up saying, "Yes, we will wait out here."

"Come in, dear," she said to Hannah and took her by the wrist. The woman shut the door and led her to the bathroom. The little boy stood and watched the stranger in his house.

Hannah looked around the dark living room. An old wooden rocking chair with a well-worn woven seat cushion sat alone near the window. Ancient photographs decorated the drab walls, and odd-shaped end tables bracketed a tan-colored couch.

That couch. Papa never liked the color. Mama wanted the 'modern look' as she called it. I wonder what the Warsaw house looks like now.

"You will be safe here, my dear. Put that gun in the corner and your coat with it."

"I'm sorry, but I must keep the weapon near me," Hannah said, looking the woman in the eye without a flinch.

"Alright then," the woman said, pointing to a corner of the bathroom. "Give me the coat." Hannah rested the gun against the faded beige, vertical-seamed paneling. It was the same as on Bubbe Rachel's bathroom wall, which always caught Hannah's eye.

"Thank you. For helping me. I'll try not to be any trouble for you."

She is so much like Bubbe Rachel. I miss my Bubbe.

"You need a bath, dear?" the old woman said, sniffing Hannah's clothes and inspecting clumps of her hair. "Yes, you do."

"My clothes are so dirty," Hannah said, looking down at her trousers. "I don't want to put them back on when I'm clean."

"What is in there?" the woman asked, touching the satchel hanging off Hannah's shoulder.

"I don't know. Something from Itzhak."

The woman slipped the strap from Hannah's shoulder and pulled out the contents. She unfolded a small Soviet army uniform with no insignia and a compact field kit, hammer and sickle emblem on the leather flap. She opened it to find a toothbrush, paste, comb, and razor. There was a little note inside. It read, "From Yuri."

The woman smiled but said nothing. She put a washcloth and

soap next to the tub.

"Now I see. You really do need a bath."

Hannah could feel her face turning red.

"Help me with the water," she said, directing Hannah to the kitchen.

They pumped water, heated it, and poured it into the bathtub. Hannah tested the water with her fingers. Nicely warm.

"Get out of those dirty things and into the water," the woman said. "I will see what can be done with these dirty clothes."

She held the uniform up in front of Hannah for size. "Looks like it will fit fine."

Hannah started to undress and stopped. Her hands would not move. She stared at the floor.

"Are you alright, dear?" the woman said, looking Hannah over. "I will leave you alone. There is soap and a cloth and towel for you. Leave your dirty clothes on the bathroom floor." She turned and left.

Struggling, Hannah shut the door and slowly unbuttoned the shirt. Leaving her clothes in a pile, she stepped naked into the tub. The uniform was neatly placed on a small straight-backed chair in the corner opposite the submachine gun.

Hannah got into the water and smelled the soap. A flowery fragrance seeped up her nose. It was not lilac, but so familiar. She dunked her head and all under the water and started scrubbing. Lifting up, warm water streamed down her face, hair matted and clinging to her cheeks and over her shoulders.

Beginning with her head, she worked her way down. Hannah lay back into the curve of the tub and let the bathwater seep over her chest and shoulders. She could feel her eyes filling with tears. *Mama.* It was lavender. Mama's soap.

She lay still for a moment, soaking. A dull knock on the door broke the silence.

"Just picking up the dirty clothes," the woman said. She reached in with one hand, grabbing the trousers and the rest from the floor. She set a bra, panties, and socks on top of the uniform. "Do you need help with your hair?"

"No, thank you, no, I can manage it."

Softly the door was closed and she was alone again. Hannah heard muffled voices outside and realized the bathroom was adjacent to where the boys were gathered. She washed her hair and was wringing out the water when the voices grew into hoots and laughs, too much to ignore. She stood up in the tub, hunched over, and peeked through the old lace window curtain.

Oh no! Put that down! Help! Get him, lady, stop him!

The little boy was running around the yard with Hannah's dirty bra over his head, giggling and falling down. Even Joseph was chuckling. The Russians thoroughly enjoyed the scene, pointing and laughing.

"Come here, Piotr! Stop that right now," the woman shouted, getting hold of the boy and the bra. She shushed the young men and they backed away playfully.

Hannah sat down in the tub and put her hands over her face. How could she face those men now? She'd be the new camp joke!

She got out of the tub and dried off with the towel. Her hair would take a little more time to dry, but she felt wonderfully clean. The underwear and uniform fit fairly well. The sleeves ran down to her knuckles, but the pants were adjustable and comfortable. The stained, scratched mirror reflected a face she had not seen for a long time. She was afraid to look deeply into the eyes staring back. She combed her hair and watched its shine come back to life.

Strange to see yourself after so long.

The uniform was impressive. She smiled.

They will see me differently now. Thank you, Yuri.

Hannah picked up her submachine gun and field kit and stepped out of the bathroom. Piotr was standing next to his grandmother with his head hanging low.

"What do you say to Hannah, Piotr?"

"I'm sorry," he said and looked up for approval.

"You may go play. Go on."

Piotr skipped off to another room. Hannah put her old shoes on. They looked out of place with the new uniform. The woman handed her the satchel.

"Your old clothes are in here. Not enough time to dry so hang them up when you get back. A few personal items as well."

"Thank you."

"Remember, I hate these Ukrainians almost as much as the Nazis," she said. "If you are fighting any of them, you are always welcome here to clean up and get warm, my dear."

"Thank you for your kindness. You've been so good to me. If you ever need help, please get a message to me. I'll come."

They stepped into the yard. The soldiers were still joking. They noticed her uniform immediately and stopped to stare. Hannah looked at them and back to the woman.

"Wait. I want to talk to these boys," the woman said and moved quickly toward the group. Hannah walked past the boys and stopped.

"If you give her a tough time, you'll answer to me. Understand?"

"We…we understand, yes," Joseph said, backing away. She looked at Hannah with a smile and sparkle in her eye.

"Good-bye, Hannah."

"Good-bye. Let's go, Joseph," Hannah said, waiting for the grinning, joking Russians to move out first. She waved them on. "I'll take the rear guard. You lead, Joseph."

Hannah caught one of them making gestures and acting silly. She pulled back the bolt on her gun and glared at them. Their faces froze for a moment. She waved the muzzle of the weapon slightly toward the woods. They started moving.

At least they were on their way. Some words in Russian were passed that Hannah didn't know. Occasional chuckles broke the silence. Thankfully, they all settled down after a time. The trip back was uneventful. Hannah suspected she would hear plenty more jokes around the camp after this mission. But her new uniform might bring her some respect.

Chapter Seventeen

It was the first of November when Itzhak called the group together. Everyone was tired from the year's work, but no one complained.

"We have another mission," Itzhak said. "Another concert before the snow."

"Am I with *you* this time?" Hannah asked. She would rather not be the one they count on to find the target.

"We're all going," he said. "Maybe some of our Russian comrades will join us as well."

Oh great! As long as Itzhak's the leader, Hannah thought.

"Maybe tonight or tomorrow, I think," Itzhak said. "I'll try to get an update."

Everyone was quiet. Itzhak turned and walked toward the Russian commander's tent. The breeze ruffled crispy brown leaves still clinging to the branches overhead. Hannah looked up and focused on one lone leaf. Her chest felt tight, breathing uneven. The tree, nearly bare, could no longer hide behind its cover. They all could've been killed last time. The Ukrainians were dead. If Hannah hadn't spoken up, Mr. Kazieba would be dead, too, she was sure of it.

I should already be dead. Maybe Adonai is giving me another chance. Hannah shivered in the wind. *That's a strange way of thinking. I don't like it. Papa said that Adonai would keep us safe if we kept the Torah. I think Papa was wrong. Was God at the pit? Not for Papa and Mama. Things should be simple, right? But nothing is simple. When is it going to be my turn?*

Looking around she saw Itzhak returning to his hut from the commander's tent. He glanced her way and then turned back and slipped into his hut.

There's always something that makes things more dangerous. What will it be this time? I don't know. Maybe I'm thinking too much. Hannah yawned and went to her hut.

Trying to sleep, she lay down, but her mind kept racing. The more she tried not to think, the more her mind wandered. After about an hour, she slipped on her shoes. If Joseph was up, she needed to ask him more about Itzhak and the Russian, Yuri. She stepped outside into the night air. Sitting down next to the hut, she pulled her coat around herself. The sky was clear. She could see stars glimmering through the spaces between the branches.

Out of the shadows, she heard footsteps. She felt for her gun. It was in the hut.

"Well, you could not sleep either?" Itzhak said quietly.

"Oh, it's you," she replied. "I was worried for a moment."

"You are safe here. Do you mind if I sit with you for a while, Hannah?" he asked.

"No. Please sit," Hannah said, looking up at the face in the shadows.

"Some nights are, well, uneasy for me."

"They killed the Ukrainians, you know."

"Yes, I heard. Appears you didn't like that."

"They were captured…no guns. I guess it doesn't matter. It's not how I thought it would be," she replied, searching for his eyes in the dim light.

"No, I guess not," Itzhak replied.

I wonder if I should say something about Zosia? Maybe that is why he can't sleep? She glanced at Itzhak. He stared into the fire, his face blank. *No. Better not.*

"The night sky is very beautiful and not to be wasted," he said. "Do you agree?"

"Yes. But very cold."

Hannah thought about the wonderful times she and Papa had in the forests in the summers before the war. There was nothing to fear then. All was good.

"I remember when my Papa, ah…my father and I spent time in

the forests camping," she explained. "At night we would sit by the fire and talk about science and plants and animals and the stars."

"He was an engineer?" Itzhak asked.

Hannah felt tears welling up in her eyes. The glue holding her together was still weak, like a deep pond topped with thin ice. Too much weight behind even a careful step and hairline cracks might form and give way. But Itzhak was so easy to talk to. She didn't know what to think about Yuri.

I think Itzhak likes me more than just as a comrade. If I look like Zosia, it must be hard for him to see me every day. It's all so confusing now.

"Oh, I'm sorry, maybe I am getting sleepy. Yes, he is—was—an engineer. But he was much more than that," she said, looking away as a tear tickled her cheek.

"You have proven yourself in the forests already. He taught you?"

She cleared her throat and swiped the tear away with her palm.

"He loved science, the earth, and the stars. We talked and wondered about the universe. And he knew about everything—astronomy, biology, chemistry, physics. He said that in the forests, nature happens all around us."

"He sounds like a wonderful father," Itzhak replied.

"Papa was my best friend, too," Hannah said. "I lost my best friend."

Hannah felt tears well up in her eyes again, then streak across each cheek.

Itzhak moved close to Hannah and put his arm around her shoulders.

"I didn't mean to make you cry, Hannah," he whispered as he wiped her cheeks with gentle hands.

"My father is a villager, a good man, a righteous Jew," Itzhak began. "My brother and I had a good childhood, I guess you could say. We had very little money, beyond what was needed to feed us. We wore secondhand clothes and shoes, but we were happy."

Hannah was not sure how to respond to Itzhak's arm around her shoulders. But worrying if others saw them together didn't seem as important tonight. And it was easier to focus on someone else's story. She took a deep breath and exhaled slowly.

"What is your father like?" she asked, hoping he would continue.

"Well, he is much different than your Papa, I imagine," Itzhak said with a wistful smile.

"How?"

"Not very educated, but has a natural understanding of things. Good with machines and understands people. He can make things with his hands. He works hard and prays at Shabbat and some of the holy days. I would say he is a righteous man, as I understand the term. Far more religious than me."

"Do you think he would like me?"

"Oh yes. You are honest. You mean what you say," Itzhak replied. He picked up a stick and poked at the dying fire. Some sparks flickered.

"I'd like to meet him someday," Hannah said.

"I am sure he would like to meet you... if he is still alive," Itzhak replied, swallowing hard and lowering his head.

The night was still. They sat in silence for a long time. Campfires were mostly dark. The dying embers and aroma of burning wood was familiar, like sitting inside a memory. Hannah could feel the night chill touching her nose and cheeks. She felt a bit self-conscious that her hair looked unkempt and her complexion ruddy. She had forgotten about her looks. But now with a young man's arms around her, that seemed to be important. Finally, Itzhak broke the silence.

"Why do you want to fight and kill the Germans and their friends, Hannah?" Itzhak said, looking up at the sky.

What kind of a question is that?

"I don't know what you mean," she replied, folding her hands over one knee.

"The German in the train wreck. You wanted to help him?" Itzhak said. "That shows me you have a kind heart. Maybe your hate for these people who murdered your family has not overtaken you yet."

"Well, I'm confused about it," she said. "Part of me wants them to pay for what they did."

"And the other part?" he asked.

"And the other part is, I guess, sad. Maybe that's it," she replied. "Maybe I thought Adonai would not let such a thing happen to us. Maybe. I don't know."

"Well, we have to do our duty, to bring just rewards to these murderers," Itzhak said. "You will be a smart and ruthless fighter. From what you have shown me of yourself, I have no doubt."

"But I'm afraid to," she started to say.

"Someday soon, in the months ahead, you may lose yourself in it."

"What do you mean?" she asked. "In what?"

"Don't let hate eat you up," he said. "Always remember who you are."

He means getting back at them. It doesn't ever go away. It always comes back. Is that what he means?

"I don't want to be like that. But something inside wants me to make them pay," she said. "To stop them from killing us all. Somebody has to do it."

Hannah could hardly believe the words coming out of her mouth. She hadn't thought much about how she felt before.

It all happened so fast, she thought. *I did what I had to do. What seemed best at the time. Not what Papa and Mama wanted, I know. If I just hid in the woods, what would stop those people? Somebody had to do it.*

"I understand. Just try to balance who you are with what you are doing," he said softly. "One day you may find yourself in that place. I hope you recognize it when you get there. I mean, don't become like them or the hate will swallow you up."

"I hope not, I guess," she replied, not fully understanding his words.

"Tomorrow is another day and it will be here soon," he said. "We need to get some rest."

They both stood up and Hannah faced Itzhak. His eyes were kind and loving. But somehow Hannah knew they would never be more than friends.

. . . . .

Morning came soon enough. Hannah went through her regular routine and met with everyone for a breakfast of soup. It wasn't like a real breakfast, but it was hot and nourishing on a cool morning. Of course, every meal—breakfast, lunch, and dinner—consisted of soup or beans or fruit. Someone had restarted the fire near her hut and everyone sat around. Hannah took the last stump. She could feel her bones pressing into the cold, hard wooden seat.

"What have you heard about the mission?" Joseph asked David. Hannah looked up.

"I think we're going out to the old tracks again," David replied.

"Where we had the big concert?" Hannah asked.

"Yes, that line is important to the Germans," David said. "They keep pushing supplies through to the front in Russia. Well, that is what the Russians tell us anyway."

Hannah saw Itzhak coming across the camp from the Russian commander's area. She was sure he had news on the next mission. Her heart began to beat faster as he approached. She hoped David was wrong. It didn't make sense to go back to the same place. No surprise in returning.

"We have to do some reconnaissance on the railroad switching station," Itzhak said.

"Reconnaissance? What does that mean?" Hannah asked.

"Soviet intelligence could not get the train schedule and the Germans have rerouted the trains from the previous times.

"What do we have to do?"

"We must get to the target during the day, then after dark, move into the station," Itzhak said, looking at everyone but Hannah. "We leave in one hour. Gather your things and pack extra ammunition." Itzhak turned and quickly walked away.

Well, that's odd. Why won't he look at me? What's going on? He's avoiding me. I don't understand.

"Itzhak, Itzhak, is there something wrong?" she asked as she hurried to catch up with him.

"No. Well, yes. We need to talk," he replied, waving her to follow.

"Let's sit over here," Itzhak said. He pointed to the tree stump seat outside his hut. Hannah looked around at the boys going to their huts for supplies. She sat across from Itzhak.

"There is more to this operation than I told everyone," he said. "We need to get into the station house and look at the timetables. They must not be aware that we got the information."

"There are people inside?"

"Sakaloff wants you to distract the switchman while we check the freight ledgers," Itzhak said. "I told him no, it's too dangerous."

"I can do it."

"By distract, he means sexually," Itzhak said, wagging his head. "No."

"I'll do it."

Barbara in Warsaw came to mind. Barbara moved like a woman. But not like Mama. Men looked at her differently. Hannah hadn't been very interested in schoolboys, being too busy with studies. But with Itzhak and now Yuri, she felt different.

"I'll need some reason to approach the station. I could be a lost girl from a nearby village. Or maybe my father sent me on an errand. I'll need different clothes. Where can I get clothes out here? Maybe from the old woman. I'll find something."

"I don't want you to do this," Itzhak said, his voice softer.

"Find me some peasant girl's clothes and I will find a way to distract the man."

The attack by the soldier at the edge of the woods was still raw, but she fought and survived and that changed what could have been. Hannah thought about that day a lot. At the time, she didn't understand what the man was trying to do to her. Now she knew. She was lucky. The knife, it saved her. She would do it again if need be. Hannah felt her pocket. It was there.

"If we can go past that little village again on the way," she said, "I can take something from a clothesline."

"I don't think we are going that way," Itzhak said, looking down.

"Well, we'll see," she said with a coy smile. Itzhak glanced at her straight, white teeth.

"Huh," he grunted and walked away.

I know – the cook. They say the Russian cook can find the strangest things out here.

Hannah grinned and walked to the other side of the camp. She looked for the man in his usual spot. Hannah suspected that the goods he sold were not necessarily gotten through the most upright means. But it was wartime and stealing a few things was allowed. Papa, of course, would not agree.

The old man was stooped over with his back to Hannah as she approached. He was fiddling with things in a big army duffel bag. He must have heard her footsteps, because he peered over his shoulder for a moment and turned back to his work.

"Ahhh, my young lady pays me a visit. Good to see you again," he said in Russian.

"Good morning," she replied in broken Russian.

"And what might you desire? Soup, goods, perhaps a whisper in a certain ear on your behalf?"

Hannah felt her cheeks blush.

He means Yuri. Was it that obvious? I must ignore that.

"I need women's clothes," she said. "Sexy things, like a blouse.

"Ha! You are more serious than I thought. Beware Yuri," he said, facing her and chuckling.

"Oh, no, this is for a mission," she explained. "I must get the attention of a German railroad man while they look at the train schedules."

"If you say so, young miss," the cook said, whispering. "I will not reveal your secret."

"No, it's really for the mission," she said.

"Out here, that is a difficult order," he said, wagging his head in mock seriousness. "When is your romantic interlude?"

"My what?" she asked, suddenly realizing he was having his fun. "Oh, yes, well, we are leaving on the hour."

"I have less than one hour," he said in jest. "Then I must be a master magician, too, not only a food magician."

"Can you find something?" she asked.

"Return in one half hour and you will see the master at work," he said with a toothy grin and a sparkle in his eye. "Have faith, my girl."

"Thank you, I'll be back soon," she said and left for her hut.

. . . . .

Hannah pulled together her gear, PPS-42 submachine gun, extra magazines, hat, and the Russian food rations the comrades provided. She double-checked the magazines to be sure they were full of bullets. She heard many stories about fellow partisans who ran out of ammunition and were gunned down. Always be prepared. Always.

It was nearly time to set off, so Hannah strolled over to the cook. He was cutting vegetables for soup and looked nothing like a magician. Hannah's spirits fell as she came near.

"Hello, I'm leaving in a few minutes, and…" she started to say.

Vladimir raised his index finger. Putting down his paring knife and wiping his hands on his tattered apron, Vladimir swiveled in his seat and reached behind the barrel he was using for a stool. Hannah stared, wondering if the magician could find clothes for a girl in this world of scruffy men. He grabbed a small utility bag and reached into it.

"I fancy this on my pretty comrade," Vladimir said, smiling. "As I am sure any mortal man would."

Hannah stared in awe as the old soldier pulled a low-cut, embroidered white blouse from the battle-worn canvas bag. It seemed to be a good fit. And it would surely show off her womanly figure.

"You are a magician," she said, taking the blouse and holding it up to her shoulders. "It's perfect, thank you. How many rubles?"

"When you come back safely, you can return it. That is the price," he said, eyes full of life. "Now go. I have work to do."

The old cook waved his hands at Hannah, shooing her away.

"Thank you. You are surely the best magician I've ever seen," Hannah said with a smile as she folded the blouse and slipped it into her knapsack.

The man pretended to be busy, but the twinkle in his eye revealed his true intentions.

He is a good man. There is still some good left in Russia.

"May God be with you," the cook called out to Hannah as she turned and started for her group.

She glanced back over her shoulder to see him look suspiciously around at his comrades.

So maybe there are some Russians who believe in God, in spite of their leaders, she thought. Papa said their leaders tried to kill God. Papa never believed a government could kill God, not really. He said God lived in people's hearts. And now she was going off to do more killing.

But what else can I do?

Chapter Eighteen

"Joseph, you lead, Hannah, in the middle, Boris, you will be the rear guard," Itzhak said. "Everyone, form a column, move out."

Itzhak made eye contact with Hannah as she quickly stepped into line.

He thinks he will have some other way to distract the Germans at the station house. But I have the best way. I'm not afraid. I can do this.

They made their way cautiously through the forest. It took longer than expected. Long shadows coated the forest floor as they reached the site of the big concert. The station house was about two kilometers farther along the tracks, and the area was usually more heavily patrolled by the German army. Itzhak needed to be in position at the station house by nightfall.

Hannah could feel her stomach flutter. She had escaped torture and death so far, but once again fear rose in her. They all knew the Germans did not like to go very far into the forests and tended to stay near the railroad cut. No partisan would attempt to bomb the tracks in this sector. The terrain provided no line of sight protection from the guards. It was too flat and straight. Itzhak moved his column deeper into the woods in a line parallel to the tracks. Hannah understood the strategy perfectly. She just needed to keep a clear head and not allow fear to get in the way of common sense.

It seemed to be hours of groping in the dark when a pinpoint of light pierced the black wall ahead. Joseph stopped and passed a message along the column back to Itzhak.

"He wants to know how we should approach the railroad house," Hannah said relaying the message to Itzhak in a whisper.

"It is probably a hundred meters from here to the tracks," Itzhak said under his breath. "Move slowly toward the light and stop near the edge of the clearing."

Hannah could feel the excitement and anxiety rising in her chest. She wanted to put on the blouse now and be ready for the diversion. But there was no discrete way she could take off her shirt and change with all these men standing around.

"Itzhak, is now a good time?"

"It is a good sign that we have not had any resistance thus far," Itzhak said, peering into the pitch toward the light. "Proceed slowly, quietly."

Someone stepped on a dry stick and the snap seemed to echo as if canyon walls carried the sound for kilometers. It didn't really, but the whole plan depended on getting in and out without a sound. No one was pleased. David whispered to everyone to be careful.

I better ask Itzhak again. I need to find a good time to put on the blouse.

When everyone reached the edge of the forest, they spread out to either side of the column to see. Everyone looked to Itzhak for some command. Hannah gazed across the open cut trying to plan a strategy for getting to the switch control building. It was about the size of a two-bedroom house. Unfortunately, the scheduler sat in an elevated room about half the height to the second floor. The lampposts extended from the house along the tracks for about fifty meters on either side. The entire area was exposed.

From his vantage point, the scheduler could peer out the large windows and spot most anyone approaching the track area or the building. Everyone seemed to come to the same conclusion at once. How could they possibly get in, get the train schedule information, and leave without being seen?

"There are at least three sentries past the building on the tracks," Boris said.

"There are three or four more about fifty meters to our left," Schlomo said. "Just Mausers, I think. No submachine guns."

"I can do it," Hannah said to Itzhak.

"You can do what?"

"Remember what the commander said," she replied and reached into her satchel and pulled out the blouse. She held the sexy, ruffled blouse up to her chest and gestured a coy smile.

"She could distract the German in the control room long enough for one of us to slip in and write down the information," Joseph said excitedly.

"No, too dangerous," Itzhak said, crossing his arms. "We will create a different distraction down the tracks to the left. They will all come running and I will slip in the office and get the schedule."

"Why would the schedule man leave with an attack happening?" Hannah asked, raising her eyebrows.

"He wouldn't," David said. "And then we would have to deal with a bunch of excited Germans with guns."

Itzhak was deep in thought and finally said in a low voice, "Gather around. This is what we will do. Joseph, Schlomo, go to the left and distract the sentries without being seen. Make it sound like an animal in the woods. Stay out of sight. David, Boris, and the rest, do the same for the sentries on the right."

Everyone looked at Hannah. She felt like they were all depending on her. And they were. Itzhak seemed edgy and nervous, not fully comfortable with exposing her to this much danger. He pulled out a small revolver and handed it to Hannah.

"Take this. If you have to, use it on them. If they capture you, use it on yourself," he said with a frown.

Hannah had not seen Itzhak so tense before. Through the underbrush and trees, the lights from the station house reflected in his eyes. Maybe this was far more dangerous than she imagined. She had escaped death more than once. If death for her was to be, it would be. Mama always said that when anything important happened, it was meant to be. Somehow, she didn't feel that this was her time. The plan would work. They would be successful.

"When you distract the sentries, Hannah and I will slip across the tracks and approach the station house. We need ten minutes. Any questions?" Itzhak asked.

David put a hand on Itzhak's shoulder. "Where do we meet afterward?"

"Yes, this is why I brought my cousin along," Itzhak said trying to smile and relieve his own fears. "We will meet at the site of the big concert."

"What if it does not go well and we are scattered?" Joseph asked.

"Then follow our route back to the camp, but make sure no one trails you," Itzhak replied. "Hopefully, we would find each other along the way."

"Good luck, Hannah," David said. "It's time."

"One more thing. If I am killed, David is in charge," Itzhak said. "Follow him and try to get everyone back. Now go."

The two teams left silently toward the sentries. Hannah watched them disappear into the darkness and then looked at Itzhak. He nodded.

Hannah moved quickly. She took off her coat and laid it over a tree branch. Unbuttoning her shirt, she exposed her chest. Itzhak turned away toward the tracks and the floodlights. She slipped off the shirt exposing smooth shoulders with bra straps looped over them. She pulled on the ruffled blouse and left the top buttons undone. Itzhak turned and surveyed her appearance in the shadows. He gave her an approving little nod, as if to say it might work.

"Hannah, you need a story to tell him," he said.

"I have a story. I'm a Polish girl visiting my uncle in the next village, went for a walk, and got lost. I am so cold," she said with a feigned shiver and coy smile.

"If it goes badly, use the pistol on him," Itzhak said. "I will be close by."

"I'll be alright," Hannah replied.

"Walk out of the woods and down the tracks," Itzhak said pointing out the direction. "I will slip across the tracks at the other end when you have his attention."

Hannah peered through the bushes, up and down the tracks. She could feel her heart pounding in her chest as she stepped out of the woods into the lighted area.

What am I doing out here? she thought. *Well, I should already be dead.*

"For Papa," she whispered, and walked up the tracks in full view of the German dispatcher.

Hannah glanced up and could see the man standing in the window. He jerked his head toward Hannah, startled, and stepped back from the window. She had to get him away from his office, to come outside and talk. Hannah went to the door on the side of the building. It was locked. Moving back into the view from the window, she looked up at the man and motioned with arms wrapped around her that she was very cold. Indeed, she was cold and could feel her cheeks and nose growing rosy in the night air.

"Please let me inside," she said, knowing the man could not hear her.

She tried motioning with her hands for him to open the door. She spread her coat, displaying the blouse, showing him that she had no weapons. Quickly wrapping the coat around her body, she sat down on a wooden barrel and pretended to weep.

After a few seconds Hannah looked up and the man was gone from the window. She heard the door latch click and the door to the station house squeaked open.

Hannah lifted her head from her lap and watched the German walk from the building toward her. He was middle-aged, perhaps forty, average height, and thinning black hair.

"I'm lost and cold," she said in Polish.

"Ahh, *sprecken zie Deutsch*?" he asked with a pained expression. "*Verstehst du mich*? Do you understand me?"

"*Ja*," Hannah replied. "Yes."

"Who are you? What are you doing out here in the cold? "

I need to keep this conversation going. Itzhak will need time to get inside, steal the information, and get out.

"I am Maria Petrovska," Hannah said in broken German. "From village over there somewhere, I think." She pointed down the railroad tracks.

"Visit uncle. Got lost in the dark. Cold and lost. Can you help me please?" she pleaded.

She tried to appear frightened and needing help. Hannah caught him glancing at her chest and figure.

"Come this way, my girl," he said, helping her to her feet and leading her toward the open door.

When he reached the door, the railroad man turned and asked abruptly, "You are not a Jew, are you? Because if you are, I could be arrested for helping a Jew."

"I am a Polish girl," she said in broken German. "I do not know much about them."

The man looked Hannah straight in the eye with suspicion. He smirked and turned back to open the door. She could sense his nervousness and thought he was probably doing something wrong by being with a girl while on duty. She hoped that his desire to be with her had taken him over. She had to keep him occupied for about ten minutes to give Itzhak enough time to slip in and out unnoticed. Feeling the pistol under her coat gave her a small measure of confidence. This man was no match for the big Ukrainian soldier. She managed to escape his grasp with the help of the farmer's knife. If this railroad man got fresh, she would handle him. He was wiry and did not seem to be very strong.

"Follow me," he said as he moved through the doorway. "And what is your name again?"

"I am Maria," she said, while following the man into the tiny, dark foyer. Only the light shining in from the outside doorway lit the area. A stairway rose to the second floor, probably to his office. On the left was a doorway into another room.

"I am the local dispatcher," he said, opening the door and flipping on the light switch. "An important job, it is."

Hannah peered into the room past his shoulder. It was a small bedroom with a desk and chair. Against the wall on the right was the bed. Hannah swallowed hard. This could be a trap. He might attack me and lock me in here. The soldiers were probably not far away and might even be on their way back.

Oh, Itzhak! Give me the sign when you're ready to leave. Please hurry!

"Why don't you sit on the bed and warm up?" he said.

"Well, I should only stay for a minute or two," Hannah replied, cautiously moving into the room.

"Here, sit down and rest yourself, Maria," the man said as he put his hands on her shoulders and steered her backward to the bed.

"I don't know if..." she said.

"You should take off your coat so the heat will warm you," he said quickly.

Through the small window Hannah was distracted by movement. In an instant, she caught a glimpse of Itzhak who motioned for her to leave. She looked at the German who was softly closing the bedroom door. She quickly glanced back at the window. Itzhak was gone.

She had to get out of there now. But how would she get past this man? She wasn't sure whether he locked the door or just closed it.

The man came across the room toward Hannah leaving barely enough space to pass by him and make it to the door.

Now is the time, go now! She got up from the bed and started across the floor.

"Oh, are you leaving so soon, my pretty *fraulein*?"

"Yes, I remember now. The way to my uncle's house. I must be off."

The German swept his arm around her, cradling her shoulder and waist as she tried to pass by him to the door. Hannah tried to squirm away from his grasp, but he was much stronger than she expected. He tightened his hold, wrapping his arms around her back and waist, pulling her into himself. With her body pressed tightly against his there was little she could do.

"Let me go!" Hannah yelled. "Help!"

Itzhak probably can't hear me. The pistol. I can't reach the gun. Images of that beast, Commander Bartowski, filled her head. The German's breath carried a faint odor of liquor, but nothing as strong as that of the vodka-drenched Polish army officer. It didn't seem possible that Itzhak would rescue her this time.

What did Barbara say to do? Oh, think, think! Yes! That's it! Stomp on the attacker's instep and grind your heel into the top of the foot. At the same time, drop directly to the floor. The element of surprise might loosen his grip. Then bolt for the door. The door. Is it locked? Did he set the lock? What if I reach the doorknob and it won't turn?

"You and I shall have a lovely time of it," the man said. A hideous smile showed yellow, stained teeth. "Won't we?"

"Let me go, I must go!" Hannah cried.

As she said that, Hannah looked down at the floor. She spotted his right shoe and immediately slammed her heel full force into his instep.

"Oww, oww," he shouted in pain.

Hannah pressed her arms tightly against her body and let her legs go limp. To her amazement, she slid right through his arms and plopped onto the floor in front of him.

Get to the door, oh, please open.

The man lost his balance in the commotion and fell backward. He stopped his fall with an outstretched hand to the desk.

"*Scheisse. Alles ist Scheisse,*" he yelled. "All is shit. *Steh' auf*! Oh, stand up!"

"Come back here!" he shouted. "*Saumensch, du dreckiges*!

With balance regained, the German stepped forward and swatted air missing her completely.

"Filthy pig. Why won't you get undressed?" he said with wild eyes.

Hannah sprung for the door and grabbed the knob. She thought her heart would stop if the thing wouldn't turn. He would be on her instantly. It all seemed to be happening in slow motion. She twisted the knob and it turned easily. Pulling the door open, she gasped the cold night air and lunged forward toward the railroad tracks. Instinctively, she shoved the door in the man's face as he started his pursuit. Hannah flung herself over the tracks and ran for the woods. Glancing over her shoulder, she saw the German trip on the tracks landing on all fours. She stepped into the woods. It was very dark and she lost her bearings for a moment.

"Over here!" Itzhak said in a muffled shout.

He found her hand and pulled her along through the underbrush.

"Are you alright?" he asked on the run.

Hannah felt sick to her stomach and wanted to stop and wretch.

Keep moving, just keep moving, she thought as the constant tug on her wrist from Itzhak's grip led her through the shadows.

Briars and tiny tree branches slapped her face and arms and legs as he pulled her steadily through the underbrush.

After several hundred meters or more, Itzhak stopped, slipping behind a large tree. He pulled Hannah to his chest and stood tall. They were both breathing hard, but he listened for sounds of pursuers. Hannah could feel her heart pounding violently. With her ear against his chest, she could hear Itzhak's heart thumping as well. The forest was quiet. They waited. Soon their breathing slowed and became more regular.

"The German gave up the chase," Itzhak said. "Now we must meet the others at the rendezvous."

Itzhak looked at Hannah's face in the dim light. Hannah felt as if she were falling away. She was numb inside. Everything seemed different. It was the German. How he touched her, grabbed her, wanted her in the station house. She wasn't really sure what was wrong. She and Beila had talked about sex in secret. But this was different. The German stationmaster did not act like Sol or Aaron back in the garden in Warsaw. It was confusing and sickening.

"Hannah, are you alright, Hannah?" he said, holding her and sensing that something was indeed wrong.

"No," she said. "I'm not alright."

"What did that German bastard do to you in there?" Itzhak said, gritting his teeth. "I'll kill the…"

"Take me home, Itzhak, please," she said softly. "I just want to go home."

"Can you walk now? The camp is a long way."

"Yes, go," she said, looking back toward the station house. "I can't do that again."

"I know. You won't have to." He lightly pressed her head against his chest. "I'm sorry I let you do it."

"Take me away from here," she said, stepping back from him.

"I'm so sorry," he said. "There should have been a better way to do it. My fault."

Hannah thought she had extended her hand to him, but it barely moved. Itzhak took her hand softly and with a gentle tug, they started off again for the rendezvous point at the big concert site. Slowly Itzhak increased his speed and Hannah followed in kind. He was much more careful this time to protect her from the briars and stinging branches on the path.

Hannah felt exhausted, mentally drained, and weak in the knees.

How much more of this running?

"Itzhak, can we rest soon? she asked. "How much farther?"

"Almost there, hold on just a little longer."

In about fifteen minutes they approached the old site. The memories of the explosion and impaled German soldier were still vivid. The boys were there waiting crouched in a defensive position, ready to tear into any enemy that approached. Itzhak took Hannah in his arms and found a soft place to lay her down.

"What happened?" Joseph exclaimed. "Is Hannah hurt?"

"I'll kill them," Boris said with glaring eyes. "I'll kill them all."

"No, we can't go back," Itzhak said. "We got the train schedule. Thanks to Hannah, they don't know I was there."

"So the mission was successful?" David asked.

"Yes, we got it," Itzhak said as Hannah turned her face away from the men.

"But at what cost?" David asked, looking at Hannah lying in the dry leaves and then glancing back to Itzhak.

Itzhak turned away, not wanting to talk.

"We should go back now," Hannah said, touching Itzhak's arm. "I'm ready."

. . . . .

They made it a few hours later to the outer sentries ringing the camp. Progress had been slow in the dark. Hannah held on feeling stronger amongst her friends. This time the Russian sentries gave them no trouble. Itzhak brought Hannah to her hut and made sure she was comfortable. He posted Boris and Joseph nearby to make certain no one would disturb her.

"Hannah, I have to report to the commander," Itzhak said as he left her. "I will check on you a little later. Try to get some sleep."

"Itzhak. Itzhak, if you weren't here, I don't think I could do this," she said. "I don't know who I am anymore."

"Just rest now. Sleep," he replied and quietly closed the makeshift door of her hut.

As she lay there, all the fear and pain of the past weeks flooded her mind. Hannah could think only of the men who attacked her, the pit, the cattle car, the Ukrainians, the German dying at the train wreck, and now the railroad man. With no idea how to deal with it, she decided to let it go. She would not allow herself to feel any of it anymore. No one would know. She would be strong inside. She would hold herself together. She would do whatever they asked. She would survive, somehow. Confused, disoriented, and utterly exhausted, Hannah fell off into a restless sleep.

Chapter Nineteen

Early in the morning, the camp was alive with activity. Hannah awoke to shuffling footsteps and muffled voices. She didn't feel rested, but numb more than anything. Looking herself over she realized she was still wearing the frilly blouse. It was not torn nor stained from the mission. But the thought of the German sickened her and she had to get the blouse off right away. Quickly changing, she folded it and started across camp. Not finding the Russian cook, she set the blouse on his seat and returned.

"Hannah, did you sleep well?" David asked when he saw her approach. He handed her a tin cup of steaming broth for breakfast.

Hannah thought for a moment and replied, "I'm alright."

But it was not true. The hot liquid should have revived her. It brought no satisfaction. Everything seemed dull and lifeless. She drank the broth anyway, because it would sustain her. She was ready for the next mission, whatever that might be. She didn't care anymore. The train schedule mission was successful, in spite of her trouble with the railroad man. Hannah didn't want to relive the scene. The schedule was the key to inflict another blow on the Germans before the winter snows set in. She understood the importance of getting the information. But she was losing herself and she knew it.

. . . . .

Almost a week had passed and Hannah wondered if they would be going after one of the trains on the captured schedule. Everyone thought it would be soon. The winter was nipping at Hannah's nose and ears. With every new day, the air was getting colder and the nights bitter. Even the sunlight looked dim. Memories slowly faded away. The old days no longer seemed to matter. The war and the death it brought left a dingy film on everything. Hannah wanted to cry, but no tears would come anymore. She worried that the old Hannah was disappearing. The new Hannah was empty. Except for the occasional clean-up at the old woman's cottage, there was little to look forward to.

. . . . .

Itzhak paced over to the group with a faint smile on his lips.

"I have news," Itzhak said. "A big shipment is scheduled for later today. We have a concert to do, so get yourselves ready. We set out in one hour."

Everyone seemed glad to be doing something other than sitting around waiting. The usual comments of bravado were passed around the camp. Hannah just watched them from her seat by her hut.

"I'm ready," Hannah said with no fear. Her own words sounded hollow and far away to her.

"You will be our best bomber," Boris said. "Your timing was perfect last time!"

"Yes, you will feel better when we move through the forest again," Joseph said with a smile.

Hannah just stared at the ground.

. . . . .

The forest was bright and the air crisp. The sharp sound of breaking sticks under Hannah's feet seemed to echo off of the tree trunks as they walked.

Could they make any more noise if they tried? She looked through the trees for an ambush. *We're going to be killed by careless feet.*

Everyone was toting a bag of explosives, about ten or so kilos each. It would make a big explosion. The trail looked familiar in the bright morning light. Hannah had traversed this path several times now. She guessed that the railroad tracks were only minutes away.

It's always heart-pounding as they approach a target. This time was no different. But this time Hannah felt strangely indifferent to the danger.

"Stop!" Itzhak said suddenly, holding up his hand to halt the column. "What is this?"

Hannah moved up with some of the others to get a better view. The tracks were not at the opening. As a matter of fact, the clearing was huge. Everyone stood speechless, with mouths gaping. The forest was cleared for nearly a hundred meters on either side of the tracks as far up the tracks as she could see. Anyone trying to reach the rails to place explosives was an easy target for German patrols or snipers. Even if someone were to place the charges without being seen, who could wait out there in the open to detonate the blast? This was bad.

"What are we going to do?" Joseph asked, glancing up and down the tracks.

"I'll go out there myself, I'm not afraid," Boris said, chin up in defiance.

"Wait. I need to think about this," Itzhak said.

Hannah could tell he was weighing alternatives. But there appeared to be little they could do to limit the risk. Then she remembered the first mission and what Itzhak had said.

This section of track is on the curve and blocked from view at both ends. That's good, she thought. Still, someone had to risk getting out to the tracks and placing the charges. Sitting out in the open waiting for the train, avoiding sentries, and having no trees for protection from the blast…that was suicide.

"I know a way, but it's still high risk," Itzhak said, his eyes gazing down the tracks toward the first curve.

"Well, how, Cousin?" David asked.

"I hope we have enough twine," Itzhak said.

"You mean to reach from here?"

"It's a hundred meters or more," Hannah said. "I'll go, place the charges, and wait."

"I will go with her," Boris said, stepping forward.

"No, wait," Itzhak explained. "We can tie all the detonators together and each line from the grenades we'll tie to one long pull cord."

"So all the grenades will detonate all the powder bags at the same time," David said. "Ingenious."

"Well, yes, if it works, and if we brought enough twine. Everyone, check your line," Itzhak said, determined to make his idea work.

"The good thing about it is that we might not get blown over by the explosion. Cut a piece for the section from your detonator to the endpoint of the main pull line," Itzhak explained. "Make each length a little longer as you place a bag away from the main pull line."

"Oh, I understand now," Joseph said. He helped the others measure the twine sections and they worked together to lay out a fan shape.

They quickly assembled a geometric pull string, moved out toward the nearest rail with packs, small shovels and weapons, trying not to tangle the separate lines of twine. Joseph located the center bag and then pointed to the spots where the other charges should be placed. Everyone frantically dug into the stone and gravel railroad beddings beneath the outside rail, placed the powder bags, and carefully set the grenades on each powder bag praying that none would detonate prematurely. Joseph signaled to Itzhak that all was ready.

"Let's get back to the woods. Be careful not to trip on the pull lines!" Itzhak shouted, louder than he wanted. As she turned to go, Hannah felt something tug on her leg and she stopped. She looked down at her trailing leg and in horror saw two pieces of twine taut as they pulled on the detonators. If a grenade exploded, they might all be killed in the blast.

"Hannah, don't move," Itzhak said, surveying the twine. "Everyone else, get back to the woods. I will take care of this."

He approached her, careful to avoid touching any of the lines.

"I am so stupid," she said, disgusted by her carelessness.

Itzhak got in front of Hannah putting his hands on her shoulders and applied a slight push to back her up.

"Itzhak, I'm losing my balance. Stupid, stupid."

"I won't let you fall. Straighten your back leg, make it stiff."

Hannah felt vibration under her feet and a distant rumbling. Itzhak looked up for a moment and listened.

"The train. It's coming now," she said, ready to panic. "Hurry."

I thought I didn't care about my life anymore. Then why is my heart pounding like this?

"I am going to push you backward. Let your back foot slide along the ground," he said.

"We're going to die here," Hannah said, eyes wild with fear. Somehow she thought to lock her knee and tense her body.

"No, we are not," he replied, placing his hands on her sides at the waist.

Hannah felt him shove her whole body backward. The soles of her shoes slid across the gravel freeing her from the twine which was left limp on the ground. Regaining her balance, she stepped carefully over the lines and was free.

"Run!" said Itzhak as he glanced over his shoulder in the direction of the rumbling sound.

I'm free! I'm free! It's coming. Forget everything, just run! Fast! Hannah pumped her legs with all she had in her. Itzhak stayed beside her running with long strides across the clearing.

They made the woods as the steam engine rounded the turn and came into view. Hannah and Itzhak got into position with the others. It was a freight transport with more than a few German guards on the engine and the following cars, all sporting weapons. Hannah saw the swastika emblem on the front of the locomotive and more markings on some of the train cars as they passed. David handed the end of the long detonator line to Hannah. She hesitated, not wanting to take responsibility after foolishly getting tangled in the twine.

"Hannah, take it. You have the luck," David said. "Remember the last concert. It was perfect."

Hannah looked at Itzhak. He nodded and gave her a reassuring smile.

She could feel the little voice rising up inside her—*take it, take it and blow those murderers to bits.* She tried to stop her hand from shaking as she wrapped the coarse twine across her palm.

Looking out at the passing train she asked, "When?"

"Any time now," Itzhak said, his voice confident and clear.

Hannah remembered the first time she pulled the string. She tugged on the line and brought it taut. All the legs of twine lifted off the ground. Dragging in a huge gulp of air, Hannah lunged away from the tracks and felt the tug of the line on her side and the wrapping squeeze her hand. The explosion was deafening. She was slammed forward by an invisible force punching her body face-first to the ground.

Hannah looked up and over her shoulder as a large cloud of dust and dirt spread over the whole area. Because they were positioned over a hundred meters from the blast, the concussion and flying debris was far less than the earlier mission. Bits of wood, rocks, and earth rained down into the trees and pelted the dry leaves around her. She rose to see everyone running toward her. Behind them off in the distance was the German train still derailing with the sickening moan of deforming steel and the crash of freight cars breaking apart over the bare ground.

"Move out! Move out!" Itzhak screamed as he bolted toward Hannah.

"What's happening?" Hannah cried, trying to clear her eyes from the gritty dust and acrid cloud of gunpowder. "Why are they running away from the tracks?"

She peered through the trees at the broken train once more. There were Germans everywhere. It was a trap! From the edge of the woods, Boris and Schlomo opened fire with their submachine guns.

Get out of here! She slipped on dry leaves and fell to one knee. Someone grabbed her arm and pulled her up into a run in one motion.

"There. Up there! Behind the fallen tree," Itzhak yelled, waving everyone to follow him. His jacket snagged on a briar bush. He yanked and pulled the cloth to free his sleeve and lunged forward toward the downed tree trunk.

Bullets ricocheted off the trees and thick branches as everyone ran for cover. Bark flew off of the downed trunk as bullets sprayed splinters into the air. Bullets whizzed by Hannah's head. She saw some of the others dive over the top of the trunk just ahead. One man tried to jump up on the tree and roll over it. He was hit in the back. It was a hollow thud and Hannah was sure he was killed. He fell forward, slumped over the trunk. From her left machine gun bullets were cutting along the trunk like a saw toward her. In a flash the deadly spray was on her.

Jump or be killed! Now! Hannah dove over the trunk.

She felt her foot snap back with a jolt up her leg, as if someone smacked the sole of her shoe with a hammer. Her body flew over the trunk and she crash-landed sliding headfirst into the dirt, sticks, and rocks. She could feel a burning sensation along the edge of her leading hand. But worse than that, her leg struck the trunk on the way down. A dull throbbing made its way to her consciousness from her bruised knee. Hannah gathered herself and quickly moved up against the backside of the tree trunk. The strap from her submachine gun was twisted around her neck and shoulders from the fall. She got untangled and pulled the lever back to cock the gun for firing.

Everyone from her side of the tree was firing frantically into the oncoming wave of German soldiers. She peeked over the trunk at the scene. Bullets grazed the bark around her head and Hannah snapped down behind the shelter. Her knee ached and her hand burned. She noticed that the sole of her shoe on the edge was torn open. The slap of her shoe on her dive over the tree must have been from a bullet. But she saw no blood and felt no foot pain. A near miss.

Peering down their line of fire, Hannah could see Itzhak shouting orders. It was clear what to do. These people were trying to kill her. She felt the cold steel of the PPS-42 in her hands. In spite of bullets flying all around, Hannah felt strangely calm, no fear. Her old life was gone. This was her new life.

She stood up exposing her upper body and opened fire against the oncoming soldiers. She waved the gun like a garden hose spraying a stream of water across the wall of charging uniforms. Men fell as they approached the tree trunk. Bodies piled up and the onslaught slowed and dispersed under the intense fire from Itzhak's squad. She dropped behind the trunk. The shelter was working well, but the Germans took cover behind trees and held their ground. More soldiers were pouring into the fight from behind their line. Itzhak made his way to Hannah, his eyes intense. Hannah thought she caught a flicker of doubt in his face. She rubbed her sore knee as more bullets tore at the trunk above her head.

"Three good men, good fighters, dead, so far," Itzhak said. "We have to give this up. They have too many men."

"What should I do?" she replied, searching his eyes, hoping he had a good plan, one of his tricks, anything. David crawled toward them. Hannah could see a trickle of blood streaming from his hairline down his temple to his cheek as he drew closer.

"Itzhak, we need to flank them or we will not get out alive," David said, peeking over the trunk.

Hannah was ready to do whatever was necessary.

"David, you and I can crawl through that depression to the left," Itzhak said, pointing to the spot.

"Flank them. Attack their right side while they are busy dealing with the frontal attack," David explained to Hannah. "Oh yes, I remember," she said, thinking back to Barbara and Pawel.

"I can do it!" she cried over the din of the fight. "You need to command the rest, Itzhak."

"She's right. You need to keep them busy while we get to their right flank," David said.

Itzhak looked at Hannah and David and nodded for them to go. She glanced back at Itzhak. *He's not comfortable letting me go. But I don't care anymore. If I'm going to die, then let it happen.*

She flipped on the safety lever of her PPS-42, got on her stomach, and crawled after David. Her knee was still aching, but crawling was less of a strain on it. She hoped the leg would support her when she had to stand or run.

Hoping the enemy did not spot their backs or heads above the slight rise of earth that provided them cover, they crawled along. About five or ten meters from the end of the tree trunk, the little depression turned at nearly a right angle. David kept moving forward five, ten, twenty meters and more. He stopped behind a tree. Hannah thought that was probably the best they could do for cover when they emerged from the ditch.

"Get ready, Hannah," David said, his forehead touching the hair above her temple.

She nodded and released the safety on the gun. They each got another magazine ready. David looked at her long and hard. With his hand, he mimicked how they would prop themselves up over the rise and fire into the enemy's right flank. She gave him another nod. They both lunged forward onto their stomachs and opened fire. A German was no more than three meters away, shooting at the main line of fire and Itzhak. David fired directly at him. Blood sprayed out the back of his neck and head. His helmet tipped forward coving his eyes and he slumped over in place. Hannah pulled the trigger on her gun and it fired into the enemy flank. Some turned in her direction, completely surprised, dropping in place. Many were close. Close enough to see the confusion and fear in their eyes. Hannah cut them down like they were paper targets. The image of the impaled soldier from the train wreck pushed into her head. *No, you people are going to die, too.* One soldier was about to throw a grenade. Hannah put her gun sights on the man's chest and fired into him. He went down face-first. The grenade hit the ground and exploded. The sound carried over the din of the battle. Shrapnel sprayed in every direction, taking down more Germans. Hannah felt something slap her forehead. She touched her skin with the back of her hand, checking for blood. Just dirt.

A wounded soldier crawled along the ground. She kept her finger down on the trigger. He raised his hand for help, but it went limp. He lay still as the other Germans pulled back from the heat of the crossfire. It was working. David fired in spurts. Hannah's gun stopped firing. Out of bullets. She pulled off the spent magazine and snapped a fresh one in place. Pulling back the bolt to cock the weapon, she looked over at David.

Sweat beaded on his forehead at the hairline. He was red-faced, jaw set.

"Let's go back to the group," he said and pointed. "Run and stoop low as you go."

Hannah started to run but her leg had stiffened up considerably and she could only hobble along.

"Are you hit?" he asked.

"No, I banged my knee," she yelled over her shoulder.

Sporadic fire continued as the pair reached the squad behind the trunk. Itzhak had three weapons slung over his head and was tugging at one of the wounded men.

"Are you alright?" he asked without looking up.

"We are mostly," Hannah said.

"Move out now," he said, waving the others to abandon the shelter and retreat into the deep woods before the Germans regrouped.

David grabbed another wounded man. Hannah pulled a couple of submachine guns off of Itzhak's shoulder to lighten his load. She found that if she locked her knee joint, she could stiff leg an awkward type of run. But she expected that that style of running would not carry her far. Following Itzhak and David, Hannah looked back toward the German lines and saw Boris, Schlomo, and Joseph still shooting to cover their retreat.

Itzhak moved at a moderate pace but made good progress and left the train far behind. Hannah figured the Germans must have had enough and not pursued them into the deeper forest. No one talked. The moans from the wounded being supported or half-dragged along the trail were the only sounds to break the silence. Hannah's leg ached now. She would have begged for a rest stop, but if the others carrying the wounded kept going, how could she complain?

A rustling from behind caught Hannah's attention and she tried to look over her shoulder without tripping over her sore leg. It was Joseph and only one other. Where was the third one? Which one was missing?

"Don't fall down, girl, or we'll all end up on our faces," said the gruff fighter behind her shouldering another wounded man.

Hannah thought his name was Slusky, but not being sure she just said, "I won't."

She had to know if Boris and Schlomo made it out alright.

I don't want to lose anybody else. Be back there, somewhere. Please… She grabbed her thigh with her free hand to help move her stiff leg back and forth. Finally, she saw a hand raised up ahead. Itzhak signaled that they were stopping. Looking up, Hannah saw a depression in the ground several meters wide and two or so deep. It would easily shelter the squad.

She reached the edge and tried to step onto the down slope with her good leg. The slope was steep. Damp leaves and pine needles gave way, her shoe sliding forward. She felt her weight shift and her rump hit the cold ground with a thud. Her bad leg got trapped under her body twisting her sore knee further. Wincing from the pain, Hannah could not hold back a yell. Skidding to a stop, the weapons jabbed her in the back and the leather straps tangled around her neck. Itzhak was lowering the wounded man to the ground at the edge, stopping short to avoid following Hannah who tumbled to the bottom.

She rolled off her hurt leg and stroked her knee. *Stupid*, she thought, expecting to hear the usual chuckles. The knee throbbed so that her eyes welled up with tears. *I'm not going to cry*. She clamped her jaw tightly.

"Let me help you, Hannah," David said softly as he untangled the gun straps from around her neck and lifted away the submachine guns.

Dried red streaks on his temple and cheek glistened with a thin coating of fresh blood trickling from his scalp. With the guns removed, Hannah rested on her back on the soft slope of the little crater. Men carrying wounded slowly negotiated the slope to the bottom of the depression.

"Where are the others?" she asked, rubbing her leg.

"Boris is here. We lost Schlomo," David replied.

"What? What do mean we lost him?" Hannah said, searching his eyes.

David shook his head slowly and then moved away. She laid her head back on crusty, brown leaves and closed her eyes. The soft moaning and occasional sharp yelps of the wounded kept her from drifting off. Everyone needed a rest.

A man jumped into the hole, stepping and sliding down to Hannah. She opened her eyes to find Boris sitting by her side.

"David says that Schlomo was killed. How did he die?" she asked. "Are you sure he was killed?"

"You don't want to know," Boris replied, eyes distant.

"How?" Hannah said, clenching her teeth.

"I am not going to tell you."

"I know what it is like to be all alone with killers chasing you through the forest." Boris looked away for a moment and said nothing. Itzhak settled next to him.

"Are you sure he's not out there alive and alone?"

"We all knew the risks, Hannah" Boris said, shaking his head in disbelief. But he did not seem to accept his own words.

"We had no choice to make," Itzhak said. "The Germans made it for us."

"He was shot through the head as we retreated," Boris said, head sagging. "He was my friend. He is not alone. He is with his family now. I am alone."

"Yes," said Hannah as she closed her eyes. She felt like a ghost. She didn't feel good or bad. Other than her throbbing leg, she didn't feel anything at all.

. . . . .

As the day wore on Hannah's leg ached and stiffened more. The badly injured got worse and the return passage to the camp slowed to a crawl. Well past sundown, the perimeter guards called for passwords. Hannah couldn't remember the code. Some came out from the camp to relieve the men carrying wounded. She wondered how any of them made it home alive. Her knee radiated a numbing pain so intense it took all her strength to take another step. Vladimir, the old Russian, saw her struggling. He grabbed her wrist and swung her arm across his shoulders. As he hoisted Hannah up off her bad leg, she let go with a sigh of relief.

"Thank you," she said, breathing heavily. "My knee. Not working anymore."

"You are safe now," Vladimir said, his brow wrinkled, eyes pained. "I will take care of you."

The men in the camp were surprised to hear three were dead, and most of the returning men were wounded. Some wanted to know about the transport train and how much was destroyed. Hannah couldn't talk about it. At her hut, Vladimir gently laid her down. He removed her shoes and covered her torso with the musty blanket and her coat. Totally spent, Hannah dozed in and out of sleep. She vaguely felt Vladimir checking her leg. He rolled up her trouser leg to inspect the injured knee. "Swollen, but probably nothing broken. I will get some things. Rest now," he said, leaving the hut.

Shivering, Hannah pulled her coat up to her chin. "Schlomo is gone, Papa," she said to herself. "Is he with you? Make him feel at home, Papa." She tried to look for Vladimir, but her eyelids were so heavy.

Vladimir returned with a wet rag, propped her leg up, and wrapped her swollen knee. "Better if this water was ice, but it is very cold. Need to get the swelling down."

"Huh, huh," Hannah groaned, half awake.

"Be still, my pretty girl, rest. I need to help more wounded. I will be back later. Try not to move your leg," Vladimir said, and he left.

Chapter Twenty

A few weeks later, the talk in the camp was that the Germans would be back in full force, but not until early spring with the snow melt. A couple of months to heal their wounds would be little to ask, in spite of the bitter cold of the forest. Hannah's knee was already healed. Vladimir had been right when he said it was only bruised. But Hannah developed a habit of rubbing it, even though it no longer hurt. Gazing at the snow lighting on the dark green pine branches surrounding her hut, she heard a couple of young men as they passed by.

"December third," the shorter one said. "It's the first night of Hanukkah. I wish we had a stack of latkes. I would eat the whole plate." They laughed, but Hannah could hear the emptiness in their voices. Bubbe Rachel and Mama made the best latkes. And the menorah. Papa always lit the center candle. Hannah held the honor of lighting each candle for the eight nights as they all sang the blessing. *We have no menorah. No candles to light.*

As she looked around the camp from her seat, a piece of firewood protruded from the pile lying next to the campfire. It was a split log of white birch. The wood was soft below the white bark. *Maybe we do have a menorah. I can try.* The farmer's jackknife was in her pocket. She punctured the wood, cut a circle, and stripped off the bark. Gouging out the soft wood, she carved indentations. Along the length of the log, she notched marks for candles, nine of them, and cut more spots evenly spaced. Maybe she could find something that looked like candles or candle flames.

Later that day, walking across the assembly area, her shoe struck something and it bounced along the footprints in the snow. A pinecone. Like a dreidel, it spun and rolled to a stop. Hannah picked it up and decided to search just outside the camp for more. Plenty lie hidden under the crusty snow. She chopped away with the toe of her shoe and uncovered a treasure of them, some rotten and some in good shape. She gathered a bunch.

On the stump outside her hut, she placed the log menorah and three pinecones, like dreidels, on the seat. One of the pinecones was sitting up on end. *A candle flame. It looks like a flame!* She placed it on the log at the center. *That's it. I don't need real candles. I'll set nine pinecones along the log.* She left the other three lying on the seat as dreidels with the menorah.

At the end of the day, as the sun set, beams of light glistened off the snow. Hannah removed all the pinecone "flames" except the center one. She placed one flame on the far right of the log menorah. *Sing with me, Papa. Sing.* She started singing softly to herself. "*Baruch ah tah Adonai, elo heynu melach ha olom.*" A man from behind added his voice. "*Ah sher kidish shanu bo mitz vo tav, vitsi vanu l'chod lik nair, shel Hanukkah.*" Hannah turned, red-faced. She thought no one would hear.

"My family stopped singing the blessing a long time ago," Joseph said. "But I guess you never forget the memories. I like your menorah, Hannah." He started to walk away.

"Would you sing with me each night, Joseph?"

"I will try, Hannah. It seems important to you.

"I didn't think so anymore, but I guess it must be."

"They refuse to be forgotten."

"What?"

"The memories," Joseph said, smiling as he walked away.

. . . . .

A few days later, reports came in about German troop movements. Hannah had seen Itzhak talking with the Russian commander for about an hour. Two other Russian team leaders were there also. One was Yuri. Hannah had not seen Yuri for some time. She thought he had gotten reassigned to another etrad. She watched from a distance hoping for a clue as to what was coming next. When Itzhak finally got up and walked toward her and the boys, she pretended not to be spying on the leader's meeting.

"Hannah, I need to talk to our group," Itzhak said.

"Is there news?" she replied, her eyebrows raised and forehead wrinkled.

"I am sure you know where I was just now," he said, glancing back at the Russian commander and his officers.

"The boys think we're finished with missions until spring," she said with a little smile.

"Well, we were until now." He waved the others to come.

"Another train?"

"No more concerts for now," he replied with a sigh.

Hannah repositioned herself on the tattered, stained remnant of a blanket she was using as a seat cushion. Even though her knee was healed, she occasionally felt the need to test it by bending the joint. It worked fine.

"Everyone, gather around," Itzhak said, waving them into a circle.

"What is the situation?" David asked.

"Well, the Germans are getting too much information through to their field commanders," Itzhak said. "At least that is what Soviet Intelligence thinks."

"So what are we supposed to do about that?" Hannah asked.

"Tellie lines?" asked Joseph.

"Yes. Three teams will strike the telegraph lines at different places along the main route," Itzhak replied. "Two Russian teams and ours."

"When?" asked Hannah, voice flat.

"I am not sure yet. In the next couple of days I think," he replied.

"We need saws, cutters, tools," Joseph said. "Do the Russians have them? We don't."

"They are supposed to supply us with tools and our target location along the Vilna Road," Itzhak said. "But we might have to pay a visit to one of our not-so-friendly farmers on the way."

"Can't we just blow up the telegraph poles?" David asked. "Much quicker and easier."

"Well, I can think of at least three reasons why we shouldn't," Itzhak said, suppressing a smile.

"Like what?" David asked with his hands on his hips.

"First, too noisy, might bring the Germans running," Itzhak replied. "Second, we need the powder for the transports."

"So what is the third?" David said in disgust.

"Well, it's that you are getting too fat, Cousin," Itzhak said as he poked David in the belly. "Must be all that fine vegetable soup! Some exercise is certainly in order."

Everyone looked at Itzhak and then at David and all burst out laughing at once.

Hannah watched the reactions of the others who were pointing in jest at David's stomach. It was David's expression. He was always so serious. Trying to convince anyone that he was not chubby was pointless. Hannah felt herself let go inside and a laugh started. She caught it.

"Oh, it's not *that* funny," David said, trying to act serious while failing to hold back a grin.

At that, Hannah couldn't hold it in anymore. It was alright to laugh. Free of the weight, she let it all go, laughing out loud. Everyone could hear her, her white teeth glistened, her eyes filled with tears. They laughed together, like a family. Like they were all home again.

Hannah looked over at Itzhak. At that moment she knew he was a great leader. He knew how to command. He knew when his people reached the breaking point and needed relief. She laughed with everyone but could not take her eyes off of him. He was smart, but that was not all. Everyone liked him. He was brave, yes, but more. It was all those things put together. Most of all they trusted him with their lives. He never lied to them.

He's never lied to me, thought Hannah. *I trust him. I think I might even love him.*

She thought about everything they had been through together. She wondered what love should be like. She had no idea what to do about her and Itzhak.

. . . . .

Over the next few weeks the weather turned raw. Snow on the ground did not melt off in the sun anymore. Hannah wondered if she could stand the cold living in the hut. When she saw David in the camp, she had to smile. The memory of their laughter was healing, as if it were medicine covering a wound. Her wounds were too deep for a small bandage of laughter. But it numbed the pain inside enough for her to think clearly and go on.

Itzhak called the team together and handed out tools, a couple of two-man wood saws, work gloves, and wire cutters. Hannah packed up extra ammunition, some carrots and crackers somebody took from a local farmer, thick leather gloves, and wire cutters. She assumed some of them would have to climb up the telegraph poles and clip live wires. Or maybe they would saw the poles off at the ground. She wasn't sure how they did it, but she definitely did not want to shimmy up poles and risk getting shocked.

"Time to move out," Itzhak said to the team as everyone gathered around him.

"Ready," Hannah said, slipping her gun strap over her shoulder.

Itzhak took the lead with Boris covering the rear as usual.

Hannah was worried about Boris. He looked sad, his mind far away since seeing Schlomo go down. Boris had been nice to her from the beginning and she never forgot his kindness. He was a great fighter and could be trusted to give up everything if need be. Hannah stayed near the back of the line, just ahead of him.

. . . . .

The target was the telegraph line along the Grodno-Vilna road. It was an important communications line and the three units needed to do considerable damage. Whether Germans or Ukrainians would be guarding the road, Hannah no longer had much fear of them. The boys said that this far north, Lithuanians might be with the Germans.

No matter.

Itzhak would choose a section where the enemy was not patrolling or he would do away with them. They'd be alright. Too much ground for the Germans to cover. At the worst, a German squad or two might be on the road.

Hannah was more concerned about climbing telegraph poles and clipping live wires. The city worker in Warsaw stuck in her mind. She was only nine when the accident happened. Burnt hands, eyes staring into the sky. The man lay on his back on the sidewalk, dead. Papa said he was shocked with electricity.

Despite the snow-covered ground, the three units made very good time. Hannah felt warmed by the fast pace through the forest. The last of the Russian units were just ahead of Itzhak. Following the Russians meant that they would make enemy contact first and the shooting would be an early warning to take cover.

The groups ahead stopped to rest. Itzhak signaled a stop, too. Hannah looked for Boris. He had brushed snow off a fallen tree, sat down, and stared at the ground between his feet.

"I have carrots and crackers, Boris," Hannah said, approaching him.

"No, thanks."

"I have enough to share," she said between chews. She held out a carrot to Boris and took a sip from her canteen. He shook his head no. The carrots snapped as she bit down and tasted the raw vegetable on her tongue. Hannah scanned the group. Most of the squad carried something to eat. Stale bread, crackers, apples, or whatever was taken from the Nazi collaborators. *They're all talk, no fight, until we turn our backs. I don't care if those traitors starve. I have to eat.*

"I have more for later if you want, Boris," she said, worried that Boris seemed too quiet.

By noon the lead Russian unit reached the road. Word filtered back through the second Russian team. They would be at the road and exposed in minutes. Hannah could feel her heart pounding as the men ahead of her stepped up their pace. She emerged from the woods into the clearing and glanced up and down the road. They would be exposed to German patrols, Ukrainians, Lithuanians, reconnaissance planes, local villagers, and farmers, anybody who might come along at any time.

I don't like this at all. What if we're spotted? This could be another trap like the last mission. The only way out is back into the forest. If the enemy crept into the woods behind us…well, I don't like it.

Looking left and then right, Hannah guessed the distance could be a couple of kilometers. Uneasy, she stepped up to talk with Itzhak.

Itzhak was watching Yuri for a sign. Yuri led the team in the middle. He coordinated the Russians up ahead and his own platoon in the middle. He was signaling everyone to spread out as far as they could stretch and start cutting wires and sawing poles.

Hannah watched Yuri for a moment. He looked impressive in his army uniform, giving commands. *I wonder if we will ever be friends…maybe more.* Boris stepped up to her side.

"You do not like to be out in the open like this, do you? The Russian. Brave, yes?" Boris said, pointing with his finger at Yuri. "I hope smart, too, or he'll get us all killed on this road. I need more time to kill Germans."

"He was very kind to me on our mission to get the artillery shells."

"Ah. You like him then," Boris said, a quick smile replaced by clenched teeth.

"I don't know. He's not easy to understand."

"He's a communist. They have their own way of seeing the world. Me, I see it one way. Kill the ones that kill your people. Schlomo did not have much time to think about the world. Someone will pay for that."

"I'm sorry for Schlomo," Hannah said, head hanging low. "I miss him, too."

"We'll see how this Russian does when things go bad." Boris stepped ahead for a better look up the road.

I don't think Yuri cares about politics. He seems to know how different people think and who to watch out for. I hope he thinks about me.

She watched Yuri move his men farther down the road. Itzhak

positioned his group on the next set of telegraph poles. No one seemed to be covering the approaches.

Stop Yuri-daydreaming. Ask Itzhak who is guarding the approaches. I can do one side. Don't want to climb poles.

"Itzhak, Itzhak," she said, touching his arm. "Does anyone have the road covered at either end?"

"What do you mean?" he asked, sounding annoyed and a little confused.

"I mean, we are totally exposed to the enemy," she said. "What if a patrol comes along? We will have no warning."

"Then we will fight it out," he said. "If too many men, then we will jump back into the woods and sting them good before retreating. Besides, we have too few fighters to spare from doing the work."

"But what if…" she started to say.

"It will be alright. We have done this many times," he said, pointing to the top of a pole. "Can you climb that pole and cut all those wires?"

She was afraid he would ask her to do that. A trickle of fear ran through her.

"No, I don't think so," she said, while remembering how she would climb the small tree in their backyard when she was only five. Papa wondered how such a little girl had so little fear of falling. But things had changed. There was no Papa under the tree to catch her now. The face of the electrocuted worker in Warsaw flashed in her mind.

"Hannah, the men are all sawing. I need someone to go up there and cut wires," Itzhak said. "You are small, I'll give you a boost to get you started."

Reluctantly, Hannah put on the thick leather gloves that were much too large for her hands and stuck the wire cutters in her jacket pocket. He also handed her a carpenter's hammer. Not sure what that was for, she took it rather than argue.

Hannah shimmied up the telegraph pole feeling sharp splinters poke her inner thighs through her coarse trousers. At about five or six meters up she reached the wires suspended from the adjacent poles and stopped to rest. She looked around. *Actually, we pole climbers have a much better view than they do.* She felt a wisp of a smile on her lips. *I can do both jobs at once, lookout and wire-cutter.*

"That's it. Now be careful not to touch anything. Just snip each wire and smash off the insulator with your hammer," Itzhak called up to her. The gloves were cumbersome and she struggled trying to get the wire cutters in position on the wire with one hand while holding onto the pole to keep from falling with her other hand. It was colder being high up in the air and she welcomed the warmth of the thick leather. Looking down the pole, she could see the tops of the men's hats and her submachine gun lying at the base of the pole.

If somebody comes down that road now, I'm really in trouble. I'd never get down there to the gun in time. She squinted at the distant stretch of road and saw nothing. Not sure whether she would feel an electrical shock through the tool and gloves, she positioned the tool and squeezed the handles together as hard as she could. The wire snapped and went careening down to the ground. It didn't hurt at all. As a matter of fact, it was easy. It was the easiest damage she had done in her short career as a partisan. Hannah couldn't stop grinning. She snapped and snapped as wires tumbled down in a contorted mess on the cold ground.

"Excellent! Now take your hammer to those ceramic and glass insulators," Itzhak called up to her.

"These?" she asked. She pointed the hammer at a dull white insulator that kept the wire from touching the wooden crossbar and pole.

"Yes, try to smash it with your hammer," he replied.

Hannah had seen Papa and other men hit nails and stakes with hammers but had never tried it herself. She gently set the hammerhead on the insulator and threw it up and back over her shoulder. She gritted her teeth and took a healthy swipe at the object. Missing it, she nearly lost her balance and barely checked her fall.

"Maybe we'll do that on the ground," Itzhak said, chuckling.

Hannah felt a bit insulted at his laughter, but agreed it was better to swing hammers from the ground than from hanging off a pole high in the air. Suddenly, she felt a vibration from the pole through her inner thighs. Looking down, she spied David and Joseph handling a two-man saw, already partway through cutting her pole off just above the ground.

"Hey! Let me down!" she yelled and started to make her way down the pole.

"Oh, look! It's a little kitten caught up in this tree," Joseph said, grinning ear to ear. "Maybe she needs a rescue."

"Oh, you two just wait," she said, playing along. "The kitten may be a tiger!"

"Alright, you two, let her down," Itzhak said, sounding more serious than before.

"Yes, Cousin, but I thought perhaps we would win an award for this daring rescue," said David.

"You have, Cousin. An extra ladle of soup will be your prize," Itzhak said, patting his stomach.

"You are too generous," Joseph said, tipping his hat while removing the saw from the pole.

"Thank you," Hannah said as she shimmied to the ground and stepped away from the pole. "Hsss!" she said, making a claw and scratching motion at the boys as she passed by.

She spotted the next pole down the line that was already sawn down and lying on the ground. Taking hammer in hand, she strode over the dead telegraph wires and began smashing the insulators to bits. One after another, Hannah worked feverishly, leaving small deposits of slivers and nuggets of the material on the frozen shoulder of the road. It felt good to hit back, and swinging the hammer was warming her body. She gritted her teeth and slammed another insulator to bits. A tiny smile of victory spread over her face. Out of breath, she finally dropped the hammer at her feet, stood up, and looked back at her handiwork. Fifteen poles were destroyed. And that was just part of the damage Itzhak's unit accomplished. The best part was that none of the enemy appeared.

They were just about done when Yuri yelled down the road to Itzhak. He was pointing to the sky and signaling all teams to move quickly into the woods. Just then Hannah could hear the distant sound of an airplane. She grabbed her submachine gun and tools and ran for cover into the trees. Looking up and down the road, everyone was yelling, waving, and running. Everyone, that is, except Boris. He stood on the shoulder of the road with submachine gun pointed up toward the sound of the plane.

"Boris, Boris, get out of there! Run!" Itzhak screamed.

"Boris, Run! Now!" Hannah yelled, bobbing up and down on her toes from the edge of the woods.

Bullets ripped up the shoulder and road in two lines as the German fighter roared overhead. Hannah saw the black crosses on the fuselage and wing tips as the plane streaked by. Boris fired at the propeller and engine and continued with short bursts into the soft underbelly of the fighter. Miraculously, the rain of bullets from the fighter plane passed on either side of Boris. He was jumping up and down and screaming wildly. Itzhak and Hannah looked across at each other, silently acknowledging what needed to be done. She dropped her tools with the nearest man and together Hannah and Itzhak ran fast for Boris.

"The plane is coming back. Get into the woods," Itzhak yelled as they approached the distraught Boris.

"Leave me alone!" he shouted. "They killed Schlomo."

"The plane is coming back," Hannah said. "Schlomo would not want us to die here like this."

"No. I will shoot the German down," Boris said, looking into the sky.

Hannah looked at Itzhak and shrugged. Itzhak frowned. They could hear the plane's engine way off in the distance. This time the pilot wouldn't miss.

"Boris, three of us will die here," Itzhak said. "One German, three of us."

"No, you two go back," Boris shouted, waving them off and pointing to the woods.

The Messerschmitt appeared over the trees. Hannah could see fire from the plane's machine guns. Streams of bullets tore up the ground about two hundred meters away and closing. The bullets were only seconds away from cutting the three of them down. Itzhak signaled Hannah to follow his lead. He grabbed Boris's bicep slipping his other arm under the wild man's armpit. Shoulder to shoulder, Itzhak pushed Boris backward toward the trees. Hannah did the same, grabbing and pushing Boris from the other side. The air sizzled just behind their heads as the bullets whizzed by, spraying dirt, snow, and ice particles as the lead melted harmlessly into the ground.

"Alright, alright, let me go!" Boris said, twisting against their grip. "I'm alright. I'm going."

Hannah glanced at Itzhak. He gave her a slight nod and they both let go at once. Boris hesitated and then moved toward the trees. They all entered the woods together and joined the others. Nobody said anything. The men probably understood about Boris. The Russian teams were already moving out as they approached. Hannah saw Yuri look back at her. His face showed no expression. She wanted to tell him somehow that her unit was alright, not to be concerned. Maybe he understood.

Sometimes I think Yuri wants to protect me. He's been away for a while and things change quickly in this place. Maybe that's why he looked back at me? I don't know.

"Pick up your tools and move out before the whole German army is on us," Itzhak said. "They sent that fighter plane for reconnaissance when their communications dropped. They might come looking for us. If we get separated, follow the Russians and make your way back to the camp."

Boris normally took up the rear guard, but Hannah was not sure that was a good idea. She told Itzhak she would cover their backs with Boris. Itzhak nodded. Hannah knew Boris was on the edge over losing Schlomo, but acting like a madman put the whole team at risk. Everyone missed the trustworthy, dependable fighter, but not the way Boris did. He hurt badly. They would finish a sentence before the other spoke. Like brothers. Everyone assumed that time would do the healing.

Itzhak won't let that happen again. That cannot happen again.

The teams moved quickly through the forest to the encampment without incident. The sentries just nodded to Hannah as she passed through the outer perimeter line. She was now a familiar sight to the Russians. It was always a relief to reenter the camp with no one injured and most important, no one dead. Hannah wondered how many more times she would return from a mission unharmed, or return at all.

This was a good day. Itzhak and Yuri said they took down seventy-three poles in total and set the Germans back a few weeks. The operation was well worth the effort. Hannah was hungry and tired and cold. The hot supper warmed her insides. She was grateful for their good luck. With Yuri on her mind, she settled into her hut and fell off to sleep with little effort. She tried to think of a prayer to say to thank Adonai for her safe passage but drifted off before any words came to mind.

. . . . .

Hannah awoke to a commotion not far from her hut. She could hear yelling in Polish, Russian, and Yiddish. Pulling off her old blanket and putting on her coat, she stood up and took one big step to the flimsy hut door. Peeking through the cracks, she saw one of the Russians from Yuri's platoon. His dark stubble beard and fierce black-as-coal eyes were menacing. Boris was waving his arms about, his head bobbing in and out only millimeters from the Russian's face. The two pushed and shoved fingers at each other's chest to emphasize their points. As she struggled to interpret, Hannah heard something about putting the whole etrad in danger and something about the German pilot. Boris switched between Yiddish and Polish, neither of which the Russian seemed to know. Hannah could make out some of the shouting.

"Who are we here to kill?" and "Was that a German in the plane?"

This can't go on for much longer. Maybe I should try to stop it.

Hannah moved back into her hut and put on her shoes. As she stepped out of the hut, Yuri and Itzhak came running from different directions, converging on the scene. A fistfight was about to break out and many in the camp now stopped to watch.

"Boris, back off!" Itzhak shouted, glaring at his man.

Hannah did not grasp the Russian commands spewing from Yuri directed at his fighter, a man at least ten years older. Itzhak and Yuri got between the men to break up the argument. Itzhak put his hands on Boris's shoulders and stepped toward the man. Nose to nose, he said, "I need you to stop this. Now. Right now!" Itzhak's eyes were strong and unbending. Hannah had not seen Itzhak's power before. Not like this. Boris shifted his eyes from the Russian man to Itzhak's stare. His shoulders dropped and he nodded, eyes still intent on Itzhak's face.

Yuri was taller, and his man could now see only Yuri's chest. His man took a few steps backward, then half-saluted, turned, and walked away. Hannah moved toward Boris and tried to talk with him as he went by. He shrugged her off, angry and frustrated, still playing the fight over in his head. Hannah gazed back and saw Itzhak walking away and Yuri just standing in the middle of the camp staring at her.

Why is he looking at me? He wants to talk?

Yuri slowly strolled over to Hannah. *He's going to say something about Boris, I suppose.*

"Good morning," Yuri said in crisp Polish. "Would you talk with me for a moment?"

"You sound so formal," she replied. "I hope my people have not caused a big problem."

"No. Not really," he said, clearing his throat. "Can we take some breakfast and perhaps walk a little?"

"It *is*, well, it *was* a good morning, until they started that argument, I guess," Hannah said, stealing a quick glance to read Yuri's expression.

"Would you mind some old-fashioned Russian cooking?" he asked.

"That would be a welcomed change from breakfast soup," Hannah replied, curious about this "chance" meeting.

"I am afraid the menu is not much different from yours," he said, chuckling.

"It'll be fine."

"This way then?" Yuri asked, pointing toward the Russian side of the camp.

"Yes," Hannah said, feeling an odd sensation, like a girl rather than a soldier.

A few men passed by in the opposite direction. One gave Yuri a quick salute. Two men sat by their huts, talking quietly while cleaning their weapons. Hannah spotted Vladimir up ahead, hovering over a steaming kettle on a charcoal fire. She breathed in the smoky food scent drifting on the breeze as they approached.

"Ah, good morning, young miss," Vladimir said, a toothy smile covering his face. Hannah caught the sly eye contact he made with Yuri as he passed two large tin cups to him.

There was something different about the soup. It was so rich, not like the regular stuff. She noticed that he poured it from that smaller pot on the fire.

"This is the old-fashioned Russian breakfast, then?"

Yuri's cheeks reddened as he looked away.

"Well, I will not lie, it is a special mixture concocted by our 'Vladimir the Great' here," he said, glancing at the old cook and back to Hannah. The potato was sliced into little pyramid-shaped chunks, like Bubbe used to do it. Carrot strips, too, floated to the surface.

Hannah sipped the special brew. "It smells and tastes like home," she said, thinking of Warsaw and the little suitcase under the tree in Sokolka.

The concoction warmed her. Hannah could see the gray landscape brighten a little. She was on a date with a boy, a very handsome young man. He was polite, but much more than that. She felt safe with him. More than that, *comfortable.*

"Thank you, Vladimir," Hannah said, nodding.

"Yes, a fine meal, thank you," said Yuri, handing back his cup to the cook. Vladimir just smiled and went back to stirring the kettle.

"Let's walk," Yuri said pointing toward an opening in the trees beyond the cooking area. "There is a small open area not far off camp on the east side," he said, once out of earshot of Vladimir.

Obviously, a secret place. Vladimir knows it. He knows everything.

"I go there sometimes to think and to be alone. Very peaceful."

"I'd love to see it," Hannah said. She looked at the ground, afraid to make eye contact.

"This way, then." Yuri pointed to a small path through the evergreens and brush.

"Oh, I don't have my gun with me," Hannah said, realizing she was breaking the first rule of combat.

"I have a pistol. You'll be safe."

They strolled on for a couple of hundred meters. The woods became very dense and dim.

"You know what that argument was about, do you?" he asked.

"Was your man complaining about Boris and the German plane?" she asked.

"Yes, he said that your Boris gave up our safety by letting the Germans know our location."

"We lost several fighters on the last transport mission. One was his best friend."

"Yes, I remember that well."

"Boris is still suffering."

"I saw you out there trying to get him to shelter," he noted. "I was worried you might be hit by the fighter plane."

"Oh," Hannah said, feeling a little embarrassed and excited at the same time.

"We are close," Yuri said, pointing ahead and glancing down at Hannah. His smile looked tight. She thought maybe he was nervous, too.

Up ahead, the path narrowed. Yuri took hold of Hannah's hand and led the way. His hand was large and warm. It engulfed hers. Calluses on his palm felt coarse against her skin. She was supposed to be soft. Soft like a girl. She had been trying so hard to be like men, but she didn't always feel like one. Hannah thought of Beila as she ducked under low-hanging sapling branches and followed him in. On the other side, they emerged into an open area a half-dozen meters across. The morning sun broke through the winter sky and warmth streamed into the little isolated world that Yuri had discovered. Yuri turned and faced Hannah. He gently rested his hands on her shoulders. She looked up into his eyes.

Yuri bent over and slowly moved his face to Hannah's. His stiff whiskers brushed and poked her chin as their lips met, soft, delicate, tender. Yuri slid his arms around Hannah's sides and back. She felt his arm muscles harden as he pulled her into his body. Her breasts pressed hard into his expanding chest. She had a brief thought to stop him, but that fleeting notion was gone in an instant. Lips parted, she opened her eyes, the pores of his skin and the hint of an old scar just under his eye were so close now. She could feel his heart pounding strongly, or was it her own? His body smelled like a man. She closed her eyes again. Their lips met. Hannah had only imagined how love and kissing would feel. She quickly realized that she had no idea how wonderful it could be.

As their lips parted the world slowly came back into focus. She had never experienced anything like that before. She didn't think much of boys her age. This was different. This was another world. She craved for him to do it again.

Yuri looked gently into her eyes. His were penetrating, but kind and safe. Her body rose to meet his lips. She felt Yuri's arms tighten around her lower back. One hand slid smoothly up her spine between her shoulder blades, his bicep sliding across the side of her breast. His large hand cradled the back of her head, softly sweeping over her ear, fingers sifting slowly through her long hair. He gently tilted her head. She let go and just let him move her body any way he wanted.

Nothing could be as good as this. I wish we could stay here like this forever.

All the pain and hate and sorrow of the past months were suspended. She knew nothing could make war or grief go away. But this was heavenly. Yuri was gentle. So gentle.

Hannah vaguely heard men's voices in the distance. She pushed back on Yuri's chest. Their lips separated.

"Did you hear that?" she whispered.

"Yes, don't worry, they are Russian," he said quietly, releasing his arms.

The voices trailed off in another direction.

"It's not good if we are seen like this," she said, looking around.

"No, I suppose not," he replied. "We must get back."

"Yes," she said, wishing the moment didn't have to end.

"I hope you do not think that I tricked you to come here."

"I don't feel tricked," Hannah said and smiled.

"Good. Let's go back," Yuri said, his hand lightly on her shoulder. "Perhaps we can meet here again soon."

Hannah nodded and started for the path, the only way out of the little clearing. No one was around as they made their way back. Hannah split from Yuri and waited for him to enter the camp. Then she strolled in from another direction. Nobody seemed the wiser.

Chapter Twenty-One

January 20, 1943. No one knows it's my birthday. Sixteen now. Not much to celebrate. She clutched her tin cup of soup. *Nobody is baking cakes out here. Where would they put the candles? In the soup?*

Hannah stared at the cup. She figured she had paid for her share of the food in more ways than one. But she didn't consider herself entitled to anything special. Being alive meant something. No longer did she think herself a newcomer. She felt as much a partisan fighter as anyone. There was nothing more to do but keep going.

Winter brought with it colds, fever, and chills that afflicted the undernourished. Many were sick, but none would complain. The food stock was almost gone. Thus far, Hannah had only contracted a cold and with it an incessant snivel. All and all a minor condition, considering the influenza and fever others in the camp were dealing with.

It was Hannah's turn to pay a visit to the local farmers and villagers, the German collaborators. The usual targets were hit on a regular basis, so Boris and Hannah were assigned a less frequented villager.

The camp was quiet. Many stayed to themselves, nursing their sicknesses. Crisp, pungent evergreen-scented air filled Hannah's lungs, a relief from a stuffed-up nose. She spotted Itzhak moving toward her, red-faced and hulking under an old blanket.

"It's time, Hannah. You and Boris? What do you think?" Itzhak said, breaking into a hoarse cough.

"I think I can trust him. He usually listens to me. In the end anyway." Hannah caught a faint whiff of liquor on Itzhak's breath. *I hope that is "cough medicine vodka" and not "vodka for Zosia." Maybe I better warn David to keep an eye on him.*

"Alright, but this one is a Volksdeutscher. Don't let him open his mouth outside the house or half the village might show up. There are a few of them in that village," Itzhak said, peering through bloodshot eyes.

Hannah knew the term—Poles who proudly claimed to be of German descent. These people were some of the worst, according to Boris. Never trust them. At the slightest suspicion, they would contact the SS. Stealing food from them almost guaranteed it.

They moved briskly through the forest and approached the hamlet. A dozen cottages, drab shacks, and unpainted wooden outbuildings dotted the open area. Most trees were bare, not many evergreens. Without natural cover, Hannah could see more and more houses as they approached.

Volksdeutscher. Open line of sight. Not a good feeling here, Hannah thought, looking around for anyone who might be watching. She also hoped that Boris had gotten more accustomed to Schlomo's death by this time. Acting brave is risky and not helpful. Surely not for moving about secretly.

"Itzhak told me this collaborator, this Bekel, lives at the north end on the outskirts of the village," Hannah said, spotting some movement behind Boris. "Do you know which house, Boris?"

"I was here a long time ago," he replied, gritting his teeth. "But I will find this miserable Volksdeutscher."

"I want to get in and out without attracting attention," she said, hoping Boris could restrain himself. A blue and white bird fluttered about in the trees and cried out a warning for the rest.

"This man will scream and carry on," Boris said. "When he does, I'll take him down."

That sounds like trouble. He is still a quick fuse, ready to explode.

They moved along the outskirts to get a better view.

"There. The one with the tin roof."

"And the red brick step, that one?"

"Yes, let's get him."

She needed a plan and one popped into her head when she saw where Bekel's house was situated. Remembering her first real action with the villager, Kazieba, Hannah thought to approach the house alone and place her submachine gun just out of sight.

How am I going to get Boris to follow my plan? He'll want to slam open the door and poke his weapon into the man's face. If he starts yelling outside the house, we'll really have problems.

"Boris, I will knock on the door and play the hungry peasant girl. Maybe they will let me inside without a fuss? Then you follow behind."

"No, I can slam the door open and we will go in fast," he said, glaring at the cottage.

"No, I am in charge. We will do it my way."

"This Volksdeutscher," Boris said, pointing at the cottage. "He will start shouting and we will have to kill him."

Scanning the hamlet again, the place was quiet. "Look, nobody is around. I'll get inside. I need you to follow me, Boris. Will you do that?"

Boris let out a deep breath and looked away. He nodded.

"Alright then, let's go," Hannah said, slipping the gunsling off her shoulder. She carried the weapon at her side as she approached the house. At the door, she gently placed the gun just out of sight from the doorway, but still within easy reach. She glanced back to Boris who gave her a slight nod. She then knocked on the door, lightly. No response.

Not home, she thought, and glanced back to Boris hiding behind the large tree off to the side of the cottage. *Be a hungry farm girl.* She knocked four times, and louder than before.

Suddenly, the door latch clicked and a paunchy, middle-aged man stood in the doorway.

"What do you want?" he said, lips puckered and eyes watery.

"Excuse me, sir, but I am lost and very hungry," she said, pulling her coat tight. "Could you spare a little food?"

"Who are you?" he said, looking Hannah up and down then glancing out into the yard. "You look like a Jew, no?"

Hannah felt a twinge of fear and stepped back out of the doorway. She swept up her submachine gun in a flash and pushed her way inside. The man was startled when the barrel of the gun pressed into his chest.

Seeing Hannah's movement, Boris came running.

"Oh, so you are a bandit and a Jew too," he exclaimed, red-faced and pouting. "I should have slammed the door in your face. This is what I get for being polite to a Jew."

Just then Boris burst into the cottage. Hannah motioned him to stop, but he just kept coming at the villager.

"Oh, so more bandits come to rob me," the man said with a smirk. "I should, no, I *will* turn you over to the SS. You can be sure of it."

"Bandits! Bandits! Papa, Papa!" a young boy about five or six yelled from the doorway of the next room.

"Yes, Jew bandits, Jozef, here to steal from your poor grandfather," the man said to the boy, his nose now bright red, mouth scowling.

"We will take whatever food we want, from an SS collaborator like you," Boris said. "Why don't you tell the boy what you really are?"

Hannah could see the mix of fear and anger in the little boy's eyes. She felt as much a thief as the man accused her to be. But they were pushed to it, backs to the wall. It was take or starve. Hannah stuck the muzzle of her gun in the man's face and backed him into the kitchen.

"Move," she ordered and gestured with her chin.

The little boy ran over to Hannah and began punching her wildly. She looked down and saw the determination on his face.

They are teaching him well to hate us. Not his fault. She gently pushed him away with her leg. Boris had found a couple of burlap bags and was busily stuffing cans, vegetables, fruit, and flour into a bag. Hannah stood guard over the man while his grandson continued to strike at her legs and side. The boy had no real force behind the blows. She remembered when she was little. So simple then. She would let the boy be but would not back down from the Volksdeutscher traitor. They'd be gone in a minute or two.

"Ahhh, ahhh," a woman screamed from the back door.

Boris dropped the bag and rushed across the kitchen to the

woman in the doorway. He reached her in a moment and grabbed her by the throat. The screaming was cut short, but not soon enough. Through the multipaned window in the dark living room, Hannah could see a neighbor step outside and look around.

"Shut up, woman," Boris said, nose to nose, grinding his teeth.

"So you bandits attack my defenseless wife, a gentle grandmother," the man said, scowling. "I will be most happy to turn you over to the authorities."

Glancing back to the window, Hannah saw two men in a yard talking and pointing toward the cottage.

"The SS are not authorities. They are murderers, but of course if you are one of them you would not agree with me," Boris said, easing his grip on the woman's throat. He pointed a warning finger in her face.

"Do not make a sound or the boy dies," he said as he glanced at Hannah. Hannah turned her gun toward the boy and stared the woman in the eye. A hand wave to Hannah made it clear she would be no trouble. Boris slowly released his hold on the woman's neck and returned to the bag of food. The woman swallowed hard and cleared her throat.

"Come here, Jozef," the grandmother said to the boy. He gave Hannah one last punch and ran to his grandmother. He hid behind her blue cotton housedress. The boy rocked back and forth throwing punches into the stale air. The place smelled of a mixture of cooked food and a lit candle sitting on the cracked countertop near the stained, porcelain sink. *The cottage in Sokolka. The suitcase. Gone.*

"We have enough," Hannah said to Boris, motioning out the window that the neighbors were already aroused. "Time to go."

He nodded and handed Hannah the smaller of the two bags. She swung it over her shoulder and held her weapon in the other hand.

"Don't do anything stupid," Boris said as he left the house. "Or my friends and I will be back for you. And the boy."

Hannah stepped out into the road and faced a group of men with clubs and pitchforks. Boris was in no mood for resistance and stepped toward the group.

"Go home now and live," he said, moving forward.

Hannah pointed her gun at the sky over their heads and pulled the trigger. A quick burst of fire cracked the silence of the quiet village and echoed off the trees. She motioned them with her weapon to move away. Most looked intimidated and slowly scattered. One man stood tall with feet apart, holding an ax diagonally across his torso. He was blocking the path at the edge of the woods. Boris lowered his weapon as they drew near the villager. Hannah was afraid Boris would cut the man down.

"Move out of the way," Hannah called out as she hurried to keep pace with Boris. She held the bag of food over her shoulder with one hand and her submachine gun with the other. Both were heavy, but she was strong now after months of soldiering.

"Another Volksdeutscher, no doubt," Boris growled. "Dirty Nazi collaborator."

"You Jews are nothing but filthy thieves and murderers," the villager shouted back.

"Out of the way, Nazi!" Boris exclaimed, jamming the submachine gun muzzle into the man's throat. He directed the man away from the path and gave him a sharp shove. The man feigned a strike with his ax, but quickly fell back. Boris moved to the path and slipped into the woods. Hannah followed, pointing her gun at the man and stepped past him without flinching. She felt calm, confident that she could respond instantly to any situation. She had learned a great deal in a short time.

I was lucky again today. But I think one of these days, my luck just might run out.

. . . . .

The pair moved at an even pace through the forest. Hannah occasionally looked over her shoulder for anyone trailing them. No one did. She smiled with the sense that Boris seemed to be back in control. No one was hurt, except perhaps the pride of an arrogant collaborator. After a few kilometers, the food bag weighed heavily on her shoulder. Boris was not about to stop. Hannah knew she had to keep going and forced herself on.

No weakness. Show no weakness, she kept telling herself. They made the camp ahead of schedule. The men appreciated the food and Itzhak gave them a "well done" at supper. Itzhak drank more vodka. He seemed a bit unsteady by the end of the night. One more thing to worry about, she thought as she drank a cup of hot water and sat by the fire. All in all, Hannah was glad her turn for foraging food was over. It would come around again, but for now she was done.

The Volksdeutscher's words bothered her for a while, but the sting of the name-calling soon blended into a cloud of gloom and sadness. The winter moved in in full force and suspended the war. Everything halted, waiting for the spring. There was no sign of a Russian counteroffensive. Spring would surely bring more of the same ugliness and death. Hannah did not feel particularly hopeful for a quick end to the misery. With influenza in the camp, she understood the danger of getting sick with no doctor or hospital available to them. She tried to keep to herself so as not to get infected. The enemy now shifted from the Germans to nature. Everything was so cold—her feet, her hands, her mind.

Chapter Twenty-Two

With a covering of snow, March 1943 dragged in spring kicking and clawing. Hannah was encouraged by the prospect of warmer weather. But the change was double-edged, as the thaw meant that the danger would rise and the killing would resume. Word filtered down that the resistance coordinator, "Barbara," in Warsaw requested a mission to get people out of the city. Things had become desperate in the Ghetto. The underground fighters needed weapons, ammunition, explosives, and anyone with fighting knowledge to support a last stand.

"I need volunteers to infiltrate the Ghetto," Itzhak said in a gathering of his team.

"I'll go," Hannah said with no hesitation.

"If Hannah goes, I go," Boris said, holding out a fist.

Maybe I am his replacement for Schlomo. I could do worse.

"I will go, too," said David.

"And I," said Joseph, nearly in unison.

A half dozen more volunteered and Itzhak had his squad.

"Are the Russians going in?" Hannah asked, hoping to see Yuri again.

"No. The commander says this is not of their concern," Itzhak replied flatly. "And too risky for no gain."

"No gain? What about the lives of our people?" Joseph said. "They mean nothing to them?"

"No. Not their fight. The Soviets only protect their own," David said. "If they happen to help us along the way, then so be it."

I wonder if that is how Yuri sees it. How he feels about me…

"They are good allies. They treat us as fellow fighters," Itzhak said firmly. "Don't forget that. Without them, we might be wiped out by now."

There were a few nods in agreement. No one else spoke about it, but Hannah could read the bad feelings on her comrades' faces. It was the way it was. She hoped Yuri would not act that way toward her. But deep down, she knew Yuri would have to follow orders. Lots of people seemed to be following orders, regardless of what was normally right or wrong.

"Thank you all for volunteering," Itzhak said. "This will be very dangerous. Do not get caught. We move out at sundown and travel to Warsaw by night. Pack up by four o'clock. Everyone should carry wire cutters. Pistols only. Cyanide."

Hannah looked at David. She knew that some of the partisans carried cyanide pills. Deadly poison in glass capsules to be broken with their teeth and swallowed. Death would be in seconds. Avoiding the excruciating pain of torture so as not to give up the detachment's location was the primary purpose. Hannah was presented with a capsule before but refused to carry it. She knew in her heart that she could not take her own life. After all, she should already be dead lying in the pit. Adonai must have other plans for her, Hannah hoped.

"Only hidden weapons in the city," he whispered, anticipating her question. "Try to look like everyone else in the Ghetto."

She nodded. *Already decided I'm not taking a capsule. I'll make them kill me first.*

. . . . .

The day passed quickly. Hannah felt her excitement and anxiety mount. No one was happy about leaving the relative safety of the forests, let alone sneaking into the city. Warsaw was heavily occupied by the Germans. As she remembered so clearly, it was a treacherous place for a Jew or a partisan. For a Jewish partisan, capture meant brutal torture and death. The SS and Gestapo would love to get their hands on her. Hannah knew firsthand that the partisan detachments were a nasty thorn in the side of the German army. Everyone bragged about it. But Hannah never bragged.

Itzhak was always saying that our missions to cut enemy

communication lines and bomb the supply trains headed for the front meant a lot. We were only a few fighters against their whole army, which must make the Nazi generals angry. The Germans wouldn't go deep enough into the woods to find our camps. Itzhak was right.

Hannah felt her stomach flutter. She held out her hand to see if it was shaking, even a little. The others bound for Warsaw seemed on edge too. The mission was very risky. Hannah checked her pistol. Cleaned, loaded, with extra bullets stuffed in her jacket pocket. The steel felt cold and smooth on her skin. An acrid scent from a smoldering, dead cooking fire crept up her nose as she passed by on her uneasy stroll around the camp. That smell always made her nauseous. She had to get her mind focused. To think. Going back to Warsaw seemed crazy. She was safe here. Well, sort of safe. But she knew Papa would not think it smart to go. *Papa.* She shook her head and looked up ahead.

Vladimir was stirring the pot as she passed. Her little wave was returned. The fresh scent of vegetables stewing broke her concentration. Yuri's "special breakfast" for her was sweet. She had to smile. *I need to be with him soon. I want him to touch me again. Closer this time. Much closer. I hope he feels the same. Maybe when I get back. Then again, maybe I'm not coming back.*

Continuing around the camp, she could not resist passing by Yuri's spot and nonchalantly glancing around. *He's not here. Why isn't he here? Maybe he doesn't want to see me.*

Hannah kept walking and thinking and trying to convince herself that Warsaw was the right thing to do.

Her group stayed hidden and always used hit-and-run attacks. They must have killed a lot more Germans than the Germans had killed of her comrades. So far, the German guards near the railroads had only hurt them once, but that was a bad attack. Schlomo and a lot of others, dead.

If caught, the SS might be especially brutal with any captured partisans. Especially Jewish partisans. Although she had not seen it, Hannah heard the stories about the SS making a statement by hanging them in a public square of a nearby village and putting signs on the bodies labeling them bandits against the Reich. *Ha! Bandits! We are the bandits? Don't they think everyone knows who they really are?*

Soon the group gathered for the mission. There was nothing more to think about. Hannah was going. They made their way much the same as she remembered getting from the city to the forests. That trek seemed a distant memory now after many months living in the forests. Going back to Warsaw was a betrayal of her vow to Papa and Mama. But she did not want to dwell on why she did anything anymore.

. . . . .

"We must split into groups of two or three to avoid suspicion," Itzhak said quietly.

Some gestured to him who would pair together. He nodded agreement.

"David, you and Joseph come in from the south, the others from the north," he said.

"What about us?" Boris asked, pacing around behind the group.

"Hannah, Boris and I will enter from the east. All make your way to Mila Street, to the underground headquarters," Itzhak said. "And if anyone gets caught, don't let them know you are partisans of course. And be careful no one sees you slip into the sewers."

"They will know who we are by looking at us," Boris said. A defiant smile crossed his face then vanished. "We know what to do."

The teams split and all moved out into the darkness. Itzhak led the way with Hannah following and Boris in the rear. They slipped through the city to the Ghetto quarter and located the fenced-in section. Each one clipped at the wires, quickly creating an opening, and all slipped inside. It was easy to mix in with the crowd. Hannah saw middle-aged men, women, and children, and old men in the hundreds milling around. The streets and buildings were overcrowded, rundown, and smells were strong and unpleasant. But the most common sight was the look in their eyes. It was the same everywhere. Uncertainty and fear shone from the inside out. Hannah shivered at the thought of living in the nightmare surrounding her.

Itzhak found a narrow, empty alley a few meters from a sewer cover in the street. He ventured into the center of the street, cautiously looking up and down for patrols. He waved Hannah and Boris on. Producing a hand tool, Itzhak pried up the manhole cover and Boris got his hand between the cover and rim and the two hoisted it off to the side. A black hole in the street was an open door into the underground. The stench pouring from the hole was overpowering. Hannah had to back away into the clean night air to keep from throwing up.

She could not even imagine what could be growing in the dark cavity before her. The thought of crawling into it seemed out of the question. Boris went down first as always.

I have to go down there… She stared into the hole.

Taking a huge gulp of cold, clean night air, she positioned herself over the entrance. Hannah grabbed the iron rung at the top of the manhole and groped with her foot to find another rung on the ladder. Her shoe made solid contact and she carefully lowered her weight onto the metal ladder. The next step was easier, but now the air in her lungs was exhausted. With lips barely parted, she gently drew in the disgusting mixture of stale, humid air and sewer gas. Her eyes were burning and watery.

It took a mammoth effort not to vomit, but she kept taking tiny swallows of saliva until her senses adjusted to the stench. She wondered if this was the worst of it, or if things in the sewer would get vile beyond coping. Stepping into the foul, black water at the bottom of the sewer tunnel was yet another challenge. Her shoe met with something slimy at the bottom of the pipe. She could feel the filthy water seeping into her shoes and soaking her trousers.

Oh, my feet! I'll never get this smell out. My shoes and clothes, ohhh… What else lives in here, animals, snakes, rats? Well, too late to worry now. Just never mind all that. Move on. Go.

Itzhak stepped off the ladder and Hannah heard his boots splash the dirty water as they hit bottom.

"Boris, move forward about a hundred meters," Itzhak said with labored breath. "We will come to a junction with the main branch. Then turn. It should be about forty-five degrees to the right and it enters the larger sewer main."

"I understand," Boris said and slogged forward through the pitch-dark, eye-tearing tunnel.

Hannah felt light-headed. *If I pass out I'll drop into the filthy water. Whatever I do, not that!*

"Keep moving," Itzhak said. "We don't have much time."

"How will you know where to turn off?" Hannah asked, already disoriented and sick to her stomach.

"I have been here before. I know," he said. The splashing of their feet echoed off the walls.

Boris called out from the darkness ahead, "Here it is, turning right.

Hannah could feel Itzhak's hand on her back. He was gently guiding her forward through the darkness. *I hope he doesn't think I'm too scared for this, but his hand feels good. Stay with me Itzhak. Please.*

After a time, Boris stopped slopping along and no sound echoed back from his position. Hannah panicked a bit thinking he had been taken by the Germans. But not much chance any Germans would climb down into this stinky hole.

Suddenly, the answer came. A light flashed for a moment and extinguished as quickly. "I found it! It's Mila Street! The name is stenciled on the wall," Boris called out, his voice echoing through the tunnel.

"Turn there, left, and go about a hundred meters. We should find some of our people in the tunnel near the central headquarters," Itzhak said.

The three groped along with shoes sloshing and hands patting the walls in the pitch-black sewer. As they moved down the tunnel, Hannah noticed a glimmer of light far ahead.

Who is that? Germans? No. Might get their uniforms smelly. No, it's probably the Ghetto fighters. Be careful, Boris.

They moved forward to the intersection, and Boris waited for the two to catch up. Turning up the Mila Street sewer, it all seemed unreal to Hannah. She was caught in a dream with sounds and smells and the touch of wet shoes and clothes on her skin. Deep inside enemy territory, there was almost no hope of survival if caught. Not what Papa had in mind for her. She thought about the glass cyanide capsule that she refused to carry. No mercy from the Gestapo if they were trapped and taken alive. She tried not to focus on the risks.

"You up there! Stop!" a voice echoed in clear Yiddish. "Identify yourself or be shot dead."

"Itzhak Grozsman, to meet with Mordecai Anielewicz," Itzhak called in reply in Yiddish.

"How many of you?" the guard asked gruffly.

"Three," Itzhak said.

"Come…slowly with hands over your heads," the voice echoed.

They moved forward sloshing in the sewer water, now only ankle-deep. In the dim light near the guard's post the man appeared haggard with drooping sacks under his eyes. His skin was a sickly yellow pallor and eyes bloodshot.

"Sorry, brother, but we can trust no one, even down here in this hellhole," the guard said.

The man eyed Hannah and Boris in the dim light and grunted.

"Where is Anielewicz?" Itzhak asked, trying to see the numbers and hands of his watch through the scratched crystal.

I guess we are already behind schedule. Hannah looked past the guard.

Another guard stepped out of the shadows where Hannah could see his face. A teenaged boy, younger than her by maybe a couple of years, stood silently. The expression on his face seemed unreadable, but she could feel his desperation, like the sweat on his face. Hannah slipped past him, grateful that she was not condemned to live here in his world. She felt bad for him, but he should have run away from the city. Maybe he would come back with them.

"Follow me," the man said, crouching and stepping into a dimly lit tunnel off the main street sewer line.

Itzhak bent over, entered the low shaft, and followed the man in. Hannah and Boris crouched down and kept moving after Itzhak.

The guard quickly reached a dead end in the low tunnel. He knocked a few times on the wall blocking the tunnel. It was some sort of code or password, Hannah guessed. Someone responded from the other side of the wall. Suddenly the wall moved with a metal-to-brick scraping sound. More light filled the low, narrow tunnel from a large sewer junction chamber. People moved about inside the room. The guard and Itzhak stepped carefully through the doorway and entered the chamber.

Hannah stepped into the dimly lit space and immediately confronted the mixture of sewer odor blended with human sweat and urine. The atmosphere was strange, as she imagined a morgue to be. She breathed in the thick, stale air that seemed to give her lungs almost no relief. The place seemed to reek of death. But she sensed something more than that.

What is it about these people? It's hard to tell… What is it? A fight for good, maybe? They know they are right? It's how I feel when a good mission is done. But they must know they can't win.

Hannah looked into more faces as she stepped over rusty pipes and junk on the chamber floor that no one bothered to clear away. They were like heroes in a fairy tale book or something. These people were staying to fight to the end. *They're better than me. I'm the one who ran away from the pit. Maybe I should have stayed to fight to the death. Who is right? How am I supposed to know?*

"Where is Mordecai Anielewicz? I have business to discuss with him," Itzhak said, an edge to his voice.

"Wait here, I will bring him," the guard said, although his tone lacked enthusiasm.

They waited impatiently for ten or fifteen minutes. There was a commotion at the doorway from the sewer tunnel into the chamber. The young guard stepped into the room and looked around. Hannah saw David and Joseph crouched, stepping into the room.

"There they are," Hannah said, pointing and relaxing her shoulders.

"Good, very good," Itzhak said, acknowledging them with a curt wave. "Where is Anielewicz? We can't wait much longer."

"Do you have guns?" the young guard asked. "We need whatever weapons you have. It is only a matter of time and the Germans will come in force. We have very little to defend our people."

We have our pistols, but no submachine guns or rifles here, Hannah thought.

She was about to reply when she caught Itzhak's eye. The slight sway of his head and pursed lips broadcast a clear message that she should keep quiet. She did not understand why they should not help the Ghetto fighters. They were of course fellow Jews and fighting the same enemy.

"Not many," Itzhak replied.

"Here is Mordecai," the guard said, looking up.

"Later," Itzhak said softly to Hannah.

She nodded. *Itzhak must have good reasons. Our group's survival comes first. But we have several pistols and could spare a few.*

Chapter Twenty-Three

"You were sent by the coordinator in the city?" Mordecai Anielewicz asked Itzhak.

"We were. I am Itzhak Grozsman. We are an attack etrad and have done major damage to the Germans. I can take as many fighters out of here as you wish," Itzhak said. "I need to replace my lost men and you need to save more of your people, as I see it. I expect a major German action against us anytime now as the winter is over. I don't think my Russian comrades will wait around to defend us."

"No. I cannot spare anyone," Anielewicz said wearily. "I believe the SS intend to purge the Ghetto any time now. We have no illusions of defeating them or that they will not stop at killing all Jews within these walls."

"Then get out now!" Itzhak exclaimed. "What are you waiting for?"

"I cannot abandon the families and the old," Mordecai replied. "If we must die, we will show the world that we fought for something. Something more than ourselves."

"But we can arm them in the forest where they can do the most good against the Germans."

"Itzhak Grozsman, I only ask that you spare us the few weapons you carry to help our cause," Mordecai said. The sagging bags of flesh under his eyes drooped into hollow cheeks. "You can take pity on us if you must, but I promise we will take as many as possible down with us. That will help your cause some."

Hannah heard the whole conversation and had to do something. She could not hold back any longer.

"Here is my pistol and some spare bullets," she said, holding the weapon out to Mordecai. She glanced over at Itzhak's face expecting his anger at her disobedience. His face was solemn as he held out his own handgun for the senior leader to take.

David stepped over to offer his pistol, but Itzhak waved him off.

"We need some protection to get back," he said to Mordecai.

"I understand. Thank you for these guns," Mordecai said, though his eyes begged for more.

"Why not give..." Hannah started to say.

"We must go now. We're already behind schedule," Itzhak said, with a sharp glance at Hannah.

"Mr. Anielewicz, the word I got is consistent with your assessment," Itzhak said to Mordecai. "They will come and soon. If you change your mind, let us know through the Warsaw contact and I will come back for you."

"One day in Zion!" Mordecai called to them as they moved toward the doorway to exit the chamber.

"Yes, one day," Itzhak said, hesitating. He then slipped through the opening into the sewer tunnel. Hannah looked back at the scene. It was clear. All of these people would die here. In the back of her mind she could see Papa and Mama lying in the pit. Turning away she crouched down and stepped through the opening into the tunnel starting the long journey east, back to the forests.

. . . . .

Itzhak backtracked through the sewer system to the manhole by the alley. The group moved at a moderate pace, taking care not to slip or stumble into an ambush. Hannah found herself growing accustomed to the pungent smell and filthy water. As they sloshed through the tunnels, she nearly forgot about the stench, although the water had long since soaked into her shoes, socks, and pant legs. She did not want to think about how to clean up the mess. When they reached the manhole, Boris moved ahead of everyone and started up the iron rung ladder to the street level. He poked his head up into the dark street. After looking around in every direction and seeing no one, he waved the others up.

As they moved through Warsaw in the shadows, Hannah felt uneasy about their return. Having donated weapons to the Ghetto fighters, they could no longer shoot their way out of a situation. Hannah now understood why Itzhak did not give up every gun. She remembered Barbara's words – *"When it comes to survival, protect yourself first."* Hannah felt sorry for the Jews in the Ghetto, but she lessened her own chances for survival by helping them.

Why is everything so difficult? Even the older people doubt themselves. So we helped the Ghetto fighters, but now we have to sneak out of the city without being seen. Nothing is ever easy.

Boris reached the fence where they had cut openings on the way in. Something did not feel right to Hannah.

"Wait!" Itzhak called out in a muffled shout.

"Something is wrong here," Hannah said, looking into the shadows and alleys.

"Yes, I feel it too," he replied.

Boris hesitated for a moment, looked around, shrugged his shoulders, and moved to the fence.

"Don't go…oh, too late," Itzhak said.

Hannah noticed movement in the shadows off to the right, and then far off to the left. She swallowed hard.

"I think someone's out there," she whispered.

"A trap, maybe," Itzhak said, eyes darting. "Too late. We're committed. Everyone follow Boris. Be quick now."

Hannah could feel her heart pounding loudly in her chest. She had no pistol. Only the farmer's jackknife. She found it in her pocket and clutched it. Focusing on the line of men ahead, she fought off the panic rising up inside. Suddenly shots rang out!

"Go, go, go!" Itzhak yelled. Everyone was running toward dark side streets, alleyways, and buildings.

Hannah spotted a narrow, dimly lit street off to the left. Her mind raced back to the basement where she and Itzhak hid from the German chasing them. They were lucky, then. More than she had realized at the time.

"Itzhak, this way!" she called out, pointing ahead.

"I see it," he replied, waving the others on. "David, Joseph, everyone, this way."

Sporadic gunfire echoed through the quarter.

The others fired toward the shadows where muzzle flashes broke the night. A few bullets ricocheted by and Hannah flinched.

"Are we trapped? No one seems to be up ahead on this street," Hannah said, surprised at her own calm.

"I think we ran into some sentries around the Ghetto fences, that's all," Itzhak said.

"Where's Boris?" Hannah asked, turning back toward the main avenue. "He is always in trouble."

"I don't think he made the turnoff to this side street," Itzhak replied, his hand touching the gray stone side of the building as they moved farther into the shadows. "He will have to find another way out."

The men behind David and Joseph guarded their rear. As they continued from street to street keeping to the shadows and moving fast, the gunshots grew distant and sparse. The look of the neighborhoods changed as they got farther and farther from the center of the city. They were deep into the fringes of town when Hannah realized the gunfire had long stopped. Everyone with her appeared to have escaped without a scratch. But Boris and some of the others were still missing and that weighed on her. She occasionally looked over her shoulder for her odd new companion.

"Hannah, he will be at the meeting place. You know Boris is a good fighter and very tough," David said, smiling and placing his hand on her shoulder. "You will see. He will be there."

Hannah looked back at David and tried to smile. She didn't want to lose any of them. They were her family. They were all she had left.

. . . . .

The meeting place was in a wooded area off the main country road leading east out of Warsaw. It was patrolled by the SS, but so were most of the city outskirts. The farther out from the city limits, the lighter the patrols. A little clearing in a small wooded area off an abandoned farm was the designated regrouping point. Most found a makeshift seat on fallen tree trunks or soft patches of grass and leaves. Hannah lowered herself to a tree stump and stretched out her aching legs. A few logs were strewn around that the now gone owner of the farm must have cut for firewood and left.

"Who is missing?" Itzhak asked the group.

"Boris," Hannah said, staring at her legs.

"And three more," someone said. "Have not seen them since we scattered."

"We will wait ten minutes," Itzhak said without emotion. "No more."

I'm not leaving without Boris, Hannah thought. *I don't care what he says.*

Hannah glared at Itzhak in defiance. She was sure he knew her mind.

The time went agonizingly slow. Still no one approached. Itzhak checked his wristwatch about every minute. The lookouts were silent.

"Any sign of them?" he asked.

"No. No one is out there," someone said flatly.

Itzhak looked at his watch, then at Hannah.

"It's time," he said, and rose from the ground.

"I am not going without him," Hannah said, looking away into the darkness.

"Everyone is going," he replied, standing rigid and pointing the way.

"I will wait for him and then we will catch up," she said, her arms crossed.

"I can wait here with her," Joseph said, looking at his cousin with eyebrows raised.

"No. Everyone leaves, that is an order," Itzhak said. "I cannot spare a single fighter. Boris and the others are experienced men. If they are alive, they will make it back on their own. None of them expect us to wait."

Everyone got to their feet except Hannah. Itzhak turned away and walked from woods toward the country road.

"Hannah, take my hand," Joseph said with his arm outstretched. "He will find us. I know it. Come."

"I'll go this time because I have no gun," she said. Her eyes were aimed at the back of Itzhak's head. "But next time will be different."

"Come," Joseph said, holding out his hand to her.

Hannah rose and started after the others. Joseph followed her, his pistol at the ready. Hannah reached the road and searched the shadows for some sign of her friend.

"Traitor," she mumbled to herself.

Turning her back on Warsaw, Hannah stepped up her pace and followed the others leaving Boris behind to fend for himself.

As usual, Itzhak kept to the small farm roads, avoiding any major routes that the SS and German patrols might travel. Hannah looked back occasionally for Boris and the others, but no one was there. Hannah hated to admit it, but maybe he was gone. She imagined him lying facedown in a Warsaw street, bullet holes in his back, blood everywhere. The ugly image returned as quickly as she erased it from her mind. Barbara's words echoed in her head, that she would lose all of her friends by the time this was over. She wondered about Joseph, David, even Yuri. Would she lose them too? Itzhak, she would not even consider losing.

About ten o'clock, Itzhak turned from the overgrown farm road toward the main route as there was no other way to get around the wide, mucky swamp that lie directly ahead. As they approached the road, a small farmhouse came into view. A light was shining through a yellow-stained lace curtain. Itzhak stopped to review the situation. "I don't see a safer way around the swamp," he explained, "so we will have to travel the main route for a while."

"We need food, mostly water," David said, pointing his nose at the farmhouse.

"Some water and bread," Hannah said, "would be enough to get us back to the camp."

"There are people in there. They will have food. We can take what we want," another said.

Itzhak noticed wires overhead running along the street and one from the mainline to the peak of the house. Very few had electric and telephone.

"We have done it before, many times," Hannah said.

"I don't know this farmer," Itzhak said, wagging his head and sensing danger.

"It will be alright and besides, everyone is thirsty. We have no more water," Hannah insisted.

"It's still a long way to get home," said David. "I agree with Hannah."

The house appeared fairly new with white clapboard siding. The residents seemed to have some means. Probably plenty of food.

Itzhak peered a long time at the house and surroundings.

"Alright, but be very careful," he said. "I still don't like it."

David knocked on the sturdy, black front door. There was a commotion inside and a long delay. Everyone who had one held their weapon out as the pale light streaming from the doorway cast upon each fighter. David and Joseph pushed their way into the house and moved deeper inside. Joseph waved the others in and took control of the place.

"Who are you? Bandits?" the middle-aged Pole exclaimed from the sparse living room.

"Oh, oh, Balik, do something!" a pudgy, red-faced woman screamed in Polish from the bedroom door.

"What do you want with us?" the man asked, red-faced and jumpy.

"We want only water and maybe some bread," Hannah said. "Then we will leave."

Itzhak noticed four place settings at the kitchen table. There must be at least two more people around somewhere. He caught Hannah's eye and held up two fingers, pointing at the table and then at the next room. Hannah understood, but she had no gun. What could she do?

"Drop your guns," someone yelled from the doorway of the house. A loud bang crashed outside the front door.

"Who, what? We're under fire!" Itzhak exclaimed, confused. He wheeled around spotting an old man holding an ancient shotgun with barrel smoking.

"I can still shoot this gun. Hands up, all of you!" he yelled, sputtering into a coughing spasm.

A man moved swiftly from the shadows and stuck his revolver into the old man's right temple.

"No, you drop your gun," Boris said solemnly. "Or you are a dead man."

"Don't hurt him, please, my father is old and stubborn," the woman said, frantically rushing across the room to the front door of the house.

"You better get him to drop the gun," Itzhak said, "or we will have no choice."

Hannah was so happy to see Boris alive. But he was a hothead and quick to act, in a deadly way. She thought she understood him well enough now to try and calm the scene. She stepped outside and slowly moved toward the old man.

"Mister, my friend is a very good shooter. He will surely kill you. All we ask for is a little water to wet our throats," Hannah said, her hands spread wide and palms up.

"You will hurt my family if I don't stop you," the man said.

"Father, listen to the girl," the peasant woman pleaded. "We have plenty of water to give. Then they will go."

The woman glanced at Hannah for some sign of truth. Hannah looked into Boris's eyes and then back to the woman. She gave a slight nod.

"Father, please!" she said.

The old man pointed the shotgun at the ground and then dropped it into the dirt.

Hannah waved off Boris with a slight head motion. After a few seconds, he removed the pistol from the man's head.

"Thank you, Hannah," Itzhak said.

"We need water and a little something to eat," said Hannah to the woman.

"We are poor and have little to give," the farmer said, still angry at the intrusion.

"There are many of you. We have water, but not much else," the farmer's wife said, shaking her head.

"I see bread and apples," David said.

"That will do," Itzhak replied. "Fill some bottles, gather up the rest. Time to go."

"You leave us nothing. We are just trying to survive," the farmer complained.

"So are we," Hannah said, sympathy gone.

Hannah moved over to Itzhak and whispered, "Where is the fourth one?"

"I'm worried. They have electricity and a telephone line," he replied under his breath. "Few have this, even fewer who are not informers."

"Yes, need to leave now," she said, looking up the country road toward the city.

The farmer's wife collected a few empty glass bottles from under the kitchen sink and filled them with well water. The boys grabbed the half-loaf of bread and the half-eaten vanilla cake from the counter. Joseph handed out apples to everyone from the woven wood basket sitting on a small table near the back porch.

"Everyone, outside now," Itzhak called from the front yard.

Hannah glanced up the dark country road toward Warsaw when a flicker of light in the distance caught her eye. It all seemed to have happened before.

"Itzhak, lights, up the road," she said, poking her nose in the direction of the approaching vehicle.

"Move out! Follow me. Quickly!" he yelled.

"Oh, so now you will pay for your stealing! You bandits will get yours this time! Ha!" the farmer shouted in glee. "Thanks to my son."

"Germans, SS are right behind us," Hannah called out. "Boris, come on, it's a trap!"

"I'm going to kill this miserable Volksdeutscher!" Boris said, pushing the old man to the ground and heading for the farmer.

The farmer's expression changed to fright and he bolted into the darkness, as Boris started after him with pistol raised.

"Boris, no time. Come now!" Hannah pleaded, grabbing his arm with both hands.

Hannah spotted another set of headlights pop up over the hill in the distance. Suddenly, the first vehicle came over the rise in the road and the light beams struck the side of the house. Boris stopped resisting when he saw the lights.

"Yes, go, go now," Boris said.

"I hope we're not too late," she said. They broke into a run after the others who had already left and seeped into the shadows.

Hannah slipped out of sight into some brush along the roadside with Boris close behind. Her heart pounding in her chest and ears, she ran as fast as she could. A car pulled up to the house behind them and another vehicle squeaked and squealed, then roared past the first one. Hannah could hear the engine as it ran past them on the road maybe fifty meters to her left. The headlights pierced the shadows creating an eerie sight. Military trucks. *Run.* She kept moving with brush, small tree branches, and briars slapping and whipping her face and body as she scrambled for the dark shadowy area up ahead. Boris was still on her, his heavy breathing and footsteps hanging close behind.

The ground ahead opened and appeared flat in the nighttime shadows. She could make out the dark patches in the distance now. Trees, woods, shelter were in their reach. She could hear German voices behind them in pursuit. Hannah wondered where Itzhak and the others were.

"Look, up ahead to the right," Boris said as they ran for the trees. "It must be our boys. That way, quick!"

Hannah veered off slightly to the right and entered the woods. The briars ripped and pulled at her clothes. She felt herself falling forward. Smashing into a sapling, she was down. Two dark shadows lifted her out of the brush. Dazed, she could feel her feet dragging behind, snagging on bushes and sticks. Gunfire broke the stillness of the woods behind them. Boris was no longer there. Suddenly they stopped.

"Are you alright, Hannah?" Itzhak said, wiping the damp hair out of her eyes. His face was nearly touching hers as he squinted to see if her cuts were serious.

"I tripped in the brush," she replied, regaining her senses, still out of breath.

David approached and reported, "Only a squad, they took a few hits and backed away from the trees."

"Any more coming?" Itzhak asked.

"Don't think so," David said, "but we are almost out of bullets. Any more Germans and we're done for."

Hannah stood up and got her balance. "I'm alright, sorry for being clumsy," she said.

"You're not. Everyone, move out. Boris, too," Itzhak said with a sly smile and a sparkle in his eye.

They moved through the woods carefully and made it out the other side to an abandoned dirt road. The weeds were thick, but the original stone base made a hard surface. They moved quickly east to home.

Chapter Twenty-Four

Sunlight streamed through the young, green leaves of the broad leaf trees and the hearty evergreen branches as the new season emerged. Hannah strolled through the camp hoping to "accidently" run into Yuri. Late April brought warmer air, and with it earthy smells seeped up from the moist, black soil under her feet. Hannah breathed in pine-scented air, filtered through the branches overhead. With her Warsaw mission, she had not been alone with him for a couple of weeks now. She checked his area trying not to appear interested. He was not around. Vladimir looked up for a moment and smiled, then went back to peeling potatoes. The skins dropped into a tarnished metal bucket. She breathed in deeply. *I wonder where he is. Well, more than that, I wonder when we can be together again. His arms around me, up my back. That feeling. Strong hands. Well, I'll try later. Maybe he'll be back.* She continued around the camp and then sat down by her hut to plan her strategy to get with Yuri.

Boris sauntered up to Hannah and flopped to the ground next to her.

"I can't say much good about Warsaw," he said, yawning. "I almost killed some old man. We did nothing to help our cause."

Putting Yuri aside and thinking about the mission, Hannah thought it was probably not worth risking all their lives. If they had taken ten fighters out or five, even two or three, then maybe. And poor Itzhak had to tell the Russian commander about the Ghetto fighters. Not that the Russian cared about the Jews in the Ghetto. What was it he said? *"Not their concern."* Hannah felt better about giving their people a few guns anyway.

"Maybe our pistols will help them," she replied, sighing.

"They're already dead. Should've come with us," Boris said,

shaking his head.

"I was afraid *you* were dead back there," Hannah said, not looking up.

"Yes, me, too," he said, smiling. "You look sad. That's not a good way for a fighter to feel. Eats away at you."

Hannah thought for a moment. "I don't feel very much of anything anymore. But I'm happy you're still with us, Boris."

"Oh, I've been in worse," he replied, waving the thought of danger away like a gnat or a pesky mosquito.

"I'm going to lie down for a while.

"Are you sick or something?"

"No, just a little tired I guess," she said.

Hannah got up slowly and walked to her hut. *A part of me is already dead, Boris, can't feel it anymore. The rest of me, I don't know. Maybe it's all of me that is dying. I just hope Yuri can help me.*

She removed her shoes, coat, and belt, and lay down. The coarse blanket felt scratchy on her cheek. She rarely took naps, but today was not a good day. She needed Yuri. There was hope with him. Instead she just felt drained and a little sad that her real home in Warsaw might be lost forever. Hannah fell off to sleep.

Chapter Twenty-Five

It was May 10th when the rumor circulated through the camp. The Warsaw Ghetto was liquidated.

Such a scientific term—*liquidated,* Hannah thought. Like diluting a solution in chemistry class. Titrating. She knew they were all dead. No more hoping, wishing. Just dead.

The forest was alive with birds and other small animals tending to their young. The trees were full with greenery and the brush and leaves provided ample cover for their operations. It was good to feel nature in bloom. Another mission was planned. "A double-pronged attack," as Itzhak explained it. Hannah would lead the second group. Itzhak's team would make the northerly hit, closer to the German outpost, and Hannah's team about a quarter kilometer below that point. If successful, they could cut communications at a key juncture and isolate three elements of the enemy. It was well worth the risk and Hannah knew she had to be successful.

. . . . .

The mission went as planned. Hannah's group scored a major hit and she proved herself once again to be a leader. As summer began, Hannah's fame spread throughout the region as a mysterious, fierce Jewish tigress. The Gestapo heard the stories as well. They would have to do something about it. A price was circulated to the peasants in the area, if any were brave enough to turn her in and collect.

"So, my brave comrade, you are becoming a legend," Yuri said, loud enough for anyone around to hear. He held up a wanted poster. It had no picture, only a vague description of the girl, a Jew and bandit, the Gestapo were seeking.

Sitting in her usual place near her hut, Hannah looked up and smiled. "I don't deserve such an honor."

"One of my men found it nailed to a tree in a village near here."

Yuri squatted, thighs resting on his calves and balancing on his toes. He whispered, "Hannah, can you get away now?"

Yes. I want to more than anything, but what excuse will I use to leave. I guess I won't worry about it.

"Can I meet you where we met before?" Hannah whispered, looking around the camp. David, Joseph, and Boris were off foraging for small game. The others did not seem to pay her much mind. Itzhak sat near the edge of the Jewish section of camp, in conversation with a Russian, his back to her.

Yuri nodded. "In ten minutes?"

"Yes."

Hannah could feel her heart starting to pound as she watched Yuri stand and walk away. He moved past Itzhak without a word, pacing toward his own area and out of sight. Hannah got up and stepped into her hut. Pouring a little water into her tin cup, she dipped her toothbrush into the water. Hannah slid her hand into the drab green satchel and reached for the crumpled tube of toothpaste among the personal items that the peasant woman gave her on the bath mission. After quickly brushing her teeth, she shook the water off the brush and placed it in the satchel with the tube. Taking a mouthful of water from the cup, she rinsed her mouth. Hannah grabbed her submachine gun, stepped through the hut doorway, and spit the water onto the ground. A glance over her shoulder, then a few steps into the woods, and she was gone.

"Hannah, over here," Yuri said in a low voice as she approached the secluded spot.

How will we get back to where we left off? They slipped through the mesh of underbrush into the secluded hideaway. Yuri was right behind her and she could feel his hand on her waist. Hannah turned to him and started with, "I've waited so long…" But his arms slid around her waist and he pulled her close. He stopped her voice with a kiss. His lips pressed hard into hers for a long time. At last, she drew in a breath through her nose. He smelled good, something smelled very good. An earthy scent. Together they broke off the kiss. "Yuri," she whispered. "You're squeezing me too tight." She looked up into bright, blue eyes, smiling, and rested her forehead on his chest.

"Sorry, I could not wait a second longer," he whispered, relaxing his arms and resting his cheek on her hair. A bird fluttered about in the bushes. Hannah glanced toward the sound. It seemed to be afraid of the intrusion into the secluded spot. Maybe a mother protecting her babies. Then it was gone. Only the sound of their breathing remained. Hannah slipped the strap of the gun off her shoulder and the weapon lowered to the ground. Yuri did the same, then increased his hold. As their lips met again, she watched his eyelids close; the lashes were soft and light like his hair. Safe, happy, she closed her eyes and felt her breasts pressed against his chest. His heart was beating almost as fast as hers. She felt her mouth opening as Yuri drew a breath from deep inside her. Startled, she struggled with the urge to stop him. But in a moment their breathing was natural, flowing easily from one to the other. Yuri's tongue gently explored Hannah's mouth. She let him in. She could not stop him. *Oh God! It's like we're inside each other. Like we're one person. I can't stop! Yuri!*

Hannah felt Yuri shift his stance and his forearm press into the back of her knees. Their lips parted. Up she went in his arms and then down to the soft grass. He gently laid her head onto the ground. Stretching out next to her body, he rolled over onto her, supporting his weight on his elbows. "I think we will be more comfortable lying down," he said, brushing the hair from her forehead.

"Yes, much better. Maybe too comfortable."

"Don't you trust me?" Yuri smiled, eyebrows raised.

"I don't trust myself." She ran her finger across his lips.

"Well, then, I must proceed with caution."

"A little more time, then maybe we should get back."

"A little more." Yuri lowered himself and their lips met once more.

Hannah placed her palms on his face. His skin was smooth, shaven. *He feels so strong and so gentle with me. My cheeks are so warm.*

Can't let him see.

She felt his lips pressing hers to open again, but she closed her mouth and continued the kiss. They held it for a long time and then broke it off. *I'm not going to be able to stop myself if we go on like this.*

Yuri rolled onto his back, holding Hannah to his body so she lay on top of him. Turning her head to the side, she rested her cheek on Yuri's chest. They lay together talking for nearly an hour. Hannah could not remember the last time she felt so happy.

Worried that someone in the camp might miss them both, she whispered, "We should go back."

"Are you sure? I want to give you every opportunity to change your mind," he said with a big grin.

"Yes, I'm sure," she whispered, lightly touching the tip of his nose with her index finger. "I hope."

Yuri shook his head, chuckling, "Alright, but there must be a next time for us."

Hannah nodded. *I wonder how far we will go next time.*

Yuri stood up, brushed off his uniform, and extended his hand. She placed her hand in his and felt a firm squeeze and a powerful arm raise her from the ground.

"Here is your weapon, notorious bandit," Yuri said, smiling as he slipped the gun strap over her shoulder. Yuri put his arm around Hannah's shoulders, leaned over, and gave her a kiss. "Let's go."

Chapter Twenty-Six

Mosquitos darted on and off the surface of the now stagnant water that filled old natural depressions and animal diggings embedded in the black mud. Last night's rain proved helpful for catching drinking water and growing vegetables back in the camp. Unfortunately, the unwanted moisture soaked the air. Hannah stared at the frail insects, dutifully working at generating more of their breed. She was not really watching or thinking. She raised her canteen to her lips and took a few measured swallows. She tried to think about Yuri, but he could not help her out here. The air was too miserable for anything, even for thinking or doing. The brief rest stop to reconnoiter an escape route to the big swamp region was going painfully slow. David and the others in her squad weren't even complaining anymore. That took too much energy away from walking and simply breathing. She wanted to get back to the camp as soon as possible. The dense forest was cooler, but hardly free of the merciless, ear-buzzing mosquitos and irritating bugs of all kinds. Thanks to Papa's nature trips, she understood much about the pests, but that did nothing to stop the summer onslaught of the miniature bloodsuckers.

"Hannah, can we go now?" David said, swatting and missing a few attackers. "It's better to keep moving then sitting here with these buggers."

"Did everyone take some water?" she asked, checking each face for some sign. Ragtag, half-bearded warriors all stared back, most nodding in agreement. She could feel the beads of sweat trickling down her sides from her armpits.

"Ready? Let's go. Boris, take the rear guard. Move out." Heading into the dry leaves, skirting the mud puddles, Hannah trudged on. It was about two hours later when she stepped over a slight rise in the ground that blocked the view ahead. Before her lay the big swamp country—an open plain of water, islands with clumps of trees, some areas to hide in, and open areas where if trapped they would be slaughtered by the Germans.

"This is the mission target. No point in going any further. It took longer to get here than Itzhak thought. That's not good," Hannah said, looking across the expanse for the best route into the swamps.

Boris moved up to the front and peered off into the distance. "Won't stand much of a chance trying to cross that."

"If the Germans don't get us, the snakes and mosquitos and whatever else is out there will," David said, wiping the sweat from his forehead as it dripped off his nose and ran down his chin.

Snakes. I hate snakes. Maybe we can make a stand in the forest and never retreat this far. I really hate snakes.

"You think they'll come soon?" someone asked.

"We're due. The Germans have had enough of us by now. They'll come soon and lots of them, maybe thirty or forty thousand," Boris said, motioning to Hannah that it was time to get back.

"All that is for another day. Take a ten-minute rest and drink water. David, did you draw up the map?"

"I have it." David put his paper against one man's back and added some figures and annotations. The pencil point was dull and some of the graphite was smeared from his sweat. "I'll redraw it when we get back."

Hannah waited about eight minutes. Swatting mosquitos, she could not wait any longer.

"Move out. If we get split up, make your way back to the camp. Boris."

"The rear, got it."

The trip back was worse because everyone was nearly spent reaching the swamps. They got as far as possible before nightfall and began to lose the trail in the dark. Hannah found a large grassy area, soft and clean enough to handle the group for a few hours of sleep until daybreak. Food was scarce and there were no farmers to raid along the way. She posted two of the boys to keep watch but figured they would probably fall asleep. Hannah pulled her coat up over her head to fight off the mosquitos. Exhausted, she dozed off into a restless sleep.

"Hannah. Hannah, wake up," David whispered, his hand on her shoulder, gently shaking her. Hannah opened her eyes to faint brightening of the sky. Stars were still visible and a fading moon sat high overhead through the branches.

"What is that noise, David?" Hannah whispered.

"It sounds like motors, armaments, Germans or Ukrainians? Don't know."

"Do you know how far we are from the camp?"

"Only a guess, but I would say five, maybe ten kilometers. They are close."

"It could be starting."

"The German Aktion? Yes. Maybe."

"We must get back to warn Itzhak. Quickly, break camp."

David got everyone up and packed to move.

Hannah felt that sour feeling deep down in her belly, the one when what you knew would someday come had arrived. Her mouth was dry and her voice cracked. "Be as quiet as possible. No talking. We could run right into them." She looked them all in the eye, one by one. "Move out."

The sounds lessened as they progressed toward the camp. Hannah tried to think like Itzhak. Would they even be there in the camp? Where was Yuri? Could they rely on the Russians or was everyone else right about them? Would Yuri wait for her? Maybe the Germans were forming nearby and not ready to attack. She knew she better get to Itzhak soon or they could be overrun.

No outer sentries stopped them as they approached the camp. *This is bad.* Hannah raised her hand and stopped. Shiny, black crows squawked and took to the air, sifting through the evergreen boughs to escape. David looked up and back to Hannah. Everyone crouched down in the tight clearing, brush up against their backs. No one made a sound, just stared at her waiting for a command.

"Gather 'round," she whispered. "It's too quiet. No guards. It's all wrong."

Boris fidgeted, crunching leaves beneath his shoes. "I'll go in from the other side. Just give me two men."

"Yes, but I want three teams. One team goes inside, the other two wait and see what happens."

"Boris, you and you," she said, pointing. "David will take three and I will take the rest." She eyed the three men squatting behind David. She wished she had Joseph with her, but Itzhak had needed someone he could trust. His cousin would give everything if need be to help him manage the camp.

"Boris, you go left, David right. I'll give you five minutes to get into place. Wait and see what I run into. Then come in firing if you have to. Just don't shoot each other. Or me," she said with a little smile. Hannah felt strong, she liked her plan. The jitters gone, she said to her team, "Be aware, let's go."

Hannah looked at the men gathered around. She couldn't believe they would follow her. But they were. The eyes were steady, no fear, no out-of-control hate in them. They were soldiers.

"Five minutes are up, be careful, follow me." A few nods were enough for her. She stepped forward to approach the camp.

All was quiet. The camp was abandoned. Smoldering campfires scented the air. They must have left in a hurry. Where were the Russians? Where was Yuri? He could have at least left her a message or something.

They strolled through camp, slowly, guns ready. Hannah looked at her hut. From the corner of her eye was movement. "Hannah, don't shoot. It's me. Joseph." Joseph stepped out from behind a tree, his hands raised over his head.

"Where is everyone?"

"They're coming. The Germans." All eyes were on Joseph. Guns were lowered and he dropped his hands to his side.

"Where are the Russians?"

"They got word and moved out the day after you left."

Yuri. He must have known something. Didn't tell me. I don't believe it.

"Where are Itzhak and the rest?"

"He sent out scouts. They saw enemy units gathering by the railroad and alerted us. He couldn't wait, so I volunteered to stay behind. To warn you," Joseph said, looking up to see David and the other teams approaching.

"We heard them too, about ten kilometers southwest of here," Hannah said, wiping sweat from her forehead with the back of her hand. "Which way did Itzhak go?"

"He went east away from the Germans, then intended to turn south later, trying to make the swamps. We can catch him if we move fast."

Hannah looked around. The door of her hut was partially open. "Alright, everybody, check the camp for anything we need like ammunition, food, water, clothes. We move out in five minutes." A few grunted and went to check their areas.

My hut. Maybe he left a note or something. Have to check. Maybe Itzhak was right about the Russians, but I didn't think Yuri would just leave me.

Hannah looked around. All were walking away. She rushed into her hut hoping for a note, a sign, something.

It was as she remembered it. Nothing was changed. She picked up a spare magazine full of bullets for her gun hidden under a rag in the corner and turned to go. Something shiny caught her eye. A tin cup hung by a string off the back side of the hut door. *The special breakfast. It was something.* She tugged on the cup snapping the string. Inside the cup was a faded yellow paper, neatly folded and pressed to the bottom. Digging it out, she stared at the little paper square in her palm.

"Hannah, are you in there?" David asked.

"Yes. Coming." She stuffed the paper into her pocket and stepped out. "Ready? Move out. Lead, David." She looked at Boris. He knew. Rear guard.

They moved swiftly through the forest. A sapling branch smacked her in the face. Hannah brushed it away. Her cheek stung and her eyes teared up. *He's gone. I know it. The Russians left us for dead. He probably had no choice. Orders. None of this is fair. Never was.* Hannah ached to read the letter. She wanted to believe he wouldn't leave her. The truth was in her pocket. *Too late now. Be a soldier. Just do your job and let it go. Let it go.*

. . . . .

"David, where are they? We're probably moving at double their speed. We should have caught up to them by now. Are you sure?"

David put up his hand, pivoted back, and stopped. Sweat dripped off his upper lip and chin.

"Itzhak said he would go about two kilometers east, then try to stay due south to the swamps hoping you made it back alive. Maybe he had to redirect his path." His eyes flashed the anxiety running through his head. Hannah sensed his embarrassment and the hope of finding the others draining from him. "I'll take the lead for a while, David. Follow me."

"We'll find them if we keep moving," Boris said, nodding to David. "Don't worry." The others nodded, some took a swig of water. Everyone looked at Hannah as she capped her canteen and wiped her mouth on her grimy sleeve. "Go."

It was just before sunset when they came upon something odd. "Look, straight ahead! Something white, a rag or something?" David said, pointing forward. "Hey, another thing to the left," somebody said. "And to the right."

"Maybe it's a sign."

David ran ahead and picked up a piece of light gray cloth. "It must be from Itzhak. See, part of the arm and sickle. Stuff we got from the Russians. It wouldn't be just lying out here. Boris came over with another piece. "Same stuff. It might be from our Soviet comrades."

"No. It's our people. But which way is Itzhak going?" David said, holding the material up in the dimming light. The sky ahead burned red through the gaps in the trees in the background. "No message on it."

"He's moving southwest. He just crossed our path from left to right. See it?" Hannah said. She traced the route with her finger and pointed to where they found the scraps of material. "He is smart." Hannah grinned. "We turn southwest. And hope we don't find Germans before we find Itzhak."

They moved on until dark, picking up scraps of material as they went. The energy of the group rose with every scrap found. With legs aching, Hannah felt the ground under her feet soften as they moved farther and farther away from the old camp region. "I think we'll stop here for the night." Peering into the shadows for enough clear, level space to accommodate the squad, Hannah heard a popping sound way off. Then another. And another. Everyone stared into the shadows to the southwest.

"Guns. Rifles and submachine guns, I think," Boris said, looking to Hannah for a command. "We've got to go down there."

"I know. It might not be Itzhak, but..."

"It *might* be them, and that's good enough for us, right?"

"Everyone check your weapons, get extra ammunition ready," Hannah said as she fumbled in the dark for her backup magazines. She found the farmer's jackknife in her pocket. A sharp corner of the folded note from Yuri poked her finger. *I don't think you had any choice, Yuri.* She slid two magazines of bullets into the waistband of her trousers for quick access. *This might be my last night, Papa. I hope I can make it a good one.*

"Protect your face and eyes from the brambles in the dark. Take it slow and steady. We don't know who is down there." Bearded, smudged, sweating faces gathered around close to Hannah. Body odor overpowered the sweet scent of pine needles surrounding them. "One day in Israel." A few nods and grunts responded in the pitch. "Move out!"

Hannah's heart pounded in her chest and ears as they approached the gunfire. It was loud now and close. Maybe a hundred meters away and closing. Fire flashes broke the darkness.

A heavy machine gun sounded over the din. "That has to be German, maybe an MG42. Tough to take out. We need some grenades," David said.

Hannah had seen pictures, but never encountered a "machine gun nest," as they called it. "We don't have any grenades," Hannah said.

"Well, I have one," Boris replied, patting his side.

I need to see who's in the fight. Flank the enemy. Take them down. Best thing is they have no idea we're out here. Move in close to the sound of the big gun. Think. Think. "Forward. See which way the gun is firing and come up behind. Maybe we can use the grenade. Let's go."

They all moved up through the brush and peered out. German helmets where silhouetted in the gunfire. Who were they shooting at? Unknown. More soldiers were positioned on either side of the machine gun. Bullets whizzed all around.

Hannah figured there must be dozens of them, maybe more. They could take out the nest from the left side. Push the others south and try to join with Itzhak, if that was Itzhak. They were taking his fire, too. They couldn't stay there. Hannah pointed to Boris to come with her. David and the others needed to hit the enemy on their left flank, then go to Itzhak. Itzhak should understand. And not shoot them, she hoped.

David moved left with the men. Hannah checked her gun and looked into Boris's eyes. He was a great fighter. If she was going down, at least it will be with the best at her side.

"Ready?" she whispered. A quick nod. Grenade armed, they stepped forward. Boris tossed the grenade into the nest. They both dropped to the ground. The explosion was loud, even over the din of the constant gunfire. The big machine gun stopped. Hannah raised her head. Four bodies lay blown apart by the blast. The Germans on the gun nest flanks froze with the explosion. Boris and Hannah lay prone and cut them down. Hannah's gun stopped. More Germans streamed in from the right. Hannah fumbled with a spare magazine in the dark. A huge blast of fire poured into the oncoming wave from the other side, Itzhak's side. Finally it snapped in and she pulled back the bolt. "Ready."

"Boris, go left, we'll join up with the others," she yelled. "Now!"

Leaping forward, Boris skirted the nest and headed left. Hannah pushed off following Boris into the shadows. *Yes. Yes. Stay left, Boris. Or they might fire on us. I hope it is Itzhak over there. Please be there.*

Machine-gun fire crossed her path as she approached the battling Boris. Hannah turned and fired into the Germans as more and more spewed out from the trees.

"They should see us firing into the Germans. I hope they can see us. Follow me." Hannah moved past Boris toward the fighters.

A steel gun barrel hit Hannah in the chest and stopped her cold. She raised her arms, holding up her submachine gun. "Don't shoot!"

"Hannah? Is that you?" a voice in the black shadows asked. "Yes."

"It's me, Joseph," he said, pulling the muzzle of his gun away from her chest. "Where are the others? We are overwhelmed. It's a German Aktion, Itzhak is sure of it."

"Which way to Itzhak, Joseph?"

"He's this way, come quickly."

"I have a map to the swamps."

Joseph patted her shoulder, then moved around to the right, behind the firing line. Hannah heard bullets sizzling by in the air, hitting trees and bodies with thuds and ricochets. *We can't stay here any longer. Why is Itzhak trying to hold position?*

Joseph lunged forward and then stopped behind a tree where two or three figures appeared as shadows huddled together. "Itzhak, it's Hannah. She made it."

He was sitting at the base of the tree on the opposite side from the firing. Hannah could see the shining stream of blood flowing down his jacket from his left shoulder each time a gun fired and lit the shadows.

"Itzhak, we can't stay here any longer. There's too many of them." His face seemed pale and his eyes told her that he had lost control. "Hannah, get us out of here," he said, coughing, throat dry and cracked. "Yes," Hannah said, straining to see a way out in the dark.

"Boris, where's David and the others?"

"On the other flank, they are with us. You lead us out. I will hold the Germans off for a minute. Take him. Go. Go." Hannah felt the calm in Boris's voice. *Yes, he is the best. Take Itzhak and retreat.* "Joseph and you boys, pick up Itzhak. Everyone, spread the word down the line. We are falling back."

Everyone tapped the shoulder or back of the man in front. The message spread quickly and some started to pull away from the firing line.

Itzhak couldn't move fast. They needed more time. Hopefully, Boris would delay them a minute or two. Joseph and another man pulled Itzhak to his feet. With shoulders leveraged into Itzhak's armpits, they carried the groaning Itzhak away from the firing line into the shadows.

Hannah needed the map to figure out how to pick up the trail to the swamplands. She waved the men coming off the firing line to follow her and got ahead of Joseph and Itzhak. Shuffling through her pockets, she found David's makeshift map. *How am I going to pick up the trail on the map? Maybe in the daylight. Southeast? Go southeast and we should find something familiar in the morning. We've got to keep moving until daybreak.*

Chapter Twenty-Seven

Tearing steadily through the brush and small trees in the dark, they moved on through the night. The gunfire was growing distant. Hannah could hear Itzhak's moans not far behind her. *He must be in a lot of pain or he would never make a sound. We're going to lose him if we don't stop soon. I hope Boris got out alive. No time to check.*

Hannah broke through the last tree line and stood at the edge of the forest. The expanse of swampland sat before her at a lower elevation. As far as she could see, it was flat and covered with shallow water and islands with clumps of trees. She hoped it was large enough an area to hide in. They had no other way. She looked up and filled her lungs with cool, dry air. A clear blue sky sat overhead with a fading moon, flanked by two or three bright stars still holding on to the night. It must be an hour or so before sunrise. Swamps. Snakes. No tanks and artillery could chase them down there—the enemy would have to put men on the ground and in the water to get close enough. It was their only chance.

"Hannah. Itzhak. We've got to stop," David said, panting, the sweat dripping from his hair. "He can't go any further."

"Yes. Here is good. Put him down. Water. Drink water. Share what's left if any. We will have plenty down there," she said pointing toward the big swampland below. The men came out of the forest into the clearing and breathed deep. Grins appeared everywhere as they took in the expanse of water below. Finally Boris came through the trees, into the open. Hannah looked up to the dying night sky and closed her eyes in thanks. She knelt next to Itzhak, who was propped up against a tree. Joseph tried to get some water into him, but most ran down his chin wetting his already sweat-drenched shirt. She put her hand on his forehead. He was hot. *Fever maybe. I don't know.*

"Itzhak. We're going to try to make it deep into the swamps. On the islands. Try to hold on a little longer. The water will cool you down."

"I have to tell you something, Hannah. Before I go," he said, reaching out for her arm and missing it.

"No, you're not going. I can't manage this without you. Drink some water."

She caught Joseph's eyes and his almost imperceptible headshake. *No, you're wrong. He is stronger than that. He will pull through.*

Hannah stood up and looked over the terrain. She didn't know exactly where they were. Must be far south of the other place they found. She looked back at Itzhak. *The artillery shells. Yes. A stretcher. How stupid I am. Should have thought of it before now.*

"Someone. Make a stretcher for Itzhak. Then we will head into the swamps before the Germans catch up."

Three men worked quickly to carve out poles. They fastened several leather belts and gun straps together with the poles. David, Joseph, and the others moved Itzhak to the crude stretcher. Two men picked it up and Itzhak groaned. It held, for now. The morning sun peeked over the horizon with streams of sunlight reflecting off the pools of water down in the valley. *No more night to hide our position. We have to get away from here, now.*

"Everyone ready?" Hannah asked, glancing around. "Boris, take six men and guard our retreat. Let's move."

They started down the long, sloping grade to the lowlands. Hannah could feel a headache coming on with the blinding reflection off the water. No food, too little water. *We need rest. Germans at our backs. Hurry, hurry.* She was afraid to look back at Itzhak. She just wanted to believe he would make it. The ground softened under her feet as the group descended toward the pools. The air below was damp and the heat of the day was already on the slight morning breeze. She splashed into the first pool feeling the cool water soak through her trousers. The others hit the water seconds later. It was over her knees, halfway up her thigh and waist-deep before it started to level off.

"Keep weapons and ammunition dry."

The bottom felt slimy under her feet, even though the water looked mostly clear. She wanted to dunk her head in and drink full gulps to soothe her cracked throat. *Probably make us sick. Need to boil it first. Keep going. The big island up ahead.*

A geyser shot up off to her right about ten meters away. Then another. And another much closer. Popping sounds from behind echoed through the valley. A bullet sizzled by her ear and a little geyser rose up just ahead. Hannah turned her head back. *They're on us.* Enemy soldiers were pouring out of the woods high above and starting down the long slope to the water.

"Keep pushing on!" *Come on legs, move, move through this water. It's there, ahead, a few hundred meters. Move.*

She could feel her feet slipping on the bottom the more she rushed. The wall of water was up her torso now and pushed on her body like a hundred-kilogram sack of flour. Holding her submachine gun over the water, she twisted around to see behind. The men were floating Itzhak with the stretcher on the water surface. They were doing fine. She peeked back again to see the Germans entering the first pool; splashing water sparkled and flashed in the sunlight. Turning forward, her left foot snagged on something deep below the surface. She lost her balance, careening forward face-first into the swamp. The gun went underwater. A mouthful of swamp water coated her tongue. *Ugh. I would have to swallow this stuff. Stupid girl. Get up. Move.* Hannah lunged forward, her head surfaced, and she spit out the musty water. Wet hair streamed down her face, over her eyes, nose and mouth. Geysers sprayed all around them. Then a sickening *thud* sound. Someone was hit. *Itzhak, Not Itzhak. Please.* Hannah wrenched back to survey their position. Another thud and another. *They've found the range and they're gaining on us. Got to make the big island.* Hannah kept pulling her legs forward, pumping and pumping against the wall of water pressing back. She swept the soggy mess of hair from her face and looked up ahead. The water was getting shallower, now below her waist.

Keep moving. We need to slow their advance. Get into those trees for cover and hit them hard. We'll put up a stand on this little island while the rest keep going for the next island with Itzhak. Boris. Where's Boris?

Hannah stepped up onto the little island, her shoes sinking into the mud. Soggy clumps of grass and black earth sucked her shoes down as she tried to pull away. Finally on more solid ground, she could see Boris at the end of the line. Last one to make the island.

"Boris, Boris!" Hannah yelled. He stepped into the muck at the water's edge and pulled his foot out of the black earth, water gushing from his boots. "Can you slow them down? Take whoever you need. Hide in those trees for cover. I'll take the rest through the woods and out the other side. We need to make the next island. It's big. Lots of woods. It's our only hope."

Boris looked around. An occasional bullet slapped the tree leaves and skinned the trunks. He did not flinch. "I need seven or eight. I can give you maybe half an hour lead. Those Germans have to get through what we just did. Not so easy with guns blasting you in your face. We will hold them for a while. Go." Hannah nodded and turned. "Hannah," Boris said, giving her a thumbs-up. "Take care, my friend." His eyes were glaring with fight, but underneath was something more.

"Take care, Boris," Hannah said. *So much pain in those eyes.* She broke her gaze and stepped away. The Germans were struggling waist-deep in the swamp. More bullets hit the trees as Hannah ran for the clump of trees to join the rest of the group. They moved quickly in and out of sight of the oncoming Germans. The roar of gunfire close behind echoed across the water in all directions. *I hope he makes it.*

They moved quickly through the clump of trees, found an open area about a couple hundred meters square and then another clump, much bigger. The gunfire was muted now, but still on everyone's mind. No time to stop. The ground was soft but seemed able to support the weight of the men. *Itzhak. He's quiet. Too quiet. I don't want to look.* Hannah trudged on half-walking and half-running. She looked back at Itzhak and caught David's eye.

"He's a little cooler," David said, pointing to Hannah to keep going. She turned and felt her foot catch on a tree root or something. Stumbling, she checked her fall and kept going. *Clumsy. Move it.*

Finally, the trees thinned out and the sunlight glistened off the next expanse of swamp through the gaps. They were almost there. She hoped this pool was no deeper than the last one, but it looked three times farther across. No choice. They were going in. Water splashed up around her as her shoes plunged into the pool.

"Keep your weapons and ammo dry." *Not like me, in the last pool.*

David and the others floated Itzhak on the stretcher like before. All seemed to be going well, but the depth was slowly increasing. Hannah was up to her chest in cool water and only about halfway across the pond. She looked back and most of the men were still only waist-deep. She might have to swim if it got deeper. Walking on tiptoes, Hannah bounced her toes off the slimy bottom. The men were up to their chests now and Hannah had to backstroke to keep her head out of water. It was hard to keep her gun from getting dunked more than a few times and she wondered if it would jam or even fire at all now. Something slithered across the surface just ahead, cutting a path through the shimmering image of sunrise reflecting off the pond. *What is that…oh! Don't think about snakes. Keep going.*

They continued along for a time and she noticed the level on David's shirt dropping. Thrusting her toe deep to the bottom, it contacted with her knee still bent. She could stand now, and walk. She righted herself and felt her shoes digging into the mud below. Another fifty or seventy-five meters to go. No sign of Boris. How would they ever make it across this deep water with the Germans on them? *Think. Think. Boris, please make it. I need you.*

Hannah stepped up onto the mucky shore and pulled her shoe out of the sticky stuff and onto the spongy ground of the big island. "Hey! Look! Boris and the others. They are starting into the water." Hannah looked across the big pond and scanned the edge of the woods for his pursuers. None yet. *What can I do to help him? My gun won't reach. Rifles, get the rifles ready. Shoot over Boris and others. Slow down the Germans. Yes.*

"Everyone with a rifle, get under cover at the edge of the woods. I think you have enough range. When the enemy shows, let them have it. Shoot high over our men. Keep the Germans busy," Hannah called out. "I'll keep moving on with the rest." She hoped that six rifles might slow them down enough to keep Boris from getting shot in the back. "Everyone else, follow me," Hannah shouted, stepping over to the stretcher and resting her hand on Itzhak's forehead. His head felt cooler, better.

"I'm worried about infection, but it is a clean wound. The bullet passed through without hitting the lung," Joseph said. "I poured all the vodka we could find into it. Maybe he will heal."

Hannah bent over the wound and inhaled. No foul odor. Only sweat. "I hope you're right, Joseph." Waving the troop on, she glanced back at Boris. The men were already up to their chests in deep water, weapons held high. She couldn't resist a little smile at the man's fight. *He is a great fighter.* As she stepped forward to lead the group, her riflemen opened fire behind her. She kept moving into the thick woods, not looking back.

Many of the trees were dead and rotting. Too much moisture in the lowlands. One of Papa's lectures came streaming into her mind. The ground was spongy. Mosquitos and other pests swarmed around the shallow pools and patches of mucky black soil.

The ground is bad here. Maybe they'll get sick of this muck and stop. Maybe it will stop the Germans. But it won't stop the Ukrainians. Haven't seen them yet. Hope they're not part of this action.

Hannah kept moving on deep into the woods. Birds squawked and flew away as the troop approached. The earthy scent of black earth filled her lungs. Mouth open, breathing hard, Hannah kept up the pace. She spit out a flea or something. Miserable bugs. Up ahead, and on all sides was endless forest. The island had looked massive from up on the ridge. No end in sight. Natural protection, she thought. *Where is Boris? I need to know what happened back there. And everyone needs a rest. Especially Itzhak.* They continued on for another half hour making good distance. Hannah happened upon a wide clearing in the trees. Almost a true circle. *Alright, this is far enough. Plenty of dry ground and fairly good protection. We can defend it.*

Hannah stopped and turned to face the group. "I am stopping here. Everyone rest. Take water. Any food? Does anyone have any food to spare?" she asked, panning the faces around the big circle. No one seemed to have any. No food. Water was probably getting scarce, too. They all dropped in place, thankful for a moment off their feet.

"I need a few lookouts." Hannah scanned the faces around the circle. Three men raised their hands. *Three, that's all? All of them are exhausted. I'm exhausted. It will have to do.*

"Fan out about a hundred meters. Left, right, and center. A few nods and the three dragged off into the woods. Hannah walked over to Joseph and Itzhak. The crude stretcher was propped up at the head end so Itzhak could take some water without choking.

"Hannah. Leave me here. I'm only slowing you down," Itzhak said in a scratchy voice, weak and soft. His underside was still wet from the pools in spite of the heat.

"I'll never leave you. You can believe in that. Besides, who else will help me keep Boris in line?" Hannah smiled when she noticed a flash of the old confidence in his eye. Itzhak winked and then shivered in spite of the heat.

"Try to take some water. Maybe we can scavenge some food for you. I'll try." Hannah stood and looked around at the clearing. The secret spot with Yuri. Another odd growth of nature. A moment of relief. Hidden. Precious seconds to stop and think. She walked around the open area, her people ringing the perimeter. *I'm safe. Well, safe for a moment anyway. The letter. I'm all wet. My pocket is wet. It's ruined. I'll never be able to read it.*

Carefully, Hannah eased the folded letter from her pocket. The paper was damp. She could see ink smudges through the nearly transparent outer skin. Slowly she unfolded it and held it up to the light. It was smeared badly, but some of it still legible.

Dear Hannah, This …no what…want for us…something, something…orders...choice…damn war…time…tell…you…try mee someday…soon…

What was that last part? It said, "love Y'. Love Yuri." He never said that before.

He wants to try to meet me, I think? When? How? How will this ever happen? One of us or both will be dead by the end. Still. Maybe I could…

"They're coming," shouted one of the men on guard duty as he ran into the clearing.

Hannah folded the paper and carefully tucked it into the driest pocket she could find in her coat. "Are the Germans on them?" she called checking her PPS-42 and moving toward the man.

"No. Not in sight," he replied, eyes wide and looking for an order from Hannah.

Hannah looked at David and Itzhak. David's eyes met hers. He looked tired and worried. Hannah motioned for him to move Itzhak behind her.

"Set up a firing line. Over here," she shouted and pointed. Everyone moved up and took cover behind thick pines and birch. Leaves crunched under her shoes and the dry dust rose up into her nose. The tickle was irresistible and the following sneeze unavoidable.

"Here comes two, moving fast," someone shouted.

"Wait, it's our men! Don't shoot!" Hannah barked, throat dry and cracked.

"They're ours," another said. "Hold fire."

Hannah saw a movement on the right. The other one was coming in, too.

The first two reached the clearing and ran through the firing line. "Commander, Boris is behind us a few minutes. No sign of the Germans. He held them up good, but we should think about getting out of here," the older one said. He was breathing heavy, sweat beading across his forehead.

"I will, as soon as Boris and his group get here." The third man came in from the right. The pained look on his face was not what Hannah wanted to see.

"Everyone, get ready to move out!" Hannah shouted.

He moved up close to Hannah, dark beard bristling over pale white skin and lines of sweat streaking down from his temples. He smelled strong and Hannah turned her head away slightly. "What is it?" she asked.

He hesitated. "Germans to the west. Thousands of them. Coming our way.

Hannah could see the concern in his eyes.

"Are we surrounded?"

He looked around. "Not yet but that's their plan. Sure of it."

"Boris! It's Boris!" someone yelled. "No one behind them."

Boris spotted Hannah, then looked past her to Itzhak and David. He walked over to Hannah and flipped the strap of his PPS-42 over his head. The gun hung down over his chest, his sweat-stained shirt soaked through with pond water.

"He's still alive. Wasn't sure he'd make it this far," Boris said, lifting his face in Itzhak's direction behind Hannah.

"Itzhak is holding on. I think the bleeding has stopped for now."

"Can we move him?"

"Yes. And are you alright, Boris?" He nodded. "What is the situation back there? I'm hearing there are lots more coming."

Boris leaned in, face to face with Hannah. "There's thousands. It's an Aktion as they call it. Hannah, I'm not afraid to die, but we might not make it out of this one. I held them off for an hour maybe. Not much more."

"What about the east? They're moving to surround us?"

"I saw them. On the east side, too. We're going to have to go deep into the swamps and hope they can't find us."

Hannah rested her hand on Boris's shoulder. It was damp and warm. "Thank you, Boris. I'll get them moving. Can you take the lead?"

Nodding, Boris pointed to a few of his men and waved them forward. He stopped at David and glanced down at Itzhak.

"He needs food and water, but he is stronger than you think," David said, trying to smile.

Reaching into his pocket, Boris pulled out a bar of chocolate. He reached out and grabbed David's hand, placing the bar with the water-damaged wrapper into his hand. "Try to get this into him. It's better than nothing."

"Thank you, Boris," David said, patting Boris's arm. "Thank you."

Boris nodded and looked back at Hannah who signaled him to move out.

I've got to keep south and move faster than the Germans. Can we win that race? I don't know. I don't think so. Oh, Itzhak, I need your help. Tell me what to do next.

Deep into the marshland forest, Hannah felt the ground getting spongy as her shoes squished up water. Her feet felt cold and wet in spite of the oppressive air. Hours in, she decided sunset was close. Tonight would not be easy. The miserable mosquitos were so irritating during the day. But given the choice of Germans or insects, there was no choice. During the day, swatting and slapping. She'd have to manage. It was torture at night, trying to sleep. And snakes and rats.

They bedded down for the night. Itzhak took some water and actually ate half the chocolate.

. . . . .

The Germans were nowhere in sight. Actually, nothing was in sight. The marsh island was as dark as pitch. No one could produce a dry match and the smell of smoke might help the Germans locate their position. "No fires," Hannah ordered. She tried to find a dry spot on the moss-covered earth, but the best place was damp and musty. Fighting off the mosquitos, she pulled her jacket over her head and tried to doze. The thought of the German advance continuing while she rested was frustrating. More than that, fear was eating away her confidence. Hannah rolled around for an hour. The imaginary crawlers and some not-so-imagined kept her mind racing. Sleep was out of the question. She got up and walked around. Most were so exhausted, they dropped in place and fell asleep.

I need help. I need Itzhak to tell me the best way to deal with this German Aktion. Thousands, tens of thousands. What am I going to do?

Hannah stepped silently across the clearing toward where she knew David and Itzhak sat. The slightest light from the stars lit her way. The shadow that must be David looked up.

"Hannah, is that you?" he said.

"Yes, how is Itzhak?" she asked, crouching and squinting to find his face in the shadows.

"I am alive, Hannah," Itzhak said. "If this wound doesn't get infected, I might make it."

"Does it hurt bad?" Hannah asked, tears filling her eyes. She couldn't hold back any longer.

His voice soft, "You did what a good commander would do. You did what I would have done. You saved us. The only thing anyone could have done."

Hannah was not convinced she had made the best decisions. She felt more scared of making a mistake than getting shot. "Itzhak, there are thousands of them out there. I think they are going to surround us. We have no way to escape and I don't know what to do."

"Stay in the marshlands. Move around in the forest. Just what you are doing now. Hit and run. The Germans don't like the swamps either."

"We have no food, Itzhak. How long can we keep going in these swamps? I am going to get us all killed."

"No. No, you're not. Think how we could get food, Hannah. You know. Your father would know. Remember things he said. You can do it." Itzhak coughed and moaned as his wound was disturbed.

"I'll try to look for food in the morning. We need to go deeper in. Maybe they won't find us. Maybe Boris can pick away at the Germans. Find an escape route east into Russia. I'll try." With Papa's lectures swirling around her head, she tried to focus. Plants, fish, what else?

"Thank you, Itzhak. Rest." Itzhak did not respond.

David put his hand on Hannah's shoulder. "He trusts you, Hannah. We all trust you." Itzhak's breathing was labored. "He's sleeping now."

Chapter Twenty-Eight

Hannah lay flat on her back. *I wish this would all go away. But I know it won't. Get up, Hannah. Get up.*

She opened her eyes. A faint rim of pale light seeped into the black sky, fading the brightness of the low-lying stars. Morning would break soon. The enemy was probably moving already. The men in the camp were stirring. With jacket pulled up over her head, Hannah sat up and slipped it down over her shoulders. She flicked away a mosquito. The pesky attacks resumed with her overnight head protection now removed. She grabbed the pistol grip of her PPS-42. *I hope this gun is not going to jam from rust. If I wasn't so clumsy, I wouldn't have dunked it under water. So stupid. No time to clean it now.*

Several bumps on the back of her hand itched and puckered red. She couldn't protect every part of herself from the miserable mosquitos. She stood and walked around the clearing. As the sky brightened, shadowy figures turned into men. It was time.

"Everyone up! We are moving out in five minutes," Hannah said. No one spoke, short of a few moans and complaints about stiff muscles. She looked over at David, hoping Itzhak was alright to travel. He caught her glance and nodded.

Everyone is hungry. Why are they looking at me? Stop looking at me. Food. Figure out what we can do for food. Think.

The trees and underbrush were visible now. Boris took the lead with several men. David, Itzhak on the stretcher, and another man took up the pace near the middle. Hannah positioned herself immediately behind Boris and the forward guard.

"Joseph, can you take the rear guard?" Hannah asked, his face now visible in the pre-dawn light.

"Yes, I'll take a few of the boys and we'll lie back a little."

"Be careful, Joseph," she said, trying to smile. *I guess I'm not sounding very confident? I'm no Itzhak.* Joseph nodded and dropped to the rear.

They moved further into the island forest. The sun beat down all morning and the humidity rose steadily during the afternoon. *Glad we're not out in the sun. I hope those Nazis bake out there.*

By midafternoon, no one had the strength to carry on without water. Looking for food along the way, Hannah saw only the telltale signs of squirrels and possibly rabbit. Small groups of nutshells and rabbit pellets, or maybe possum droppings. Not much to feed a detachment of starving men. That assumes they could find any small game to hunt. In the water, she had no time to think about fish. How would they fish anyway? No string, no bait, no hooks. She didn't know what to do about it. *Do what Itzhak said. I'll just keep moving on.*

Gunshots rang out ahead. Rifle and submachine gun fire. Then a big machine gun sounded.

Big guns. How am I going to stop the big machine guns? Grenades, we have no more.

"Boris made contact. He must have reached the outer fringe of the woods," Hannah said. "We might be surrounded."

"Hannah, where can we put Itzhak?" David shouted, frantically searching for cover.

"Let me down, I'm alright, I'll walk," Itzhak called out. "Get me a gun."

Boris and the others appeared running through the trees, firing behind as they ran.

"Go left, left!" he screamed, waving his arms wildly and looking for Hannah.

"This way, this way," Hannah yelled, waving her fighters to follow her. *I hope he knows what he's doing or we'll be flanked.*

German soldiers moved in between the trees behind Boris and began firing into the camp. Bullets cut into the tree trunks, bark flying into the air. "Fire, fire!" Hannah screamed and twenty PPS-42's and rifles laid into the oncoming German line. She heard the thud and the fighter on her right went down. A dozen or so Germans and black uniformed soldiers hit the soft ground face-first. *Black uniforms, damn it! Ukrainians. No wonder they are in this deep. We're not going to outrun them this time.*

Itzhak was stumbling along, pistol held against his chest near the shoulder wound. Moving toward him, Hannah grabbed his wrist and pulled his arm from across his chest. She ducked under his arm, rising to lift him up from his armpit, wrapping his arm across her shoulders. She could feel the strap from her gun pressing into her throat. The pistol fired loudly in her ear. Itzhak shot a German soldier in the head. The man dropped only three meters away. Hannah's ears were ringing. The image of blood spurting out of the dead man's temple and running down his cheek stayed a brief memory, then was gone. She looked for a way out. The only possible direction seemed to be north, as Boris said. *This sling is choking me. Get the gun better positioned.*

"Stop, Itzhak. Let me fix my strap," she said in his ear, looking up at his face. He nodded. She slid the gun strap around her shoulder, collapsed the shoulder brace, grabbed the pistol grip, and pointed the barrel forward. *Better. At least I can try to protect us.* "Ready. Let's go," she said looking behind and to her left. More Germans were coming through the trees. The boys were cutting them down but it wasn't enough. Three, four, maybe five of them down already. They couldn't hold this position.

"Retreat. Retreat. This way!" Hannah screamed, but none could hear her. She had to keep moving. David was firing into the oncoming Germans, backing up toward Hannah.

"This way. This way!" he shouted, motioning the others to follow. A few partisans heard or saw him and started in his direction. Hannah spotted Joseph in the group. But where was Boris? He hit them head-on. He'd never get out alive. Hannah felt Itzhak's sagging weight on her shoulder. Her back muscles were aching already. *But he is Boris. Count on Boris to survive if it's possible. Keep moving. Look! Black uniforms. Shoot!*

Hannah lowered her hand to pivot up the barrel of her PPS-42. She pulled the trigger and the gun fired, spent shells pouring out of the weapon. Surprised Ukrainians stopped short and fell backward in a heap. More came through the trees, and David, Joseph, and the others opened fire. A dozen or more black uniforms lay dying as Hannah kept Itzhak moving forward. She looked down at one who was still moving. Tilting her gun down, she fired a short burst. Blood sprayed up from the black uniform. The soldier lay still. *Keep going, Hannah. Just another dead one.*

Struggling on, the boys got ahead of Hannah and Itzhak. They cleared the path ahead for a long way. But two or three of the boys went down. Joseph checked for pulse and shook his head no. *David is hit, I think. Leg maybe. Not my friends, please. Oh Lord, please. Not my friends, too.*

Hannah lost count of the enemy bodies she passed since the last one she dragged Itzhak over. She could see David limping along now, barely able to keep the pace. The trees were thinning out, the forest brighter. They must be near the end. More ponds and marsh. Open territory. No protection.

Gunfire was steady in the rear, although no longer so close. *We can't go back. I'll have to take my chances in the swamps.*

"Joseph, stop. We need to rest for a minute," Hannah called out, back aching from supporting Itzhak. The boys stopped and returned to Hannah. She helped Itzhak down to the ground. "Gather 'round," Hannah said, making eye contact with everyone. She glanced at the wet bloodstain on David's pant leg. "Look, we are leaving the forest not far ahead. It will be open marsh. No cover, and we don't know the enemy situation. I think we have about five or six hours to sundown."

"What do you think we should do?" David asked, his hand pressing on his wounded leg.

Hannah made eye contact with Itzhak. "You are in command, Hannah," he said.

She hesitated a moment. "I think we should get to the forest edge, survey the marshes from cover, wait for dark, and proceed across the water," Hannah said, checking Itzhak's expression again. "If they find us before dark, we fight and run."

Itzhak was smiling. "See. I told you, you were in command. Let's move out. Joseph, can you help me and give Hannah a rest? And David, how bad is that wound?"

"David, sit down," Hannah said, gesturing. "Let's have a look."

"I'll be alright."

"You're bleeding. Sit." With a frown, David sat on the ground and Hannah reached for her pocketknife and knelt next to him. She made a small slit in his pants and peered at the wound. "The bullet came in the front and out the back. No bone hit, just muscle I think."

"If it hit an artery, there would be lots of blood we couldn't stop," Itzhak said as he peered over Hannah's shoulder.

"Somebody have a cloth we can use to wrap it?" Hanna asked looking around. Blank stares all around. "David, your undershirt. Are you wearing one?"

"Yes, but its real dirty."

Joseph paced back and forth. "We have to get moving. They're going to catch us."

"I think we lost them for now, Joseph. Take five minutes and sit down," Hannah said calmly.

"Alright, alright. Just get Joseph to shut up!" David said, grinning through the pain.

"Open your shirt. I'll cut a piece off the bottom hem. Will have to do." Hannah sawed at the shirt with her knife cutting a long rectangle. Pull your pant leg up or pull your pants down. "

"What!"

"Look. One or the other. I don't care either way. Hurry."

"Up. Be careful."

Hannah grabbed the pant leg just below the wound and carefully slid the material over the bullet hole. She wrapped his leg placing the cleanest-looking side of cloth toward the wound. As she tightened the knot, Papa's voice echoed in the back of her mind—*"firm but not so tight as to cut off circulation."* She was young, about nine. They were in the forest and she slipped on a downed tree trunk and gashed her calf. It bled a lot. There were tears. It stung and burned. *"It will have to do for now,"* Papa said, and he was right. Eventually, it healed well.

Pulling the pant leg slowly over the bandage, Hannah looked up.

"Time to move out."

Joseph jumped to the lead. Hannah smiled at Itzhak. He smiled back.

They moved on slowly for a couple of hours and reached the north edge of the forested area. Hannah pulled back the low-hanging branch of a young sapling and scanned the terrain. Marshland and pools stretched out before her. German, Ukrainian, and some other soldiers were sweeping the area. *This is going to be difficult.* They would surround the forested areas and then tighten the noose. Hannah knew she was already trapped. Soldiers would start moving into the woods very soon. They had to find a way out through the enemy lines. The only way was at night.

"We will have to wait until dark. Find a gap in the lines," Hannah said, looking back at the men while scratching the mosquito bites on the back of her hand.

"You mean through the water? And with Itzhak so cold? Too risky. Impossible. There must be a better way," David said, waving his arms toward the water. "We would shoot a few and the whole battalion would be on us. No good."

"Maybe we can create a distraction?" Itzhak said, muffling a cough in his sleeve.

"How? No grenades? Shoot and run? Draw their attention?"

"That's what I was thinking, Hannah."

"I'll do it!" Joseph said, peering out through the low branches of the sapling.

"No. My responsibility," Hannah said, gazing at the enemy in the distance.

"You're the leader. We can't lose you. I want to do it," said Joseph, eyes roving between Hannah and Itzhak.

"We'll see. Wait for dusk."

• • • • •

Streaks of red and yellow coated the horizon, sparkling off the pools as far as Hannah could see. *It is so beautiful sometimes. Oh Papa, the sunsets. If only things were like they were before all this.* She breathed in the musty air and flicked away another flying bug.

Hannah looked at Itzhak. "Almost ready to go," she said. "Can you travel?"

"My shoulder, it's sore, but I feel better. Wish we had some liquor to kill the pain," he said. "But I can go on for a while." Hannah thought it was probably better that they didn't have liquor.

"Alright, my plan is to wait almost an hour. Then move through the shadows to the next island. Get outside of their circle. They won't hunt us out there. They think we're trapped inside the noose."

"I'm going to make the diversion, right?" Joseph said, eyes intense on Hannah's.

She didn't want to lose him, too. It was hard sending them into danger, to always know what to do. She had to stop caring so much.

Itzhak nodded to Hannah. She nodded and looked away toward the water, glancing along the pool in front as it meandered along the forest edge. *Reeds. Natural snorkels. Papa. Yes. There is a way. Underwater. Thank you, Papa.*

"Yes, Joseph. You need to move along the water's edge about a hundred meters. Fire into them. Empty the magazine. Make sure they see the muzzle flashes. And then run back to this spot and enter the water here. Head for that island over there," Hannah said pointing. "We should be into the pond some distance by then. Stay low and catch up to us."

"Alright, I understand everything."

"One more thing. Come with me." Hannah pulled the farmer's knife from her coat pocket and moved along the trees at the water's edge, careful not to be seen. Through the brush, she could see the reeds growing along the pond all within a meter or two from the shoreline. Propping her submachine gun against a tree, she crouched low and stepped into the shallow water. Cool water filled her shoes and her wet pants clung to her calves. Fingering the reed stalks she picked a hefty one. Reaching underwater with knife in hand, Hannah sawed off the plant stem and pulled it out of the pond. Water dripped off the stalk.

"What is this for?" Joseph asked. "I don't need anything but my gun and knife to kill those people."

"You getting killed won't help our cause much, will it?"

Hannah rested the reed against the fat end of a fallen tree branch nearby. Estimating about a third of a meter up, she cut off the top end of the stalk. She gouged and blew out the inside of the stalk. Blowing hard into the tube, water and plant particles sprayed out the opposite end.

"A straw," Joseph said, frowning. "What am I going to do with that?"

"Think water. And air," she replied, pinching her nose and mimicking a submersion. "A snorkel."

"We stay low in the water and dunk under if we need to disappear?"

"Help me, Joseph. We need a bunch of these."

Joseph pulled his knife, crouched, and waded carefully into the water. They gathered several stalks and stepped up to dry ground to work on the snorkles.

"You are really smart, you know," Joseph said, a little smile breaking through. In a few minutes they had the tubes ready. Hannah looked over their work. *Papa would be proud, I think.*

"My father was very smart. Maybe I learned a few things. Let's get back to the others. Almost time to go."

Chapter Twenty-Nine

The forest was dark and dusk settled over the pools of water across the marsh. Everyone sat quietly, waiting for dark. Shadows lurked in the gray distance. Ukrainians mostly, Hannah thought. A few miserable Germans. She hoped they would take the bait. Maybe she could get Itzhak through a gap in their lines. Sneak through. That was the only way. She hoped she wouldn't lose Joseph with this plan. "No choice," as Itzhak says.

"It's time, Joseph," Hannah said, resting her hand on his shoulder. "Take care. Get back here quickly. If you can't find us, head on your own for the island across the way."

"I'll make it. Please get Itzhak through. We need him."

"Don't let them take you alive, Joseph." She always thought a younger brother would have been fun. *Be careful, my brother.*

He nodded, moved away into the shadows, and was gone.

"Take care, Joseph."

Itzhak opened his eyes. "You have no…"

"I know—choice," Hannah said. "Ready? We move into the water as soon as he starts firing."

"Ready," David said. "I'll stay with Itzhak. How deep is this water?"

"Too late to ask that now," Itzhak said chuckling low, smothering another cough. Snorkles ready."

Submachine gun fire broke the stillness. Hannah moved forward stepping slowly into the water. The rest followed.

Water always feels colder at night. Those weasels, like rats. I hope we scare them off. And the snakes. It's too dark to avoid them. Yuri's letter will be gone then, if we make the other island. I can't worry about it all.

Men's voices echoed over the water. Hannah dipped lower into the shallow pond, her front immersed in the brackish pool. *Can't make it out. German, Ukrainian probably. Not far.*

The bottom sloped down and she would be about waist-deep if standing. It was perfect. *Squat with your head out. Dunk out of sight if they get too close.* Hannah looked back at the shadowy figures following behind. Everyone was good. Except Joseph. Where was he?

She turned back, feeling one foot slip on the bottom. It held. Straining to see the dark figures ahead, she realized there was an enemy group coming directly toward her from the left. They split off from the main group and were moving diagonally toward Joseph's diversion. *We're found out! Yes. No. They can't see us either.*

She reached behind and groped in the dark to find David's sleeve underwater. She tugged sharply downward, hoping he would understand. *Ukrainians. They will split us up. Snorkels. Go under. Now!*

Blowing gently on the reed, Hannah cleared the tube of water without making a sound. The enemy soldiers were about five or six meters away, talking low and moving fast. Hannah pinched her nose and lowered her head underwater. She could feel David's hand on her back. She kept moving straight ahead. The air was hard to draw in but it worked. *Papa's trick. The nose. Hold your nose, then tilt your head back. I forgot to tell them to hold their noses. They'll choke! Too late, keep moving. Keep moving and we'll pass by before the Ukrainians reach us. Move!*

Hannah could hear the pops of gunfire above the surface.

Are we past the main line? Did everyone make it? Joseph, they found Joseph! I have to see. Did the main force close the gap up ahead? Or are we clear?

Hanna surfaced to eye level. The salty water dripped off her eyelashes and burned her eyes. Blinking over and over, she stared into the darkness. Crossing through the gap in the main force was working. The island was maybe fifty meters away. She turned and looked back to the shore. The diversion worked. But no sign of Joseph. More gunfire echoed off the water. She felt David's gentle tugging on her jacket. Reaching behind, she found his forearm and pulled to signal him to keep going. Still holding on, David nudged her forward. She hoped Itzhak could keep going. They were almost out of danger. Turning forward, Hannah dipped her head underwater and swallowed a mouthful of marsh water from the snorkel. *Papa said don't panic. Stop, blow out, and breathe.* Quickly blowing into the tube, she cleared out the remaining water and sucked in air. *Keep moving. Almost there.*

The pool bottom was rising as Hannah approached the island. She crouched more and more to stay submerged. Underwater, she felt for David's chest. She stopped and he ran into her open palm and stopped. She turned and lifted her head to the surface. It was dark now. The Ukrainians moved by with muffled voices and sloshing water hidden in darkness.

We made it. Some of us made it.

Hannah grabbed David's shirt underwater and pulled up. He rose from the water and lifted Itzhak. They stood belly-deep, water draining off their faces, heavy breaths all around. Turning back toward the enemy, he ran his hand down his face and pushed back sopping hair. Hannah stepped into the muck on the island beach. David reached out his hand and she latched onto his wrist with both hands and pulled on his arm to get the two men out of the pond. The others helped push them onto the shore, everyone's boots being sucked into the soft earth.

In the darkness, Hannah found David's eyes. *He's not coming with us. I'm sorry, David, I'm so sorry.*

They crossed the clear area, entered the tree line on the little island, and disappeared into the safety of the woods. The plan worked. But once again, at what cost. Hannah felt more of herself crumbling inside as Barbara's words pounded in her head. She was slowly losing all her friends.

The night was long and lonely on the island. The boys took turns on watch through the night. David was quiet. Too quiet even for him. *I got his brother killed. He blames me. It was my plan and now Joseph is gone. And I can't bring him back. I used to think God would protect us. I guess not.*

Exhausted, Hannah rung out her hair and tied it back with a

string. She rung out her jacket and laid it across a low tree branch to dry. Pulling the magazine off her PPS-42, she shook the water out, opened the chamber of the submachine gun and tried to blow out the barrel. Some of the others were doing the same. *It'll probably jam when I need it most, then I'll be dead. This will be over.* Laying down on the leaves, Hannah stared up into the hazy night sky. No moon. *Why is all this my fault?* The tree branches overhead were the last thing she remembered. The night passed quietly on the little island.

. . . . .

"Hannah. Hannah?" Itzhak said softly, gently shaking her shoulder. Cold and damp, a shiver passed through her. Eyes open, Itzhak's face appeared a bit gray, but his smile looked hopeful. Swallowing hard, she could feel the roughness in her throat and the mucous trickling from her nose. Swiping her upper lip with the back of her hand, she sat up and scanned the group.

"Any sign of Joseph?"

"No. You can't blame yourself."

"When I look at David…"

"I know. It takes time," Itzhak said.

"We don't have time."

"Give it time or it will turn you sour."

"I know. I know. I have to check on our Ukrainian friends."

Getting her things together, Hannah moved through the woods and crouched low as she approached the lookout. She thought his name was Moshe, but unsure, she decided not to address him.

"Where did they go?" Hannah said, looking through the brush.

"Started moving into the big island forest to squeeze us. Tighten the noose as you say," he replied.

"When?"

"Daylight. They're afraid of the dark," he said grinning.

Hannah patted him on the shoulder. "We'll stay a few days until we're sure they're gone, then go back."

"A game."

"Yes, a dangerous one." Hannah went back to the group, looking for berries, mushrooms, anything they might eat. There was little to be found on the tiny island.

. . . . .

A week passed with no enemy activity. The Aktion was over. They had to get food and clean water. Hannah decided it best to cross over to the big island under darkness. There was no dry path back, but at least they did not need snorkels. The big island had some game and berries. After seeing no one for days, she risked a few gunshots to kill a couple of small animals. Now well into the island forest, no enemy would notice the smoke or noise. They would need to make a fire. One of the boys had matches dried out enough to light. *Papa's cooking stick will work, I think.* She carved up a couple of skewers and "Y" sticks for supports the way Papa did it. Hannah roasted the meat over a small campfire. Everyone ate what there was of the meat, mushrooms, and blueberries. No one was full. Nobody complained about anything. *I guess hunger treats everyone the same. Not real happy about eating weasels, but I suppose it is better than starving.*

Moving through the woods at a moderate pace, Hannah stopped for the night. No sign of the enemy.

Hannah looked around the group. David looked lost. She knew he blamed her for Joseph. Itzhak was alone, now was her chance. She sat down next to him.

"Itzhak, do you think we should go back to the old camp?" Hannah asked, talking low.

"We can't tell if the Germans are gone without trying. When their last Aktion was over they left the whole area. Officers back to the cities I'm sure," Itzhak answered. "Regular army men went back to the Russian front, I figure."

"Are we safer in the forests to the north than down here?"

"If the Soviets come back, yes. They won't come here. And we can get food from the peasants. Better cover. Yes, we need to go back."

"I don't know what to do with…with…"

"David? Yes, I've been watching him," said Itzhak. "Joseph is my cousin, but he is David's brother. This is harder for him. I'm afraid there is nothing you can do to help him. Like an open wound. Raw and angry. We don't know for sure Joseph is dead. Wait and see."

Hannah nodded. *I'd like to kill every German and Ukrainian I can find. Those pigs need to pay for all this. For Joseph.*

"Alright, it's decided. We move back toward Bialystok, to the forests in the north."

. . . . .

Hannah backtracked across the big island and the large pond. The thought of getting wet again was not pleasant, but necessary. The cautious trek through the forests seemed endless. Almost two weeks later they dragged into the old camp. Hannah strolled carefully around the Soviet huts, looking inside a few. Old bedding, rags, junk mostly filled them. In one she spotted a clean canteen with a sickle emblem lying on the hut floor. Turning it over she found the hidden side was crushed and cracked open. Worthless for holding water. It was the color of the inside of the suitcase Papa buried in the woods at Sokolka. This place felt like an empty house. Yuri, Joseph, Boris, all the others, gone.

The camp was partially destroyed. Obviously, the Germans found it. Her hut was standing, the flimsy door torn away and off to the side. In the corner of the hut was the tin cup. *The letter. How am I going to find Yuri now? He could be anywhere. Even dead.*

Itzhak and David gathered around the old huts with Hannah looking over the damage.

"You think we are safe here, Itzhak?" Hannah asked. "The Germans know this place now."

"I'm not worried. They come in big numbers, try to kill as many of us as possible, and run back to the cities. Like I said before, the soldiers are sent back to the eastern front." Itzhak waved her off.

"Not sure about that."

"Look, we put sentries on guard no matter where we are. It will be alright. Trust me."

Hannah hoped he was right. They couldn't afford to lose any more friends.

Everyone helped each other to reconstruct their damaged huts. One of the new boys found a discarded leather belt and cut it up for hinges for Hannah's hut door. No one wanted to take another's hut. It didn't feel right. The huts were like caskets, waiting to be dropped into their graves.

"We need food and water. Who will go?" Itzhak asked, raising his voice and panning the group. Checking her repaired door, she glanced around the assembly area and the Jewish quarters. No one looked up.

"Hannah, will you do it?" he asked.

Why me? Haven't I done my share of stealing food? She looked over in David's direction. David stared at Hannah, not moving. Two of the boys got up ready to go. *Not them. Too green. I need to push David or we'll never get over this grudge of his. Do it. Now.*

"David, please come."

"I will stay with Itzhak," he said, arms crossed.

"One of the others can stay. You know the peasants better than me. We need food. I need *you*. Please."

"You should have sent me to do the diversion. My brother was too young."

"We are all too young," Itzhak said. "I know it is painful, David, but we must keep fighting. Joseph would have wanted us to avenge him. I would."

David stared at the ground. It seemed forever to Hannah, then he lifted his head.

"I guess you're right, Cousin. But I just left him back in the swamps. Not even a proper burial. How can I live with that?"

"Hit that miserable Volksdeutscher in the east village. His stinking sons, too. You know the ones, David."

"The ones that probably killed Dyadya?"

"Yes. I'm certain they did it, though that crooked mayor sided with *them*," Itzhak replied, resting his hands on David's shoulders, looking him in the eye.

This must be old village business, Hannah thought. *Itzhak, just get him to go with me.*

Itzhak spoke quietly to David for a moment. Finally David nodded and looked toward Hannah, his face grim, eyes sad.

"If you can get me there, I'll hit them hard," Hannah said, eyes glaring and jaw set firm. She was finished with that scum.

Hannah took David and the two new boys eager to make their mark and they headed off to the village in the east. The Germans were gone. No one was around. They moved with renewed confidence, quickly through the woods.

Chapter Thirty

The village was typical—farmland bordered by thin woods with several dozen cottages nestled in the trees. Hannah scanned the village for threats. A few peasants, mostly women, moved around near the houses, hanging wash, tending gardens. The farmers only planted small portions of the fields. The group moved along the woods past a tilled field. The earthy scent of open ground reminded Hannah of digging for earthworms with Papa on their first fishing trip. *Papa is gone now. Forget. Focus.*

"Which house, David?" she asked.

"I'm not sure now. It was about a year ago." He searched for something familiar as they walked.

"Take your time. Be sure."

They walked on between the crop fields and the houses at the edge of the woods, submachine guns exposed. Hannah was looking to intimidate the peasants. They needed food, but not as much as usual.

"There. The big house with the dark brown trim. The Nazi lovers."

"You're sure?"

"Yes, yes. I remember the fat pig standing in the doorway yelling out that all Jews would soon be gone from Poland forever."

"Follow me," Hannah said, slipping the gun strap off her shoulder and extending the shoulder stock on her PPS-42.

"Guard the back. David and I are going in," Hannah said to the boys. "Let us know if anyone comes this way."

Knocking on the door, Hannah looked at David. He gave a slight nod. *Not sure he is ready for this yet, but one way to find out.*

The door opened a few centimeters. Eyes peered out through the crack and the door started to close. Hannah thrust forward ramming the door with her shoulder. The door hardly budged. There was weight behind it.

"Help me, David!"

He stood dumfounded for a moment watching the struggle. Then he slammed into the door with his full weight. The two lunged into the room.

"Bandits! Bandits! Rous! Get out, Jew bandits!" the man yelled. "Where's my gun! Greta, call the boys." The woman ran out the back door screaming for her sons.

Hannah ran to the back door. She could see three men in the crop field running toward the house. They might be armed.

"Boys, come in here quickly," Hannah shouted. The two came in through the back door. "Let the woman go. Collect as much food as you can. I'll deal with the sons.

David pushed the man into a corner of the room and he fell over an old tufted chair. We need food, old man."

"Thieves! I'll turn you in to the Gestapo. Or I'll kill you myself. I'm authorized," the old man yelled.

"So you are a Nazi too, you stupid old Volksdeutscher," David said, glaring at the man as he climbed to his feet. He glanced over to the boys who were stuffing burlap bags with cans, potatoes, a blackened old pot, and some utensils. He looked back to see the old man pointing a German Luger at his chest.

The gun was loud as bullets tore through the old man's body, his blood spraying over the worn beige fabric of the couch and burgundy rug. He keeled forward landing face-first on the living room floor, Luger in his hand. Hannah stood feet apart, expressionless, smoke drifting from the barrel of her gun. She glanced at a speechless David, turned, and stepped out of the house to greet the three men as they entered the yard. She sized them up quickly. The oldest was maybe late twenties, stocky, wispy hair, an obvious limp, and carrying a bolt action rifle. The middle one, thin, early twenties, a revolver at his side. The third, young, about her age, ruddy complexion, carried a sickle.

"We are starving and just need some food. We will be gone in a few minutes," Hannah said. "Stop." She raised the PPS-42, but they still kept coming. At ten meters, the oldest raised his rifle. Hannah pulled the trigger. A short burst hit him in the chest. He went down. She focused on the middle one. The two stopped, stunned, looking at their fallen brother. The older one stepped forward and raised his pistol. Hannah cut him down. Blood sprayed into the young one's face. The second one dropped to his knees and fell forward into the dirt. The young one just stared at Hannah. *Don't make me kill you, too. Go back or you die, too.*

"Hannah. Enough. Let the boy go," David said from the house. "We have the food. Time to go. Run, boy. Help your mother back there. Go!"

Hannah's gaze froze on the boy's eyes. She pointed the PPS-42 at his chest and gently motioned him to back away. He seemed cemented into the ground. No one moved. Finally, the sickle dropped from his hand and he backed slowly away, turned, and ran toward the field where his mother stood at a distance.

"Hannah. Hannah? Are you alright?" David asked, placing a hand on her shoulder and whispering in her ear. "We have the food, let's go home."

She nodded and stared at the ground. "Yes. Home."

They moved quickly through the forest. No one spoke. No one could. Hannah led the way.

Back at the camp, she went into her hut. *Stupid people. What did they think I was going to do? If they're not with us, they're against us. I don't know what's right anymore and I don't care. I'll kill them all.*

Itzhak walked over to her hut. "Hannah, I heard what happened," said Itzhak, peering into her hut, his arm in a sling. "They told me about the Volksdeutscher. You did all you could. They gave you no choice."

"Really. What's the difference? They want us dead, we want them dead. I'll make it so, or die trying. What else is there?"

"Can we talk about it?"

"No. Nothing to talk about." Hannah rested her weapon against the hut wall and lay down in the bed.

"Hannah, I'm worried about you. What you're carrying

inside…let it go."

"There will be more of them to pay back tomorrow, Itzhak. Be ready."

She closed her eyes and turned away from him. "You got your food," she said.

"Hannah. Hannah," he said, shifting his weight. "Alright, we can talk later. But we *will* talk." She heard his footsteps as Itzhak walked away.

• • • • •

About a month went by with little action. In September the Soviets began parachuting behind enemy lines and made their return to the camp. Sakaloff's officers showed up in the first wave. They recognized the Jews and welcomed themselves back into the camp. Slowly, the numbers grew. Hannah figured they must be very confident now of beating the Germans on the front. She heard about Sakaloff's schedule. His new push would get more Jews killed for sure.

The spring and summer had been brutal enough. Now with the Russians back, two missions each week took an awful toll. Boris and Joseph never came back. It took months before David would say more than "yes" or "no" to Hannah. She couldn't get Joseph out of her head. Hannah gave up on trying to fix things over with David. Itzhak healed and regained most of the mobility in his arm. She could still talk with him. Itzhak understood.

Hannah watched early December snowflakes drift to the bare ground. *I never thought I'd make it through '43. But here I am, or what's left of me anyway.*

A second wave of Russians entered the camp. Hannah spotted a familiar face. The Russian cook was still attached to Sakaloff's brigade. Hannah only recognized a few faces from the earlier Russian group. No Yuri yet.

"*Zdravstvuj,* comrade," Vladimir the cook said to Hannah as she strolled by.

"Hello," Hannah said, expecting to see Vladimir perform some new magic, but she was in no mood for tricks.

"Are you new here?" he said, craning his neck and squinting.

"New? I am Hannah Gould, Vladimir. Don't you know me anymore?" She tried to smile, but her jaw tightened, lips pressed hard together.

Vladimir studied her face. "Oh, forgive an old man. You look…ah, older. I guess I don't see so well these days." His bloodshot eyes pleaded for some relief.

"It's me. I suppose I am different."

"The fighting. It changes all of us."

"I guess I was mostly a schoolgirl when we first met. Now I kill people," Hannah said, her voice sharp and spiteful. Vladimir stared, then nodded.

"Well, I have news about Yuri. Do you want to know?"

"I want to know why you all left me and my group behind?" asked Hanna. "Why did Yuri leave? You left us alone with all those Germans and Ukrainians."

"Moscow. Generals. They give orders. Don't care about people. When the spies heard about the German action, well, we got ordered to leave."

"Yuri. What happened to him?"

"We were all ordered out. But Yuri was sent to the front. They needed young commanders. Many were lost," explained Vladimir.

"He left me a note. But now I'll never see him again, will I?"

"I have heard a few things. There will be a counteroffensive, as they call it. He will be back."

"So he had no choice? They forced him to go?"

"No choice. Sakaloff would have shot him."

"I lost good fighters. My friends." Hannah started to walk away.

"Come and see me again. Please."

"Yes. Sorry, none of this is your fault. I will stop by again, Vladimir." Hannah looked at the black iron pot of soup starting to boil. Wisps of steam circled the rim and disappeared into the cool air. She walked away, toward her hut.

Soviet soldiers walked all around the camp and congregated in the assembly area, between the Russian huts and the Jewish section, close to Hannah's spot. Most were strangers, new recruits. None of them seemed to know the old camp rules and wandered around the Jewish huts, looking at her. A few more Jews straggled in from hideouts and the forests, scared and hungry. By luck they found their way to the camp. A year ago, Hannah would have welcomed them. Now everything was changed.

Itzhak, David and the others are not the same. It's like meeting old friends who are no longer as I remember them.

. . . . .

After five more months and forty-some missions, Hannah was tired of it all. Some partisans impressed by her daring wanted to see the Jewish girl the Germans hunted. Some thought her reckless. No one thought of her as a girl anymore. Just a fighter. Hannah thought it only a matter of time and she would be dead, like the others.

She walked in the woods alone, just outside the camp all the time now. Spying young buds on the ends of the birch tree branches, a smile crossed her lips but quickly melted away.

Papa loved to show me how all the plants bloom. But I grew up and didn't really care anymore. I only cared that I was with him. The forest near Bialystok. The first nature trip of the year, always in May. What a relief from the dirty snow and cold wind in Warsaw.

Hannah stepped on a brown and gray stick. It snapped under her weight. *Especially on a sunny day like this. The warm sun and cool air on my skin. Why doesn't it feel like it used to? I guess I might as well get used to being alone. I am alone.* She sat down on a fallen tree trunk. She felt like crying. After a while, Hannah walked back to the camp, dry-eyed.

That night, sitting by the campfire between her hut and Itzhak's, Hannah felt the cool night air drift up the back of her neck. The summer sun and humidity would be back soon enough. The thought of summer did not stop her from shivering. She had wondered once if people in graves got the shivers. They were already as cold and dead as dirt, how could they shiver? The firelight cast shadows on the hut walls and evergreen branches above, dancing in rhythm with the flames. From the shadows Itzhak came toward her. He swayed a bit as he positioned himself to the tree stump stool next to Hannah.

"I'm feeling good tonight," he said, looking at her with glassy eyes. Firelight reflected off his face. "How about you?"

"You want to talk now?" *He's had enough war, too, I suppose. But drinking won't help.*

"If you're ready."

Gazing into the fire, she searched for words to say. *I'll never be ready. My life is so mixed up now. I don't even know myself. Why is it always so hard for me to talk about how I feel? Some girls never stop.*

"I can't keep doing this, Itzhak."

"What do you mean? The Germans?"

"My family, my friends…not much longer."

"Yes, you can. You're stronger than you think, Hannah," he said with a slight slur. "You can do it."

"No," she said. "I'm not you."

"The new ones—they look up to you, you know."

"So many gone. Joseph. You might as well say it, I killed him. And the new ones don't know me. They don't respect me," Hannah said, wagging her head.

"Hannah, you didn't kill Joseph. No blame. We all know the risks. David and the new ones, they already respect you. Even the Russians do. You know that."

"When I kill a German, I don't feel good or bad. It doesn't bring anyone back. My Papa and Mama are lying in the ground."

"Hannah, I can't bring them back. We just can't deal with losing you."

"I used to like our partisan songs. They make everybody strong. Once I thought we were winning. But everything looks empty now. Every time I beat them back, there are more to kill. I'm afraid I haven't much left. For me now there's no victory like in the songs. Singing helps. Makes us feel stronger. Laugh at danger. I forgot how to laugh, Itzhak. You have to feel something to laugh."

"Maybe we need to sing. To know we're still alive."

"I sang with Mama. When I was little. It's so long ago."

"You will," Itzhak said in a whisper.

"Itzhak, I'm afraid," Hannah said, wanting to cry. She rubbed her dry eyes and searched his eyes for something to hold on to.

"These Nazis will be gone someday. Don't let the killing and hate wash you away. Don't disappear with them, Hannah."

"What should I do?"

"Stop hating them. Don't let the hate swallow you up. Save yourself, for me. Forgive them, Hannah. It's the only way I know. I had to forgive Zosia and myself. It was killing me."

"What? I don't understand, Itzhak."

"I know you heard about Zosia. It's alright. You must let go of the guilt."

"What? What guilt? Zosia? Oh, I don't know what you are telling me."

Sliding off the stool, Itzhak moved to his knees in front of Hannah. He rested a hand on her shoulder and touched a finger to her lips. "You will find yourself. Hold on a little longer. The end is near, I know it."

"The Germans are losing, right?" she asked, vaguely noticing the men standing around the assembly area. Itzhak's hand went to her other shoulder and squeezed gently.

"They are. There will be no mercy on those murderers. We'll join the Russians in tearing them down. Or not. It will happen either way."

"I'm not guilty, am I?"

"You can never make it equal, Hannah. You can only lose yourself trying. Leave it behind. When you do, the tears will come, streaming down your face like a river," he said.

"But everything is so far away. Too far to touch anything."

"You will find yourself. Trust me, you will."

Itzhak got to his feet and helped Hannah up. Some of the new

Jewish fighters were staring at them across from the assembly area. Hannah glared at them and they turned and walked away. *They don't understand where we've been.*

"Think about what I said, Hannah. Get some rest." He turned, looked around the camp, and walked unsteadily back to his hut and disappeared inside. Hannah looked at the dying fire, the Soviet tents across the camp in shadows, and walked to her hut.

Chapter Thirty-One

The Germans were frustrated with the increase in attacks on their trains and telegraph lines. The Gestapo nailed up more reward posters for Hannah's capture. Some part of her enjoyed taunting them. Fear was always in the back of her mind somewhere. Some fear she told herself was healthy. The words of Itzhak and Boris. But the Volksdeutscher incident still laid heavy on her. She woke up in the middle of the night, sweating and screaming. The image of the sons lying in a pool of blood mixing with Papa's and Mama's blood, soaking her bare feet, would never go away. *How much longer? This counteroffensive better happen soon or I might just leave camp and keep walking. Maybe being dead would be better than this.*

. . . . .

Hannah roamed the camp alone, day after day. She saw more and more Soviets arriving each week. The camp was expanding into another section. The Russian soldiers couldn't resist bragging about the glorious Soviet invasion that would not stop until Berlin. How they would stomp every last German into the ground. Hannah didn't care about victory. Whoever came her way, she'd kill. Nothing else about Nazis and Germans mattered anymore.

One day a Soviet reconnaissance team left Hannah word that her peasant woman friend needed help. The Russians thought the source to be suspect and warned her. It was many months ago since she paid the woman a visit. But Hannah owed her. She was kind, like Bubbe Rachel, when Hannah needed help the most. A promise she couldn't ignore. After all, she'd let Hannah take a bath whenever she got really dirty. But it was more than a bath. The woman revived her. And the scent of her soap. It's all Hannah had left of Mama.

It was risky to go alone, though. It was hard to tell the difference between being brave and being stupid. Something else Itzhak once said. These peasants were starving and money could change things for them. Anybody would be tempted to turn her into the SS for the reward. She doubted the Gestapo would actually pay them in the end. Hannah sat on the stump outside her hut. She looked toward Itzhak's hut.

I wonder if the old lady is sick or hurt. She blames the Germans for her daughter's death. What if she said something to the wrong people? It's a trap for sure. But I promised her I would be there if she needed help.

Hannah got up and started walking to Itzhak's hut. The campfire between them was long cold. Her boot caught on a firestone and she nearly tripped. Things were quiet for the moment. The old woman was probably in real trouble or wouldn't have called for help. She wouldn't turn on Hannah. Hannah had to go now. Itzhak's door was open, no one inside. Looking to the far side of his hut, she spotted him sitting behind it on a log, between David and Joseph's huts. Hannah avoided Joseph's hut. It took too much effort to even look at it now. She focused on Itzhak, reading some papers. Probably from Sakaloff. He looked up.

"I'm going to the old woman's house, Itzhak."

"I heard she got a message out, but it doesn't sound right."

With an open hand, he rubbed his chest over the old gunshot wound. She nodded at his shoulder. "Is that still bothering you?"

"I'm alright. Everything works in there. A little tender, that's all."

"I'll go alone. No use risking more fighters."

"You can't go alone. Take the new boys. They are looking for a fight. "

"They'll slow me down."

"Hannah. I can't stop you, but you know that's not smart. Teach them something."

He scanned the camp area. Soviets were moving about around Sakaloff's tent. Two were sitting between Boris's hut and the Jewish latrine on stumps, talking out of earshot. The other three hung together across the assembly area near Vladimir's area. They probably smelled the food cooking.

"Those two over there. Take them with you," he said, pointing.

"Alright. But if they don't come back alive, remember this was your idea."

"Fine. Go, then, but remember what we talked about."

Nodding, she paced off toward the new men, her boots crunching dry sticks and leaves.

"I have a mission. A small one. I need you two."

They stood up, almost at attention. "Yes, when do we go?" said one, eyes wide.

Hannah stood with her feet apart, satchel and gun straps across her shoulder. The submachine gun hung muzzle pointed at the ground. "Extra magazines and pistols, bring water and food," she said.

"Where? When, Commander?"

"Now." Hannah watched as they pulled their things together. *They seem nervous. Probably because it's me. I bring bad luck. Itzhak's right, I am dangerous and tired and probably reckless. Or somebody will turn me in for the money. Only a matter of time.*

She drew in a deep breath and let out a long one.

"Meet me over there, past my hut," Hannah said pointing.

They nodded. Hannah walked to the edge of the camp and stood, arms crossed. The boys hurried over to her and the three moved out of the camp into the brush. Hannah set a fast pace.

One of the boys slipped and tripped over a downed tree branch, falling face-first into the leaves and pine straw. Hearing him fall, Hannah stopped and looked back. He got up, red-faced, and brushed himself off. With a scowl, Hannah turned away and continued forward.

Yuri. What happened to us? It's like a dream now. I only know how to kill people. Would you love me like this? Papa is so far away from me. Mama, I can't even think about. Itzhak. What a sad place this forest is for me now. Cold and lonely.

They skirted a large puddle of black water blocking the path through the woods. Hannah glanced at the reflections in the puddle as they passed by. She continued on for a few minutes. The village was close now. There was good ground cover and plenty of pine to hide them. It might be a good time to go over with the boys how to approach the village and the house.

Hannah picked a spot and stopped. Crouching down, she grabbed her canteen and took a gulp of water. The two boys crouched next to each other facing Hannah.

"From here I don't know exactly where the woman's house is. But it should look familiar to me when we come upon the town."

"Alright, tell us what to do."

"No matter what happens, if we get split up, try to meet here."

"How will we know…?"

"Look up. See the crooked branches growing flat across to each tree. Looks strange. Find this rendezvous point. Understand?"

"Yes," one said. They both nodded.

"Let's go." Hannah stood, scanned the forest all around, and started off. The boys followed. She turned her head to make sure a gun barrel was not pointed at her back.

"Make sure the safety is on and your weapon is secure," Hannah said, turning her head forward. She heard a click from behind. *I really don't need to be accidently shot in the back. This was your idea, Itzhak.*

Ten minutes later, they approached the edge of the village. The path was closer to the peasant woman's home than Hannah expected. The house looked shabby. More so than she remembered. Rusty streaks from rainwater leaking out of the torn gutter marred the faded gray siding. No one was around. The cottages farther up the road looked abandoned. Hannah remembered how Itzhak and David approached the houses in their village. Familiar places need extra caution. *Don't let your guard down. Check the windows before going in.*

"You two. Each take a wall and peer inside the windows. I'll take this wall here. Should only be an old woman. Be quiet. If it looks suspicious, come back to me. Now go."

Hannah watched the boys crouch and run silently to their positions. She moved up to her wall and kept her gun low. Her cheek touched the siding as she peered in the window. It was hard to see past the reflection of the woods off the glass, but after a few seconds, the woman inside moved through a doorway and disappeared. She went into the kitchen. No one else seemed to be in the house. She had to risk it. Hannah moved along the wall to the corner of the house. She motioned to the boys and they came back to her.

"Stay here out of sight. I'm going in. If you see someone coming, knock on the window and hide. If there's a commotion inside, come in ready to shoot. I can't tell you everything that could happen. Do what seems right."

They nodded. "But what if the Germans come?"

"Do what seems right. I won't leave you, try not to leave me."

They nodded again. Hannah looked at their eager, scared faces. She peered around the corner to the front of the house. No movement up the road. She stepped out and walked to the door.

Moving her gun behind her leg, she knocked on the door and waited. Footsteps approached the door.

"Who is there?" a woman said. Hannah thought she heard another voice, low and deep. She swallowed hard, her throat dry.

"Hannah Gould. You sent for me." The door opened a crack, then more. The woman's face was white against the dark room. Her eyes showed fear. Her pupils centered and then moved to her lower left. Hannah nodded ever so slightly.

"May I come in?" she said.

"Yes." The door opened halfway. In one movement Hannah swung the PPS-42 past her leg and thrust it into the space to the woman's left. The barrel contacted a heavy body and she pulled the trigger. Spent shells tinkled off the dry wood floor. A groaning sound and a man's body fell away and dropped to the floor in a pile. Hannah felt a steel barrel push into her temple.

"Don't move, Jew," a man said in a deep voice.

"I am so sorry, Hannah."

"Shut your mouth, old woman," the man said as he closed the door.

"This miserable pig calls himself our village police chief. He has my grandson. I had to do this," the peasant woman said.

"You shut up, woman. Move slowly into the room, Jew." Hannah noticed a younger man with sandy brown hair in the corner behind the chief.

"Drop your gun, Jew bandit," he said, pushing the pistol hard against her head.

Hannah lowered her submachine gun to the floor.

"Go and alert the captain. He can pick up his Jew right here," the chief said.

"Alright, but I don't trust the Germans. They might kill us anyway. Papa, you hearing me?"

"Go! And don't worry about the money. I'd do it anyway."

The chief's son rushed past Hannah and out the front door.

The boys heard my shots. Why didn't they come in? Maybe they tried and saw the door close. Hannah scanned the room for more people. None. *Where's the grandson? Not here? If the SS arrives, we won't have any hope. I need a distraction. Before the chief's son comes back with them.*

"Why do you want to help the Nazis? You're a good Pole, right?" Hannah said, looking for an opportunity.

"Get two chairs from the kitchen, old woman," the chief said, motioning with his head. "Go!"

The peasant woman did as she was told and carried one at a time to the living room.

"Put one behind the other in the middle," he ordered. The room was small and the old couch left little space.

"Sit, girl," he said. He had his pistol at Hannah's head, slowly moving her to the seat. He then moved around and sat behind her in the other chair and pointed his gun at the back of her head.

Smart. I can't see him. Come on boys, help me. Do something, anything.

"We'll just have a little wait now," the chief said, adjusting his chair. "This will all be finished soon."

The old woman passed by Hannah on her way to the kitchen.

"Where are you going, woman? Stay here where I can see you."

"You're holding my grandson at your house. What can I do?"

"Yes. And remember that. My assistant chief will take good care of him. As long as things go as planned," the chief said with a little chuckle. "I would guess another twenty minutes or so and you will have this dump of a house back."

Moving her head slightly, Hannah caught movement in the window to her right.

"No, no. Don't try anything stupid, my little Jew. A bullet is much faster than you."

It seemed forever, sitting and waiting. Finally, the sound of vehicles far off broke the silence. The chief stood and his chair moved back scraping the floorboards. Glass splattered into the room. Hannah dove forward and slid on the bare wood floor trying to reach the kitchen. She heard a blast of submachine gun fire and slid to a stop at the doorway. The police chief dropped to his knees and keeled over on his side, pistol in hand and not moving. Hannah got up and stomped the back of his hand and the gun slid away. She ran across the room grabbing her submachine gun and looked up. Itzhak's face was framed in the broken window. "Back door," he said, through the remaining shards of glass. "Hurry."

Hannah looked at the old woman. "I'll try to save your little boy."

"No, you get away. They don't want him, they wanted you. I know the assistant's wife. She'll beat the shit out of her husband if he harms my grandson. I couldn't do anything with this one alive. The bastard is finally dead. You go. Quickly!"

"Thank you," Hannah said, their eyes locked for a second. She escaped out the back door to find Itzhak and the two boys. "Run! They're on us."

Four SS soldiers and an officer rushed the cottage. Three came around the side of the house as Hannah ran from the backyard into the woods. She looked over her shoulder and spotted the officer near the back door. The old woman stepped out on the landing and watched the chase. *I hope they don't kill her for helping me. I can't save her and myself. I've brought more bad luck.*

"Run!" Hannah yelled. Hannah, Itzhak, and the boys thrashed through the underbrush. She stopped, turned, and fired into the oncoming soldiers to slow them down. Return fire from the Germans rang out behind her as bullets ricocheted off trees and rocks. Hannah started running again and saw that in another two hundred meters the forest was thinning out. *No cover up ahead. They'll shoot us down!* She caught up to Itzhak who was now running slower than the boys.

"We have to make a stand somewhere," she shouted. "Ambush them."

"From where?" Itzhak called back over his shoulder.

The boys had run ahead through a big puddle of black water crossing the pathway. Water flew up from their boots as they entered a small clearing with two large trees, their trunks forming a V at the base. Perfect cover for an ambush.

"Itzhak, you stop with the boys on the other side of that clearing. I'll ambush from the right."

"I see it. Go!"

Hannah veered off the trail to the right, jumped between the two tree trunks, and turned and squatted low in the V. *Don't think they saw me. Here they come. One chance for surprise. Make it good. Only three Germans. Where are the other two?*

She aimed her sights at the second German. She pulled the trigger and the gun pumped rounds into the man. He went down and the third soldier ran into her stream of bullets and was also hit. Still alive, he tried to fire in Hannah's direction. A bullet struck the tree trunk over her head. More gunfire broke through from the other side of the clearing. One gun, then two. Itzhak and the boys were firing now. The lead German went down.

Catching her breath, she felt a familiar calm come over her. Her hands steadied. The officer and the remaining soldier hadn't followed the others. Where were they? She waited a few seconds and stepped out from behind the V of the two trunks. The downed man was no longer moving. He probably bled to death. She had to get to Itzhak.

Hannah started into the clearing. She could see Itzhak and the boys. They stood up.

A single gunshot rang out.

Hannah felt a burning pain in her left thigh and she dropped onto her knees over the puddle on the trail. As her face hovered over the black water, her reflection came into view. She saw her fierce eyes staring back—the eyes of the SS officer in the pit so long ago now. *I'm a monster like him. What have I done?*

"Hannah. Get out of there! Come with me," Itzhak shouted, running toward her. She looked down at the dark bloodstain spreading across her thigh. He wrapped his arm around her waist, tugged and supported her weight on his hip. They moved closer to the shelter of the big trees where Hannah had been hiding.

"Almost there. Almost..." Itzhak said, straining to move her to cover as another rifle shot echoed through the trees.

The thud Hannah heard was familiar. Solid. Permanent. Hannah felt the power leave Itzhak's arm as they both fell forward hitting the cold mud and leaves together. Her mind stopped thinking for a moment. *Please God, no.* The hole in his back was small, but Hannah knew the front of his chest would look different. Her thigh burning, she looked back through the trees, but she couldn't see the SS officer or his rifleman.

Another shot was fired and one of the boys cried out. He dropped to the ground moaning. The other boy reached Hannah and tried to pull Itzhak back behind the sheltering tree. Another shot rang out. Blood shot out of the boy's chest and he went to the ground and lay still. It was cruel, but at least she knew the direction of the rifle shots. The shooter was probably a hundred meters away, but a deadly shot. She dragged Itzhak around to the other side of the two trees making the V.

Hannah spread her legs wide for stability and pulled on Itzhak's shoulder to turn him onto his side. She checked his wound. As she imagined, his chest was much worse than his back. Just above her a bullet tore bark off the tree. Splintered wood sprayed down on her head and shoulders from above. She laid Itzhak down on his back. He moaned as his body twisted then came to rest.

"Itzhak, don't leave me," Hannah cried. Her thigh throbbed. Dizzy and nauseous, she struggled to think clearly.

"I'll get you back. The Russian doctors, they'll fix you." The words came out of her, as if someone else was mouthing them. Faint wisps of steam rose from his warm blood and the hole in his chest. Hannah turned away. He was alive, but his body looked like the other dead strewn around her.

"Hannah, listen to me. I am going to die here. Listen."

"Itzhak, don't leave me. You can't." Hannah held up her blood-soaked hands, helpless to stop the bleeding. His face grew pale.

Itzhak whispered, "I love you, Hannah. God help me, but I've always loved you." Hannah cradled his head as the sparkle in his eyes froze.

"Itzhak." She looked into his eyes, hoping for a sign. "Itzhak." She shook him gently, but his eyes stared blankly up at her.

She gently rested his head on the ground and lowered her forehead to his. Itzhak was gone.

She didn't think it would happen like this. Shot in the back. She had hoped they would take down many more than their number, and go down fighting like Boris. Not this way.

A submachine gun burst jolted Hannah and she looked up to see the German rifleman stagger and drop to the ground. The SS officer walked calmly over to Hannah's last man and fired three shots point blank into the partisan. The SS officer hesitated, then gazed in Hannah's direction. He moved differently than the killer in the pit, but his eyes were the same. He held his Luger by his side and walked toward Hannah.

He thinks we're all dead. Quietly, Hannah got her hand on her PPS-42 and gripped the handle. She flipped off the safety and rested the gun in the V out of sight with the muzzle pointed upward at the German. Staying low, she lifted her head enough to see the man approaching. She smeared some of Itzhak's blood on her face and pretended to be dead with her eyes open. As he came into view between the tree trunks, he stopped, leaned forward, and raised his Luger. Taking aim, he pointed the pistol at Hannah's head. She nearly froze when their eyes met. Hannah pulled the trigger and held it, emptying her gun into the German's body. He fell away from her sight and hit the ground with a thud. The gunshots echoed off the trees and then drifted away. The forest was quiet. She lay still next to Itzhak's body, her eyes dry, her leg aching.

Chapter Thirty-Two

Hannah lay still for a long time. Birds moved about in the branches above. Cold from the ground seeped into her back. *I've got to get him out of here. David and I, we need to bury him properly. I can't leave him like this.* She looked at her thigh. The bloodstain was no worse. Pulling her pocketknife from her coat, Hannah made a slit in her trousers and peeked at the wound. The burning grew more intense. It was a deep flesh wound, but she thought it missed the bone. That's why she could still move her leg. She had to stop the bleeding. When the leg stiffened, she wouldn't be able to walk.

She struggled to her feet and looked around. One of the dead boys had a shirtsleeve sticking out below the sleeve of his coat. That would do. She unbuttoned his coat and cut the shirtsleeve below his armpit. It seemed disrespectful, but she needed a bandage. *I feel like I did when I pulled the slippers from the feet of the dead woman in the pit.* Hannah shook her head to erase the image from her mind. She grabbed the protruding sleeve and yanked it out of his coat. Sitting on the ground, she fed the cloth through the slit in her trousers. She wrapped the wound and held her breath. Cinching the bandage tight, Hannah let out a scream and almost lost consciousness. After a minute, she got back to her feet. It was done. Good enough for now. She needed the peasant woman's help, and the woman needed her.

Hannah took a step. The searing pain stopped her breathing for a moment, but the leg supported her weight. Itzhak, eyes partially open, arms spread out on the cold ground, looked so vulnerable. Hannah grabbed him under the arms and pulled, wanting to sit his body upright, resting his head in the V of the tree. She glanced over at the dead Nazi officer, his chest torn open from her bullets. Blood-red leaves surrounded the black uniform. Pulling again on Itzhak's body, her leg throbbing, she managed to move him enough to prop his head up on a tree root. She unbuttoned his coat and pulled it up to cover his head. It would have to do for now. *I'll be back soon, Itzhak. I won't leave you here. Not for long.*

Picking up her submachine gun and collecting Itzhak's gun and the extra magazines from his coat pockets, she checked on the two boys. She felt no pulse on either and their skin was already getting cold and rubbery.

"I'll bury you, too," she said over the boys' bodies. After checking the dead strewn around the clearing, she set out for the old woman's house.

Close to the edge of the forest, Hannah could see the houses through the trees. *I wonder if…? Stupid. There are always more. Watch out.*

She moved quietly through the white birch and ash, hiding behind a thick pine at the edge of the woman's backyard. After a minute, Hannah moved as quickly as her stiffening leg would carry her. Leaning against the back of the house, she knocked lightly on the door. A curtain in the window moved. A face surrounded by thick, gray hair appeared, then the yellowed curtain swept closed. Hearing the door latch, Hannah stepped away and raised her submachine gun. The door creaked open enough for Hannah to see the woman clearly. In the dim light, she looked frail and older than Hannah remembered.

"I heard shooting far away in the forest. None of the SS came back here. I was afraid you were dead. I tried to get my grandson back, but…" she said, shaking her fist at the house down the road. "Can you help me?"

Hannah nodded and motioned toward the kitchen.

"Yes, come in, dear."

Hobbling up the step, Hannah limped into the house. She scanned the living room through the doorway. The police chief's body lay in the middle of the room. The other villager lay near the front door where Hannah killed him. She lowered her gun. The blood on her Bubbe Leah's burgundy rug shot through her mind. *We must get rid of these bodies and clean up the blood. The SS will be back sooner or later and kill her if they think she has helped me.*

Glancing down at Hannah's thigh, the woman grimaced. "Oh, oh, you're bleeding. I'll get soap and water. I have iodine, too."

She started toward the bathroom and Hannah clutched her arm. "Wait." The old lady stopped and saw Hannah wobble.

"Feeling dizzy," Hannah said, moving to the kitchen table. She lowered herself to a spindle-back chair.

"I need to sit. Water. Please." The woman nodded and stepped to the sink and reached into the cabinet for a glass. Hannah placed the PPS-42 over a hairline crack in the wood tabletop and Itzhak's gun next to it.

"Your grandson, where is he?" Hannah asked, as the woman started back with the glass of water.

"He's being held by that snake down the way. When the Germans left I went to the assistant chief's house. My grandson was not hurt. He called out to me to help him, but the bastard slapped my face and pushed me away. My boy is so frightened, Hannah. That stinker is waiting for the big bastard chief to come back."

"That one is not coming back," Hannah said, looking down at his body. "My friends are not coming back either. I—*we*—need to bury them."

"And the SS?"

Their eyes met. "All dead. We'll need to hide their bodies. In case others come looking for them."

"They will. I'll do what I can. I have friends in the village who may help. They will know what to do."

The woman handed the glass of water to Hannah and she gulped it down and coughed. "Let's go get your grandchild before my leg stiffens and I can't move," Hannah said, holding up the water glass, gazing at its blue and yellow hand-painted flowers. Like the glass in her Bubbe Rachel's kitchen that had held the daisies that Hannah picked each summer. Hannah placed the empty glass at the center of the table the way she used to, but now next to the guns. "Let's go."

Checking her weapon, Hannah got to her feet. "Lead me to the house."

"The other end of the village. Can you walk that far?"

"Let's go."

As they walked along, the woman looked at Hannah. "This man we're going to see. He's stubborn, but old and afraid. He's only holding my grandson because of the chief. You don't have to kill him. As I said before, I know his wife and she would not survive as a widow."

Hannah looked at the woman. "Do you want your grandchild back or not? I'll do only what he forces me to do. If that means he dies, then he dies."

The old woman looked worried, but Hannah figured she could handle one old man. The two approached the house from the front. The few peasant women in the neighboring yards stared and then moved quietly into their houses. Hannah checked for any sign of resistance. None. She tried to turn the door handle, but it was locked. Positioning herself on the hinge side of the sun-bleached brown front door, she motioned the woman to knock. Three light taps on the door received no response. Hannah reached across and pounded on the chipped paint four times with her fist. She was about to knock again when a floorboard creaked. Hannah heard a click and watched the pitted, rusty door handle slowly rotate. The door swung open about halfway.

"Oh, you again. Haven't had enough yet? Well, now I'm really going to..."

Grabbing the edge of the door, Hannah swung it open and stepped into the room, jamming the muzzle of her gun into the man's throat. Startled, he fell away, turning and hobbling toward the kitchen. Hannah scanned the room. The little boy cried and yelled from behind a closet door on the left. A wooden kitchen chair was propped under the door handle to hold him in. The peasant grabbed his old rifle that leaned against the wall by the kitchen doorway.

"Drop the rifle or I'll cut you down," Hannah said, taking a close look at his weapon. *Wait. That old thing probably doesn't even work.*

"Your miserable chief is dead. All the SS are, too. Give up, you old fool," the woman said, gritting her teeth.

"How do I know you're not lying?" he said, pointing the rifle over Hannah's head.

That's an old Polish make. No magazine in it. It's not even loaded. He doesn't know what he's doing. Scare him.

"Drop the gun, old man," Hannah shouted and shot a burst over his head into the wall. The sound was deafening. Bits of plaster sprayed into the room. Spent shell casings tinkled and rolled across the hardwood flooring. The old man threw the rifle to the floor between himself and Hannah.

Limping across the room, Hannah grabbed the chair lodged under the closet door handle, and yanked it away. The chair tipped over, hitting the floor with a bang. She opened the closet door, releasing the little Piotr. He looked up at Hannah, blonde hair ruffled up, and then he spotted his grandmother.

"Grammy, Grammy," he yelled. Hesitating a moment, he stepped around Hannah and ran to waiting arms.

"It's over, old man. If you ever do anything to this woman or her family again, I'll be back for you."

The old man held his arms up.

"Do you understand?" Hannah hissed through gritted teeth.

"Yes, yes."

A floorboard creaked as Hannah stepped forward and leaned toward the man.

"If the SS come back, you don't know anything about anything. Understand."

"You're the one they are looking for, aren't you?"

Hannah gave a slight nod. The man looked at the woman, the PPS-42, and back to Hannah.

"Are you sure the chief is dead?"

"He is right now staining my rug with his miserable blood. And you can make doubly sure, because you and your stupid friends are going to bury him," the old woman said, shaking her fist at him.

"I can't..."

Hannah raised her submachine gun and pointed it at his head.

"Yes, I will get the villagers. When?"

"Now. Bring shovels. You have to bury ten men."

"Ten! Why ten?"

"Because you caused all these deaths. You and your chief. Now move!"

The old man hustled out of the house and down the road. Hannah watched him from the front door. She leaned on the doorframe to take some weight off of her leg.

"Can we trust him?"

"He'll do it out of fear," the old woman said. "Don't worry about him. Now we need to look at your wound."

They took Piotr and walked back to the house. Hannah was limping badly. She wouldn't be much use for a while with her leg like that. Sakaloff will be wondering what happened to Itzhak. Maybe even her.

At the house, the old woman told Hannah to lie down on the kitchen table. She brought two pillows from the bedroom and propped up Hannah's back and head.

"Take off those trousers," she said. She carried over a bowl of water, a sponge, clean rags, and a dark glass bottle of iodine. Hannah looked at the hole in her trousers and the bloodstain. Years ago she hurt her leg in the forest. Papa had bandaged it, but she worried because they were so far from a doctor and hospital. There was blood, but not like this. The trouser leg was soaked through and clung to her skin as the woman gently pulled the material over the wound. Streams of blood from the new wound passed by on either side of the scar that lie just below her knee. She stared at the scar, trying not to focus on the bullet wound.

"Have you done this before?" Hannah asked, feeling nauseous and looking away.

"My husband and sons were farmers. Somebody was always having an accident. I saw plenty in my time." She took two bottles of liquid, one clear and one dark, from the kitchen cabinet. Hannah couldn't see the labels, but one looked like the vodka Itzhak had in his hut. She poured some into Hannah's hand-painted glass, then filled the glass with red wine and stirred it with a tarnished spoon.

"All I've got to kill the pain," she said, holding out the glass for Hannah to take.

Hannah put the glass up to her lips. It smelled strong. "I don't know. I don't feel so good."

"Hold your nose and drink it down, all at once. It will help."

"I'll try." Pinching her nose, Hannah took the mixture in four big gulps. It burned her throat as much as the pain in her thigh. She almost threw up, but clamped a hand over her mouth and kept swallowing over and over.

"Water," she gasped, hoarse and choking. The old lady was ready with another glass full of water. Gulping it down, Hannah took a deep breath and lay back on the pillows.

"Try and relax your leg muscles. Let me clean this wound and take a better look."

The woman's touch was gentle, unlike her disposition with strangers. She cleaned the wound quickly.

"From what I see, you are real lucky. I would guess the bullet passed through muscle, skimmed the big bone, and then out more muscle on the other side. Another centimeter or so and you wouldn't be walking. Lucky girl. Real lucky."

The room was spinning, like when she hit her head jumping off the train and later in the bedroom with Barbara, the spy in Warsaw. Even though the kitchen was cool, Hannah could feel sweat dripping down her sides. She lay back exhausted. Itzhak's body lying in the cold mud stuck in her mind. Her leg seemed far from her body. An occasional tugging on her skin jogged her back to consciousness, then nothing.

. . . . .

Loud knocking on the front door roused Hannah from a groggy sleep. She opened her eyes and focused on a water stain on the ceiling above her head. Still lying on the kitchen table, she tried to get up but the room seemed to be floating around. *They're back. Where's my gun?* Turning her head to the side, she spotted her submachine gun in the corner of the room, out of reach. She could hear people talking by the front door, but couldn't make out the words. Hannah recognized one voice.

Two old men, one the assistant chief, walked into the living room. "Oh, God. He's dead," the assistant said, hands on his hips. "How are we going to get him out of here? We'll have his blood all over us."

"You stupid old fool. You should have thought of that before you listened to that bastard of a police chief," the peasant woman said. "Get those two bodies out of here."

"If the Germans come back and see all this and find their soldiers dead, they will kill our whole village," the assistant said.

"Idiot," the old woman said, throwing her hands up. "Of course. That is why you people need to bury these two and the other eight lying in the forest behind my house.

"We can't dig that many graves," he said, looking at Hannah, glancing at the dead bodies and then back to the woman.

"Get more neighbors to help!"

Hearing where the conversation was going, Hannah wanted to get to the gun to help persuade the men further. She looked at the bandage on her bare thigh, still clean though it felt wet underneath. Sitting on the table in her underwear with these old men looking at her was not going to help matters. She slid her buttocks to the edge of the table and dropped her feet to the floor. The skin over her wound pulled tight. Shocked, she took a moment to adjust to the pain, and then stood up. The others stopped jabbering and stared. Her army jacket barely covered her privates.

"I'll lead you to the other bodies," Hannah said, gripping the table to keep from falling. "Get more people to help. You know the Gestapo and SS will burn this village to the ground if they find that we killed their people."

The assistant chief backed away from Hannah. "I have four more coming, I think."

"Look, we need to hide or bury the SS. All five. Where can we put them?" Hannah asked, leaning back on the table.

"You mean dig graves or hide them in the forest somewhere?" the assistant asked.

"Anyplace where we can cover them up. And not too close to the village," replied Hannah.

"The old, abandoned well," the woman said. "We could dump them into it."

"That might be alright…where is it?" Hannah said from the kitchen doorway. "Have to cover them with dirt so the animals won't get to the bodies. And keep the smell hidden."

"No water in it for years. About a couple hundred meters behind the house here. That's what we'll do," the assistant chief said. He checked to see if Hannah agreed. She nodded to him.

A knock on the door stopped their talk. *The gun. Get the gun.* Hannah hobbled to the corner of the kitchen and picked up the PPS-42. She took a firing position from the kitchen doorway and aimed over the living room couch at the front door. The old woman opened the door to three peasant women and an old man holding shovels and rakes. Hannah lowered the gun, limped into the living room, and leaned against the couch.

"We have a problem. You probably know this already. The SS are looking for this girl. The police chief took my grandson, to make me help the SS capture poor Hannah here," the old woman said, pointing to Hannah. "She and her friends killed the SS men, but Hannah's friends were killed, too."

"Isn't she the one with a price on her head?" a villager asked. "Why should we help her?"

"She has killed many Germans for our country. Now you would turn against her? No."

"We will tell them she…"

"You all know the SS. They will burn our village to the ground no matter who killed their people."

"Never mind him, we understand. We will dig," another woman said, waving the man off.

"I need to take you to the bodies in the woods. Does anyone have a crutch or a cane?" Hannah asked, searching the faces in the group. Someone said they had a cane and left to get it. "And we need to bring three bodies back here and move the five Germans to the well. How are *you* going to do that?"

"I have a pull wagon. I'll bring it here," an old man outside said. He set his shovel on the ground and walked away.

The old woman looked at Hannah, confused, and moved next to her.

Hannah looked her in the eye and asked her quietly, "You've always been so kind to me. Would you let me bury my people on your land? One is my best friend."

The old woman hesitated and sighed. "Not where my husband and children are buried. I promised him that my family would be together. But just inside the woods is a little clearing. Bury them there, my dear."

"Thank you," Hannah said, looking around for her uniform trousers.

"Your clothes? I have work trousers. More of my daughter's things. Couldn't bear to throw them out. Not yet." She left the room and returned in a moment with light brown trousers with cuffs that buttoned at the waist. She helped Hannah get them on over the bandage.

When the villagers returned with the cane and the pull-cart, two women helped Hannah onto the pull-cart. The cart bed was cracked and covered with bits of dry clay and straw. Splinters poked at her palms as she lifted her bottom onto the cart. The train car at the depot and the German's face filled her mind. *I was a little girl then. No more.* She led them to the ambush sight.

The peasant women gasped at the bloody wounds. No one was happy about moving dead bodies. Especially dead SS men. Hannah moved stiff-legged, pivoted on the cane, and pointed out her men to be taken back to the house. She avoided Itzhak's face. "Take the Germans to the well," she said. "Make sure you cover them with plenty of dirt."

Four of them took Itzhak's body by the arms and legs. One woman dropped his leg and the weight of his body pulled the others down to the ground. Hannah closed her eyes. What was so difficult that they couldn't just pick him up and place him in the wagon? It was a simple thing. She hobbled, awkward and shaky, to them, the cane snagging on briars and sticks. Hannah held Itzhak's head up while they placed him into the pull-cart. They lay the two other boys next to Itzhak, their arms overlapping each other.

"It's not far back to the house. Can you take the women back and start digging the graves," Hannah said to the old woman. "I'll go with the men to find the well."

"No, you look like a ghost. You'll go to my house with your friends. I will go with the assistant chief bastard to the well. Send the old man back with the cart to this spot and I will see to it that the Germans are dumped in the well. I hope to be back before dark."

Feeling weak and dizzy, Hannah nodded and turned to the old man who was ready with the cart. "Let's bring them to the house," Hannah said. He started back.

"Hannah. You can't mark the graves," the old woman called out.

Stopping and turning, Hannah's eyes met hers. "I know. That is the saddest part of it." She turned on the cane and limped after the wagon.

When they got to the house, a woman sat on the back stoop waiting. Two pudgy, red-faced girls stood next to her. The woman, probably the mother of the girls, was stocky with thick arms, no neck, and a bull head. Hannah thought she could probably lift the bodies off the wagon by herself. A shovel jammed into the ground next to her, stood like a fence pole waiting for the rails to be attached. A shovel and a rake lay on the ground in front of the girls. They seemed disinterested and not particularly bright. Nodding to the woman, Hannah looked for the place to bury Itzhak and the others.

Near the rear corner of the property stood four gravestones, thin and weather-beaten. She moved further back. A row of trees and brush marked the start of the woods, but a small, protected clearing lay on the other side. "This is the place," Hannah said. She tapped the ground with the cane. *It looks peaceful here. A good place for him.* "Bury them here," she said to the stocky peasant woman and girls. They pulled the wagon to the spot, unloaded, and lined up the three bodies on the ground. The stocky woman put her foot on the edge of the shovel, her weight burying the blade into the earth.

"I have to go back to get the Germans," the old man said. "I am sorry you lost your friends."

"Thank you," Hannah said. She watched the old man pull the wagon into the woods and disappear into the brush.

Chapter Thirty-Three

The sun was setting when the other group returned with the wagon and shovels. The villagers looked tired and worried. The old woman came over to Hannah who was sitting on a log with her leg stretched out, watching the gravediggers.

"It's done. The well was not far from the bodies. We dumped them all and covered them up with plenty of dirt. I don't think the animals will find them," the old woman said.

The three graves for the boys were nearly completed, but a bit shallow. Everyone pitched in and quickly finished the holes. Hannah was spent from the loss of Itzhak and the nagging pain from her thigh.

"I have some big burlap bags in the shed that we can wrap them in. I was saving them to hold vegetables, but this is important. Is that alright, dear?"

"Yes. It's more than my parents…" Hannah said. "Yes."

As they wrapped the three bodies in burlap, Hannah sat quietly. The only other burial she could remember was when Bubbe Leah got sick. They wouldn't let Hannah see her. There was a lot of whispering and "don't upset the child" talk. She remembered Bubbe's funeral and shiva. Hannah was only seven years old. The bare wood casket smelled like the trees in the forests. The funeral place looked like Bubbe's apartment. Dark curtains guarded the windows from any sunlight entering. The rug under the casket was burgundy and gold, like Bubbe's rug. She looked for bloodstains, but there were none. The bare, light wood casket did not belong in such a fancy room. Bubbe Leah would never have approved. Hannah watched the villagers lower Itzhak and the boys into the ground.

"Do you want to say anything, dear?" the woman asked. "Like a prayer, I mean."

Hannah looked at the faces, watching her in the dimming light.

"I remember some of it, Kaddish, prayers for the dead."

"Why don't you say them, Hannah?"

Hannah nodded and looked at Itzhak covered in burlap lying in the open grave. *What will these people think? They won't understand Hebrew. I don't even know if God is listening anymore.*

"Go ahead, Hannah," the woman said softly.

Hannah looked up at the villagers standing around and then down into Itzhak's grave again. She only remembered parts of the prayer for the dead.

"Yitgadal, v'yitkadash sh'mei raba…" she recited then paused. *"U-vi-z'man kariv, v'imru amein,"* She looked at the old woman. "I don't remember the middle part."

"Say what you remember. It's important that you tried. It's more for you than for them."

Hannah looked down and continued. *"Oseh shalom bi-m'romav, hu b'rahamav ya'asehshalom aleinu v'al kol yisrael, vimru amen."* Picking up a handful of dirt, Hannah wanted to cry as she threw it onto Itzhak's body. But no tears came. She threw a handful of dirt on each of the boys and looked up. "You can cover them up now." Leaning on the cane, she turned and limped away toward the house with the sound of shovels and dirt hitting the burlap behind her. The smell of open earth was familiar. The smell of the pit.

• • • • •

Hannah stayed the night with the old woman and her grandson. The woman took her uniform and gave her a blouse, sweater, and baggy pants she said were her daughter's clothes. Hannah had planned to take the cane and make the long walk back to the camp in the morning. The wound was agonizing and she hardly slept all night.

"I can see you're struggling. I have a friend, a Home army man, about three kilometers from here. He may be able to get some army medicine. I'll leave this morning," the old woman said. "You'll have to care for my grandson, Piotr. You can't leave him alone. Can you do that, Hannah?"

"Yes, he will be good with me. I won't sleep. And please try to find something strong," Hannah said, gently rubbing her upper thigh above the wound. "I know you don't want me to know your name in case I'm tortured, but…"

"Call me Rifka. I will be back as soon as I can." Piotr was in the kitchen eating breakfast. Rifka went into the kitchen and told the boy that she had to leave and would be back soon. Hannah hoped the boy would behave. She was not able to run after him. Rifka put on a drab gray coat and fleece hat that used to be green, now faded beige. "Good-bye Piotr. I'll be back soon. Give me a kiss." Piotr ran over and hugged the old woman. Rifka looked at Hannah and nodded. She opened the door and left.

The door was scratched and faded like the rest of the place. The green door from the warehouse in Warsaw flashed in Hannah's mind—the door she stared at when waiting for Itzhak, Barbara's young partisan who was to take her away to the forest.

Piotr sat on the floor in the living room, playing with his toys. Hannah watched for hours how the boy would make up stories and talk to his stuffed animals. He made up his own world and ignored adult life around him. Hannah remembered the stuffed bear on her bed in Sokolka and forced it out of her mind.

"Where is Grammy?" Piotr asked. "When is she coming home?"

"Soon, I hope. Do you love your Grammy a lot?" Hannah asked, forcing a smile.

"Yes. When is she coming home?" he asked again.

"I had a nice grandmother, too. Her name was Rachel. She baked cakes and pies for me. I loved her very much."

"Where is she? Will she come to my house?"

"I wish she could, but she lives very far away," Hannah said glancing out the window up the village road. A peasant woman with a fleece hat, carrying a satchel, moved steadily along the road toward the house. *Rifka, I think. Yes. No one following her. Good.*

Footsteps on the doorstep got Piotr's attention. The door opened.

"Grammy! Grammy!" Piotr shouted and ran to the door.

"Well, well. How are you and Hannah doing?"

"I like her," he said.

Rifka looked at Hannah half-lying on the couch. Their eyes met. Rifka motioned if they had any trouble. Hannah mouthed no, but her eyes couldn't hide her desperation for relief of the numbing pain as she gazed at the satchel.

"I owe him. A couple of shots of morphine was all he could spare."

Hannah hated needles and her expression probably gave that away. Little choice. She needed the painkiller now.

"Can you do it quickly?"

"Yes, let me put these things down and wash my hands."

Rifka got everything ready, filled the syringe, and injected Hannah. She lay back on the pillows and tried to relax her thigh muscles, stroking the skin above the wound.

Soon the pain lessened and Hannah fell asleep on the couch.

. . . . .

Late the next morning, a knock on the door startled Hannah out of a light sleep. Her eyes popped open. Her gun leaning in the corner of the living room slowly came into focus. *Get to the gun, quick!* She tried to rise from the couch, but her leg was stiff and burned as she moved. From the kitchen, Rifka grabbed the submachine gun and handed it to Hannah on her way to the front window. Peeking through the slim gap in the curtains, she turned back to Hannah.

"I think they are yours, but I don't trust anybody now," Rifka whispered.

Hannah checked the weapon and flicked off the safety latch.

"Ready. See what they want." She pointed the gun barrel toward the door.

Rifka opened the door only partially so Hannah remained out of sight.

"Who are you and what do you want?" she said in her usual tone reserved for strangers.

Hannah could hear boots scraping on the front step. "I am looking for Itzhak and the others. I am from the fighters in the forest. But you already know that, don't you?"

"What is your name?"

"I am David, Itzhak's cousin."

Rifka glanced back toward the couch. Hannah nodded and Rifka swung the door wide open.

David looked past the old woman and saw Hannah sitting there, submachine gun pointed at him.

"Hannah, you're alright? Where is Itzhak and the others?" David asked, scanning what he could see of the room.

"You can come in," Rifka said, stepping aside. "Tell the rest to wait around the back of the house. I don't need any more attention. My village has already seen enough." David nodded and motioned his three fighters to wait in back.

"Be quiet and stay out of sight. Knock on a window if you see trouble. I will be out soon," David told them. He stomped his boots on the cracked stone step to clean off the mud and stepped into the living room.

He looks taller than usual. Or maybe the room is small. Maybe it's me. Hannah clicked on the safety and put the gun down on the couch. Rifka closed the door and returned to the kitchen.

"Your leg. Is it bad?" he asked.

"I'll live." Hannah rubbed her thigh above the bandages.

"You didn't come right back so Itzhak left to find you. I argued with him that it was too dangerous to go alone. He said he would have plenty of support when he met up with you. Where is he? And the rest?"

Hannah tried to look David in the eye. *This is going to be so hard for him. And the blame. My fault, I guess. Always seems to be my fault.* Hannah looked up and their eyes met again.

David looked at her face a long time. His eyes narrowed.

"No. Oh, no. Tell me he's not dead." David closed his eyes. He stood limp and without color. Then Hannah could see his jaw tighten. His body became rigid as he slowly opened his eyes.

"You killed him. Just like you killed my brother. Joseph, now Itzhak. You've killed what little family I had left. Now I'm alone. I have no one left."

Hannah hung her head down. *Maybe he's right. Maybe I should put the gun to my own head. Papa, what should I do?*

"She saved my little grandson," Rifka said from the kitchen doorway. "The German bastards killed Itzhak and your other friends. Don't you dare blame this brave fighter. She saved me and this whole village."

Hardly hearing Rifka's words, Hannah looked down at the submachine gun lying next to her on the couch. Rifka picked up the gun and put it on a high chest in the corner of the living room, and looked at the closed door of the bedroom where Piotr lay sleeping.

"Sit, David," Rifka said as she moved a kitchen chair into the room near the couch. "Sit."

Absently, David leaned on the chairback and then dropped himself into the seat. He put his gun on the floor and rested his head in his hands. After a time, his stomach convulsed and short bursts of air shot from his nostrils. As he cried, Rifka walked to him and stood, gently rubbing his back.

"It is best to do it now. I learned that a long time ago. It is better for the soul. Let it go," Rifka said.

Hannah leaned back on the pillows, the drug taking hold of her again, and she fell asleep.

. . . . .

An hour or so later, David and his three fighters were in the kitchen eating. Hannah was awakened by Piotr climbing onto the couch. She felt Piotr's stuffed bear hit her shin. It was close enough. The thigh ached and burned, but much less than overnight. David came into the room. Standing with feet apart and hands on his hips, he towered over Hannah. His head seemed to touch the ceiling of the room, though it really didn't.

"The woman tells me you buried Itzhak and the others in the back here. I thought you left them to rot in the forest," he said to Hannah.

He's trying not to hate me. But he does. Why shouldn't he?

"Help me up, David and I'll show you."

Reaching out her hand to David, Hannah sat up on the couch. With her other hand she grabbed the cane that rested against the seat cushion. David just stared at her for a moment. Nodding to herself, she pushed off the couch armrest and stood on her good leg. She leaned on the cane for balance. The wound pulled and burned. She gritted her teeth and put weight on the bad leg. It hurt but held her upright. She hadn't tried to walk for a couple of hours since she made her way to the bathroom.

"Out the back door. Less noticeable to the villagers," Hannah said, moving slowly to the kitchen. The cane knocked on the wood floor with each step. Getting through the doorway was awkward, but Rifka grabbed her arm and helped her outside. Hannah noticed the scowl on Rifka's face as she bumped David out of the way. Hannah heard David order the three boys outside to stay alert. Hannah and David went alone to the grave site.

"Where are the dead Germans? And I don't care if they rot in the woods."

"We hid the bodies. I didn't want them killing this whole village if they found their dead."

He nodded. "How did my cousin die?"

"Sharpshooter. Sniper probably. He shot every one of us from a long way off."

They walked on to the tree line at the back of the property.

"They're in the little clearing behind these trees. It's peaceful there, I thought." Hannah hobbled between two trees and stopped. "The three are here. Itzhak and then the others," Hannah said, pointing out the position of the three graves.

"It is a good place, but there are no markers. No stones or anything?"

"Rifka, the old woman. She will put up markers after the Germans are gone from here. I thought it was safer for everyone if we hid the graves."

"That was your idea, was it? Why do we care what happens to these people?"

"I didn't want the SS to dig up their graves looking for partisan maps and orders."

"I doubt they would bother. How did Itzhak go down?" David asked, looking Hannah in the eye.

"Do you really need to know that?"

"He came out here to protect you. Is that what he was doing?" David asked, reaching down and picking up a stick.

"I was hit in the leg and he was helping me get to cover."

"And then what?"

"German's bullet hit him in the back and we went down."

"I thought so. He'd still be alive if…" David said, throwing the stick hard into the trees.

"If what?"

"If he wasn't risking his neck for you."

"That's not fair."

"No?" David said. "You're reckless. You've killed what's left of my family. I've got no one left."

Hannah hung her head and wanted to defend herself, but no words came to her.

"There's nothing more I can do here. Time to go back," David said and turned toward the house. He took long strides and left Hannah behind, struggling to keep up.

Back at the house, David's three men were standing around. The younger one kept watch from the rear corner of the house. *Haven't seen that one before. Must be new. The other two, well, not too disciplined.* They were sitting on stools in the backyard, close to the house and smoking cigarettes. As Hannah approached the group, she could hear David speaking. "Get ready to move out, I'll be right back."

David walked into the house. When Hannah reached the house, the young fighter asked, "You are Hannah Gould, aren't you?" *I guess David didn't tell 'em much about this mission.*

"Yes." She hobbled past the three, sensing their eyes on her. The back door opened and she stepped inside.

"Everybody says you're a hero. I just wanted to meet you."

"I'm not a hero," Hannah said. She tried to climb the step to the back door. The door opened and Rifka grabbed Hannah's forearm, helping her up.

"Hannah, do you want to go back to your camp or stay here another couple of days?" Rifka asked. "I think you need more rest, but if the SS come back, you can't be here. And they will be back looking for their people."

Hannah looked at David. "I'll need help. Maybe the boys can help me.

"You said Kaddish over the graves," David said, looking at Rifka and back to Hannah.

Hannah nodded.

"We will get you back. The Russians have plenty of medical supplies at the camp. Things are going to change very soon. Rumors are stronger by the day," David said. He glanced around the kitchen. "Do you have a blanket or something we can use for a stretcher?"

"I have blankets, but they might tear," Rifka said shrugging.

"Burlap," Hannah said, making eye contact with Rifka.

"Yes, that will do." She opened the pantry door and rummaged through layers of material and canning jars on the closet floor.

"Get your things together and I'll have the boys make some poles," David said, stepping to the door.

Rifka rolled up a sheet of burlap and a length of rope and took it to the men outside. "Tie the ends with the rope to make a loop for the stretcher poles." One nodded. She watched them cut small holes in the material and feed the rope through. Satisfied they were on the right track, Rifka returned to the kitchen.

"My trousers, I can't wear these things in the forest," Hannah said to Rifka as the old woman came through the doorway. David glanced at Hannah and left to join the boys in the yard.

"I washed out most of the blood and mended the holes in your uniform," Rifka said, scowling at David behind his back. She went to the bedroom closet and returned with Hannah's uniform. "I'll help you get dressed."

Rifka changed the dressing on the wound. It looked very red and ugly to Hannah, but Rifka said it didn't look infected.

"He will blame me forever," Hannah said. She watched the old woman bandage the wound.

"Maybe not. You can only try. The rest is with him."

David took the lead and the men took turns carrying Hannah on the stretcher. She lay on her back, gun across her stomach and the cane at her side. She watched the trees above and wondered about Rifka and the child. How long before the SS come looking for that officer? If they bothered to look in the forest, they might find the well. She hoped David was right about the Red Army coming back. Maybe that would keep the SS busy.

Approaching the camp area, the Russian sentries knew Hannah and stared as the group passed through the outer perimeter. They thought she was invincible. *I see them looking at me. I should be leading, not David. Damn, I hate this.*

Too tired to fight, Hannah lay back on the burlap and closed her eyes. The group entered the camp and brought Hannah to her hut. Even more men than before were moving about the camp. The Soviet quarters had expanded over half of the assembly area. The Jewish section and the latrines were no longer set apart. David was right, things were changing quickly. She got off the stretcher and leaned on the cane. More eyes than ever were on Hannah.

"I'll ask their medical man to see you," David said as he walked toward Sakaloff's area.

"Thank you, David," she said and hobbled into her hut to lie down on the musty bedding.

He grunted and kept walking.

Hungry and thirsty, Hannah asked one of the new boys for water and food. Looking around, she spotted the tin cup. Yuri's note that was stuffed in the cup flashed through her mind. The smeared words on the damp paper soaked with swamp water. And worst of all, Joseph begging her to pick him to be the diversion in the Pripet marshes. A suicide mission for sure.

"Here. Take this to Vladimir, the old Russian cook," she said, holding out the cup. "Tell him Hannah asked for a good Russian breakfast."

"But will he…?"

"He'll know." The young Jewish fighter nodded and left her alone.

Later on, refreshed from the soup and tea that Vladimir sent over, Hannah saw an army medic at her door.

"I am to treat your wound and change the dressing," he said in Russian. He was a little younger than Itzhak perhaps and looked a little like Yuri. Hannah understood enough and nodded. "I have to remove your trousers," he said, his eyes glancing up to Hannah's and nervously looking back to her thigh. He removed her boots. She unbuttoned the trouser waist and crotch. The medic gently tugged on the material. Leaning on her elbows, Hannah lifted her buttocks. The material slid down her legs. Their eyes met for a moment and then he pretended to rummage in his satchel for something. His ears were red. *He's embarrassed. Well, I can't worry about him. This hurts!*

"Are you ready?"

"Yes," she said in Russian. "Get on with it."

The medication was wearing off and the pain was quickly rising.

"Wait. Give me a shot for the pain?"

He held up his index finger and proceeded to undo the bandage. Taking a quick look, he folded the bandage back over the wound. Searching through his satchel, he pulled out two small glass vials of liquid and a syringe. He gave her two shots and Hannah lay back to rest.

"Whoever treated this wound did well," he said as he worked. "No infection. It should heal fine. Once the swelling goes down, you should be able to walk much better."

"How long?"

"I am not sure. Probably three weeks or more."

"I may not have that long."

He shrugged and finished cleaning and dressing the wound with a fresh, white bandage.

"Do you want to put your trousers back on?"

Looking through the doorway, past the medic, Hannah could see fighters milling around outside.

"Yes. Help me."

He was gentle and her trousers slid over the bandage with little difficulty.

"I will be back every day or so to check the wound."

"Thank you," Hannah said, lying back on the bed. The throbbing slowly lessened. Drowsy, she fell off to sleep.

Chapter Thirty-Four

Over the next month Sakaloff continued the attacks on the trains and telegraph lines. For Hannah, walking around the camp became easier and she finally left the cane in her hut. Her slight limp seemed to add to her reputation in the camp. Some young fighters actually saluted her, even though she told them she was not in the army. She figured David must have asked Sakaloff to leave her alone until she was fully healed. She hadn't been on a mission since Itzhak died. The rumors of the Russian counteroffensive continued to build. Everyone could feel it; 1944 seemed like it would be the beginning of the end for the Germans.

. . . . .

It was a Wednesday morning in late June, just after sunrise. The Germans passed by to the north, although nobody knew, except maybe Sakaloff and his senior officers. The cool dampness in the forest would turn to a nagging heat and humidity by midafternoon. Hannah thought she heard thunder, but the sky was blue through the trees above. Then she realized it was artillery booming off in the distance. The armies were close. Sakaloff was strutting about, giving orders. The Soviet men were rushing to close the camp and move out.

I don't feel like fighting anymore. But once again, the Russians will leave us Jews alone to fend off the Germans. If this is to be the end, then I'll die fighting.

David was up directing the Jewish fighters. He and Hannah hadn't talked much for weeks. She made herself a promise, a secret one that she would not break. She walked up to David and looked him in the eye.

"That is artillery. It's close. This must be the big offensive, right?"

David repositioned the gun strap on his shoulder and nodded. "Yes. Sakaloff tells me the Red Army started the attack days ago. The Germans are on the run moving west. They're north of here. Maybe twenty or thirty kilometers. He was ordered to move north and join up with his comrades. We can join with them. Sakaloff heard it's going well. We can help drive the Germans back to Berlin. Revenge will be sweet."

"Do all our people want to join in?"

"Yes! We can lead our boys to victory. And kill every German we can find on the way. Pack up, Hannah. We move out in an hour."

Hannah nodded, but she knew she had had enough. It wasn't safe in the camp anymore. She would go with them north and then see what happened. She went to her hut and collected her gear. The tin cup hung from the rusty nail. *So much for Yuri,* she thought and turned away. Picking up her canteen, extra magazines and jacket, Hannah stepped out into the sunlight. The weight of her extra equipment put more of a strain on her bad leg. Sometimes a sharp twinge of muscle pain would break her stride. She met with David and they divided the Jewish boys into two squads between them. David and his group took the lead and Hannah's group followed. She fell back to the rear guard position.

Today could be my last mission. No matter what comes, I'll make it through or I won't. These Germans won't just lie down. Don't fool yourself, David, it'll be a fight. And more of us will die.

. . . . .

Sakaloff's troops moved out of the camp first. David fell in behind them. There was some comfort in the numbers as the whole detachment marched together through the forest. By noon, Hannah's shirt was soaked. Even Sakaloff must have felt the heat as he ordered regular ten-minute rest stops along the way. Though her leg was well-healed, the strain of a twenty-kilometer march was wearing on the muscles. Hannah sat as soon as the order was passed back. The boom of the artillery was much louder now. *Are we going to run into the Soviets or the retreating Germans? Comes down to luck, I guess. And I haven't had much of that lately.*

The march continued until about six o'clock, when small arms fire cracked in the distance. The line stopped up ahead. Everyone waited, listening and peering through the trees for the enemy. The faint sound of machinery, trucks, and tanks droned on in the distance. They were close. But close to which army? They were no match for tanks and artillery. Looking ahead, over the heads of the Russian men, the sky looked brighter. They were near the edge of the forest. Farmland. She supposed the big armies needed open areas to move tanks and trucks. Word was passed back to proceed. Hannah could hear her heart thumping in her chest and ears, but her hands were steady. She looked behind every so often for enemy soldiers.

Finally, shouts and hoots up ahead broke the silence. Men were yelling in Russian and laughing. Some poked at the sky with their guns and rifles. The line slowly moved forward. David turned back and called to Hannah. "It's the Red Army. The Germans passed through here already."

Hannah nodded; she didn't smile. She made the clearing and stepped out into a field. The night she left Warsaw with Itzhak and stole the farm truck to pick up David, Joseph, Schlomo, and Boris flashed through her mind. It looked like the same ground. But the whole area looked like that. Trucks pulling artillery, tanks, and hundreds of Soviet soldiers stretched across crop fields and pastures. *Maybe it's alright to hope now,* Hannah thought, and sat down to rest her leg.

. . . . .

Sakaloff gave the order to camp by the edge of the forest, and everyone unloaded their gear. It was about seven o'clock and too late to press on. Hannah watched as two of Sakaloff's officers went off toward the army vehicles across the field. Everyone had field rations, but Vladimir started a cooking fire and boiled water for coffee. At sunset a Russian officer was driven up to the campground. Out in the open, away from earshot, the officer, Sakaloff, and his staff talked in private. They passed a bottle of vodka around. From a distance, in the dimming light, Hannah could see big smiles and some pointing fingers. Then the man saluted Sakaloff and drove away.

One of the officers got everyone together and the commander stepped into the middle of the group.

"I give you good news. The German has been pushed back from the Motherland by our glorious Soviet forces. We have met with the rear guard of our army. I am ordered to move north to join forces with our comrades moving west to liberate Warsaw and the northern cities from the Nazi. We will join them in crushing the German invader."

The Russian men hugged and slapped each other's backs. Hannah watched David and some of the Jewish boys. They whispered to each other, "What about us?"

David stepped toward Sakaloff. "Commander, what should we Jewish fighters do now?"

Hannah noticed a slight change in the Russian's expression and then a toothy grin crossed his whiskered face.

"Yes, my Jewish comrade. Your people have been good fighters to help us free the Motherland, and I am grateful."

"But what are we to do now, Commander?"

"Well, comrade, you are welcome to continue the fight with us."

"Thank you for that honor, Commander."

Hannah watched David nod to Sakaloff and then step away. *I don't care what you do, David, but I won't be with you.*

. . . . .

The night was peaceful, in spite of the rumbling artillery far off to the west. Tired from the day's march, Hannah drifted off to sleep with her gun lying across her torso. At first light, the army assembled and started moving north. Sakaloff's detachment joined in with the Soviet army as did all of the Jews. Hannah decided it was still too dangerous to leave them. They continued on for five more days. She figured they must be close to Bialystok by now. Hannah watched David up ahead as they stepped through unplowed fields and empty pastures. *David wants revenge. I know all about that. But him and me, we're not doing so well anymore. He's not going to be happy if I leave now. I'm too good of a killer. But I don't have much fight left. It's Itzhak. It hurts too much.*

About midday, Hannah heard more shouts and cheers. In the distance vehicles and people were moving back and forth across the horizon. As they marched closer, she could see a major road crossing their path. Trucks and tanks marked with red stars and Soviet soldiers overflowed the road. Most of the traffic was moving southwest. Sakaloff halted up ahead. Everyone came to a stop. Hannah told her people to follow David's group and she moved up to talk to him.

"I would guess we are about thirty or forty kilometers northeast of Bialystok. This is the road between Bialystok and Grodno. Looks different with all this traffic," David said. He coughed on the dust in the air kicked up from the tire and foot traffic.

"Where we took down the telegraph lines with Boris and…"

"Itzhak and Joseph. I remember."

And the train ride from Warsaw, with Papa and Mama, before all this started. I remember.

David looked up and down the rail line. "I heard that the main army pushed the Germans back to just west of Bialystok."

Not far enough. If they break through we'll die in the field or worse, be taken alive. I've got to do something soon.

"We will follow Sakaloff," David said, turning away. They watched up ahead as Sakaloff's detachment merged into the flow going to the city.

I used to ask Papa about everything. But now, I need to find my way back.

"David, I'm leaving," Hannah said.

He turned back and faced her. "What do you mean, leaving?"

Hannah stepped to the side out of the way and David followed her. She turned around. I'm going east, David. Where I should have gone all along."

"You can't. Not now. That's away from the fighting. We need you to finish the Germans off."

"Good-bye, David."

"Wait. Do it for Itzhak. Do it for your family."

"I'm done. I can't do it anymore."

"I must avenge Itzhak and Joseph and the rest of my family."

"Good-bye, David. Good luck. I hope you make it to Berlin."

Hannah slung her submachine gun over her shoulder and across her back, muzzle down. She passed her fighters who started calling out to her. "Follow David," she said.

"Hannah," David called out. She stopped and turned. "Shalom," he called. Hannah tried to repeat the word, but nothing came out of her. She nodded to him then turned back, walking against the endless flow of men and armored vehicles.

. . . . .

Along the road, peasants moving away from the fighting formed a small stream in the opposite direction from the river of army men and machines heading toward Warsaw. She let the stream carry her away. Daydreaming, she thought of going back to the old building, the familiar courtyard where they played as children. If these people chased the Germans from the city, she could go back someday. But she doubted their house survived anyway. Why go back? Only a memory now.

Hannah looked straight ahead or at the ground. *Strange I suppose, a girl with a gun out here with all these men.* Occasionally, Hannah glanced up at the faces passing next to her. Some were smiling and some looked angry. The eyes of others were weary and sad. She wondered if her eyes held that hard glare anymore or were they just tired and lost? Up ahead was a building along the rails. No trains sat waiting to board passengers. As she approached the building, the sign came into view. "Sokolka Station." The station building had survived with little damage. Hannah left the stream of escaping peasants, turning off onto the road into town. The area looked mostly the same, except for an occasional relic of a truck or a small crater in the earth from an exploded artillery shell.

Soon Hannah entered the village. It seemed mostly deserted. She stayed on the outskirts and headed to the cottage. *That SS man's face through the crack in my bedroom door. Forget him. It's over now.* Walking on, she spotted the cottage. It looked abandoned. Turning away, she walked by and entered the woods. The dirt road that jolted her bicycle that cold morning was still full of ruts. Her boot twisted on a rut and she felt a sharp pain in her ankle. She stopped for a moment, balanced her weight on her healing leg, and rotated the ankle. It was alright. The rustling of leaves to her left sparked an immediate reaction. Pulling on the gun strap, the PPS-42 slid into position and she dropped to one knee, gun sight targeting the sound. A fat rabbit scurried into a thicket. She held her position for a few more seconds, then stood up and moved on. *The tree. Will I know it when I…there.* Hannah stood still, unable to move. The ground at the base of the tree was undisturbed. *Oh, Papa. Forgive me. I never made it to Russia.*

She looked around and found a thick stick with a jagged end. Standing in front of the tree, she dropped the stick at the base. Hannah pulled the gun strap over her head and laid the submachine gun on the ground. Kneeling, she dug into damp soil. It smelled earthy, like the dirt she threw on the burlap covering Itzhak. The stick contacted something hard. *The suitcase.* No one found it. Digging and scratching the dirt away, she found and grabbed the handle and pulled the suitcase from the soil. Wiping the dirt from the case, she set it next to her gun.

With thumbs on the two latches, she pressed and the latches snapped open. Hannah stared at the case for a long time. Then she slowly opened the cover. The blanket, socks, and knit hats, one for each of them, were on top. Hannah wanted to cry when she saw the cans of fruit and soup. Mama in her way trying to protect her family. At the bottom was the clear glass jar. She grabbed the top and twisted it. The lid would not budge. On a second try, she gave it all she had and broke the seal. She was stronger now. She couldn't have opened it before. She dumped out the necklaces and a roll of bills. She stuffed them into her pocket. A soft, black pouch fell out, too, and lay in the suitcase. *What is that? I don't remember packing that.*

With her fingertips, Hannah pulled open the velvet pouch and shook the contents into her palm. Two rings. Wedding bands, tied together with a blue ribbon. Hannah tried to focus her eyes. They always said they would never take their rings off. Tears streamed down her cheeks as she blinked at a slice of bright blue sky above. On her face she could feel a breeze moving through the trees. *Like Itzhak said, I can feel again.* Hannah stared up at the blurry sky for a long time.

"I thought you gave up on me, Adonai, so I gave up on you," Hannah said, voice cracking. "But then, you never did, did you?"

The End

Made in the USA
Middletown, DE
18 November 2022

15427352R00217